Hilda McKenzie was born and brought up in Cardiff. She left school at fourteen to become an apprentice at a drapery store, left there to learn book binding at a local printers, was an assistant and a cashier for a grocery firm and later became a telephonist at a turf accountants' office. She was fifteen when her first short story was published, and she has written one previous novel, *Rosie Edwards*, praised by *Publishing News* as 'a nostalgic and evocative family saga'. She has a grown-up son and daughter, and still lives in Cardiff with her husband.

Also by Hilda McKenzie

Rosie Edwards

Bronwen

Hilda McKenzie

KNIGHT

First published in 1991
by HEADLINE BOOK PUBLISHING PLC

First published in paperback in 1992
by HEADLINE BOOK PUBLISHING PLC

This edition published 2003 by Knight,
an imprint of Caxton Publishing Group

10 9 8 7 6 5 4 3 2 1

ISBN 1 84067 385 0

Phototypeset by Intype, London

Printed and bound in Great Britain by
Cox & Wyman Ltd, Reading, Berkshire

Caxton Publishing Group
20 Bloomsbury Street
London
WC1B 3JH

For my much loved grandsons Jim and Paul McKenzie and Neil Crawford.

Also for my friends of many years, Betty and John Hutchinson.

Also the 'Friday Girls' without whose company I would have missed a lot of fun.

ACKNOWLEDGEMENTS

To the staff of Cardiff Central Library and St Mellons
Library, my grateful thanks for all their help.

Chapter One

In the long street of narrow grey stone houses the blinds were drawn as a mark of respect for the dead, but there'd been a lot of head shaking at the way Megan Thomas had seemingly chosen to die.

Eleven-year-old Bronwen Thomas stood at the window in the darkened parlour, the blind twitched aside a fraction, staring with eyes red and swollen at the women on the opposite pavement. There were only four of them now, goose-pimpled arms wound tightly in coarse sacking aprons against the chill of the murky November afternoon, their eyes flicking now and then towards the house, though there'd been nothing to see since late this morning when the two policemen had mounted their bikes and ridden away, leaving Dada and herself devastated by the news they had brought.

From habit Bronwen had opened the window in the tiny parlour a few inches at the top – Mama always had been one for fresh air. Gazing over the laurel hedge that pressed against the green-painted iron railings surrounding the little front garden, she strained her ears towards the women's conversation.

'Desperate she must 'ave been, poor soul, and 'er with them two lovely kids an' all, an' a 'usband what's a saint

1

to most in this street.' This from plump, kindly Mrs Coles from number three.

'But there's a way to go, isn't it, girl? The river! And in weather like last night's, mind! Couldn't see youer 'and before you by five o'clock, and them fog-'orns bellyache-ing in the channel without a break.' Young Mrs Williams unwound her apron and wiped her long thin face with a corner and Bronwen found the tears streaming down her own cheeks once more. Anger flared inside her at the woman's words. She wanted to open the window wide and shout to them, 'An accident it was! My mam would never do a thing like that.'

Guiltily Bronwen remembered standing with a curious crowd outside Mrs Roberts' shop on the day she had put her head into the gas oven. It had been last year during the General Strike. Lena Roberts had very nearly been gassed herself when she'd opened the wash-house door and found her mother. Her screams had brought help but it had been too late for her mam. A lump came to Bronwen's throat as she remembered Mama saying: 'I'd never take that way out myself. She must have been beside herself, poor soul, to put her family at risk like that.'

A sound behind her made Bronwen hastily dab her eyes and push the blind into place before turning to her little brother.

'I'm awful hungry, Bron. When's Mama coming home?'

Filled with love and pity she rumpled his short, dark curls. How did you tell a five-year-old something like this? Anyway, Dada had said not to.

'Come on, Jackie, I'll butter you a nobby,' she said, tears brimming again at the thought of what she couldn't tell. Cwtching him tight for a moment, she led him gently towards the kitchen.

'Eat it by here, there's a good boy,' she said when she'd spread the crusty end of the Swansea loaf with margarine. Soon he was munching happily, his dark blue eyes glazed with contentment, heels drumming a tattoo against the legs of the bentwood chair, and she went back to her own unwelcome thoughts.

Her mother must have left the house last evening before five o'clock. She'd sent Bronwen with a knitting pattern and needles to Aunt Polly's as soon as she'd come in from school.

'Take Jackie with you, love,' Mama had said, 'the walk will do him good.' Had she seemed eager to see them go?

The evening was darkening and a little misty when they'd set out, but on the way home the fog had descended quite suddenly and Jackie had clung to her as the fog-horns, loud in the stillness, had begun their mournful dirge.

When there'd been no answer to her knock she'd pulled the key on its string through the letter-box and opened the door, calling, 'Mam! Mam!' but there'd been no sound.

Thinking her mother had probably gone to the shop on the corner, Bronwen lit the gas ring and put the saucepan of potatoes to boil, then brought the plate of sausages from the mesh-fronted safe in the yard. The meal had been ready when her father came home and she'd covered Mama's dish of sausage and mash and put it on a saucepan of boiling water to keep hot. She could tell her father was annoyed by the way he drummed his fingers on the table after he'd pushed his plate away.

'Go and see if she's with Ivy, will you, Bron?' he'd said. But she hadn't been with her friend, and Dada had gone from neighbour to neighbour, getting increasingly worried, before beginning to search the streets, but it had been too foggy to see anything except the outlines of people, and then only when they were right on top of you, and finally, unwillingly, he'd gone to the police.

The neighbours' conversation she'd overheard still rankled. Why should they think her mother must have been desperate? What could Mama possibly have felt desperate about? Sometimes her father got angry because of the things she was always buying from Gus the Packy, but it couldn't be that or Gus would have been demanding his money instead of trying to sell Mama more things on her account.

It was always on a Thursday night that they argued – she couldn't bring herself to say rowed – especially if Mama had had one of her buying sessions in the afternoon. Every Thursday Gus came with his battered cardboard case and opened it up on the parlour table. Mama could never resist pretty things and she and Gus would joke together as she made him a cup of tea while deciding whether to have another dress for Bronwen or something for little Jackie.

Last Thursday when she'd got home from school Gus had been there as usual. They were in the parlour, the door was wide open and he seemed to have laid out his entire stock. There were things spread all over the parlour table and dresses draped over the chairs. Mama was holding a frock against herself, saying: 'I love it, Gus, I really do, but I've got enough to pay for as it is.'

Her mother had been reflected in the big oak-framed mirror over the mantelpiece, her pretty face flushed with excitement, blue eyes shining, and Bronwen's heart had swelled with pride. She'd wished, as she always did, that she'd taken after her mother instead of her dad. She herself had big dark brown eyes in a pale oval face, but at least her hair was fair like Mama's and wavy too. Most of her friends' mams were shabbily dressed and always looked tired, their hair wispy and untidy on wash days as the pins became loose from their buns. Mama's hair was bobbed and naturally wavy. Bronwen's mam always looked nice and smelt lovely, and she wouldn't go further than the gate unless she was properly dressed.

While Bronwen gazed entranced at her mother's reflection, Jackie, perpetually hungry, had been trying to drag her towards the kitchen. The scrubbed table covered by a white damask cloth had been cluttered with used teathings. She'd piled them quickly on to a tray and taken them through to the wash-house. Fetching the toasting fork from the drawer, she'd cut two thick slices of bread and held one to the fire.

Half an hour later, the cloth pushed back, Jackie had been copying his letters at one end of the table, his tongue clenched tightly between his teeth in concentration, while she did her homework at the other when she heard voices in the passage and the front door close, then Mama's light footsteps running upstairs. Faintly she heard the wardrobe door click in the bedroom overhead, the room she shared with Jackie, then Mama's footsteps coming downstairs again and along the dark little passage and down the three steps to the kitchen.

'I've put the dress I bought in your wardrobe for the time being, Bron. Ours is full.'

'Shall I put the oven on ready to start the dinner? Dada might be early tonight.'

'No, love, I've left it too late to cook. You'll have to get some fish and chips from Pritchard's.'

'What's your new dress like?' Her mother didn't often buy anything for herself from Gus.

Mama's eyes brightened. 'I'll show it to you, if you like.'

She was a long time upstairs but when she came back

5

to the kitchen Bronwen gasped with pleasure. Her mother was wearing her high-heeled shoes and had brushed the honey-coloured curls into a halo around her pretty face.

'Like it, love?' Mama swung around so that the skirt of the peacock blue dress swirled about her.

'Going somewhere, Megan?' Neither of them had heard her father open the door.

The colour had drained from her mother's face. She didn't need to explain. It was Thursday, wasn't it? His dark eyes full of hurt, Dada had said bitterly, 'You promised, Megan, when I gave you part of my baccy money towards those things for the kids, you said then that you wouldn't take on anything else.'

Not wanting to watch her mother's embarrassment Bronwen looked around the bright kitchen with its pretty chintz covers on sofa and rocking chair, matching curtains and frilly mantel cloth. Mama was standing on the soft beige rug in front of the range, her eyes downcast. There were two matching rugs covering the red and black diamond tiles – real carpet, too, not pegged rags or coconut matting – but somehow, just then, they didn't give her the usual satisfaction.

There's sure to be trouble tonight, Bronwen had thought miserably, knowing that she'd lie in bed listening to Jackie's gentle breathing, waiting for the raised voices. But they wouldn't start until they thought she was asleep. The fireplace in her room was directly over the one in the kitchen; she could hear every word. Bronwen wished fervently that Gus would go away, but even if he did Mama would soon find another pack-man and nothing would really change.

'I'm still hungry, Bron.' Jackie's voice recalled her to the awful present. She bit her lip against the terrible grief

6

that filled her whole being and threatened to drown her eyes once more.

Chapter Two

'Awful it must have been for Megan, brought up in that orphanage.' Kindly Alma dabbed her plump cheeks with a black-edged handkerchief before continuing, 'Put the children first she always did, buying them things she couldn't really afford. I don't think that Jackie ever passed the Penny Bazaar without having some little toy. Determined she was they'd have a happier childhood than her own, pooer soul.'

They were following the other mourners out of the parlour where the service had been held and towards the open front door.

Polly put her handkerchief away in a capacious handbag and snapped the clasp shut before replying sourly, 'And just look what happened. Put her in the river, it did, the worry of it all . . .'

Alma broke in quickly in a shocked voice: 'You know that's not true, our Poll. The Coroner brought in a verdict of misadventure.'

Her two aunts had left the house now and were walking with Nana towards the single carriage drawn up behind the hearse. Bronwen, not wanting them to know she'd overheard, went back to the parlour, her thoughts in turmoil.

The sickly sweet smell of arum lilies still pervading the

9

little room made her feel suddenly queasy. She clung for support to the small table piled high with hymn books which stood beneath the window, and stared sadly out at the hearse. Through the thick glass she saw the coffin piled high with colourful wreaths and sprays, the dewy blues, mauves and golds contrasting with the sombre unrelieved black worn by Grandmother Thomas and the paternal aunts as they got into the carriage. Aunt Alma had said that women didn't often go to the cemetery but her grandmother had replied, 'Well, there's few enough relatives will be attending the funeral as it is, with Megan having none of her own and Walter and Will able only to get just enough time off from work to go straight to the cemetery. Poor Jack would need someone from the family with him, wouldn't he?'

Nana had settled herself in the carriage and was sitting bolt upright by the window, a snowy handkerchief held to her eyes in one black-gloved hand. She wore a thick melton coat now against the chill of the cemetery, covering the high-necked blouse and long voluminous skirt she'd worn for the service. A pork-pie shaped hat of pleated silk rested on her thick iron grey bun. The handkerchief never left her eyes, but Bronwen suspected her tears were mostly for Dada, her only son, for she had never got on with her daughter-in-law.

Now the girl's attention was taken by the horses in front of the hearse, glossy creatures, their black-plumed heads nodding towards each other as though to indicate they would soon be on the move. A man from the funeral parlour came to stand beside them, stroking their noses gently, the sombre ribbons on his shiny top hat blowing in the breeze.

The men who'd attended the service, friends and neighbours most of them, wearing their dark Sunday suits, were forming a procession behind the carriage ready to walk to the cemetery at Cathays. Dada, his face grey with grief and fatigue, was talking to the Reverend Joshua of Bethesda Chapel who'd conducted the service and Willie Llewellyn from the choir who'd sung 'Rock of Ages', and 'Abide with Me', his deep baritone voice reverberating around the tiny room.

Through a mist of tears Bronwen saw the funeral procession move slowly along Rosalind Street, the men's breath steaming in the chilly air as they fell into ponderous step. She remembered with gratitude that whatever Aunt Poll thought, the Coroner had brought in a verdict of misadventure. Her father had told the inquest of her mother's friendship with the family in Rumney with whom she'd been in service before her marriage. She'd probably been on her way to pay them a visit, he'd suggested, dressed as she was in her best clothes, when the fog had suddenly come down. But Bron didn't think her mother had visited Mrs Wilson since last spring, when a new maid they'd just engaged, obviously jealous of her employer's warm friendliness towards Bron's mam, had shown her resentment by being very rude.

At first they'd thought it strange that there'd been no word from Mrs Wilson, no letter of sympathy, for the *Echo* had reported Megan Thomas's tragic death on the front page, but Aunty Ivy had said today that the Wilsons were away, and had been since the day before it happened.

Bronwen shut her eyes and swayed slightly as, behind closed lids, she saw her mother wandering on to the common in the thick impenetrable fog. The hesitant steps when she'd realised where she was, the horror when the tangled grass was no longer underfoot, the scream and splash that no one heard . . . and the scream that tore

11

from her own throat brought Ivy running from the kitchen. As she hugged Bron and smoothed her hair, she said softly, 'I heard what youer Aunt Polly said, but it was an accident, *cariad*, a dreadful accident. Youer mam loved life too much to want to lose it, believe me.'

'Oh, Aunty Ivy, Jackie's been crying ever since Dada told him. He's with my cousin Gloria at Nana's house now. He would only have been upset if he'd seen the coffin and the hearse.' As the tears began to fall once more, Ivy waited until Bron had wiped them away before saying, 'Well love, I left Mrs Coles making the sandwiches, shall we give her a hand?'

In the kitchen Ethel Coles looked up from the corned beef sandwiches she was making and gave a sympathetic smile as Bron took a sharp knife from the drawer and began to cut the slab of fruit cake and arrange it on a doyleyed plate – doyleys Mama had crocheted for her bottom drawer before she was married. Ivy had been washing out the big brown tea-pot they'd borrowed from the Chapel. Wiping it with a tea towel, she put it on the fender seat ready to be filled.

When at last Nana and the aunties returned they looked pinched with the cold despite their warm coats, taking hot cups of tea gratefully as they sat at the table. Some of the men who'd walked to the cemetery had gone back to work or straight home; those that returned with Dada looked exhausted and chilled to the bone.

Seats were drawn up to the fire as beer and tea were handed around. The sandwiches and cake disappeared rapidly and had to be replaced, and the tea-pot refilled several times. Listening to snatches of conversation, Bronwen marvelled that attending a funeral could give them all such an appetite; she herself had eaten nothing and Dada had just sipped at his beer.

When there was a lull in handing around the sandwiches and pouring the tea, Alma called, 'Come over by here, Bron,' and she settled herself between cushiony Aunt Alma and big-boned Aunt Polly. The latter bent towards her, saying, 'Going to live with our Mam then, are you, Bronwen?'

Staring at her aunt in disbelief, she cried, 'No, of course not! I'll be looking after Dada and our Jackie. I learnt to cook ages ago.'

'Well, that's not what I heard . . .' Polly began, filling Bronwen with apprehension, when Alma leant over her and hissed, 'Keep your trap shut, our Poll, it's probably not decided yet anyway.'

When the mourners had left and the dishes were washed and put away, Ivy folded her overall to go to her own house a few doors away, for her daughter would soon be home.

'Come and see Peggy, will you, Bron?' she persuaded. 'She wanted to come straight here after school but I told her to wait until later.'

Ivy's daughter was Bron's best friend.

'I won't come just now, Aunty Ivy,' she told her. 'I want to talk to Dada about something.'

What Aunt Polly had said couldn't be true but Bron wanted her father to reassure her. Taken it for granted, she had, that he'd need her to look after them all. Anyway, she told herself with a sigh of relief, there wouldn't be room at Nana's house for all of them. There were three bedrooms. Aunt Polly and Uncle Will had the one in the front, Nana the middle bedroom, and Gloria, Bronwen's seven-year-old cousin, the one at the back.

When she returned to the kitchen, having seen her mother's friend to the door, she found her father leaning forward in the wooden rocking chair, staring sadly into the fire. He looked up at her, the brown eyes in his haggard face deep pools of sorrow.

'Ah, Bron, I want to talk to you – '

'Aunt Polly said we were going to live with Nana,' she burst in with a shaky laugh, hoping it made the suggestion sound absurd. 'I told her I'd be looking after you and our Jackie.' She broke off uncertainly seeing the look on her father's face.

'That's just what I wanted to talk to you about, Bron. It wouldn't be fair to burden you with looking after us – you're not twelve yet. When you leave school I'd like you to get a job and make new friends, not stay at home as an unpaid skivvy.'

'But I want to look after you, Dada.'

He shook his head sadly. 'It's all arranged, love. My cousin David's got me a job in Coventry – I'll be staying with him and his wife Vera. It's only you that's going to live with your Nan – Jackie's going to Aunt Alma's. He'll be company for his cousin Tom and – '

She flung her arms about him with such force he had no breath to continue. 'No, Dada! No!' she cried in dismay. 'Please stay here and let me look after you and Jackie. I don't care about going to work and making new friends, honest I don't.'

'It's no use, Bron, you don't understand. I'll get decent money at the car factory once I'm trained. I'll be able to send enough home to pay Gus what's owing – and other things.'

'But I could save on the housekeeping. I know I could. There can't be that much owing to Gus. She paid him something every week.'

Her father was looking at her thoughtfully.

'Bron, has your mother bought anything big recently?

14

Things for the house? Furniture?'

Surprised at his question, she shook her head, saying, 'Only that dress she had from Gus.'

'No, love, I don't mean clothes.' The blue dress had hung in the wardrobe, the labels still attached, and Gus had kindly offered to take it back and credit the account. Jack Thomas sighed deeply, remembering how pretty Megan had looked in the dress when he'd found her pirouetting in front of the mirror instead of getting his tea. He wished now he hadn't shouted at her. She knew her failing for buying things she couldn't afford as well as he did.

'There's no spare bedroom at Nana's house,' Bronwen was saying sulkily. 'There won't be room even for me.'

'Youer going to sleep with Gloria, love,' he told her.

She flung herself at him again, tears streaming down her cheeks. 'Aunt Alma lives miles away – in Canton,' she sobbed. 'I want our Jackie with me. Please don't do it, Dada! Please don't go away.'

'You'll be all right with youer nan, Bron,' he comforted her, smoothing her hair. 'Loves you very much she does, and as for Jackie – it's only a tram ride. You'll be able to visit him whenever you like.' Then, pressing his cheek to hers, he said, 'Youer poor mam had such a hard life when she was young. Most people, if they'd been orphaned at birth and lived all their young lives in a children's home, would have wallowed in self-pity, but not youer mam. She was a survivor, always looking on the bright side of things. She'd never have taken her own life, Bron, I'm quite sure of that.'

A knock on the front door set Bronwen hastily dabbing her eyes before going to open it. When Jack heard Peggy's voice and the parlour door closing behind them he sighed deeply and went back to his own thoughts. Remembering the very first time he'd seen Megan his eyes misted. He'd been a van boy delivering a parcel to the house where she was employed, and when she'd answered the door he'd been smitten right away. She'd worn a lavender calico dress down to her ankles, and a bibbed apron so stiff it crackled as she walked. Her fair hair, except for a few stray curls, had been confined by a mob-cap, its lace-trimmed brim framing her pretty face. He'd waited while she'd got a signature for the parcel and when she'd returned, smiling shyly at him, she'd held out some cubes of sugar for the horses waiting patiently in the road.

Although he'd looked out for her whenever the van went that way, it had been more than three weeks before he saw her again. He could hardly believe his eyes when he'd looked across the aisle in Chapel and she'd been sitting on the end seat two rows in front of him. He hadn't been sure it was her at first, dressed as she was in Sunday best, her long honey-coloured hair falling from beneath a wide-brimmed hat trimmed with large pink roses and cloaking her shoulders in rippling waves. When she'd turned and smiled shyly at him he'd felt like throwing the hymn book into the air with joy.

As the people crowded the aisle at the end of the service he'd made sure he'd reached the door first, and waited impatiently for her to appear, sighing with relief when he'd seen she was alone.

Looking around the room now his eyes filled with tears. The house was alive with memories. They had been crowding in on him these last few days, tearing at his heart. But something unpleasant that must be faced was intruding on his thoughts. He must think about the Provident payment card that had been at the bottom of Megan's handbag when he'd been asked to check the contents. The card, badly stained from being in the river all night, was for ten pounds – more than a month's wages at

16

the ironmonger's store where he worked. The interest on the loan had been paid and the cheque itself must have been spent. There'd been no sign of it although he'd turned out every drawer and cupboard in the house. He'd racked his brains trying to think what it could have been spent on. Bron had confirmed that no big item had come into the house. How had Megan proposed to pay ten shillings a week? Come to that, how had she managed to pay the ten shillings interest in advance?

The card had been tucked away beneath all the other contents of the bag: a lace-edged handkerchief, face powder, mirror, tortoise-shell comb, a brown leather purse containing two shillings and threepence halfpenny, and a key. The key hadn't fitted any door in the house.

Hearing the girls' voices louder now, as the parlour door closed and they came towards the kitchen, he tried to put the mystery from his mind. But he knew it would be there with him every minute until it was solved, as would that even more worrying and tragic mystery: what had Megan been doing on the common?

Chapter Three

Bronwen looked from the window of the empty front bedroom at the road outside where a horse-drawn flat cart was waiting, the ancient horse neighing and pawing the road, while two men in cloth caps were carrying furniture and other things from the house to load upon it.

It was just over a week since the funeral and she'd come upstairs because she couldn't bear to watch what was happening, but had been irresistibly drawn to the window. This was the third and final journey the second-hand dealer would make, and she felt devastated by the finality of it all, as Mama's cherished possessions had been carried through the house and dumped unceremoniously on the cart.

'Bron! They're nearly finished,' her father was calling gruffly, and with a last look out, she closed the bedroom door and went downstairs.

Two shabby brown cardboard cases stood in the passage where the hall-stand had been, one packed with her clothes and possessions, the other with her father's things. Dada picked them up and put them outside and she followed, waiting for him to lock the front door.

Yesterday afternoon she'd taken Jackie to Aunt Alma's. At first he'd clung to her tearfully, then Aunt

Alma had brought him a box which contained a small clockwork train set.

'It's the same as the one ouer Tom had on his birthday,' she told him. 'You'll have one each now, Jackie love.'

As he clambered from her lap and began eagerly to fit the tracks together, Bronwen, knowing her aunt had little money to spare, cried, 'Oh, Aunt Alma! You shouldn't have.' And her aunt, smiling at Jackie playing happily with his present, had whispered, 'I hoped it might take his mind off being parted from you, Bron.'

Jackie was sending the little train racing around the track as Alma knelt beside him, saying, 'Uncle Walt will be bringing some cardboard home tonight, love, so's you and ouer Tom can make a tunnel and paint it with his box of paints.' Then looking up at Bronwen, she said, 'I'd have dearly loved to have had you an' all, *cariad*, but we've only got two bedrooms as you know. A real shame to part the two of you it is.'

There was great excitement when Tom got home from school, especially when the boys discovered that by fitting the two tracks together they could send both trains rushing around at the same time. The fair head and the dark curly one were soon close together, the boys' voices shrill with excitement. Jackie hadn't even noticed that Bron had put on her coat, but he looked up when she said, 'I'm going now, love. I'll see you at the weekend.'

He'd scrambled up quickly then and hugged her, his cheek warm against hers.

'Come on, Bron!' Her father broke into her thoughts as he waited impatiently to close the gate.

Several neighbours waved to them as they went up the street, and seeing the pity in their eyes Bronwen walked a little ahead of her father, blinking back her tears. Inwardly she was still seething with the injustice of losing the comfortable home her mother had worked so hard to make, sure that somehow she could have managed to pay Gus from the housekeeping as well as paying something off the Provident cheque her father had told her about last night. He'd given her the key that had been found in Mama's handbag in case anyone laid claim to it, but it was as much a mystery to her as it was to him.

Mastering her tears she turned suddenly to see her father wiping his own eyes, and her anger melted to pity for he had lost everything too.

Nana lived only a few streets away. As they turned the corner into Thelma Street and were nearing number twenty-four she could see the dark green chenille curtains with the strip of Nottingham lace between that had hung at Nana's parlour window as long as Bronwen could remember. Approaching the gate, they could hear raised voices coming from the front bedroom.

' – but I want my own bed, Mama. I told you, I'm not going to sleep on Nana's old bed. I want my new one back.'

'You'll 'ave to, Glory, there's no room for you both on the little bed.'

'Let *her* sleep with Nana. You promised I could have the room to myself.' Gloria's words ended in a sob.

As Jack slammed the gate shut the voices stopped abruptly and the front bedroom window was pushed up.

Bronwen glanced at her father as he raised the knocker and banged the door, her heart heavy with foreboding. He was pretending not to have heard, but his lips were set in a grim line.

Martha Thomas opened the door looking flustered, wiping her hands on her long black alpaca apron and ushering them into the narrow passage with its faded green-varnished wallpaper patterned with bowls of fruit. A long strip of green- and brown-striped coconut matting lay on top of the knotted boards as far as the foot of the stairs where a dark brown chenille curtain was looped back, cutting out any light coming from that direction.

The parlour door was shut, but Polly stood in the open doorway of the middle room, her large bosom heaving from her recent dash downstairs, smiling a welcome to both of them.

They followed Martha along the dark little passage that led to the kitchen where an appetising smell greeted them from the big iron stew-pan bubbling on the hottest part of the range. A fire burnt in the grate, the only bright spot in the kitchen with its shabby furniture and dark cushions and covers. Heavy brown curtains hung at the window which was darkened anyway by the wall it faced, on which hung two mesh-fronted food safes and a couple of tin baths.

A large square table and four shabby balloon-back chairs took up most of the space on the window side of the room, the table covered by a faded chenille cloth. On the shelf in the alcove just beyond the table and chairs was a polished wooden box, the lid fastened with a brass hook, on top of which rested a pair of head-phones. Bronwen knew this contained the crystal wireless set. A shabby rocking chair with creased brown velvet cushions was drawn up to the fire on one side of the steel fender, and a wooden armchair, its cushions crocheted from oddments of dark wool, on the other. Almost covering the flag-stoned floor were two pieces of striped coconut matting.

As Martha spread a cloth and made a cup of tea, Polly said apologetically, 'Gloria's playing upstairs. She couldn't have heard you arrive. She'll have to get ready to go back to school soon – I'd better go and hurry her up.'

Bronwen caught a glimpse of her cousin as she waited for her mother to get on her coat to take her across the busy Broadway. Gloria's eyes behind the steel-rimmed glasses she wore were red and puffy, and Bronwen couldn't help feeling sorry for her, remembering the day only a few weeks ago when the child, excited and happy, had shown her the newly decorated bedroom.

While Martha ladled out three generous helpings of pea soup, Bronwen laid the table and put the kettle to boil. As they sat down her father said, 'Good of you it is, mam, to have Bronwen like this.'

'Nonsense, Jack. She'll be a big help to me. Taught my own girls to be useful I did, but our Polly is bringing that Glory up real namby-pamby if you ask me. Too much of her own way that madam 'as and that's a fact.'

'Bronwen always helped her mother,' Dada said, 'so that's no problem.'

The train to Coventry was at three o'clock. Bronwen had wanted to go to the station with her father but he'd said he'd rather say goodbye at the house, knowing he'd only worry if he had to leave her in tears on the platform. When the time came for him to leave, she clung to him.

'You'll write to me, Dada?'

'Every week,' he promised. 'I'll be home for Christmas and that's only a month away.'

Home! She couldn't call this place home, she thought bitterly, instantly feeling guilty as she remembered Nana's kindness in having her.

At the front door she hugged her father again, pressing her cheek against his, her arms tight about him, then waved to him until he'd turned the corner.

When they went back to the kitchen Martha sat down

heavily on the sagging cushions of the rocking chair and lay back, closing her eyes.

'Fill the scuttle and put some knobs on the fire, will you, Bron?' she said, her eyes still closed. 'Feeling real worn out I am, what with one thing and another.' Best keep her busy, take her mind off things.

Blinking back the tears, Bronwen filled the scuttle and topped up the range, putting the iron cover back as quietly as she could. Martha was asleep now, snoring gently. Bronwen rolled up her sleeves and washed the dishes in the tin bowl in the wash-house, afterwards tip-toeing from the kitchen and up the stairs to put her clothes away in the wardrobe that had been put in Glory's room for her.

When she opened the door of her cousin's room she saw right away why the child had been so upset. When Gloria had shown her the bedroom with such pride only a few weeks ago it had looked so pretty: the creamy wallpaper patterned with tiny rosebuds, the little bedroom suite of bedstead, dressing table and wardrobe in light oak, the bed with a frilly, pink silk cover and the dainty curtains in a matching shade had all given the room a lovely airy feeling. Even the oilcloth on the floor was a light beige, with a single fluffy pink rug by the bed, and there'd been a pink basket chair with a big baby doll in a long gown propped against the cushions.

Now she looked around her in dismay. The basket chair had gone, obviously making room for a hideous, much varnished wardrobe with spotted mirrored doors, the varnish on the wood so thick it looked almost like tar. The pretty bed had gone too and in its place was a large brass bedstead, its mattress sagging badly in the middle, the whole covered by a dark green huckaback spread.

Poor Glory! No wonder she was in tears. The room was completely spoilt.

Bronwen was still putting her clothes away when she heard her cousin return and wondered if she'd come up to the bedroom, but after the middle room door had closed behind her and Polly, there was only the faint murmur of voices.

As she entered the kitchen, her grandmother yawned and woke up.

'What time is it, Bron?'

'A quarter past four.'

'Gosh! I didn't mean to sleep that long. I'd better bring the things in from the line and fold them up ready for ironing.'

'I'll do it, Nana.'

'Thanks, Bron. It's cold out there, mind.'

As she began to unpeg the two lines of clothes, bed linen, table cloths, and tea-towels, Bronwen wished she'd listened to her grandmother and put on a coat. An icy grey mist had come down, and as she loosened the last peg with numb fingers and held the washing against her, the cold dampness seeped through her jumper, making her shiver. Just then she was surprised to see a man's cloth cap appear above the stone wall that divided the garden from the one next door. Then a face appeared, red with exertion, a thin face, rosy and wrinkled, and two bright blue eyes twinkled at her from underneath the cap which rested on top of snowy white hair drawn into a bun. Suddenly their neighbour seemed to shoot upward and became visible to the waist, and now she appeared to be extremely tall until Bron remembered the upturned wooden butter boxes which stood either side of the wall, the one on Nana's side hidden behind the blackcurrant bushes.

Bron gave the neighbour a friendly smile and Bertha Morgan asked, 'Youer nana in then, Bronwen?'

'Yes, Mrs Morgan, she's in the kitchen.'

A button-sided black boot straddled the wall, bringing with it a tumble of red flannel petticoats and a stiffly starched white one all worn under a voluminous black skirt. The buttoned boot was searching blindly for the butter box and Bron hurried across. Clutching the bundle of damp washing against her body with one hand, she guided Bertha's foot with the other. Safely on the ground their neighbour wasn't very tall. Her face, arms and chest were thin, but below the waist the full ankle-length skirt billowed about her, giving her the shape of a corn dolly.

'Going in then, Bron, are you?' she asked, taking the peg-bag from her and hurrying on to open the back door.

As Martha greeted her friend she drew the kettle over the fire and reached for the tea-caddy. Bronwen dumped the washing on to the scrubbed table and rolled up the things that were starched, while Bertha sat down at the kitchen table waiting for the cup of tea that was always forthcoming.

'Get the clothes-horse, Bron,' Martha instructed, 'hang them other things over it, there's a good girl, then put them in front of the guard.'

While they dunked their biscuits and drank their tea the window became steamed up as vapour rose from the clothes around the fire, and when Martha lit the gas in its frosted shade Bronwen got up to draw the curtains and shut out the darkening sky.

Three cups of tea and a number of Garibaldi biscuits later Bertha was resting her elbows on the table, her hands supporting her chin, when Bronwen, looking towards her and seeing with horror that a furry creature was peeping from the neck of her blouse, went rigid with fright. As it struggled to free itself Bertha's hand flew to her throat and piercing screams filled the room. A final wriggle and the little grey mouse was jumping to the floor with Martha brandishing a poker in hot pursuit. Bronwen opened her mouth but no sound would come. Her eyes dilated with fear, she rested her heels on the edge of the chair, hugging her knees.

All the colour had gone from Bertha's cheeks and her body was shaking like someone with the ague. Suddenly her tongue lolled out and her head fell back.

'She's fainted,' Bron cried, finding her voice at last as they both rushed towards her.

'Go and ask Polly for the smelling salts, Bron, quickly!'

When she hurried back to the kitchen with Polly, they carried Bertha to the rocking chair and wafted the smelling salts to and fro under her nose.

'You'll 'ave to do something about those mice, Mam.'

'I'll put down a trap again tonight,' Martha said, then catching sight of Bron's white face, she said, 'You'd better 'ave a whiff of this an' all, girl. You look as if you'd seen a ghost.'

Bron thought she'd probably prefer to meet one of those as she sat on a chair, knees against her chin, eyes anxiously scanning the floor. She was terrified of mice. Always had been.

When Bertha came round and some of the colour had returned to her cheeks, another pot of tea had to be made, while she related over and over how she'd put her hand to her blouse and had felt the warm furry body. She couldn't seem to think of anything else, telling the story over and over again. Then, saying she couldn't trust her legs to get her over the wall, she stayed to tea, after which she allowed Bronwen to see her to her own front door.

After tea Polly came to the kitchen and stood in the doorway.

'Bron, I was wondering if you could help Glory with

her reading? If you put your coats on you could do it in the bedroom. I want to listen to a play on the wireless.'

Gloria had already spread her books on the bed when Bronwen tapped on the door and entered. Seeing her little cousin's sullen expression, Bron greeted her with a sinking heart.

'Hello, Glory.'

'You don't have to knock. It isn't my room any more.' Her voice was filled with self-pity and Bron's heart went out to her. By the look of her she must have cried for most of the day. Slightly built and thin-featured Gloria took after her father in looks, even to the straight sandy-coloured hair which was drawn tightly back from her forehead into two fat plaits tied together at the bottom with a dark blue ribbon bow. Suddenly Bronwen remembered her mother saying to her dad, 'That Gloria takes after Will's family, doesn't she? She's nothing like your Poll. But with a surname like Hole why on earth do they call her Glory? It's asking for trouble at school.'

'I'm sorry, love,' Bron said, sitting down beside her on the bed. 'I know I've spoilt things for you but it isn't my fault. I'll try to make it up to you, Glory, if I can. I'll take you to the pictures if you like on Saturday afternoon. We could go in the twopennies, I've got enough for that.'

'And we could climb under the ropes and sit in the threepenny seats.' Gloria, remembering a girl in school boasting about doing this, smiled for the first time. Then her face resumed the sulky expression.

'We won't be able to go to the pictures on a Saturday anyway. Nana will see to that.'

'Why not? I'll get up early and do the housework.'

'It isn't the work,' Glory told her with a pitying smile.

'What is it then?'

'Brimstone and treacle.'

'Brimstone and treacle?'

'Yeah! A big basin of it. She watches you eat it an' all.'

Gloria smiled again, obviously enjoying giving her cousin the bad news. 'I tell you, Bron, you won't be wanting to go to the pictures on Saturdays no more.'

Chapter Four

The following Saturday morning, as Bronwen went through the kitchen to empty the heavy galvanised bucket at the sink in the yard, there were two small bowls of sulphur-coloured mixture on the table and Gloria was already dipping her spoon into one of them. But the over-whelming feeling of dismay which came over her had nothing at all to do with the bowl of brimstone and treacle.

Martha Thomas was sitting at the other end of the table working at a hand sewing machine, the fingers of one hand guiding the material as she stitched the seam of a faded red flannel garment. Beside her lay one of Bron's lace-trimmed cotton petticoats on top of which was a tape measure and a large pair of scissors.

'Making you some warm petties I am, Bron,' Martha told her. 'There's enough in these old ones of mine to make you a couple.'

'But I always wear cotton ones, Nana,' Bronwen protested.

'I wouldn't be doing my duty to youer dada, love, if I didn't look after you properly. We'll 'ave some freezing weather after Christmas, you'll see, and top show won't be enough to keep you warm then, girl.'

Dismayed, Bronwen emptied the bucket and washed

her hands at the sink in the wash-house before taking her seat beside Gloria and picking up the bowl and spoon.

The cloying sweetness of the mixture was not unpleasant, but remembering Glory's warning about the aftereffects Bron's face wore a dubious expression as she took the first spoonful.

'It's for youer own good, my girl,' Martha assured her, noticing the way she was eyeing the bowl.

'I don't need it – ' Bron began, but her grandmother waved aside her objections.

'It's only once a week,' she told her. 'Cools the blood does brimstone and treacle. Thank me you will one of these days, *cariad*.'

At a knock on the front door Martha took her purse and left the kitchen.

'If you don't want to take this stuff, Glory, why doesn't your mam stop Nana giving it to you?' Bron asked.

'Mama had it when she was young – she says it's good for you. Have you seen all the medicines and things Nana makes, Bron?'

Bronwen nodded. The two highest shelves in the pantry were full of jars and bottles in rows three deep. She'd stood on a wooden footstool one day when she was alone in the kitchen closing the door so as not to be disturbed, reading some of the labels by the dim light from the fan-light. Oil of eucalyptus, garlic water, camphorated oil, oil of cloves, three different kinds of home-made cough mixture – dark brown, syrupy red, and pale lemon – and goose grease in a large earthenware jar. At the end of the shelf nearest the door was a jar of brimstone and one of black treacle.

There was an overpowering smell of sage, mint and rosemary which hung in upside down bunches from the shelf at the back. As she opened the door and put the stool outside Bron viewed the shelves once more with misgiving, vowing that if she ever felt ill she would keep it to herself.

'All those bits of flannel that's left over will be put away in the drawer,' Gloria told her, bringing her thoughts back to the present.

'What for?'

'When you've got a sore throat she'll pin them round your neck on top of that awful smelly stuff she rubs in. Rubs your chest with goose grease she does if you've got a cough, and covers it with a piece of flannel. It don't half stink, the stuff she puts on your neck.'

Dismayed at this information Bron was more determined than ever to keep quiet about any coughs or colds she might have in the future.

Martha came back to the kitchen, saying, 'Made a good job of scrubbing the front you did, Bron. Nice and white that step has dried and the patch in front of the gate.'

Her mouth full of the sticky mixture Bron didn't answer, and before she could swallow the mouthful her grandmother was calling her over to try on the garment. She rose sulkily and stripped off her jumper and skirt, standing before Martha in her short white petticoat with its pink ribbon insertion and dainty lace trim.

Nana took the hated red flannel one and pulled it over Bronwen's head. The frilled hem came below her knees, tickling the backs of her legs. She cried out in horror: 'It's too long. It'll show beneath my skirt!'

Her grandmother was smiling at her. Shaking her head, she told Bronwen, 'No it won't, love. You can't go all winter in them thin jumpers and skirts, and no liberty bodice neither.' She clicked her tongue disapprovingly. 'When youer dada's money comes I'm going to buy you a warm gym-slip and some fleecy blouses, and a black cardigan to wear on top. I won't take anything for your keep until I've got you some warm things. Now take it off, and I'll finish sewing it.'

She's only being kind Bronwen thought suddenly, feeling guilty about making such a fuss. As she handed over the garment an awful thought struck her. How was she to manage on the day they had gym in school, when they stripped off in front of each other down to their vest and knickers?

When the machine was whirring again Glory whispered smugly, 'I wouldn't be seen dead in one of those petticoats.' But Martha had stopped the machine suddenly, catching the end of the sentence, and noticed Gloria's superior expression.

'If youer mother had any sense,' she told the child, 'you'd be wearing them an' all – then perhaps you wouldn't be sniffling all the time.'

If Bronwen still had any hopes of going to the cinema they were dashed quite early in the afternoon as the two cousins began taking it in turns to scurry along the path to the WC, often with coats over their heads for it was a squally day.

Bron sat on the wide wooden seat thinking longingly of other Saturday afternoons spent in the company of her friends at the pictures, sucking pear drops, weeping at the heroine's misfortunes and jeering at the villain, then she gave a little moan as another cramp gripped her stomach.

It was quite dark by four o'clock and now the girls must remember to take the matches with them. Martha Thomas was justly proud of the latest convenience she'd had installed in the lavatory. It was an ornate brass candle holder which had once graced a piano. Now it was fixed on the white-washed wall, its fat candle encrusted with melting wax, and its flame flickering wildly in the wind that came under the badly fitting door.

The light from the candle was sufficient for Bron to read the scraps of newspaper that had been torn up and strung on the wall. The box of vestas beside her on the scrubbed seat, she'd search frantically through the other pieces in the vain hope of finding the rest of the story that she'd just begun. By tea-time her arms were aching from lugging buckets of water for both of them, for these were required to flush the pan, and she made up her mind that come next Saturday she would just pretend to eat the brimstone and treacle, then smuggle it out and put it in the ash-bin.

After tea the girls were playing a game of Ludo in their bedroom when Will came up to say good night. Bronwen thought he looked very smart in his best suit, his unruly ginger hair almost covered by a grey trilby, his face beaming at the thought of the pleasures of the coming evening.

When he'd kissed them both and produced a twist of jelly babies for each of them from his coat pocket, Gloria asked, 'You going out with Uncle Charlie then tonight?'

'Yes, love, and I'd better hurry up an' all,' he told her. And with a final, 'Good night, God Bless!' he was closing the door and hurrying down the stairs.

'If he's meeting Uncle Charlie, just wait 'til he comes home,' Gloria said mysteriously.

'Why? What happens?'

'Just wait and see.'

When she went to bed Bronwen couldn't sleep for worrying about undressing for gym on Tuesday if Nana made her wear the red flannel petticoats. She knew her pretty underwear had been the envy of most of her classmates. Now the shame of being seen in the old-fashioned garments that her grandmother would force her to wear, supposedly for her own good, weighed heavily upon her.

She tossed and turned, thinking of her father and Jackie, and wishing with all her heart that she was at home looking after them. She had just dozed off and was dreaming that she was back in her old home in Rosalind Street when a loud banging at the front door woke her with a start. She heard Polly go down and open the door. The singing had become louder and Bron recognised Uncle Will's voice coming from the passage: 'There's an old mill by the stream, Nellie Dean'.

Polly was shouting angrily but the singing continued. 'Where I used to sit and dream – oh, Nellie Dean.'

Her aunt was yelling, 'You ought to be ashamed of youerself, Will Hole.'

'And the waters as they flow – ' there were stumbling footsteps on the stairs – 'seem to whisper sweet and low – ' But Polly's voice, shrill with anger, rose above the singing: 'It's that Charlie. That brother of yours.'

'Shut up, woman!' Will yelled. Bron could hardly believe it was her meek-looking uncle who spoke the words. 'Shut up, will you? Who's the blutty master in this house anyway, I'd like to know?' Then it sounded as if he was stumbling back down the stairs.

'Don't stand there gawping, woman,' the voice was definitely coming from downstairs now, 'go and make me a cup of tea and be sharp about it, 'cos like it or not I'm going to be the boss from now on, see?'

By now Gloria lay propped on her elbow listening with her cousin.

'Aren't you worried about them rowing?' Bron asked kindly, remembering how she'd dreaded the Thursday nights when her parents had argued over the things Mama had bought from Gus.

'It'll be all right tomorrow, Bron,' Glory assured her, 'just wait until the morning and you'll see.'

Presently they heard the master of the house stumbling up the stairs to bed and Polly shushing him as they passed the girls' bedroom, then all went quiet.

Next morning, yawning from lack of sleep, Bron rose early to lay the fire. She paused by the open door of the middle room. Will looked up and smiled at her sheepishly, then went back to clearing the ashes from the grate. In the wash-house a kettle was beginning to boil on one of the gas burners and an egg was simmering on another. A few minutes later Will came out with a laid tray.

When the tea was made and the egg sat in its cup, Bron said, 'Shall I take it up, Uncle Will?'

'No, Bron, thanks.' He looked at her and nervously ran a finger around the inside of his collar. 'I'm afraid I made a bit of a rumpus last night. Hope I didn't wake you and Glory up? Better try and make it up to her today, hadn't I?'

A few minutes later she could hear Polly's voice, sharp with anger, and her uncle's mumbled reply, then all was quiet. When he came down without the tray, Bron sighed with relief. But it seemed that poor Uncle Will wouldn't be the blutty master again for at least another week.

Bronwen had begun to feel sorry for her uncle long before the Saturday night incidents, for she'd soon realised that Polly constantly belittled him. She supposed that her uncle being so much shorter and thinner than her aunt put him at a disadvantage. Despite her weight Polly walked tall, her large bosom puffed out in front like a pouter pigeon, while Will, whose head barely reached her shoulder, seemed to tag along behind her, glancing nervously about him with short-sighted eyes.

Uncle Will was a very kind person, Bron soon realised. Several times that week he'd brought her sweets just as he had Gloria. Whenever he'd found her looking sad he'd put his arms about her and hug her, just as he comforted his own little daughter. But Gloria was only eight while she was nearly twelve. Uncle Will didn't seem to realise she was almost grown up. Grown up enough anyway to feel embarrassed by this warm show of affection.

Chapter Five

The letter and money from her father arrived on the Monday morning. Bron could hardly wait to read his news but she couldn't help wishing that the money hadn't come until after the gym class on Tuesday afternoon, for the hideous flannel petticoats had been made a good six inches longer than the skirts she was wearing and so couldn't be worn until the gym-slip was purchased.

Her father had sent her sixpence pocket money and threepence to take to Jackie, but with Christmas only a month away she decided to try and save her money towards presents.

When she came home from school in the afternoon Martha was waiting to take her to Goldberg's Emporium in Clifton Street. She would have liked to have lingered by the long plate glass windows gazing at the lovely clothes on the models, but her grandmother marched her through the doorway and straight to the department where school uniforms were on display.

The first gym-slip the assistant brought fitted her perfectly, but Martha insisted on plenty of room for growth and would not be satisfied with anything less than two sizes larger.

Looking at herself in the mirror Bron thought she'd die of embarrassment, especially when she saw the assistant's amused expression, but she was very relieved to hear her tell Nana in a firm voice, 'You see, madam, it's far too long. If I may say so, the first one I brought is the young lady's size.'

'It's got to last,' Martha insisted. 'I'm not made of money. We'll take that one, thank you.'

Put in her place the assistant went off to fetch the fleecy blouses, and Bronwen, her face blanched of all colour, stared miserably at her reflection before taking off the gym-slip. When she tried on the blouses that were brought these were also much too large and gained her grand-mother's instant approval, as did the liberty bodices chosen to reach the top of her legs. The assistant's eyes were filled with pity as she handed Bron the parcel. Going home Bron was silent, her pale face mirroring her dismay; in vain her grandmother told her that she couldn't afford to buy her clothes every five minutes. Picturing her class-mates' reaction to her changed appearance she wallowed in her misery.

Will proved to be an unexpected ally. She had thought he must be as afraid of Martha as he obviously was of Poll, but when just after they'd returned home he came across Bron sulking in the parlour, her eyes brimming with tears, he sat down beside her and, putting his arm about her, drew her head down to his shoulder.

'What's wrong, Bron? Someone been ragging you at school like they do our Glory?'

'Not yet,' Bron told him, 'but they will tomorrow.'

Her voice broke on a sob and his arms tightened about her. When she told him about the too long gym-slip and the flannel petticoats, he was very sympathetic, saying, 'She wanted Poll to put Glory in them flannel things, but her mother said she'd be the laughing stock of the school. Poll's had a go at your nan over making them for you,

Bron. Had a real set to they did. Look, love, I'll 'ave another word with her if you like. Can't do no harm, can it? She doesn't know 'ow much it means to you, that's all.'

Will stood up and straightened his shoulders and walked determinedly to the door. Leaving it open he went to the kitchen. She heard the murmur of voices, then Martha's voice, louder now, sounding belligerent. Then after a few minutes the voices became quiet again. To Bron's surprise, her grandmother was standing in the parlour doorway dressed to go out.

'Go and see to the tea, Bron. Going to change this gymslip for the next size down I am, and the blouses too – it will save you turning up the cuffs. I may 'ave to take up them petties a bit when I get back.'

When the front door had closed behind Nana, Bron jumped up and hugged Will gratefully.

'Oh, thank you! Thank you!' she said over and over. It would have been asking too much for Nana to have changed them for the right size, but even now she was overjoyed. Noticing the way Will drew himself up tall she hugged him again and kissed his cheek. Then she went to the kitchen to prepare the tea.

The euphoria soon disappeared when she began to think about the gym lesson on the following day and undressing in front of everyone. That night she couldn't sleep for worrying about it. In the morning when Martha remarked on her pallor she seized this as an excuse to stay away from school.

'I don't feel very well, Nan.' She looked up at her grandmother appealingly.

'You don't look well either, Bron, but you'll feel better when you get into the fresh air.' Feeling the girl's forehead, she added, 'You 'aven't got a temperature anyway.'

When Bron still dawdled she said sharply, 'Hurry up now or you'll be late.'

Bron dragged her steps and was indeed late for school, hoping that the chastisement for this would be to withdraw the privilege of gym class, but Miss Phillips who had been most understanding and sympathetic about her bereavement merely said, 'Don't let it happen again, Bronwen.'

Just after lunch everyone in the class, except Millie Evans who had a weak heart, was marching in twos down the corridor to the hall where the class was taken. Bron's heart was beating so fast she wondered if there could be something really wrong with her. If only she would faint, but no, she mustn't do that, for someone would be sure to loosen her clothing, displaying her underwear anyway.

A few minutes later Peggy stood in front of her, already stripped to her vest and knickers, jumping up and down, beating her arms about her body in an effort to keep warm.

'Come on, Bron, everyone's ready.'

Bronwen had been standing with her back to the others, eyes wide with fear at the thought of her classmates' reaction when she exposed the old-fashioned underwear. Now she really did have everyone's attention simply because she was the only one still not undressed. Red with embarrassment she tried to raise the garment over her head at the same time as the gym-slip, but the red petticoat fell back about her legs. There was a shocked silence, then someone burst out laughing. Soon they were all falling about laughing, all except Peggy who said anxiously, 'Take no notice, Bron. Miss Pickering will be here to take the class in a minute.'

'Did you borrow that from youer gran, Bron?' a girl asked between giggles, and the others, enjoying the unexpected entertainment, laughed loudly at the joke.

Swallowing hard, and with her eyes bright with tears of mortification, Bronwen followed Peggy to the corner of the hall where Miss Pickering had just arrived to take the class. As she swung her arms downwards to touch her toes she was seething with anger. 'I hate her,' she muttered to herself, 'I'll never live it down – never.' If only Nana had listened to Aunt Poll. I hate Thelma Street too, she thought. She'd been so happy living with her Mam and Dad and Jackie in Rosalind Street. Mama had known how much clothes mattered to a girl.

If only she was home and could fling herself on the bed and sob her heart out, but even if she could go home to Thelma Street there was no privacy at all at her grandmother's house.

When she did get home from school Polly was waiting at the door and didn't even seem to notice that she was upset.

'I want you to take a message to my friend in Splott, Bron. Glory, you can come in and peel some potatoes for me.' She handed Bron an envelope with an address written on it. 'Wait for a reply, will you love?' And Bron heard the door shut as soon as she left the gate.

The letter handed over and another put into her hand to give to Poll, she crossed Splott Road. Walking with her head down she didn't notice the second hand shop until she almost bumped into the settee on the pavement. She gasped with astonishment as she recognised it as the one from her home in Rosalind Street, then her astonishment turned to horror as she saw how bedraggled it looked in the flickering gaslight from the shop window. She could hardly believe it as she stroked the arm lovingly, feeling the dampness of the cretonne covers. Her own troubles were forgotten as she gazed in dismay at the flowered covers and cushions that her mother had always kept starched and spotlessly clean.

"'Ere, you, clear off, will you? I only wants customers 'anging round 'ere. Keep yer 'ands off that settee. Go on, bugger off or I'll – '

Bronwen didn't wait to hear what he would do. A great sob tore from her throat as she turned and ran over the bridge and down Pearl Street, but she didn't stop at Thelma Street even though by this time she had a stitch in her side, but went on until she reached the street where she'd been born and brought up and the only people who would understand how she felt, Peggy and Aunty Ivy.

Seeing Bron's distress Ivy took her straight to the kitchen, and telling a startled Peggy to make a pot of tea she put her arms lovingly about Bronwen and cradled her.

'Want to tell me about it, love?'

Bron looked up at her with drowned eyes and nodded, but even before she began Ivy was fuming with anger for her daughter had told her about what had happened at school that afternoon. She'd wanted to rush around and tell that Martha Thomas just what she thought, but she hadn't gone in case she made things even worse for Bron.

When Bronwen told her about the settee, Ivy could almost see it as it had been when she'd sat on it in Megan's house less than a month ago, the covers so fresh and pretty. But she addressed Bron with a voice kept deliberately cheerful.

'Don't upset yourself love. Someone will buy it and look after it just as youer mam did. Come on, Bron, eat youer biscuits and have another cup of tea. Youer nan will be wondering where you are.'

'No, she won't, Aunty Ivy,' Bron told her, putting down the tea cup. 'I'm on an errand for Aunt Poll so I'm all right for a while.'

'Let's have a swing round the lamp-post before you go home,' Peggy said, taking the rope from the cupboard under the stairs.

'Don't be late going back now,' Aunt Ivy told her as they went through the passage.

Throwing the rope over the arms of the lamp post they took it in turns, and when she wasn't swinging Bron stared longingly at the house that had been her home until a short while ago. A lump came to her throat as she saw that it looked just the same. The paper blind that Dada had left behind was drawn, and the gas light in the room threw shadows on it that flitted about, shadows that could have been her mother and father, Jackie and herself, just a few weeks ago. Peggy had told her that a family called Evans was living there now. She gave a shuddering sigh, glad of the darkness as she moved to the shadows and watched Peggy make a perfect circle on the swing, and the light from the lamp blurred by unshed tears seemed to scintillate and dance in front of her eyes.

Martha Thomas had been sitting by the fire waiting for Bron to come home from school. She'd got up and lifted the lid of the stewpan and decided it would be ready by the time Bron came in. Then Polly had come to the kitchen door and announced calmly that she'd sent the girl to her friend's house in Splott with a message.

Polly hadn't waited to see what she'd say. Really, that one took the biscuit for cheek, Martha didn't know who she took after. Her father, God rest his soul, had been a gentle, kindly man.

There was a tap on the kitchen door and Bertha came in, holding a cup.

'Can you spare a bit of sugar, Martha? Just for supper. I can get some in the morning.'

'Come and sit by the fire, Bertha, nearly boiling the kettle is. I got some Garibaldis. I know they're youer favourites.'

Bertha sat in the armchair, carefully lifting her skirts so that they wouldn't touch the floor and glancing anxiously around her.

'You caught that mouse yet, Martha?'

'No. It's a fly one. Even took the cheese last night it did without setting off the trap.'

Soon they were settled either side of the range cradling their cups of tea.

'See you been sewing for Bron,' Bertha said, pointing to the garment still draped over the back of the chair. 'Remember when our kids were small, the struggle we 'ad?'

Martha nodded, recalling the nights when after the children were bathed in the tin bath in front of the fire and put to bed, she'd wash out their only set of clothes in the lukewarm water, wringing them as hard as she could and drying them over the guard. The kitchen would be filled with steam and her hair all damp and wispy. When the clothes were dry enough she'd heat the flat irons on the range and press the top petticoats and embroidered pinafores, lace-trimmed drawers and Jack's little shirts, and leave them in the warm room to air ready for school next morning.

'To be poor and look poor is the Devil all over,' her own mother used to say, and Martha had never questioned the logic. Going off to school the children would look like new pins and she'd feel so proud of them. Only her friend and long standing neighbour had known the effort it had cost, for Bertha had been in the same boat.

Martha glanced worriedly at the clock. Bron had had plenty of time to do that errand. Be round Rosalind

Street, she would, hankering after the house where she used to live. Better it would be if she forgot that Peggy and found a friend here in Thelma Street.

When Bertha left with the cup of sugar Martha moved the heavy stewpan to the back of the range, telling herself that if Bron didn't come soon she'd have hers and be done with it. Settling herself back against the lumpy cushions she rocked to and fro, sighing when she thought of Polly's high handedness and how rude she'd been about the petticoats. A well-earned rest she should be having at her time of life, not having to put up with Bron's moodiness. Just look at all the fuss she'd made about them clothes. By God! Lucky she was to have new clothes to wear.

Leaning sideways and looking again at the clock on the high mantelshelf she tutted with annoyance and brought a soup dish from the pantry. She wasn't going to wait any longer.

Ladling out the soup she thought angrily of Polly's interference over the sewing she had been doing for Bron.

'What's wrong with them?' she'd asked her daughter. 'I'm making them to last, that's all.'

'They're so damned old-fashioned,' Polly had replied bluntly.

'Honestly, Poll, you don't want Bron growing up like her mother, do you?' She'd had a job to keep the exasperation from her voice. 'Made a God of clothes and pretty things she did. Worried our Jack something awful.'

'Megan was a real good sort,' Polly told her. 'Our Jack could have done much worse, believe me. Kept the house lovely she did, and the children. Our Jack worshipped her. You'd better not let him hear you talking like that.'

'Well, I can't see anything wrong with them. Are you suggesting that I should dress young Bron like a flapper?'

Polly had burst out laughing, saying, 'Don't talk such nonsense, Mam.'

'None of you seem to realise what a responsibility I've taken on,' Martha had complained in vain, for Polly had just rolled her eyes ceilingwards, shrugged her shoulders, and muttering, 'God give me strength!' had marched out of the kitchen and back to the middle room. But she hadn't given in to her. Polly should know by now that she didn't get anything by showing off. But she'd listened to Will, he'd always treated her with respect. Martha chuckled. Polly wouldn't like that.

When Bron opened the door and stepped into the kitchen, Martha took one look at her stricken face and bit back her angry words. She took the soup dish and, filling it, said gently, 'Sit down, *cariad*, and have something hot. You look frozen girl.'

Chapter Six

It was Christmas Eve and her father was coming by an evening train. Bron could hardly contain her excitement at the prospect of seeing him again.

All day there'd been a bustle about the house, a coming and going, as first the plump chicken arrived from the farm in Rumney – the farm that delivered fresh brown speckled eggs every week of the year. Then the baker had come with extra bread, humping the heavy basket to the door on his hip, and Martha had chosen three Swansea and two tin loaves, and would make some of her delicious soda bread if they should run out.

The milkman had been early, putting the dipper deep into the milkchurn and filling the two big flowery jugs that Bron held tightly. He promised to deliver half-a-pint of cream with the Christmas day milk.

Glory had helped her hang brightly coloured paper chains the week before, but Bron, remembering the decorations her mother had made last year, thought they looked pathetic. Her mam had been a dab hand at making paper flowers, Victorian ladies in poke bonnets and crinoline dresses, and tiny red-cloaked Father Christmases out of nothing more than bits of cardboard, crêpe paper and cotton wool. And the celluloid doll she'd dressed for the tree each year had been as pretty as a picture in a frilly white paper dress edged with tinsel, holding a wand topped with a glittering silver star. Thinking of last year and her mother, so very much alive and happy, Bron's sadness, which was never very far away, enveloped her once more.

In the afternoon the two cousins went to Clifton Street for some last minute presents, gifts they couldn't buy until they'd had the proceeds of last night's carol singing. The sixpences Bron's father sent each week had not been nearly enough for all she wanted to buy, and anyway she'd already had to break into her pocket money. Glory had suggested carol singing and at first Bron had thought that at twelve she was too old to be singing at people's doors, but her cousin had persuaded her and she was glad.

Knowing that their grandmother would never have approved they took library books to change and went to the library first. The third time they were supposed to be at Band of Hope and took a real risk of her finding out they weren't there.

Gloria had quite a good soprano voice. Bron had been surprised the first time they'd sung, and stopped singing herself to listen in admiration. After that it was agreed that Gloria should sing 'Away in a Manger' on her own. They made one and threepence each that first night.

By the time they had returned from Clifton Street they had a present for everyone, most of them bought at the Penny Bazaar, and a few at Woolworths, but the muffler for Bron's father had been chosen carefully at the gent's outfitters. It only remained to wrap up the gifts and tie on the pretty labels they'd made and decorated with painted Christmas trees.

Downstairs the kitchen smelt lovely, with spicy mince pies cooling on the rack and the ham simmering in the stew-pan on the range. And soon, very soon, Bron thought excitedly, Dada will be here.

He arrived about half-past eight. When she rushed to the door to open it she flung herself into his arms and hugged him, and he held her tightly and pressed his cheek to hers. But a few minutes later when he stood beneath the gaslight in the kitchen she was shocked to see that his face was gaunt and grey, and although he smiled at them, obviously glad to be back amongst his family, his eyes held such a look of sadness that a remark a neighbour had once made to her mother about a man they both knew, a remark that had startled the impressionable Bronwen, came to her mind.

'Looked just as though he'd been to Hell and back,' the woman had said. Now why should she remember that suddenly?

After supper Jack went to the middle room to chat with Will. A few minutes later he put his head around the kitchen door, saying, 'Just going for a pint with Will. Tell your gran I won't be long.'

Martha was clattering the dishes in the washing up bowl. When Bron told her, she cried, 'Oh my God! See if you can catch him 'fore he goes.'

When she opened the front door it was dark and misty and there was no one in sight. She ran half way up the street but they must have turned the corner and Bronwen hadn't stopped to get her coat.

Gloria was reading a book in the armchair by the fire as Bronwen passed the middle room on her way to the kitchen. She looked up to say, 'Mam's gone next door to take a present to Mrs Morgan, and my dad's gone out with yours.'

Back in the kitchen Martha was fretting.

'Polly will go mad,' she told Bron. 'Will promised to stay home tonight 'cos it's Christmas Eve.'

'Where've they gone?' Polly demanded the moment she came in.

'Our Jack took Will for a pint.'

'Oh Mam, no! That Charlie will be there. I'm going straight round.'

'Leave it, Poll. Jack will look after him. Looks bad for a woman to go and fetch a man out.'

By ten o'clock Bron couldn't persuade Nana to let her stay up any longer, but as she lay by Glory's side, listening for any sound, sleep was far away.

Some time later there was shouting outside, then a loud knocking on the door. She heard Polly go through to open it and there was the sound of tuneless singing from the street, and as the front door opened her father's voice saying, 'Shut up, Will, you'll wake the street.'

Then Polly was shouting, 'You ought to have had more sense, Jack. Christmas an' all.'

Bron had rushed to the landing and was leaning over the banister, her bare feet freezing on the chilly oilcloth.

'We only went for a pint,' her father was explaining. 'He met his brother – he didn't have that much, Poll.'

The gaslight had been turned down awaiting their return. Will was weaving about, his shadow suddenly growing enormous as he toppled towards the wall. Polly, her hair bristling with steel curlers, her hands resting on her hips, was standing by the stairs. Suddenly Will was upright again and trying to push his wife towards the kitchen, crying, 'Get out there, woman, an' put the kettle on.'

Then, when she didn't budge, 'Go on, Polly, put the kettle on. Do as youer told 'cos I'm the blutty – ' He stopped and chuckled as though something had struck him as funny, then began to sing, 'Polly put the kettle on, Polly put the kettle on, we'll all 'ave tea.'

'Give over, Will,' her father said again as he pushed his brother-in-law towards the middle room.

'Make him a cup of Camp coffee,' he said to Polly, holding on tightly to Uncle Will. 'Make it black.'

With nothing more to see Bronwen went back to bed and lay there worrying about tomorrow. Christmas Day had promised to be a happy one with the fat chicken and a goose waiting to be cooked, and the pantry shelves bulging with all the good things her nan had made, and the presents waiting to be given around.

Now Polly would be sulking, and Will looking shame-faced and scurrying around trying to make up for last night, and her father would be blamed for taking him to the pub.

She went down early to rake the ashes from the grate but her father, who had slept on the front room sofa, had already lit the fire in the range. Will was scurrying around just like before, but this time when he took it up the breakfast tray came down untouched. Aunt Poll wasn't falling for any of his soft soap.

At breakfast Martha looked anxious and Jack uneasy. Bron had flung her arms about her nan to thank her for the cretonne-covered sewing box she'd found at the foot of her side of the bed. Then she'd hugged her father for the *Girls' Own Annual* and the box of chocolates he'd brought her.

It was an uncomfortable meal and, glad to get away at last, Bron took the presents she'd bought for Polly, Will and Gloria, and went to the middle room. The door stood ajar and she was about to tap on it when she heard her uncle pleading, 'Couldn't you forget it just this once, Poll? It's spoiling our Glory's Christmas and you don't want that.'

'You should have thought of that before you – you – '

Words must have failed her aunt. Creeping away, Bron went up to the bedroom where Gloria was playing with the stack of presents that had been placed on her side of the bed. She looked up glumly as Bron entered the room.

'It isn't all right this time, is it?' she said. 'They're rowing down there, an' it's all youer father's fault.'

Bron was quick to defend him. 'It isn't my dad's fault if your dad drinks too much.'

Gloria glowered at her. 'Yes it is, Dada wouldn't have gone out if Uncle Jack hadn't taken him.' She turned her back and picked up a book.

Going downstairs Bronwen found her father getting ready to cycle to Canton to see Jackie and give him his presents. He had borrowed a bike from Bertha Morgan's son-in-law as there were no trams running this morning. If only she had a bike, Bron thought, then she could have gone with him. Her mother had always said she'd buy her one when her ship came home. She remembered worrying when she'd been small about Mama's ship getting home with no water in the street, but she'd soon realised that her mam always used this expression about things she'd like to buy for people but couldn't.

Before he went out Jack braved the atmosphere in the middle room and went to apologise again, but Polly was in no mood to listen and he came out shaking his head.

Martha bustled about the kitchen, basting the chicken, and preparing the vegetables. As Bron went to help her, she said, 'I hope Poll won't spoil things. We'll all be having dinner together out here today.'

At last it was time to lay the table with the best damask cloth and put out cutlery for six. Bronwen had just placed a red and gold cracker at the top of each setting and Martha had basted the golden chicken for the last time when Jack returned.

'Tap on their door, Bron, and tell them it's ready,' her grandmother instructed. 'Polly's supposed to be cooking the goose tomorrow. I hope she'll get over it by then.'

When the others came out and everyone was seated Bron held a cracker towards her aunt whose face looked like a thundercloud, while Will twitched nervously, easing his collar as if it was choking him, and Jack glanced worriedly from one to the other. Somehow Martha kept the conversation going, drawing her daughter and son-in-law into it as often as possible, but the decorations, the sprigs of holly and mistletoe, the paper hats and the novelties from the crackers, did little to encourage a festive spirit. Polly glared at Will and refused to pass him even the condiments.

After the dishes were washed and Martha had settled for a nap in the rocking chair, Jack said, 'How about going for a walk, Bron?' She jumped up quickly to get her coat. She'd been waiting for an opportunity to mention the petticoats and ask him to tell Nana that she couldn't wear them to school.

Glory was playing upstairs again and the middle room door was firmly closed, so they put on their outdoor things and closed the front door quietly behind them.

Bron shivered as she linked her arm in her father's. It was bitterly cold and the watery sun made little impression on the frosty rime-coated pavements and rooftops.

'I had a long talk with Will last night before he met up with Charlie,' he told her. 'He's a good sort is Will. Told me he'd look after you as though you were his own, Bron. Be a father to you, seeing I'm so far away.'

'Do you like Coventry, Dada?'

'I miss youer mam very much, love, and there's nothing I can do about that. I miss you and Jackie too. Coventry's all right, I suppose, but I didn't realise that I was going to miss you both so much.'

Hope flared in her. 'Couldn't you come back, Dada? Please! We could find a place – be together again.'

He shook his head. 'Oh, Bron, it's too late for that, love. My job here is gone, and the house is already let.'

Swallowing her disappointment, she asked hopefully, 'Will you come home again soon?'

'I won't be able to come very often, love. There's money to send home for Gus and the other. Has he been round for the money?'

'Yes. He brought me a box of handkerchiefs with my initials on.'

'That was kind of him. And that Provident cheque I'm paying for – you've still no idea what it was spent on?'

'No.'

'It's a complete mystery to me as well. Has anybody claimed the key?'

She shook her head, saying, 'Perhaps they don't know where we are now we've moved, but Aunty Ivy would tell them, wouldn't she?'

Her father was pulling the string through the letter box, and she still hadn't mentioned her troubles. Looking at his hunched shoulders and pinched face she knew she couldn't add to his burden.

'You go through, Bron,' he said, shutting the door behind them. 'I'll leave my coat in the front room.'

When she opened the kitchen door Martha looked up and smiled at her.

'Poll's come down off her high horse,' she whispered. 'And about time too.'

'Oh, I'm glad! Dada will be pleased an' all.'

'Getting the tea for us all in the middle room she is, and Will can't do enough to help.'

Bron was thankful that they'd made it up so soon. They'd be a happy family again. Her father would have to go back tomorrow evening. She was so glad things were going to be all right, something nice for him to remember.

When Jack had taken off his coat in the parlour he went over to the fire. Sitting on the edge of the chair he broke up the glowing coals and put a few nobs of coal on with the tongs. He leant forward and held his palms towards the blaze. What a fool he'd been, he reflected sadly. He should never have given up the house; he should have let Bron look after them just as she'd wanted.

His thoughts went to the cold little bedroom he had in Coventry. Vera didn't want him there, he'd soon become aware of that. She'd never said as much, of course, but he was made to feel that he was in the way, whether it was the faces she pulled whenever he lit his pipe, or the way she was always in a hurry to clear the dishes before he'd finished his meal. And when they had visitors, which was often, he'd make an excuse that he had letters to write and could almost hear her sigh of relief as he got his coat and went up to the freezing bedroom. His eyes wistful, he stared into the fire remembering the bright little house in Rosalind Street, with Megan singing as she went about her work.

When Bron called him for the second time he was reluctant to leave his memories, but hearing her call again he got up, turned down the gaslight, and went to join them for tea.

Chapter Seven

'Got a clean handkerchief, Bron?'

'Yes, Nan, I've got one.'

'Take them sandwiches I made, *cariad*, in case he lets you stay in to have youer dinner.'

Bronwen looked anxiously at her reflection in the mirror as she combed the front of her fair wavy hair which her grandmother had insisted she grow, and was now pulled back into a single heavy plait.

It was a warm September morning in 1930 and Bronwen was getting ready to go to her first job.

Their neighbour Bertha Morgan had seen the notice in the window of a grocer's shop in Cathays. When she'd told them about the job she'd seen advertised Martha had insisted that Bron go right away to see if she could get it, taking her school leaving certificate to show the manager.

Bron wished that Bertha had never gone to Cathays and looked into the grocer's window, because Peggy was being apprenticed to the drapery at Goldberg's Emporium in Clifton Street and Bronwen would dearly have loved to go with her.

'Youer not slaving all them hours for half-a-crown a week,' Martha had said. 'You'll get six or seven shillings at a grocer's.'

And seven shillings a week was what Mr Jessop had

told her she'd receive when he'd interviewed her and said she could start the following Monday. Seven shillings seemed a lot of money until she'd remembered that it would be two tram journeys to Cathays. If she had to go home at mid-day that would be eight journeys a day for five days of the week and four on her half day. Three shillings and eight pence would go on fares.

She'd found the shop to be much bigger than she'd expected, with freshly strewn sawdust covering the floor and that special aroma of the grocery store, a mixture of odours from sides of bacon hanging from hooks in the ceiling, salt fish dangling above the provision counter, spices and herbs, strong cheese, and the tangy smell of vinegar coming from the barrel whose slowly dripping tap was soaking the sawdust beneath it.

Mr Jessop had lifted a flap in the counter and taken her through to the warehouse at the back, where two of the staff looked up at her curiously before going back to weighing sugar into blue paper bags. Here a more pungent, and definitely unpleasant, smell assailed her nostrils, which she traced to a galvanised bucket boiling on top of a gas-ring.

'Lights cooking for the cat,' Mr Jessop explained, seeing her wrinkle her nose. And there, just a few feet from the gas-ring, was a large ginger cat stretched out on a sack in a pool of sunlight.

Now, as the tram rattled along City Road taking her to work, she was thinking about her grandmother. This morning when she'd reached the top of the street and looked back, Nana had still been at the gate, a tall upright figure in her dark blouse and long black apron, waiting to give her a final wave. Yet she hadn't shown any concern at all when Bron had told her she felt nervous about starting her first job. It was as though she found it hard to show any tender emotions. But, thinking back over the past few years, Nana had always been there when she came home, with a meal waiting and a warm dry towel and a change of clothing if it was raining, ready to dip into her medicine cupboard at the slightest sign of feverishness or sniffles.

Of course her grandmother cared, she told herself, but often Bron longed for a comforting arm about her and a few words of endearment. The only one to show any tenderness in the house in Thelma Street was Uncle Will. He would put his arm about her shoulders when he thought she was unhappy and by now she was becoming really embarrassed about it, but was afraid she'd hurt his feelings if she told him how she felt.

Suddenly Bron was remembering her mother's long ago plans for when she left school.

'We'll see if we can send you to Blogg's College, love,' she'd told her. 'That's if something turns up by then.'

But Bron had known even then that something turning up was about as likely as Mama's ship coming home. One thing she did know, her mam wouldn't have worried about it only being half-a-crown a week at Goldberg's; she would gladly have let her go to work with Peggy.

Even though she was fourteen her grandmother still insisted on making every decision for her, choosing all Bron's clothes even now.

'He who pays the piper calls the tune,' she said cryptically when Bron had dared to complain.

Martha made everything except the outer garments herself, choosing the materials and cutting them out by one of the patterns she kept in the sideboard drawer. Even Poll couldn't remember when the patterns were new. Martha would adjust the size, altering length and width according to the measurements required.

Bronwen looked down at the flowered cotton dress she was wearing for her first day at work. The long sleeves were buttoned at the wrist. The high neck had a demure white Peter Pan collar. If only she could have gone to work at Goldberg's, she thought wistfully, then she'd have had to wear a green uniform dress like Peggy and she'd have looked like everyone else.

The tram reached her stop and finding herself early she walked slowly towards the shop. But Mr Jessop was already there, the door open for business. He took her through to the warehouse and she hung her cardigan on one of the pegs on the wall.

'You've brought a white coat, Miss?'

Filled with dismay she shook her head. He must have forgotten to tell her. In any case her grandmother had had difficulty finding even the tram fare.

'Oh well, never mind. There's one you can borrow over there.'

Her heart sank as she lifted the coat from its peg. It was hopelessly big for her and a strong cheesy smell seemed to envelop her together with the coat, which was stained with grey grease across the front.

Looking at her dubiously, Mr Jessop added, 'You'd better stay out here or on the cash desk for today.'

When the staff began to arrive Bronwen was so embarrassed she could hardly raise her head to greet them. There was a fair young man who worked on provisions with Mr Jessop, and two younger men who worked behind the grocery counter. A girl of about sixteen went straight to the cash-desk after greeting her, and sat on a backless wooden stool counting the bags of money which Bron heard her refer to as the float, afterwards tipping the silver and copper into their respective sections of the till.

A young man named Chris from the grocery side came

out to show her how to weigh the dried fruit that came in bulk, and flat wrap it ready for the fixtures, and after she'd packed it away she had to familiarise herself with the stuff behind the counter, for when she could serve.

'If the customer wants something on tick,' Mr Jessop told her, 'you enter it on the bill book. And if you take an order, remind them of what they might want. You got to jog their memories like this:

'Butter, Margarine, Cheese, Bacon, Eggs, Dried Fruit, Tinned Fruit, Jam, Tapioca, Rice, Macaroni, Semolina, Custard Powder, Cornflour, Blancmange, Jelly, Biscuits, Coffee, Cocoa, Brasso, Soap, Polish – ' Mr Jessop, who had given the list without a pause, stopped now for want of breath, but Bron felt sure he could have gone on and on. 'They'll soon stop you when you come to something they need,' he added.

Just then the provision assistant came to show her how to skin a cheese and Mr Jessop went in to take over the counter.

The more Bron clawed and tugged at the cloth binding the cheese the more it broke off in her hands. Soon her fingers and nails stank to high heaven and the coat became even more obnoxious than before.

'You'd better wash youer hands and go in with Miss James to see how the cash-desk works,' Mr Jessop told her, eyeing the cheese she'd skinned almost on her own.

'I'm Marcia,' said the other girl as Bronwen stepped in beside her. Then wrinkling her pretty nose, she added, 'Ye Gods! You're wearing the cheese coat.' Her blue eyes appraised Bron carefully then she said, 'Look, you're about my size. I've got a spare coat I took off to wash. It's a lot cleaner than that.'

'Thank you,' Bron said fervently, noticing as she slipped it on that the coat was hardly soiled.

The last member of staff to arrive was the errand boy, a freckle-faced lad with a cheeky grin. His name was Alby. There were few orders to be delivered on a Monday morning, but he seemed to be a Jack of all trades – opening up crates, polishing the windows, sweeping up and laying fresh sawdust. He kept grinning at Bronwen as he passed the cash-desk, and she felt she could soon have at least one friend.

Marcia showed her how to enter from the bill-books into the ledger, and how to check the warehouse sheets from the wholesalers. At one o'clock the shop was due to close until a quarter-past-two. Bron hesitated about asking Mr Jessop if she could stay in the shop to eat her sandwiches, but looking at her impatiently he said briskly, jingling his bunch of keys, 'Come on, love, I haven't got all day.' As she hurried through the door where he'd already turned the sign to 'Closed for lunch' she vowed to pluck up the courage to ask tomorrow.

Hurrying to the tram stop, she wondered what she could do about getting a white coat to wear to serve on the counter, and worried about it all the way home, having to wait so long for the second tram that when she arrived home it was nearly time to leave again. As Martha chided her for not having the courage to ask about staying in, she swallowed her soup too quickly and began to cough and splutter, and still coughing and spluttering had to leave again for work.

'You're late, Miss,' Mr Jessop informed her with a meaningful look at the watch he took from his waistcoat pocket. But Marcia was even later and when at two-thirty she still hadn't arrived, young Alby was sent to her home to find out why.

'Bad, she is,' he announced when he returned. 'Says she'll come in tomorrer if she's better.'

'With Miss James poorly you'll have to go on the cash-desk, Miss,' Mr Jessop told Bron. 'She showed you what to do, didn't she? And Monday's a quiet day.'

Sick with apprehension Bron took her place on the stool and thumbed through the bill-book to the last entry that Marcia had ticked, then began entering the amounts into the ledger, double checking that she had the right page. Some were whole orders from Saturday, others just scribbles at the foot of the page: 'Mrs Williams, 8 Lesley, bacon 1/6'. Then there was a pile of warehouse sheets to check – Marcia had told her that morning that they must be checked today – and often in the middle of adding a long column of figures a face would appear in front of the cash-desk and a mouth would apply itself to the aperture in the glass, saying, 'Tell me 'ow much I owe, love, will you?' Or the two overhead cash-carriers whizzing to and from the counters would interrupt Bronwen's concentration.

At four o'clock Alby brought her a cup of tea in a cracked cup, his cheerful grin widening into a beam of happiness as she gave him the sandwiches she'd forgotten to take home.

At five to six she was told to cash up. She counted the notes and the silver and copper just as Marcia had told her must be done, but no way would it balance with the figures she had added up. Over and over them she went, and the money, but they wouldn't balance.

'Is it going to take you much longer, Miss?' Mr Jessop stopped at the aperture to ask.

'No, I've nearly finished.' Now why had she said that?

The staff were all still busy stacking up the fixtures so she wasn't keeping anyone waiting. Bron counted the money and added the figures once more, sick to her stomach as she knew for certain now that she was ten shillings short.

Now Mr Jessop was going over the figures and the money, growing more and more annoyed, the colour deepening in his florid cheeks until they were a dull brick red. Finally, aware that his meal would be spoiling in the flat overhead, he said, shovelling the money into a cloth bag, 'You'd better come in half an hour early tomorrow, Miss, so's we can go over it again before I open the shop.'

Miserably Bron boarded the tram, turning her face to the window, keeping it averted from the other passengers because her eyes were brimming with tears. It didn't have to be her fault, she told herself, she hadn't been in charge of the cash-desk during the morning. But Mr Jessop had made her feel responsible. The tears spilled over, and sensing that the woman on the opposite seat was staring at her she didn't dare dab her eyes.

When she'd reached Thelma Street and had pulled the key through the letter box and opened the door she was thankful that no one was about. Turning the handle softly she went into the parlour and closed the door quietly behind her, then crossing to the sofa she flung herself on it, buried her head in her hands and began to sob. A little while later, hearing the door open, she looked round anxiously and saw Uncle Will. He came and sat beside her and put his arm around her, saying sympathetically, 'What's wrong, Bron? Tell youer old uncle, *cariad*, and I'll do what I can.'

When she told him he was indignant with Mr Jessop for assuming that she was to blame.

'But he didn't actually say that, Uncle Will, he just seemed to take it for granted, 'cos I was new, I expect.'

'Well, you'd better remind him tomorrow that you weren't the only one handling the money.'

She began to cry again, and he drew her towards him and cradled her. Soon she grew quiet but still he kept his arm about her. When the door burst open and Aunt Poll stood there, her face red with anger, they quickly pulled apart, but by this time her aunt was screaming: 'So that's what youer up to, the two of you, when youer in here all alone! Thick as thieves you've been for a long time but I never suspected this. Get out, you little slut! Get out before I do something I'll be sorry for.'

'You don't understand,' Will shouted above Bron's despairing sobs, 'I promised youer Jack I'd look after her – '

'Look after her!' Polly gave a short mirthless laugh. 'I wouldn't call it looking after her, you lying sod. Why don't you admit that you were carrying on?'

Bron fled to the kitchen where Martha was listening with dismay.

'Whatever's wrong in there?'

When Bronwen explained haltingly, she tutted a few times, nodding her head and saying, 'I thought it might come to this, the way he acts with you. There's no harm in Will, it just makes him feel good protecting you. Oh, I know all about his promise to youer dad, but I'm sure our Jack didn't mean him to put his arm around you at your age.'

'What will happen now, Nan? Will Aunt Poll let me explain?'

'Not for a while she won't. Seems to me she's got the rats proper this time. One thing's for sure, she'll make Will eat humble pie for a while. Why was he comforting you anyway?'

When Bron explained about being short in the money, her grandmother said, 'You'll 'ave to be more careful. Will you 'ave to put it in?'

67

Bron, feeling utterly miserable, shrugged her shoulders, then decided that as she was in for a penny she might as well be in for a pound.

'I've got to have a white coat for the shop, Nana,' she told her. 'Mr Jessop won't let me serve on the counter 'til I do.'

Chapter Eight

Seeing Martha's look of dismay Bron wished she hadn't mentioned the white coat. Poor Nana! The tram fare had been found at the cost of last week-end's joint, though they hadn't done without. The dinner her grandmother had made with two small rib chops had been just as delicious as usual, the potatoes roasted golden brown, the flavour enhanced by her favourite mint sauce.

As Bron left unwillingly for work on Tuesday morning she noticed the worry lines about Martha's mouth, the lips tightly closed, and hastened to assure her, 'I can probably borrow Marcia's coat a bit longer, Nan. I'll ask her today.'

Martha nodded, her face still grim. 'Dreading today I am,' she told herself, watching her grand-daughter hurry up the street and turn the corner. She envied Bron getting away from Polly's tantrums. But the girl would probably have a lot of unpleasantness to face herself if they didn't find that missing money.

Going through to the wash-house she rolled up her sleeves and filled the washing up bowl with hot water from the kettle.

What was she to do about them coat overalls Bron needed for the shop? God knows they'd scrimped enough this week already. For a moment she wondered whether

69

to take the money she'd put by to pay the Co-op grocery bill. She'd done this before in a dire emergency, when she'd bought that black outfit for Megan's funeral for instance, but you had to face the consequences sooner or later. The day of reckoning always came.

Just after Martha had closed the door and was putting the dishes away in the pantry she could hear Polly slamming things about in the wash-house. By God! In for a day of it she was. Real sorry for poor Will she felt, knowing Poll would make sure that he suffered.

If only it was Alma sharing the house, she thought. Even as a child Alma had been sweetly reasonable, while Polly had wanted things all her own way. But Polly had been the first to marry and it had been only natural that she and Will should take over the middle room and the largest bedroom. Polly had her good points, Martha had to admit. She could be very generous when she liked and had stuck up for Bron more than once. Not after what happened last night though. 'Lot of fuss about nothing,' Martha muttered to herself, 'but Poll will make sure she has her pound of flesh.' Too many of them trashy books she reads. Love stories she called them. Rubbish was a better description!

When Bronwen arrived at the shop half an hour early as she'd been asked to do, the door was still closed and she had to knock. When she went in Mr Jessop had the books and money laid out on the cash-desk. Shaking his head at her, he said, 'I haven't found anything, Miss, it's still ten shillings short. Perhaps you gave change of a pound for a ten shilling note?'

But how could she have? No one had paid a big order while she had been in charge, and the change she'd sent whirring back to the counters in the cups would have been counted into the customer's hand by an assistant. Besides, she'd always been good at sums. Arithmetic had been her best subject.

Bron sighed with relief when Marcia, apparently recovered, came through the door, then looked down at her feet as Mr Jessop told the cashier about the discrepancy. Feeling uncomfortable, Bronwen was glad to be sent to the back room to weigh sugar into bags and pack it. Even Alby, when he arrived and got out the delivery bike, didn't seem his usual cheery self.

As she passed the cash-desk with an armful of bags to put away in the fixture, Marcia turned towards her, saying, 'Don't worry, Bron, everybody makes mistakes, and the money could still turn up.'

Would Mr Jessop take it from her wages? Bron wondered miserably. It would take more than a week to pay back. Where would she find the tram fare and the money for her grandmother towards her keep? Anyway, she'd tell him she hadn't been the only one to handle the cash yesterday.

At lunchtime she ate her sandwiches surreptitiously as she walked along the street, going into a cafe for a cup of tea when she'd eaten. In the present atmosphere she'd thought it best not to ask about staying in the shop when it closed at midday. If anything went missing, she'd be sure to get the blame.

Walking back along Whitchurch Road she was joined by Alby who seemed very subdued. When Bron offered him the sandwiches that were left he looked uncomfortable, his pale blue eyes fringed by fair spiky lashes not meeting her gaze.

Suddenly he turned to her, his eyes anxious. 'I gotta tell you, Miss, 'cos I know you're in trouble an' it isn't fair,' he burst out.

'Tell me what, Alby?'

'Yesterday morning I saw that Marcia fiddle about with the notes then go to 'er 'ambarg.'

'But she could have been just getting change from her bag.'

'I know, Miss, that's why I 'aven't told. But it ain't fair the way you got the blame.'

Could Marcia have taken the money? There must be some other explanation. Marcia was a nice girl, had been really decent to Bron about lending her the coat. As she passed the cash-desk after lunch, Marcia smiled warmly and Bron felt guilty for doubting her even for a moment.

That evening as they were leaving the shop Marcia said apologetically, 'Sorry, Bron, but Mam says she must have the coat for washing by tomorrow night.'

'Thanks very much for lending it to me, Marcia.' Bron tried to smile back at the cashier, but she was remembering the look on her grandmother's face when she'd told her she had to have one of her own. Poor Nana! What a lot of problems Bron seemed to be making for her.

When she opened the door of the house Gloria had her hand on the banister and was about to go upstairs.

'Hello, Glory.'

There was no answer as her cousin ran up the stairs and slammed the bedroom door.

Bron sighed and went through to the kitchen where the first thing she saw was a new white coat neatly folded over a chair.

'Oh, Nan!' She flung her arms about her grandmother who said in a gruff voice, 'It's Bertha you want to be thanking, my girl.'

'But Mrs Morgan didn't buy it?'

'No, of course not, Bron, but she let me have her money club because hers was due to be paid this week.

Mine isn't due for another two months 'cos I drew a late number.'

Bronwen said 'Oh, Nan!' again, and Martha told her, 'You'd better go in and thank Bertha for swopping with me. Go in now before she goes to visit her niece in the next street.'

Bertha Morgan was dressed ready to go out when she opened the front door. In place of the usual flat cap she wore a wide black hat adorned with a single red rose, and a black coat now green with age that fitted tightly at the waist and fell over the full skirts to her ankles, covering most of her button-sided boots. Her rosy cheeks beamed a welcome as she ushered Bron into the passage.

'I've just come to thank you Mrs Morgan. It was very good of you to swop with Nana so's she could get me the coat to wear at work.'

'Do the same for me she would. I'm glad youer pleased though, *cariad*. Would you like a glass of ginger beer?'

'No ta! My tea is ready, Mrs Morgan. Thanks again about the club.'

As she passed the middle room she could hear Polly shouting at Will, 'You philanderer, you! Don't think you can get round me with a box of chocolates.'

'I 'aven't done anything, Poll, and I don't know why youer getting youer 'air off. *Daro*, woman, I've had just about as much as I can take of this.'

The kitchen door was wide open and Martha stood in the doorway listening.

'Been at it they 'ave 'ammer and tongs ever since Will came in, pooer dab.'

If Bron managed to avoid Polly and Will all evening she couldn't ignore Gloria's sulks when she went up to bed.

'It isn't my fault, Glory,' she told her cousin, seeing

her sullen expression. But Gloria pulled the bedclothes around her ears and stared stonily at the wall.

On Friday when Bron saw Mr Jessop putting up the pay packets she was anxious to know if there was one for her. He hadn't mentioned the shortfall in the money since, but he could hardly have forgotten it. She watched him come into the shop and give an envelope to Marcia, then one to Mr Evans who assisted him on provisions. Chris and Ray the two grocery assistants were next, and then he handed one to her and she sighed with relief.

The two boys behind the grocery counter were laughing at some joke they had shared. They got on well yet they were so different. Chris was about sixteen with dark wavy hair and friendly brown eyes and she had noticed the way some of the customers seemed to mother him. Ray was a little older and chatted up the girls who came into the shop. He seemed to spend all his money on fashionable clothes. Today he wore blue trousers and pale brown suede shoes. They were new shoes and he kept looking down at them admiringly. The girls who made eyes at him in the shop often went to a phone box and rang him up which enraged Mr Jessop. But she'd seen Ray shrug his shoulders, a little smile on his face which said quite plainly that he couldn't help attracting the girls and there was nothing he could do about it.

Suddenly Bron's eyes were drawn towards the cash-desk where Marcia was opening her pay envelope from which she drew a ten shilling note, then she tipped some small change into her hand and put it in her handbag. Bron's heart beat fast as she watched Marcia bend down with the note still in her hand. She could hear her pulling the metal money tray out.

A minute later Marcia was calling urgently, 'Mr Jessop! Mr Jessop! I believe I've found the money that was miss-

ing.' Then she was describing how she'd pulled the tray
out because she'd dropped a threepenny bit behind it, and
had found a crumpled ten shilling note behind the till.
When Marcia caught Bron's eye she blushed and looked
down.

'I'm glad that's cleared up, Miss. Sorry about thinking
you'd made a mistake,' was Mr Jessop's only apology, but
Bron felt angry at the way she had been used. Why had
Marcia done such a thing? She didn't understand it at all.

When Bron left the shop to hurry to the tram stop she
was surprised to find Marcia running after her.

'You won't tell Mr Jessop, will you, Bron?' she gasped
when she caught up.

'Tell him what?' Bron asked, hoping for an explanation.

'I'm sorry, Bron, I always meant to put the money back
when I got my wages though I won't be able to give my
mother her money this week now.'

Trying to contain her anger, Bron said, 'You used me,
Marcia, just because I was new here. You let him think
I'd made a mistake or even taken the money.'

'But it was only for a few days, I always meant to put it
back. Look, Bron, it was my boyfriend. He owed some
money to a man who threatened he'd beat him up. I lent
him all my savings but it was still short. I couldn't tell my
mother, she'd have a fit if she knew I was going out with
him.'

The tram was clanging to a stop and Bron boarded it
without a backward glance. She was seething with anger
when she thought of all the trouble it had caused for Uncle
Will, and for herself too. But even if she told Mr Jessop
about Marcia's deceit, it wouldn't help anyone now that
she was in the clear. She'd better not tell her grandmother
what had happened. Best just to say that the money had
been found.

As she approached Thelma Street she was surprised to see Peggy coming towards her.

'I've been waiting ages for you,' her friend told her. 'Thought I'd better not ask you at the house.'

'Ask me what?'

'They've got a dance at the Church Hall on Monday. Well we've both left school, so we're old enough to be allowed to go. Do you want to come with me?'

'I can't dance, Peggy.'

'You'll be able to waltz, it's only one-two-three, one-two-three, and we can sit out the others until we learn.'

'But supposing a boy asks me to dance?'

'Well, you could have a go.'

'I haven't got anything to wear.' Bron glanced down at the high-necked, long-sleeved dress she was wearing.

'You can borrow one of mine.'

'It's no use, Peg, I can't go in these clodhoppers.'

'I'm going to buy a pair of silver sandals, they won't cost much. I bought some lipstick in Woolworths today. If you do it carefully you can colour your cheeks as well.'

Bron began working out how much she'd have left after she'd paid her grandmother towards her keep, but as she had to put the bus fare aside ready for next week, even though it wasn't as much now that she didn't come home at mid-day, she knew that there was no way she could buy a pair of sandals like Peggy.

That evening, as she sat in the armchair munching an apple and pretending to read, she thought about going to the dance. She'd love to go. Nothing exciting ever happened to her, and it would be nice to put on a pretty dress even if it was someone else's. But her grandmother would never let her go; she'd say that she was far too young.

Did Nana have to know? she asked herself. She certainly wouldn't let her borrow Peggy's frock anyway, having frequently voiced her disapproval of the way her friend dressed, and prophesied more than once that she'd catch her death of cold.

By Monday Bron had made up her mind to go to the dance that evening, and she paved the way by telling her grandmother that she'd been invited to Peggy's for tea and would go straight from work.

When Bron arrived that evening, Ivy had just ironed the dress Peggy was to lend her friend and now it hung from the airing line strung across the kitchen. Bron looked up at it admiringly. It was of pale blue silky material with a tiny flower pattern and dainty puff sleeves, and Ivy, discovering that Bron took only one size smaller than herself, was happy to lend her a pair of court shoes with a small heel to go with it.

The girls went up to Peggy's room to dress and Bron remembered gratefully how, when she had first gone to live in Thelma Street, Ivy had saved her from further embarrassment from the red flannel petticoats by letting her come up to this room and take them off on the days of the gym class. Bron would take Glory to school early, then double back to Rosalind Street, leaving the red petticoat there until after school. And it had worked. Nobody at home had ever suspected. She hoped fervently that her trip to the Church dance would stay a secret too.

'Hurry up, Bron, or we'll be late. Ooh! You look lovely in that, but your hair looks wrong.'

Bron tore the bow from her hair and unplaited the thick strands. When it fell about her shoulders and she'd put a comb through the soft waves, Peggy gasped, 'Oh, Bron, it's lovely. You must wear it like that.'

The shoes she had borrowed were really too large and slopped as she walked, so Bron decided to carry them with her, wearing her usual pair to walk to the hall. Peggy had put on some lipstick, and rubbing a little into her palms had smoothed it gently over her cheeks. Then she handed it to Bron but her cheeks were already pink with excitement, so carefully outlining her lips, she pressed them together as she'd seen her aunt do and declared herself ready to go.

The coat she put on took most of the glory from the dress, but with her pretty hair falling about her shoulders even her dark coat didn't look so severe.

There was a queue waiting to go into the Church Hall and Bron glanced anxiously about her but saw no one she knew from the street, no one who would tell tales to her nan.

They'd paid their sixpences and handed their coats and Bron's heavy shoes in at the cubby hole, and were sitting on two chairs that had a view of the door, when Bron saw Chris from Jessop's grocery counter coming into the hall. She gasped in surprise. He glanced across and didn't seem to recognise her, but a few minutes later he was coming towards her.

'I didn't know it was you with your hair like that,' he said, his eyes filled with admiration.

Bronwen was introducing Peggy to Chris when someone asked her friend to dance just as the pianist started playing 'The Blue Danube'.

'Shall we dance, Bron?' Chris asked, and when she nodded he led her on to the polished floor.

'One-two-three, one-two-three,' she counted under her breath, remembering what Peggy had told her, but as soon as Chris twirled her round and round waltzing seemed as easy and natural as Peggy had said. She managed to keep the borrowed shoes on her feet by gripping with her toes. Despite the discomfort she was enjoying herself – she couldn't ever remember enjoying herself like this.

The next dance was a military two-step and once she'd got into the rhythm she found that easy too. She had qualms when they announced the fox-trot but Chris decided to go to the refreshment stall, coming back with a tray containing tea and biscuits. Soon Peggy hobbled towards them and sat down thankfully, nursing her toes in their open sandals, looking balefully towards the partner she'd just left, muttering, 'He's wasting his time if he asks me again.'

Chris went for tea and biscuits for Peggy. By this time there was a long queue. He's nice, Bron thought, glad she had met him while she was wearing a pretty dress and with her hair loose about her shoulders. Then her eyes clouded as she remembered that tomorrow she would have to go back to wearing her hair in a plait and one of the old-fashioned dresses Nana had made. It's just like being Cinderella, she thought. Surely her grandmother would realise soon that she was almost grown up?

While Chris was getting her tea, Peggy told Bronwen about her day at the shop.

'You ought to have come to work in Goldberg's,' she said, 'They've put me on Baby Linen now and it's great. I had to dress the models for the window dresser today. There was a boy model, a girl model and a baby doll. They looked lovely when they were dressed up.'

The evening passed much too quickly, and with a final crescendo of notes the pianist got up and bowed, and soon there was a queue forming at the cubby-hole to retrieve their coats. As they waited Chris whispered, 'Can I see you home?'

'I'm not going home, Chris, I'm going back with Peggy.'

They were going through the door now. As she took a

step into the street Bron was grabbed from behind, and turning around looked straight into her grandmother's wrathful face.

'You deceitful little madam, coming here without asking permission! Not that I'd have given it – ' Martha's eyes had swivelled towards Chris, but the quick-thinking Peggy had linked her arm in his, and with a 'Good night, Bron' they were walking up the street.

Martha marched her home in outraged silence. When she'd opened the door and pushed the girl into the passage she saw the dress underneath her coat. Dragging the coat off Bronwen, she lunged for the dress, attempting to pull it off. At the same moment Bron turned quickly away, crying, 'No! No! Please let me take it off.' But her plea fell on deaf ears as Martha grabbed at the sleeve which came away with a rending sound. Bronwen, sick to her stomach, yelled, 'Look what you've done! What can I tell Peggy? It was one of her new dresses.'

Then she saw that her grandmother's face had gone very white. She knew she hadn't meant to rip the dress, but almost at once Martha recovered herself, shouting at Bron, 'That's nothing to what might 'ave 'appened to you if some fellow had picked you up at that dance. You might 'ave landed up like that Maisie Jonas up the street. A bun in the oven and no 'usband.'

Bronwen was sobbing now. Holding the ripped off sleeve against her she dashed up the stairs and opening the bedroom door saw Gloria apparently asleep in bed. But when she heard Bron's sobs she sat up, and lit the candle. She put her arms comfortingly about her cousin's heaving shoulders, the bad feeling of the week before apparently forgotten.

'What's the matter, Bron? What was Nana yelling about?'

While Bron told her what had happened Glory twined the long wavy hair about her fingers, interrupting once to ask, 'Why don't you wear your hair just pulled back into a slide? Lovely it is out of a plait.'

When Bron had finished anguishing over the torn dress, Glory assured her, 'It wasn't me told her where you were. I didn't know anyway.'

'I know that, Glory. I expect one of Nana's friends saw me waiting in the queue before the dance started. They weren't to know I'd get into trouble. It's the dress I'm worried about. What can I do?'

Next day, puffy eyed and low in spirits, she went to work taking the dress with her, intending to return it that evening and apologise. She felt too ashamed to look at Chris but he came over to her and asked sympathetically, 'Was it very bad, Bron? I'd have stayed and stuck up for you, but your friend said it would be better if your grandmother didn't know I knew you.'

'What happened?' Marcia asked, watching Bron anxiously, hoping she was willing to be friends again.

Bron told her about borrowing the dress and leaving her hair loose and going to the Church dance. When she came to the part where Martha had ripped the borrowed frock, Marcia said sympathetically, 'She must be awful, your nan.'

'No, she isn't really,' Bron assured her. 'She's a kind person, but she's very old-fashioned, and worries about me and treats me like a child. If only she hadn't ripped Peggy's dress.'

'Let's have a look at it.'

Marcia examined it critically, saying, 'It's only come apart in the seam, Bron. My sister's a dressmaker, she works at home. I'll take it home with me at lunch-time. I may be able to bring it back mended this afternoon.'

Bron looked at her hopefully, then her eyes clouded.

'How much do you think it will cost?'

'I owe it to you, Bron. It won't ever happen again – about the money, I mean. I've learnt my lesson. We had a row and I've finished with him. I don't suppose I'll get any of my money back.'

At a quarter-past two Bron was watching anxiously from the doorway for Marcia to come back. When she did she handed Bron the parcel, saying, 'There you are. You can't even see where she's sewn the seam. Your friend need never know.'

'Thanks, Marcia.' Bron breathed a sigh of relief as she examined the dress. 'I've bought your sister a little box of chocolates. It isn't much but I'm really grateful.'

Mr Jessop had arrived to unlock the door. As they trooped into the shop Bron felt as though a big load had been lifted from her shoulders. Marcia was nice really. Bron was glad she'd finished with that awful boy, and glad most of all that Peggy would never need to know what had happened to her dress.

Chapter Nine

'It won't be very long now, Bron.' Peggy was dragging the gondola of overalls into the shop from the deep entrance of Goldberg's Emporium. Bron nodded and smiled at her friend, continuing to stare enviously at the fashionable clothes displayed on the models in the window.

Bron was enjoying being in Clifton Street on a Saturday evening. When she was working she didn't finish until all the other shops were closed, but on this late September evening in 1932 she was on the final day of belated summer holiday. The last hour had flown by although a slight drizzle was falling, misting the glow from the tall gas-lamps that threw squiggly patterns of light on to the greasy pavements as evening quickly darkened into night.

She loved the noise and bustle around her in the busy street, which rose even above the the raucous cries of the butcher, greengrocer and fishmonger as they auctioned their perishables to be rid of them before closing time.

When she'd gone into the Penny Bazaar the memories had come flooding into her mind, as far back even as when Mama had carried Jackie in the shawl Welsh fashion, and Bronwen herself had just been able to rest her nose on the edge of the counter to view the delights displayed on top.

There'd been tiny sponge bouncing balls, whips and wooden tops that you could draw patterns on in coloured chalks – patterns that would merge into fantastic shapes as you whipped the top faster and faster. Then there were little celluloid dolls with painted hair and eyes, so small they could be dressed by cutting two holes in a tiny scrap of material for the arms to go through, and a tray of brightly coloured hair slides, their 'diamonds' glittering under the lights.

If you had more than a penny to spend you could move further up the counter and choose from boxes of paints and colouring books, or magic painting books that required only water to bring out the concealed illustrations. There were cut out cardboard dolls on the cover of a book full of pretty clothes to be trimmed out carefully, especially the little tabs that you bent over to attach the garment to the doll. Oblong boxes contained balls of rainbow wool together with a pair of short fat knitting needles, or a similar box containing a Knitting Jinny, a small, brightly painted wooden lady with a circle of short-headed nails on top, around which you wound the wool, drawing the stitches over and pulling the work through the hole in the middle of the Jinny, the resulting tube of knitting being used to make such things as kettle holders or mats for resting things on.

A man came to Goldberg's main door to shut and bolt it, breaking into Bron's thoughts as he looked enquiringly at her. Leaving the doorway she waited on the pavement outside, but soon the staff came pouring out of the second entrance and Peggy was linking her arm in Bron's saying, 'You're not meeting Chris tonight then?'

'It's hardly worth it by the time he finishes,' Bron told her friend. For although Jessop's closed an hour before Goldberg's on a Saturday night, there would still be last-minute orders to be put up and delivered, fixtures to fill, bags to string and hang at the side of the counter. And Marcia wouldn't be any better off, for as soon as she'd cashed up she'd be expected to begin entering the day's credit accounts into the ledger.

'He's nice, your Chris,' Peggy told her. 'He was real worried that night your nan started shouting at you when we came out of the dance.'

Remembering that awful night, Bron sighed. Chris was a nice boy and she liked him a lot, but Alby was jealous of him and Alby was nice too. She'd got on well with the errand boy, who was the same age as her. He'd been her friend ever since she'd started at Jessop's, ever since that first day when he'd tried to make her feel at home with his friendly grin.

It was funny with Albert. He hadn't asked her to go out with him until she'd become friendly with Chris, but if he was in the shop and saw her putting up a big order ready for delivery, he'd hang about to lift the heavy box from the counter with ease and carry it to the back room for her. Somehow he always managed to share her tea break, risking Mr Jessop's wrath by often overstaying his time.

She liked Alby, he was a ray of sunshine, whistling his way happily through the day. When he did ask her out she'd already promised to go with Chris, and with his blue eyes regarding her anxiously she'd felt awful saying no.

'Going anywhere tomorrow?' Peggy was asking.

'We'll probably just walk over the tide-fields. I'm meeting Chris at two o'clock.'

Chris and Bron had been good friends ever since the awful night of her first dance. He was quiet and easy to get on with, and she'd grown very fond of him, but there'd been increasing evidence lately that his feelings for her were a little more than fond and she was waiting with some trepidation for what must surely come.

Bron wished with all her heart that she could feel more for him. It had been one of Polly's love stories, left by mistake on the parlour table, that had made her realise how woefully inadequate her own feelings were. It was as though the plain, no-nonsense clothes that she was forced to wear had stamped themselves upon her very emotions. Chris had been patient, mindful that she was two years younger than himself, but there was no hiding his love and longing for her, especially when he kissed her good night. Although she'd allow her lips to linger on his, she knew that mere fondness for him was not enough.

'We're going to cycle to Sully,' Peggy was telling her, 'we might go right across to the island if the tide is right. It'll be the last time this year for the seaside.'

If only I had a bike, Bron thought wistfully, then she too could become a member of the cycling club. She remembered the day in August when she'd been returning a book to Ivy, and had watched enviously as Peggy and her friends cycled off. Peggy had been wearing a short pleated skirt and a pink blouse. She looked very modern with her neat bobbed hair and long suntanned legs. How Bron envied her, imagining her grandmother's look of horror if she had dressed the same. Most of the girls from the cycling club wore short skirts and nearly all wore three-cornered scarves about their necks, streaming out behind them in the breeze.

Bron's hair, though still long, was now worn pulled back into a slide. At first she had unplaited her pigtail in the back room each day before going into the shop, and braided it again before leaving for home. But one day in the rush to get out she'd forgotten to do this and was surprised when her grandmother remarked that it looked very nice that way.

Martha, perhaps tired of all the work it had entailed, no longer made her grand-daughter's clothes. Instead Bron was allowed to keep part of her wages to clothe herself, and could choose her own things providing her grandmother approved.

It had been a long time before she'd taken Chris home but even Martha had soon been won over by him.

'A nice boy he is,' she'd said, and Polly had nodded her agreement as she'd added, 'Knows his manners too. I've been thinking, Bron, I would probably have played with his mam when I was at school.'

'I'm going to meet his mam on Sunday, Aunt Poll. I'm going to Chris's house for tea. I could ask her, if you like.'

When Bronwen met Chris on Sunday afternoon they walked over the tide-fields, arm in arm. It was a warm sunny day and there were a lot of people strolling along over the spongy grass.

When at last they came to the edge, and stood looking down at the sluggish water lapping the grey mud that formed a beach at this point of the Bristol Channel, Chris drew her towards him and kissed her, his arms tightening about her. When she didn't respond he looked down at her, his face flushed, and there was no mistaking the message in his soulful brown eyes.

'I love you so much, Bron. I know we'll have to wait a while, love, you're only sixteen, but in a couple of years perhaps we could get engaged?'

Bron was feeling panic-stricken. How did you know if you were in love? The only knowledge she had gleaned of the subject was from the romantic novels and magazines Polly left lying about and she'd never felt any of the emotions the swooning heroines experienced in these.

Chris was looking swiftly around him before putting his arms about her once more then pressing his lips to hers in a long hard kiss. Although her lips lay passively against his, he didn't seem to notice.

Presently he released her and they began to walk arm in arm back the way they had come until again he bent his head and kissed her, and this time she blushed furiously, looking around her in a panic to see if anyone was watching them. She didn't love him, that was obvious, or she'd have wanted him to kiss her like that. Getting engaged led to marriage, didn't it? And marriage meant sharing a double bed. The colour in her cheeks flared crimson and to cover her confusion she slipped her arm from his and walked a little in front.

'Don't you want to get engaged to me, Bron?' Chris sounded upset.

Not wanting to reply she giggled, and was sorry immediately when she turned and saw his hurt expression. Linking her arm in his once more, hoping not to answer his question, she drew him towards a little crowd gathered around a soap box orator whose meeting was in uproar, as a heckler was being dragged away by two stalwart communist supporters.

When the excitement was over and they began to stroll homewards – for Bron wanted to change before visiting his house – she was thinking wistfully that if only she could love Chris then perhaps in a few years' time they could be married and she could get away from all the restrictions of the house in Thelma Street. There was no other way, for she knew now that her father would never come back to live in Cardiff. He hadn't visited them for more than a year and Polly had even suggested that he had a lady friend in Coventry. Although Bron's heart had missed a beat at the thought, she knew her aunt could well be right.

But she didn't love Chris and being fond was not enough, and although her aunt and uncle seemed to have made up their differences there was no prospect that she could see of her getting away from Will's look of hurt misunderstanding, Polly's ever-watchful eye, and Martha's stifling, conscientious caring.

Chapter Ten

As Bron washed in the bowl of warm soapy water on the washstand, then slipped the cool green cotton dress over her head, she was feeling nervous about the evening ahead. Brushing her hair so that it fell in a warm golden cloak about her shoulders she slipped her feet into her black patent leather shoes, and hurried downstairs to the kitchen where Chris was talking to her nan.

As they turned into Marlborough Road and walked beside the big houses with their wide bay windows, she licked her lips. Chris, sensing how she felt, squeezed her arm encouragingly, telling her he knew that his mam would love her.

'You look lovely in that dress, Bron,' he told her as he held open the gate and led her up the tiled path.

A lady with greying bobbed hair and plump cheeks came to the porch to welcome her, smiling warmly. When Chris introduced his mam, Bron knew it would be a waste of time enquiring if she'd gone to school with her aunt.

'I know you must be surprised, Bronwen,' Chris's mother was saying, just as though she could read Bron's thoughts. 'Christopher came to us very late in life, and he's all the more precious for that.'

When his father came into the room he addressed Bron as 'my dear', and used the phrase all evening. The conversation never flagged; they were lovely warm-hearted people intent on making her feel at ease. However, going home with Chris, their arms entwined, she felt depressed. His parents seemed to be taking things for granted, and unless she could feel something more for Chris than fondness, meeting his parents had been a waste of their time.

Life had settled into a routine since she'd been going out with Chris. In the summer, as now, they'd go on long country walks or to the seaside at nearby Penarth or Barry Island. On winter Sundays, with little else to do, they'd wander around the town, looking at window displays in the big stores; with the city streets almost deserted, shops and cafes closed, it would be like a ghost town. On Wednesdays it would be the pictures, or a trip to Newport where the shops closed on a different half-day.

'Not going out with Chris tonight then, Bron?'

'No, Nan, not tonight.' She'd been dreading the question ever since she'd left Chris a couple of hours before, knowing how fond of him her grandmother had become over the last few months.

'Nothin' wrong, is there?' Martha persisted. 'You are still gettin' engaged?'

Knowing she couldn't dodge this one any longer, Bron sighed, 'It wouldn't be fair to him, Nan. I don't love him enough.'

'Love!' Martha snorted derisively. 'It was love caused all that trouble for Maisie Jonas, poor little dab. Be a slave to 'er mam for the rest of 'er life she will, 'cos Edie Jonas 'as given a home to that baby of 'ers.'

When Bron didn't answer, she continued: 'You listen to me, Bron Thomas. If you can respect a man an' look up to 'im then love will come later. You want youer 'ead read, my girl. That Chris would make you a good partner.

Got a good steady job 'e 'as, an' all.'

Martha flung the washing from the wicker basket on to the table and went to the line for more.

Bron was very fond of Chris, and she respected him. Nana was right, he would make someone a wonderful husband. But liking him wasn't enough. In August she would be seventeen, and it was her coming birthday that had brought things to a head that afternoon. It was a Wednesday, and they'd been to the cinema. When they'd reached the corner of Thelma Street, Chris's arm had tightened about her and he'd said warmly, 'You know how I feel about you, Bron. We'll be engaged on your birthday, love.'

When she didn't answer he'd said, his voice pleading, 'You do love me, Bron? You do want us to get engaged?'

She'd wished she could say yes. She couldn't bear the hurt look in his eyes, but she didn't love him – not enough to marry him anyway. Supposing after they were engaged she fell in love with someone else? Even worse, supposing such a thing happened after they were married? Peggy was engaged to a boy from the cycling club. Her eyes shone whenever she talked about Joe, which was nearly all the time. She was obviously in love. And Bron knew she didn't feel even a little bit like that about Chris.

'Can't we just go on as we are – ' she'd begun, but Chris had said bitterly, 'There's no point going on, is there? What is it you feel for me, Bron, after all this time?'

'We're good friends Chris – '

'Good friends!' He'd spat the words at her. 'I'm going home, Bron. I'll see you at work.' His voice was gruff, and she knew she'd hurt him deeply, but a part of her had been glad the pretence was over.

Martha came back into the kitchen and gave her a long look before asking, in her usual blunt fashion, 'You been 'aving a row with Chris this afternoon?'

'I don't think I love him enough to get engaged, Nan. It's best he knows.'

She could feel Martha's disapproval as she cried, 'Don't be stupid, Bron. Go an' make it up with 'im when you've 'ad youer tea.'

The meal prepared, they ate in a silence that was becoming uncomfortable, when Martha said persuasively, 'Why don't you go and make it up, Bron? I'll clear the dishes.'

'It's no use, Nan. It's finished I tell you.'

When she saw Martha's jaw set obstinately, Bron pushed her plate aside and went up to the bedroom.

She didn't want to discuss it. There was nothing to discuss. For a long time now, she'd felt as though she was just playing at courting, much as she'd played at mothers and fathers when she was a child. I'm glad it's over, she told herself. She'd felt such a cheat when Chris held her in his arms.

A few days later, when she arrived at the shop, Chris was talking to Mr Jessop in the back room. As he came into the shop, Mr Jessop called after him, 'I hope you'll change youer mind, Chris. I don't want to lose you.' And Chris turned back to say, 'I've already taken the job, Mr Jessop. I can start on Monday, like I said, if you'll waive the full week's notice.' Then he stepped back into the warehouse, and Bron heard him say, 'It's nothing to do with the shop, believe me. I've been very happy here. I'm sorry, I can't explain – '

Bron didn't need any explanation. She felt guilty that Chris looked so hurt and upset. She had an almost overwhelming desire to go to him and kiss it better, like you did with a child. She bit her lip, and, turning, began to tidy the fixtures.

When Bron took Marcia her tea later she learned that Chris was going to work for the Maypole. When Bron didn't comment, Marcia added, 'Well, he couldn't very well stay here, could he, Bron? Seeing you all the time would only make things worse.'

On the following Saturday evening, when Chris said goodbye to each of them in turn, Bron mumbled her own good wishes, her eyes on the sawdusted floor, unable to face the vulnerable brown eyes she knew would be looking at her pleadingly. It's all my fault, she thought miserably.

Mr Jessop didn't replace Chris right away so they were all rushed off their feet as they tried to cope. A lot of grocery orders had to be put up and delivered after the shop was closed, and many of the customers grumbled about having to wait so long to be served. Even the girls from the nearby offices and shops who still crowded Ray's end of the counter, refusing to be served by anyone else, were heard to moan as they waited.

Tempers were getting short, and like the others Bron was leaving for home later and later each night. After three weeks of being short-staffed Marcia called her to the cash-desk and whispered, 'He's going to put an advert in the *Echo* tonight. He'd better find someone soon, Bron, or Chris won't be the only one around here to give in their notice!'

Chapter Eleven

'This is Mr Phillips, our new grocery assistant.' Mr Jessop introduced him to the staff, one by one. Bron had hardly been able to take her eyes from the young man as he'd waited to be called into the back room for his interview. He was tall, and broad with it, in his early twenties she guessed, with a fresh complexion and large eyes so dark they looked almost black. His hair was a crown of tawny curls which clung tightly to his head, and which no amount of brilliantine had managed to flatten.

'Looks more like a rugby player than a grocer,' Marcia giggled admiringly to Bron.

Mr Jessop informed them that the young man would be starting work the following Monday. As Bron's fingers touched the new assistant's when she was introduced she felt something akin to an electric shock, and her cheeks flamed with colour as the young man said, 'Cyril's the name, Bron.'

She looked up and saw that his eyes were crinkled with amusement, which made her blush all the more. She was glad when Ray, having finished serving a customer, came over and shook Cyril's hand.

As he talked to Ray she took in every detail of the newcomer: the snowy white shirt, the sporty tweed jacket, and his neatly pressed grey flannels. He was big but there didn't seem to be any flabbiness to him. She could almost see the rippling muscles beneath his jacket sleeves. Marcia was right, he did look like a rugby player, and she wasn't surprised when a few minutes later he was telling Ray that he'd have to give it up now he'd found digs in Cardiff and would be working on Saturdays anyway.

His voice had the lilt of the Valleys. Bron could have listened to it all day. After he had left the shop she stood staring at the closed door until Marcia said with a laugh, 'Close your mouth, Bron, or you'll catch a fly.'

Even after he'd gone she could see the full lips, the straight nose, the strong cleft chin, and the large dark eyes appraising her as he'd gripped her hand.

It didn't make sense. She'd gone out with Chris for almost three years and she'd never felt anything like this. Now a stranger had just walked into the shop and turned her world upside down. He was probably engaged anyway, she cautioned herself, might even be married. Anyway, he'd behaved in exactly the same way when he'd been introduced to Marcia. She'd noticed that.

Bron could hardly wait for Monday morning when Cyril would start work. When it came at last, there he was behind the counter in a stiff new white coat, chatting to Ray as though he'd known him for ever.

Just before the shop closed for lunch, the girls who usually crowded Ray's end of the counter at this time of day came in for cakes or whatever took their fancy. A few of them looked towards Cyril. He smiled at them, and all unsuspecting that they were Ray's special province, invited them to come and be served by him. Several of them did. Glancing at Ray's glowering face, Bron thought uneasily, There'll be trouble over this.

It came the next lunch-time as soon as the door had closed behind the last customer. You could have cut the atmosphere with a knife as Ray said angrily, 'They don't want you to serve them, can't you see that? Those girls always wait for me.' And Cyril answered, genuinely surprised: 'This is ridiculous, mun. They don't mean anything to me. I was just trying to clear the customers, that's all.'

'Give them the glad eye, you mean! I saw you – '

'Don't talk nonsense,' Cyril broke in, looking needled. 'Why, I'd rather go out with Bron here any time than one of those silly giggling girls.'

'Why don't you ask her then?'

The colour was flooding Bron's cheeks, she held her breath. Cyril hesitated just a fraction too long before he said, 'All right then, I will,' and moved towards her.

'Doin' anything tonight, Bron?'

'Nothing in particular. Why?' Somehow she managed to keep her voice steady.

'How about coming to the pictures with me?'

'I'd have to go home and change first. We could go to the last house. Where shall we go?'

'How about the Pavilion? It's the only one I know in Cardiff. I think there's a film with Bette Davies and Douglas Fairbanks.'

'Oh, I love Bette Davies.' Bron hoped she'd managed to keep her voice as casual as Cyril's had been. She was thankful that she'd bought that new dress a few weeks ago. She chose her own things now so long as they passed her grandmother's modesty test, and this one had. It was a lupin blue and the fashionable calf-length with a round neck and short sleeves.

The afternoon dragged as she waited impatiently for closing time, noticing the way Cyril bestowed charm on everyone, whatever their age. When Mrs Thompson brought her mother-in-law shopping and settled her on the bentwood chair in front of the counter while she gave her order, Cyril paid almost as much attention to the old lady as he did to the customer he was serving, bringing her into the conversation, although as she didn't have a tooth in her head it was difficult to understand her mumbled replies. But it was plain she was enjoying being the centre of attention for once.

Bron noticed too the way he dashed to open the door when anyone struggled with it trying to get a pram load of groceries through with a baby in arms, but he sometimes spoilt his action by making remarks to Ray sotto voce, remarks that set them both laughing.

Bron wanted to pinch herself as she waited impatiently for the tram to take her home, trying to ignore the fact that it was Ray's challenge that had practically forced Cyril into asking her. Well, she wouldn't let him down. Her grandmother would want to know where she was going all dressed up. She'd tell her she was going out with a friend from work, hoping she would think it was Marcia. If she thought she was going out with a young man she hadn't personally vetted, Bron wouldn't put it past her to follow them and see for herself!

When she arrived home there wasn't much time to spare, but she ate enough of her tea to keep Martha happy, then hurried upstairs with a jug of hot water and searched in the drawer of the wash-stand for the lavender-scented soap and talcum that Glory had given her last Christmas.

Slipping the dainty dress over her head and smoothing down the skirt, she looked at herself in the spotted mirrored door of the wardrobe, pleased by what she saw. Oh, she was glad that it was summer and she wouldn't need a coat! The coat she still wore for best was old-fashioned and far too short to wear with this lovely new dress. The eyes looking back at her were bright with excitement as she twirled about, then looked down at the new white buckskin sandals, glad she'd had her own way over them.

'They're not very practical, Bron,' Martha had said, 'Best change them for something you can wear if it rains.'

But she hadn't wanted to, and the weather was perfect for them tonight. Sensible shoes would have ruined the effect of the dress.

When she approached the cinema and saw Cyril looking at the photographs displayed outside, her heart began to beat very fast. He turned as she drew nearer, his eyes widening as he took in the smart dress and sandals, then resting on the bright face turned eagerly to his.

When he returned from the cash-desk with the tickets they were led down the darkened aisle where the usherette's torch beam pointed out two empty seats in the middle of a row. People stood up for them to push past in a darkness now lit only by the screen, then they were seated and Cyril was pressing a small box of chocolates into her hands. Muttering her thanks, Bron wished that she could keep the pretty box to cherish. But perhaps Cyril would like one now? She opened it and offered the box to him. When the film began she thought Douglas Fairbanks, good-looking as he was, not nearly so attractive as Cyril, though Bette Davies's large expressive eyes held her spellbound. The film was romantic and full of thrills, and when at last Cyril took his arm from about her shoulders and they rose for 'God Save The King', Bron felt as wanted and loved as any screen heroine.

Cyril had taken it for granted that he would walk her home so when they'd got off the tram and were approaching Thelma Street she stopped suddenly in a panic and tried to explain about her grandmother and how strict she was. But Cyril laughed good-humouredly and said, 'Well, we'd better say good night here then,' and drew her into the doorway of a corner shop. Then she was in his arms and his lips were warm against hers. Her heart began to beat rapidly when his arms suddenly tightened about her and his lips pressed hard against hers, taking her breath away. As he pressed her to him and his kisses became more urgent, she was glad he couldn't see her flaming cheeks.

When at last he released her, laughing shakily, he said, 'Got carried away I did,' then led her out to the pavement, and brushed her lips with his again. 'Good night, Bron, see you tomorrow.'

'Good night, Cyril. Thank you for a lovely evening.'

Her feet hardly touched the ground as she hurried along Broadway and down Thelma Street. Letting herself into the house, she stood with her back to the door in the dark passage, trying to compose her thoughts.

When she went through to the kitchen Martha was dozing in the armchair. Blinking at Bron, she asked, ''Ave a good time then, did you?'

'It was a lovely picture, Nan. You ought to go and see it.'

Martha grunted. She didn't hold with some of them films. Gave young girls the wrong ideas they did. Still, Bron seemed to have enjoyed herself. The girl looked much happier these days, and she was glad.

Bron's thoughts were with Cyril. She'd thought of little else for days. After the way he'd kissed her tonight she was sure he felt the same way as she did. She could hardly believe it! All those young girls who came into the shop, and it was her, Bron Thomas, that he wanted to see. She hugged herself with happiness.

Chapter Twelve

Cyril didn't know Cardiff at all, and there were so many places she wanted to show him; but somehow she felt she couldn't take him to the haunts she'd frequented with Chris. Poor Chris! In her new-found happiness, Bron hoped fervently that he would find happiness with some girl who would love him as much as she loved Cyril.

Today, as she hurried to the tram stop to meet Cyril, she told herself that she'd have to tell her nan about him very soon. Martha had remarked several times lately on how much happier Bron seemed to be.

'Too young you was to be gettin' engaged, love,' she remarked with hindsight. 'Perhaps when youer older, you and Chris could get back together again,' she'd added hopefully.

Bron's legs felt suddenly weak when she saw Cyril coming towards her. His dark eyes crinkled at the corners as he smiled, the tight tawny curls shone with brilliantine. She thought he looked very smart, in a blue open-necked shirt worn beneath a grey tweed-mixture jacket, a sharp crease in his pale grey flannels. As if he'd just come out of a band-box, she thought, smiling to herself that one of Martha's sayings had come to her mind like that.

Cyril was taking her hand and pulling her gently towards the tram that had just arrived at the stop. Leading her upstairs to the open top deck, he pushed the seat back so that they wouldn't be seated facing anyone and could enjoy a clear view.

They were on their way to Victoria Park. It would be nice, on a warm day like this, to walk beside the river that flowed through the gardens, perhaps even catch a glimpse of Billy the seal.

As they entered the park, happy noises came to them from the stream, where young children paddled, kicking joyously at the water and sending it spraying over each other, while mams and grandmas watched them dotingly from the bank.

Sitting beside Cyril in the warm sunshine, Bron was enjoying herself, but, sensitive to his every mood, she soon realised that Cyril was becoming bored.

'Shall we go to see the monkeys?' she asked hopefully; but Cyril replied, 'Let's go back to town, Bron.'

'But there's nothing open on a Sunday.'

'It's early yet. I believe there's a fair in those fields by the Castle grounds. I saw it advertised from the tram.' Cyril was already on his feet.

They got off the tramcar near Cathedral Road, and could faintly hear the hurdy-gurdy music of the round-abouts, increasing in volume as they took a side turning and found themselves on a path, which led to the fair-ground, already lit with gaudy coloured lamps despite the bright sunshine.

Cyril's face wore an eager expression now, as he pulled her towards the rides. While they got into a swaying carriage, a ragged boy came to click the safety bar in place. Now they were close together, Cyril's arm about her shoulder, his face smiling down at her. Then, with a jerk, the carriage swung up and up in a backwards circle, sway-ing with a sickening motion so that she clung .to him tightly. He bent over, and, after kissing the top of her head, put his arms about her protectively. Bron kept her eyes closed for the rest of the ride, her face against the rough tweed of his jacket, her emotions a mixture of fear and ecstacy. When at last their feet touched the ground again, she was forced to cling to him still, for the ground seemed to be moving beneath her like the waves of the sea.

They strolled around the fairground eating ice-cream cones. When Cyril tried his skill at hoopla he won her a celluloid doll dressed in frilly pink crepe paper, and when he rolled the balls into all the right slots a china figure of a Victorian lady was put into her hands. She vowed to cherish them for ever, already picturing them in the bedroom she shared with Gloria, but felt suddenly dismayed as she remembered that Martha didn't know about Cyril – she'd just have to pack them away in her case until she'd told her nan and then could put them on display.

It would soon be August bank holiday, and Cyril had seen an advertisement for the grand reopening of the Empire in town. Janet Gaynor and Lew Ayres were starring in a film called *State Fair*. The cinema, it said, had been completely refurbished in the latest luxurious style, and Cyril had asked her if she'd like to go.

Again Bron told Martha that she was going with her friend from the shop, and she was, of course, but she felt awful about the way she was deceiving her nan. It's her own fault, she thought – I couldn't bear her showing me up in front of Cyril. Holding her tongue wasn't one of Martha's virtues.

The cinema was beautiful, all plush red and gold; and when the Compton Wonder organ rose slowly in a kaleidoscope of ever-changing colour, music swelled to fill the auditorium.

After the main film it was a job to bring herself down to earth. She was Janet Gaynor, but she didn't want Cyril to be Lew Ayres. He was far more handsome than any film star she'd ever seen. But when Cyril called the usherette and bought two tubs of ice cream, she'd put the first icy-cold spoonful into her mouth and the spell was broken.

Bron was running out of places she hadn't seen with Chris, as she and Cyril wandered over the tide-fields one day listening to a lone orator, whose audience contained more hecklers than supporters. As they walked towards the edge to look out over the Bristol Channel, she felt a little sad, wondering what Chris was doing now and if he was happy in his new job.

As they stared out over the water, Cyril pulled her gently towards him and kissed her, his arm tightening about her, and she didn't feel any of the embarrassment she used to feel with Chris.

Now it was early September, a warm golden day, and they were enjoying an afternoon in the country on their half-day off from the shop. She told him about her mam and dad and Jackie and the house in Rosalind Street where they used to live. She'd been hoping he'd tell her about his own family for he never mentioned them.

Then Cyril told her about his home village and how much he missed it, of how he loved to be outdoors, especially going for long walks on the mountain.

'It sounds wonderful,' she sighed. 'Whyever did you leave there?'

He looked down at her sadly and took her hand in his.

'My mother wanted me to marry a girl I didn't love, Bron. There was an awful row.'

She knew all about that, she thought, smiling at him sympathetically. Look how Nana had carried on because she wouldn't get engaged to Chris.

They had reached Morgan's tea gardens, and sitting at a long wooden table they waited for scones and tea. The sun filtered through the branches of the apple trees, dappling the path with sunshine, and behind them in the flower beds bees droned noisily.

She had never been so happy. She wanted to put her hand out and take Cyril's but there were other people at the table so she looked across at him, admiring the dark eyes smiling at her, the bright colour of his cheeks, the tawny curls shining gold where the sun caught them, the smart blue open-necked shirt. Imagine a man like this wanting to be with her! She felt like pinching herself, but it was no dream. She bit into the creamy scone, and heedless now of the people around her stretched out her hand. Cyril took it in his and cradled it tenderly.

After they left the tea gardens they walked for about half an hour, their arms entwined, stopping to rest against a five-bar gate. The field on the other side, shadowed by a tall hedge, looked cool and inviting. Cyril put his arms about her and drew her towards him. When his lips found hers Bron's heart leapt with joy and she flung her arms about him. It was so romantic, just like the stories Polly read. Her lips were pressed hard against Cyril's, her heart beating fast. Suddenly he broke away and was urging her over the gate, almost lifting her over.

'It says trespassers will be prosecuted,' she giggled, thinking they must be taking a short cut. Next moment he'd pushed her down in the long grass behind the hedge and she lay very still. Was someone coming? Must they keep out of sight? Then Cyril was on top of her, breathing heavily, his eyes glazed, pressing his body against hers. Panicking now, her heart pounding, Bron struggled to free herself, but she couldn't move him an inch and to her horror Cyril was lifting her clothes and fumbling with his own.

When she began to scream his hand came over her mouth. Suddenly she felt a sharp pain which returned again and again, and now her muffled screams were of agony.

At last, with a sigh, Cyril slumped to her side and lay there, panting, staring up at the cloudless sky. Bron, pale and trembling, pressed her face into the lush grass, her heart sick with disgust, long shuddering sobs tearing from her throat.

Cyril raised himself on one elbow to say, 'What you crying for? You wanted it, Bron. Encouraged me you did.'

'I didn't,' she sobbed. 'I didn't! How was I to know what you were going to do?'

He laughed incredulously, then lay back and stared once more at the sky.

Presently she got shakily to her feet. Still sobbing, she straightened her clothes and stumbled towards the gate, but she didn't have the strength to climb it. Then Cyril was helping her, only now she couldn't bear the feel of his arms about her and would have hurried away once she was in the lane if she hadn't felt sick and a little faint.

Seeing her white face, Cyril took her arm, saying, 'I thought you loved me, Bron. Don't worry, *cariad*, if anything ever happens – a baby, I mean – we'll get married.'

So he expected it to happen again?

A wave of sickness came over her and he would have put his arm about her but she shook it off, dashing to the hedge as her stomach began to heave. When at last she could leave the support of the hedge she stumbled along the lane, tears streaming from her eyes, and as Cyril followed he said in a voice filled with disgust: 'Well, no one's ever reacted like that before.'

So there'd been others? Oh God! She hated herself for letting it happen, but how could she have stopped him? Had she encouraged him as he'd said? She'd shown all her love for him in her kisses, but how could she have known it would lead to this?

When Cyril attempted to take her arm she shrugged herself free.

'The way you kissed me, Bron, I thought you wanted it.' He shook his head in bewilderment.

Her little hiccuping sobs were quieter now, and as they reached the tram-stop, the tears still streaming from her eyes, she stood facing the wall, thankful no one else was waiting.

'For God's sake, turn off the water works,' Cyril told her, his voice sharp with disgust. But at his obvious lack of remorse her tears flowed faster.

When the tram came she went upstairs and sat on the front seat, staring miserably out of the window, ignoring Cyril as he took the seat beside her.

Because of her grandmother Cyril had never walked her all the way home. Now, as they got off the tram, he said again, 'Thought I was pleasing you I did, Bron. You shouldn't have kissed me like that.'

She hurried away without answering, slowing her steps as she neared Thelma Street, and dabbing her eyes with her soggy handkerchief.

Passing the house where Maisie Jonas lived she remembered last week, when the girl, her baby carried Welsh fashion in the shawl, had been opening her gate. She'd looked at Bron then quickly away, barely answering her greeting. She'd looked so ashamed, so embarrassed. Now Bron was no better than Maisie whom everyone pitied. It probably hadn't been Maisie's fault either but it had ruined her life. Bron shivered as she hurried on.

Letting herself into the house as quietly as she could she climbed the stairs on tip-toe, thankful that Glory was gone to her friends to do her homework. Pouring cold water from the jug on the wash-stand into the bowl she bathed her burning cheeks. She felt dirty. Perhaps that wasn't the right word but she couldn't think of a better one. If only she could get into a tub of hot water, but nothing would wash away what had happened, nothing could.

Bron tip-toed to the door and turned the key in the lock, then tearing off her clothes she bathed all over in the icy water, splashing herself over and over, the scent of the lavender soap strong in her nostrils, wondering if she'd ever feel clean again. Surely if she really loved Cyril she shouldn't feel like this? Nothing in the tender companionship and loving kisses that Chris had given her had prepared her for this. Suddenly the full impact of Cyril's remark struck her: 'No one's ever reacted like that before.'

How many had there been? And why had his mother wanted him to marry a girl he didn't love? What a fool she'd been, worshipping him as she had.

When half an hour later she entered the kitchen, Martha was coming from the line with an armful of clothes.

'Had a good walk, Bron?' she asked, putting the washing on the table and beginning to fold the garments.

'Yes. It's still warm out there, isn't it?' she answered, keeping her face averted, but in the gloom of the kitchen Martha didn't notice her grand-daughter's pale face and red eyes, or that she'd changed her dress.

Chapter Thirteen

During the week that followed Bron swung between hope and despair, the plight of Maisie Jonas never far from her mind. She was surprised that at work she was able to behave more or less naturally, sure that what had happened must have marked her in some way. Her feelings for Cyril swung alarmingly. Sometimes she could barely stand being behind the same counter, at others, seeing his puzzled expression at her behaviour, she wanted to put her arms about him and reassure him. But when he'd asked, 'What cinema shall we go to on Wednesday, Bron?' she'd replied, 'Sorry, but I've got to go to Newport to do some shopping.'

Why had she said that? She hadn't meant to go. Was it because she didn't want to be close to Cyril in the darkness, to feel his arms about her and his cheek against hers? Or was it that after what he'd said about her encouraging him she'd feel constraint over every kiss and hug?

She thought she loved him, but with none of the hero worship and admiration she'd felt for him before. Whatever happened she would never feel the same towards him again; the old trusting Bron had gone. The worry of what might happen was never far from her mind, and she wouldn't be sure about that until early next week at least. She longed for the time to pass, but at least while she

111

didn't know she could still hope.

She didn't go to Newport on her half-day, and late in the afternoon when she was washing her hair her grandmother said, 'Not goin' to the pictures with youer friend, Bron?'

'No, I told him I didn't want to go.' Before Martha spoke, Bron realised what she'd said.

'Him? I thought it was Marcia you went with.' Martha's voice was anxious.

'No, it's Cyril from the shop.' Nan would have to know sometime, wouldn't she?

'How long 'ave you been going out with 'im then? You never told me.'

'Only after Chris left and he started work at Jessop's.'

At the mention of Chris, Martha's expression softened but her voice was still sharp as she said, 'I 'ope you know what youer doin' my girl. You'd better bring 'im 'ome. I should 'ave met 'im long before this.'

The following week, as day followed day, Bron's hopes faded. It sickened her to see Cyril joking with the customers and chatting up the girls when Ray's back was turned, apparently without a care in the world.

She couldn't bring herself to discuss her worries with him, but surely he must have guessed? Even though she didn't feel the same towards him she didn't want to lose him, so when on the following Wednesday he asked her what film she'd like to see, she said he could choose because she didn't mind. And when they sat in the darkness of the cinema with his arm about her and his lips occasionally seeking hers she wished they were alone so that she could confide her worries. But perhaps something would happen soon? Perhaps being so upset all the time was delaying it? She'd heard this could happen. But when a new week began and slowly passed, and then another, she knew she must tell Cyril without delay.

'Oh no, Bron! Not that, not the very first time.' Cyril's expression was frankly disbelieving. 'Anyway, you could be wrong. Best wait and see.'

Wait and see? It had been more than six weeks. They had been talking quietly in a corner of the warehouse. Without another word, Cyril went back to the shop. Bron felt shattered by his lack of concern. As she weighed sugar into bags her mind seethed with questions she had already asked herself over and over. What would her grandmother say when she knew? Poor Nan! The shame might be too much for her. And poor Aunt Poll too. Her father would be bitterly disappointed in her. She was glad she wouldn't have to face him at least.

She stacked the sugar she had packed into a box and took it through to put away in the fixtures, the feeling of apprehension building within her. She was going to hurt the very one who had given her a home when her father went off to Coventry. Her nan had had a hard life but had always been able to hold her head high. Now she would be shattered by Bron's news.

She had thought maybe Cyril would walk her to the tram that evening to discuss their predicament, but with a quick 'Good night' and a wave of his hand he had hurried away. It was the last straw and as Bron sat in the tram on the second part of her journey home she was numb with worry, wondering how she could face her grandmother when she told her what had happened. Martha was a stickler for decency, for having some pride in yourself. Bron swallowed hard and looked out of the window with misty eyes as she thought: Go beserk she will, I know.

She was so deep in her own dark thoughts that she missed her stop, and when at last she clattered down the twisting stairs and got off, she was half way along Newport Road where it bordered the Common.

When the tram had gone she stood irresolute. It was near here her mother had drowned in the swirling waters of the river. For years she had carefully avoided this spot. Till now. She turned and got on to the grass verge, walking over the wiry grass until she reached the river bank and stood looking down at the sluggish water, her heart heavy with sorrow. Perhaps it would be better for everyone if she never went home? The river was fairly high now after recent rain. When her mother had fallen in it had been swollen and fast flowing.

Suddenly she was a child again, reliving the heartbreak of that November day so long ago when the policeman had come to break the awful news. Again the dreadful grief flooded over her, as though her heart was being torn out. She had believed then she would never be happy again.

Mama's death had been an accident, but they would soon discover why Bronwen had jumped in. There would be an autopsy and an inquest and they would know all about the baby. There'd be headlines in the *South Wales Echo* and probably in the *Western Mail* too.

Her cheeks grew scarlet at the thought. Everyone they knew would read about it and her grandmother would probably die of shame. Oh no, she wouldn't be saving her any unhappiness by doing this dreadful thing, but giving her more grief than she could bear. She took a step back.

The tears began to flow and she let them, lying down in the tall couch grass and burying her face in her hands. If only her mam were alive she would understand, she would know what to do.

The sun had gone down leaving a warm red glow in the

sky. Feeling calmer, her tears spent, Bron got up and walked back towards the pavement. She would walk home, give her tears time to dry.

'There you are at last,' Martha said as she came into the kitchen. 'Where 'ave you been?'

'Sorry I'm late, Nan!'

'Oh well, you're 'ere now. Youer dinner's in the oven, Bron. Polly and Glory 'ave gone out. Waiting I was to go into Bertha's for an hour.'

When the door closed Bron sighed with relief that there were to be no questions.

Next morning Martha called her earlier than usual, saying, 'If you get up now you'll 'ave time for a decent cooked breakfast 'fore you go. Been looking peaky lately you 'ave. Real worried about you I've been.'

Bron sat up and rested on one elbow, then lay back again and closed her eyes. She didn't feel well. Martha had gone back downstairs and presently the smell of bacon frying came through the open bedroom door. Bron splashed water from the bowl on the wash-stand over her face and neck, looking at her sleeping cousin enviously for Glory wouldn't have to get up for at least another half an hour.

As Bron descended the stairs the smell of frying bacon became stronger and her stomach queasier by the minute. Hand over mouth she dashed through the kitchen and just managed to reach the sink in the yard. When at last, after bathing her face under the tap in the wash-house, she went back to the kitchen, Martha was staring at her wide-eyed, her face deathly pale.

'Something's wrong,' she said, and her voice was a croak. 'Oh my God, Bron! Youer not goin' to 'ave a baby?'

When Bron nodded miserably Martha's hand flew to

her mouth, and with a little despairing cry she sank to the floor.

'Aunt Poll! Aunt Poll!' Bron screamed, dashing along the passage to the middle room. The door flew open and her aunt gaped at her in astonishment.

'It's Nan. She's fainted.'

Hearing the commotion, Glory was dashing downstairs in her nightdress.

'Bring the smelling salts,' Polly called over her shoulder as she rushed with Bron to the kitchen.

Together they lifted Martha on to the sofa. As they settled the cushions behind her head her eyes fluttered open.

'What – what happened?'

'You fainted, Mam. You've never done that before.'

Martha looked from one to the other, and as her eyes rested on Bron a look of horror came over her face, and to the astonishment of Polly and Gloria she said, 'Whoever 'e is 'e'll 'ave to marry you. I don't believe for one moment that it's Chris, which only leaves that Cyril you've been goin' out with. Well?'

Bron nodded her head miserably, glad that it was out at last. Polly had been gaping at them both. Now looking at Glory, she said hurriedly, 'All this is not for youer ears, Miss. Come on and get dressed or you'll be late.'

As the kitchen door closed behind them, Bron sat down. Folding her arms on the table she gave a long shuddering sigh as she rested her burning cheeks on them.

'Pull yourself together,' Martha told her. 'It's me who ought to be doin' the sighing. I might 'ave known 'cos come to think of it I don't remember seein' anything in the wash for you last month.'

Bron's thoughts went to the hemmed pieces of flannelette neatly folded in the drawer upstairs, but Martha was continuing, ''E'll 'ave to marry you, that's for sure. Blame myself I do for not puttin' you in the picture like. Our Poll always said I wrapped you in cotton wool. Oh my God, Bron! What's youer dad goin' to say?'

When Bron didn't raise her eyes, Martha went on, ''Ave you told that boy yet? Look 'ere, Bron, I think you'd better bring 'im 'ome with you tonight so's we can talk about it. Sooner youer married the better it'll be, though God knows where youer goin' to live.'

The nausea, the shock of Martha fainting and the endless tears and worry had taken their toll. Bron sat at the table shivering, her head in her hands. Martha swung to and fro in the rocking chair, her face pale and set, sad eyes staring before her, wondering how best to handle this evening's confrontation – that was, of course, if Bron could persuade that Cyril to come.

When Polly came back to the kitchen she found them like this, and it being far too late now for her niece to go to work, she bustled about making a cup of tea. Well! she thought. What a t'do. Who'd have thought it of young Bron? Of course, there'd been that business with her and Will all those years ago, but she hadn't really believed anything was wrong, not even at the time. Will was such a fool, he'd needed a good shaking up.

When Bron went to work in the afternoon she was outwardly calm, planning to tell Mr Jessop she'd had a bilious attack. Martha had given her strict instructions to bring Cyril home with her, but how was she going to do that if he refused to come?

Cyril and Bron shared their teabreak and she saw the fear in his eyes when she told him her grandmother would like to meet him.

'Oh, not that again, Bron,' he blustered. 'I told you, it takes more than once.'

'Well, it didn't this time,' she told him, showing some of her old spirit. 'You made a promise, didn't you? Aren't you going to keep it?'

'Come off it, Bron. It can't be.'

When just then he was called to the counter, she dispassionately watched him walk away. How could I ever have loved him so much? she thought.

But she was surprised that evening when, coming from the back room with her coat, she found Cyril waiting for her. Linking her arm in his, he said, 'Better get it over with, I suppose.'

'We've got to talk about it, Cyril,' she said. 'My gran's only trying to help.'

'Couldn't we have talked it over ourselves without her putting her nose in?'

Relief was flooding through her. Cyril wasn't being very gracious about her grandmother trying to help, and hadn't she tried to talk to him herself? But he was willing to talk now. Was he going to be reasonable? If they got married quickly then no one except the family would need to know about her condition.

Bron remembered this morning when Polly had gone back to the middle room and she'd heard her telling Will. Oh, it was awful! And if Cyril didn't keep his promise the whole street would be talking very soon.

When they got home she was really surprised for Martha had put the best damask cloth on the table and a hand-crocheted lace one over it, and on this was laid the best china. There was a plate of dainty sandwiches, and fairy cakes set out on a doyleyed cake stand. Cyril was being treated like a welcome guest and was half way through his second cup of tea before Martha said quietly, 'Have you thought about making a date for the wedding yet, Cyril?'

Bron watched his mouth open and shut several times before he replied carefully, 'No, we haven't arranged anything.'

'Well, in view of Bron's condition don't you think you'd better arrange it very soon?'

Cyril just looked at her but he knew he was no match for Martha Thomas, who smiled at him disarmingly.

Bron stared at the floor, humiliation bringing the hot colour to her cheeks. It was obvious that Cyril didn't want to marry her. He was looking around him before finally bringing his eyes back to Martha. Then, putting his tea-cup down slowly, he said, his voice resigned, 'We'll go to the Register Office and make arrangements on Wednesday afternoon. Will that be all right, Bron?'

Relief flooded through her but not happiness. Why didn't she feel happy? Lots of girls would jump at the chance of marrying a good-looking man like Cyril. But she already knew the answer. He didn't want to marry her. If circumstances and her grandmother hadn't forced him into it, he would never have considered it. He looked trapped, sitting there. She watched him ease his collar and take out his handkerchief and dab at his forehead. Yes, trapped was the word.

For a moment she felt like allowing her pride get the better of her common sense and telling him he was free. But only for a moment. She couldn't afford the luxury of pride. For the baby's sake, for her own sake, and for the good name of her family she was grateful that Cyril was going to marry her.

When he had gone, Martha gave a great sigh of relief. 'Went off much better than I expected,' she confided. 'Making 'im welcome was the best thing to do, as Poll said. Didn't give 'im the chance to lose 'is temper and walk out.'

119

When at last, exhausted with the events of the day, Bron went to bed, Glory, who stayed up later now that she was nearly fourteen, was pretending to be asleep. Bron knew that she wasn't because one eye was open and watching her undress.

'What are you looking at, Glory?'

'Where are you going to live, Bron, when you marry youer Cyril?'

'I don't know. We'll have to look for some rooms.'

'If he hadn't said he'd marry you, you could have bought a wedding ring from Woolworth's and called yourself Mrs Smith or something.'

Bron could afford to laugh now. 'But everyone around here would know I wasn't Mrs Smith, silly.'

'Oh, you'd have had to go away somewhere, of course.'

'Well, we *are* getting married so I won't need to, will I?'

As she lay in the darkness with Glory breathing gently beside her Bron was remembering the expression on Cyril's face when Martha had pressed him about making the wedding arrangements. His dark eyes had looked so sad. She remembered how happy he'd looked when he'd talked about the village where he'd been born and brought up. He'd told her about the feeling of freedom he always had when, climbing the mountain and reaching the top, he would stand with the wind in his hair, looking down at the panorama of little villages and countryside below.

In the morning she felt queasy again, and got up earlier to give the nausea time to pass before she had to leave for work.

For breakfast she had a piece of dry toast, knowing that she could make up for it at mid-morning break.

'You don't look very happy, Bron. I thought you'd be

on top of the world.' Martha had been watching her uneasily. 'Don't you want to marry Cyril? Life's goin' to be very 'ard for you, *cariad*, if you don't.'

'Yes, of course I want to marry him, Nan. It's just that, well, I think he feels trapped. Cyril misses the Valleys. I don't think he likes Cardiff very much.'

'Well, 'e should 'ave thought of that and kept 'is trousers buttoned!' was Martha's tart reply.

Chapter Fourteen

Walking home, Cyril wondered why he'd been fool enough to give in so easily. He hadn't meant to commit himself, but Bron's grandmother had been so nice to him when he'd arrived he'd been taken completely off his guard.

Ironic, that's what life was. He'd come to Cardiff to avoid getting married. He remembered the way his mam had stuck up for Ceinwen. Tried to shame him she had, but he'd known Ceinwen better. He'd known she was anyone's who'd give her a good time. The baby could have been his but then it could have been any one of three men's.

Supposing he'd married her and the child had had ginger hair and green-grey eyes like Michael McDaid, or a swarthy complexion and black hair like Dilwyn James? No, he had to be certain, so he'd come to Cardiff to bide his time, hoping one or the other would marry her and settle the matter.

There'd been ructions at home before he left. 'Youer no son of mine, Cyril,' his mother had said, 'getting out of youer responsibilities like that.' And when his father had added his voice to the pressure for him to marry Ceinwen, Cyril had been glad to come to Cardiff and find a job.

He didn't have any worry of that kind with Bron; he'd known she was a virgin the moment he took her. She'd asked for it though, only now he realised that that was all part of her innocence. Oh God! Fancy being forced to live in Cardiff, maybe for the rest of his life, when he longed so much to get back to the Valleys. Now it wasn't only Ceinwen keeping him away. That old girl he'd met tonight would make sure he married Bron and settled down.

Suddenly he was remembering his own nan. She'd been real soft with him, twist her round his little finger he could. But Mrs Martha Thomas would hover over Bron like a hen with its chick, he'd known that as soon as he'd laid eyes on her. He'd never be able to go home now, for if he took Bron back to Glas Fynydd to live Ceinwen would want to scratch her eyes out. Anyway, where were they going to live? There was no room in his digs for a wife and baby.

Next day at work Bron whispered that Martha was baking a wedding cake and planning to give them a small reception after the wedding. 'I hope your family will be able to come, Cyril,' she said, her eyes bright with excitement.

She is a pretty girl, Cyril consoled himself. I could do worse, I suppose. It would be nice to have someone to look after him. He'd missed his mother's cooking since he'd come to Cardiff.

Everyone at the shop was surprised when they told them the news. Mr Jessop agreed to them having the Wednesday morning off and promised them a week's groceries as a wedding present. Marcia was excited about her invitation, even though she couldn't have time off in the morning to be at the Register Office, promising to come straight to the house when they closed for half-day at one o'clock.

Now that things were settled and Cyril was making plans for her to go with him to Glas Fynydd to meet his family, Bron almost began to enjoy the situation. The wedding ring was purchased, not from Woolworth's either, and they were desperately seeking furnished rooms. Bron had been to see a few, but the snag with renting them furnished was that the rooms were so much more expensive – and they hadn't yet found any they could afford, especially as she would be giving up work in a few months' time.

On the day before Bron was to meet Cyril's family Peggy came round with the news that Mrs Evans's daughter and her family had moved to a council house, and so there'd probably be rooms to let in the very house in Rosalind Street where she used to live.

'Furnished?' Bron asked, knowing it wouldn't be.

'No, Bron. I saw them putting their things on a lorry.'

'Go and see them anyway in case they get taken,' Martha told her. Time was running out, wasn't it? Perhaps they could all help out, just to give them a start. If they didn't find a place they'd have to live apart, and that would give the neighbours something to gossip about.

The gate groaned protestingly as Bronwen pushed it open. The door was shabby and the brass knocker and letter-box dull and spotted. The door opened and Mrs Evans was looking at Bron enquiringly, her eyes tired. She was a short, plump woman, her straight grey hair drawn back at the side into a slide. 'Is it about the rooms? You 'aven't got any children, 'ave you?' she asked.

'No, we're getting married next week.'

'Come in and look round then. The rooms are a bit of

a mess 'cos them kids of my daughter's are little terrors. You'll 'ave to take it as it is, though. Decorate it youerself, you'll 'ave to.'

Bron nodded, following her into the familiar passage, unfamiliar now with its shabby wallpaper and paint. Yet looking closely she recognised the very wallpaper that had been there when she was a child.

The front room was to let as well as the second bedroom upstairs, the room that had been hers and Jackie's. It should have felt like a homecoming, but the sight of the ripped paper and the blind – probably the one Dada had left – hanging crooked, its dirty lace hem torn, the grate and its surround as rusty brown-looking as though it hadn't seen a blacklead brush since they'd left, made Bron feel deeply sad.

She wondered if Cyril could decorate like her father used to. Jack had always been so fussy with his plumb line, peeling the paper off and on until he'd achieved perfection.

'Well? What do you think, girl? A mess it is I know, and that's why I wouldn't let to anyone with kids again.'

For a moment Bron wondered if she should tell her, recoiling instantly from the thought for it would be all over the street if she did.

'How much is the rent, Mrs Evans?'

'You can call me Bessie if you come 'ere to live. And you are?'

'Bron – Bron Thomas. My name will be Phillips when we're married. I used to live in this house when I was a child, Mrs Evans.'

'Six shillings I was thinking. Tell you what, we'll call it five shillings and sixpence.'

'Thanks, Mrs Evans – Bessie. Can I see the bedroom?'

As they climbed the stairs her heart was beating fast.

This was the room where she'd dreamt her childish dreams. Where Mama had always kissed her good night with a loving hug. Where Father Christmas had piled her bed with presents.

''Ere we are.' Bessie flung open the door. Bron stared at the badly scuffed floor, the dirty windows at which tattered curtains flapped in the breeze, the faded wallpaper, the very same of course. Hadn't they done any papering in all these long years? But she was thrilled to get the rooms even though at the moment they had no furniture to put in them. It had always been a happy house, she and Cyril would be happy here too. She'd clean and polish and buy new wallpaper and paint as soon as they could manage it. They'd have both their wages for a while. They'd have Sundays and Wednesday afternoons to work on the rooms.

When she told Cyril about them and how much needed to be done, he said, 'Can't we hang on for a while, Bron? Perhaps we can find something better.'

'Better?' she cried. 'Not at five and six a week. It's very cheap.'

'It sounds awful.'

'I used to live there when I was a child. It was lovely then. We can make the rooms nice again.'

Really! Didn't he want them to be together? She'd thought he'd be excited about doing the place up.

The family and friends rallied round to help them. Ivy promised the loan of her spare bed until they could buy one, and gave them some bedding to start them off. Martha was loaning them the gate-leg table and two chairs from the parlour and she was giving them enough china and cutlery to get by. Alma brought a companion set for the fireplace, some tablecloths and a new sweeping brush. Bertha Morgan contributed some bowls and a bucket containing a scrubbing brush and floor cloth. Polly and Will bought them a new oak clock for the mantelpiece and some lovely new towels, and Martha promised to buy them a brand new tea-set when her money club came out the following week.

Bron went to Clifton Street to order oilcloth for the living room. The bedroom floor would have to remain bare for now.

Nothing could be done about the rooms until the next week when they would be paying the rent from the Monday. Before that loomed the dreaded visit to her future in-laws. Bron would have been looking forward to meeting them if it weren't for the circumstances, but it was with a feeling of trepidation that she met Cyril at the station on the following Sunday morning. She sat in a corner seat of the carriage watching him drumming his fingers nervously on his knee. He'd assured her that she'd be welcomed but it was obvious that he was worried about something.

The whistle shrilled, there was a slamming of doors. The train lurched forward with a hissing of steam and they were on their way. Soon the flat fields gave way to hilly country, with distant mountains and sometimes the flash of the river as it wound its way between green banks. The train stopped many times and people got on, crowding the carriage now, friendly garrulous people who talked and called to each other in the lilting accent of the Valleys, drawing Bron into the conversation.

'Lovely day, innit? Going far, are you?'

'Glas Fynydd. We've come from Cardiff.'

'Went to Cardiff last week we did. Fagged out I was, traipsing round them shops. Tipping down it was too.'

When Bron and Cyril got off the train the goodbyes were still echoing in their ears as they ran down the steps from the platform. Outside the station the long street swept upwards, seemingly blocked at its far end by the mountain itself, but nearing the top, a little out of breath by now, Bron saw that the mountain was further off than she'd thought and that the street ended in a stretch of grassland that gradually rose towards the lowest slope.

As they neared the house the door burst open and a girl of about twelve was dashing towards them, flinging her arms about Cyril and burying her face in his jacket. Hugging the child, then holding her away from him, he said, 'This is Ceridwen, my youngest sister and the only one still at home.'

At the open door of the house a woman stood smiling at them, her arms outstretched. When they reached her it was Bron she folded them about, crying, 'Welcome, *cariad*! Welcome!' and drawing her into the house. The wide entrance ended abruptly at the door of a large kitchen-cum-living room where a number of saucepans were simmering on a brightly blackleaded range.

The smell of roasting lamb filled the air as a pot of tea and a plate of Welsh cakes were put on the table in front of Bron and Cyril. The room was bright with pretty chintz covers and curtains. Bron looked around her appreciatively. The wallpaper was pale, making the room look even more spacious. On the high mantel shelf a pair of prancing brass horses flanked an ebony clock with bold brass numerals on its black face, the space on either side of the clock filled with family photos in dark wooden frames. Looking round for Cyril whose tea was getting cold, Bron saw that he was now standing sideways, staring out of the window towards the mountain, and as he turned toward her when she called his name, she saw the longing in his eyes. Going to his side, she said, 'Why don't you go out for a while? I'll be all right here with your mam.' But he sighed and shook his head.

'Better not,' he said, and went to the table and picked up his cup.

Was he afraid of meeting someone? The girl perhaps? The one his mother had wanted him to marry.

When she said, 'There's a lovely view of the mountain from here, Mrs Phillips,' her future mother-in-law said, 'Call me Mam, Bronwen. I'd like that, *cariad*.' And Bron felt suddenly sad for she hadn't called anyone that since her own mother had died.

'What is it, love? What's wrong?' Jenny Phillips was all concern, and when Bron told her she cried, 'There's sorry I am. I didn't know.'

'It's all right, Mam,' Bron smiled 'I'd really love to call you that.'

'Idris has probably gone for a walk after Chapel. Ashamed of his son he is,' Jenny confided. 'Chapel we are, and brought the children up the same, but Cyril – ' She broke off as the door opened and a tall man came into the room.

'This is Cyril's dad, Bronwen. Idris, this is Bron.'

He shook hands pleasantly enough, but she couldn't help feeling that he was ill at ease, and this became even more apparent when Cyril came back into the room.

Bron helped to lay the table and made the mint sauce while Mam dished up, then they all sat down to the delicious meal followed by generous helpings of apple pie and custard. When the table was cleared Bron insisted on doing the washing up, adding, 'Cyril will wipe. You sit down and have a rest, Mam.'

Jenny looked very surprised, and Idris's head shot up from behind the Sunday paper.

'Cyril wipe the dishes?' his Mam murmured, making it sound a preposterous idea.

Cyril snatched the tea-towel roughly from her as Jenny collapsed thankfully into an armchair, and Idris retreated once more behind the newspaper.

'Where's Ceridwen?' she asked, hoping to make some conversation, but Cyril was glowering at her.

'Sunday school of course,' he said bitterly. 'Everyone in this house has had to go to Sunday school.'

The dishes dried and put away, the pull of the mountain proved too much for him, and with a hurried, 'Won't be very long,' he was out of the front door and she was watching him wistfully as he strode away from the house, wishing he'd asked her to go with him.

Seeing her expression, Jenny came over and put an arm about her, saying, 'Look, Bron, I'm really pleased about Cyril marrying a nice girl like you. Idris will come round soon, I hope, and friends they'll be again. Too much for him it's been, deacon at Ebenezer and all. First Ceinwen and now you.' Then seeing Bron's face crumple, she added, 'Sorry I am, love, 'cos it's a bad start, but I'll help you all I can.'

'Cyril loves this place. I want to love it too. I'd have liked to have gone with him up there.'

'I know how you feel, *cariad*,' Cyril's mother replied, 'but it's better people round here don't know you're getting married, not until after it's done anyway. You see, Bron, there's a girl not a stone's throw away who thinks she's got a prior claim to our Cyril. Ructions there'd be if Ceinwen knew he was getting married to you.'

131

Chapter Fifteen

'Let's go upstairs and see if I've got anything that will be useful to you, Bron,' Jenny said. And they climbed the steep stairs to the front bedroom where, taking a crocheted cloth from the top of a cabin trunk and lifting the lid, she took out layer upon layer of blankets, embroidered sheets and pillow cases, table cloths, tea-towels, traycloths and towels.

'Now, Bron, what have you got?'

She went through the list of things they'd been given or loaned.

'Well, you'll need some more bedding, won't you?' Jenny put aside a cream satin bound blanket, a pair of sheets and pillow-cases, a white huckaback bedspread, several fluffy towels and four good-sized tea-towels.

'Oh, Mam! You mustn't give us all those,' Bron cried, red with embarrassment.

'I've got plenty, *cariad*. When they were all at home I needed a lot of bedding and things. Only three of us there is now.'

The bedroom they were in was light and airy, both windows open to the crisp autumn day, and with a clear view of the mountain.

'Shall we stay up here for a while, Bron? It's pleasant, isn't it? Idris will be taking his afternoon nap in the chair though he always says he's been reading the paper.' She smiled. 'Shall we look at some photos of Cyril when he was small?'

While she was getting the albums Bron stood at one of the windows gazing up at the mountain. There were quite a few people strolling on paths worn by many feet. There wouldn't be much else to do here on a fine Sunday afternoon. Chapel morning and evening but only Sunday school for the children at this time of day. She'd have loved to have gone with Cyril and climbed right to the top, standing there enjoying the view and gulping in the fresh mountain air.

Suddenly her gaze became fixed on a spot almost at the foot of the mountain where a young man and woman stood talking. Her heart beat fast as she recognised Cyril. Was the girl Ceinwen?

A minute later the girl was walking away backwards, and seemed to be shouting something before turning and hurrying down the path. Cyril stood watching her but he was too far away for Bron to see his expression. Hearing Jenny's footsteps on the landing, she hurried over to the bed and was sitting there looking down at her hands when Mrs Phillips came in.

Looking through the snaps Bron was amazed at how many there were of Cyril.

'Spoilt he was, Bron,' Jenny told her. 'Five girls before him and we wanted a boy. Nothing was too good for him, and his sisters spoilt him more than we did.'

When they heard firm footsteps on the pavement outside and the front door open and close Jenny said in a worried voice, 'We'd better go down, love.'

Downstairs Cyril was alone in the room, reading the paper.

'Where's youer dad then?'

Cyril shrugged his shoulders. 'Went out the back he did, soon as I came in.'

His mother sighed, and as she and Bron put the things they were carrying on to the table, she said, 'Something to take home, son. I'll pack them into a case for you. We can pick it up when we come to Cardiff for the wedding.'

They left for the station soon after tea, with Cyril looking anxiously about him until they arrived at the platform.

Reaching Queen Street station they caught a tram to Roath, and he carried the heavy case to Thelma Street before going back to his digs. He hadn't been very talkative since they'd left Glas Fynydd, but Bron knew he was miserable at the thought of coming to Cardiff to live permanently. If it hadn't been for the girl Ceinwen, she would have suggested that he look for a job near his home in the Valleys, and they could perhaps have found rooms nearby.

When Bron showed Martha the contents of the case, her nan said, 'There's kind, Bron. Glad I am you'll have nice in-laws. Did they say they were coming on Wednesday?'

'Yes, Nan. At least his mam and young sister are coming. They're going to take the case back with them then.'

'We'll go round to Rosalind Street tomorrow night,' Martha said. 'Give the place a good scrub. Poll says she'll come and help.'

Bron nodded, wondering what all the oddments of furniture and the bits and pieces would look like when they were delivered to the rooms.

The first scrubbing had very little effect, and Martha tutted in disgust at the greasy floors. Neither elbow grease nor brown soap was spared and soon they could do no more. The windows were cleaned, and fresh curtains hung and a new paper blind put up. The flowery oil-cloth was laid in the downstairs room, and they were waiting for Bertha Morgan's son-in-law to deliver the furniture and other things on the horse-drawn flat-cart that he'd borrowed from work. When she saw him arrive bringing Will to help carry the things in, Bron's heart plummeted, especially when she saw them lift the blistered wardrobe and manipulate it with difficulty over the banister on its way upstairs.

'My God!' Cyril whispered when he finally arrived. 'What a load of junk.'

For a moment she felt angry with him for not appreciating the way people had rallied round to help them, then remembering the lovely home he'd left to come to Cardiff just a few months ago, she understood his feelings.

The bed looks nice anyway, she consoled herself, smoothing the dazzling white huckaback bedspread into place. The bare floor hadn't improved much for its scrubbing, being even more scuffed than before. Apart from the bed and the over-varnished wardrobe the room was empty.

Downstairs as she polished the gate-leg table in the living room she reflected that it looked little better. The two dining chairs stood against the peeling wallpaper, and Bertha had provided a rickety cane table to stand the cups, saucers and plates on until they could get some shelves put up in the recess by the fireplace. There was nothing but this, the table and two chairs in the room. There were no armchairs. They would have to save up for those. Two old saucepans stood on the fender and, despite a vigorous blackleading, the grate was still a rusty brown.

Cyril left early, making no secret of what he thought, and remembering how everyone had helped to make it possible for them to take these unfurnished rooms, Bron felt ashamed of his churlish behaviour.

That evening back in Thelma Street Bron began to pack her belongings into the cardboard case she had brought with her all those years ago. When she had packed her clothes, all except the lupin blue dress she was to wear for the wedding, her best underwear and the buckskin sandals, she started to turn out the top drawer of the chest where she kept her handkerchiefs and her bits and pieces. At the bottom of the drawer was the stained purse of her mother's that had been soaked with river water, and inside this the key that had remained a mystery all these years.

Bron knew that she could never part with it, unless of course they ever found its purpose, for it must belong to someone. She turned it over in her hand, willing it to give up its secret. That and the purse were the only things she had left of her mother's; she'd been too young to wear the pretty locket that her mother had loved. It was real gold and opened to reveal a picture of Jackie one side and herself on the other. Her father had taken it with him to keep safe for her until she was grown up; she'd probably have had it by now but she hadn't seen him for ages.

On the Wednesday morning they were all up early, busy with preparations for the wedding when, answering a knock on the door, Bron found her father standing there, his arms outstretched. She flung herself into them and they held each other close, the long years of parting seeming to melt away. She hadn't really expected him to come, thinking with such short notice he wouldn't be able to get time off from his job.

There were no recriminations but he looked worried as he said, 'I hope this young man's going to be good to you, Bron. It's a bad way to start, *cariad*, but if you love each other you'll make out all right.'

Shaking his head sadly, he said, 'Blame myself I do for leaving you like that. Poll told me the last time I was here that your nan treated you as if you were a child. She's been good to you though, your nan, and I appreciate that.'

Martha, hearing voices, was hurrying along the passage. Next moment she was in her son's arms.

'Jack,' she cried, 'there's lovely to see you. We didn't think you'd manage it.'

'Just try to keep me away from my own daughter's wedding,' he said, putting his arm about Bron again.

When the excitement was over her father put his hand in his pocket and took out an envelope. Handing it to Bron, he said, 'You'll find your mother's locket in there together with some money to buy yourself a wedding present. I was all for choosing something for you, but Evelyn said it would be better to let you buy something you really needed.' Then seeing the puzzled look on Bron's face, he explained, 'Evelyn and I have known each other about three years. She's a wonderful friend, love. We were two lonely people until we met each other. We'd like to get married if we could find somewhere to live.'

'But we never knew – '

'I'll never forget your mother, *cariad*. Evelyn had a wonderful marriage too and we respect each other's memories.'

Bron was opening the envelope. First she took out the locket and looked at it lovingly, then she drew out a pretty card and a folded five pound note, and her eyes grew wide with wonder, for although she'd handled them at the shop she'd never had one of her own. Flinging her arms around her father, she was thankful for his friend's good sense; she was right, there was so much they needed to buy.

At half-past eleven the taxi they'd ordered arrived to

take them to the Register Office and Bron, looking pretty in the lupin blue dress, her mother's locket about her neck, got in followed by her father, Polly and Alma, leaving Jackie and Tom with their mam.

Cyril was already there with his mother and sister, and he had also brought two friends from his lodgings as witnesses. Just before they'd entered the building a beribboned taxi had passed and Bron had caught a glimpse of a girl in shining satin holding a bouquet, a lace veil over her face. It was her wedding day too, the day every girl dreams about, with memories to cherish for ever, and photographs for the family album. Well, there wasn't much to cherish about hers, though Polly would take a snap of them with her box Brownie on the steps of the Register Office when they came out. Bron hoped Cyril would smile. He hadn't done much of that lately.

The witnesses left as soon as the short ceremony was over. The snaps were taken – though Polly confided she didn't think she'd got them all in. When they got home – and the wedding breakfast was over – Ceridwen went upstairs with Glory to her room, and Mrs Phillips donned one of Martha's afternoon aprons and was soon making herself useful. Marcia arrived and there was a lot of chatter and laughter, which lasted well into the afternoon. Bron had confided in Marcia, who'd probably guessed anyway from the speed of the wedding, but Bron asked her not to tell Mr Jessop or the others. In a few months anyway she would be giving in her notice, telling Mr Jessop that she was expecting a baby.

'Bron, I know it won't make any difference to you now,' Marcia said, 'but I went out with Chris last week.'

'Oh, I'm really glad,' Bron told her. 'He deserves someone nice.'

When Jenny decided to leave for the station, Jack said

it was time he went too for it was a long way back to Coventry, and so she and Cyril accompanied them to the station going back afterwards to the rooms in Rosalind Street. Bron could hardly believe it when Cyril stayed only long enough to change from his best suit into flannels and a jacket.

'I expect you've got things to do, Bron. Gives me the willies this place does. I'm going out for a while.'

'Where are you going?'

'Just for a pint. Good God, Bron! I haven't got to have an excuse-me note, have I?'

She bit her lip hard to stop it trembling as after a little peck on her cheek, Cyril went out and slammed the door.

It was this place, wasn't it? They'd have to get it decorated and furnished properly. There wasn't even an armchair for him to sit on.

Fighting back tears she looked at the adverts for furniture in the pieces of newspaper that had been wrapped around china and other things. She'd kept them to use when they needed a fire. Coal! That was something else they'd need and all. She'd have to ask Bessie where she could store it.

Straightening the pages and smoothing them flat she flicked them over. In an advertisement for Cavendish's there was a figured oak bedroom suite for seven pounds nineteen and six, and they already had five pounds from her father. But it was down here in the living room they needed something, some comforts to keep Cyril at home. If they saved for a while, and added to the five pounds, they could perhaps manage a dining-room suite. Oh, that would be lovely. She could just picture it in the middle of the room. But they wouldn't be able to afford any easy chairs then. That's what was really necessary, that and a wireless. Cyril would like that, but the walls would need

---

decorating first. But how about when she had to leave work? Then there'd be the expense of things for the baby. A cot, a pram, clothes, bedding. How were they to save for furniture then?

When a quarter to eleven came and Cyril still hadn't returned, Bron went to the wash-house and filled the kettle and put it to boil ready to make a pot of tea. Her heart felt like stone. She'd remember her wedding day, she thought bitterly.

The kettle was beginning to sing and she'd been peering around her in the dim light, at the peeling white-washed walls, at the saucepans, blackened from the gas rings, arranged along a shelf. The built in boiler for wash-day, last week's ashes not yet lifted . . . a great sadness came over her. She had so many happy memories of this house, the shabby reality was hard to bear.

She was pouring the boiling water into the pot when there was a loud banging on the front door, and before she could put down the kettle to go and answer it, she heard Bessie Evans moving about in the kitchen on the other side of the wash-house, the rocking chair protesting as she got up.

Hurrying out into the yard and back up the three steps to the main passage, Bron bit her lip hard as she heard Cyril's voice.

'Where's my wife then? Why couldn't she come to the door?'

She reached the front room to see him swaying in the doorway, his face beetroot red.

'Been celebrating, Bron,' he told her, a fatuous grin on his face. 'Met some good butties I did. Came up trumps when I told them I was married today. Bought me all the pints I could drink.'

And a bit more, she thought sadly. Oh, she'd been

141

dreading tonight, all right, the experience of that sunny afternoon at Llanedyrn never far from her mind, but she'd never dreamt that he would make it worse by getting drunk. She wished with all her heart that she was back in Nana's house, sharing a bed with Gloria.

Bessie was still leaning against the door, her plump face wearing a look of disgust. Bron's heart plummeted even further, and the tears she'd been struggling against squeezed from beneath her eyelids and trickled slowly down her cheeks.

'What's the blutty matter with you, you silly bitch?' Cyril cried, pushing her further into the room.

Bessie Evans, glaring at Cyril now, muttered, 'And to think it was kids I was afraid of 'aving. Strewth! Kids is nothing to this. There's nothin' worse than a drunk, God 'elp us.'

Chapter Sixteen

Bron washed the supper dishes and filled the big gaudily flowered jug with water ready for the morning, standing it in its matching bowl on the bedroom floor. She was really grateful to Bessie for the loan even though there was no wash-stand to stand them on.

By the time she went up to bed Cyril was asleep, lying on his back and snoring loudly, the crisp white bedspread wound round him like a shroud. Bron, determined to keep it nice, had meant to fold it carefully each night so that it would be fresh to put on the bed in the daytime. Oh, well! It was too late now.

She got into bed carefully so as not to disturb him, relieved that tonight, drunk as he was, he would make no demands on her; but as she lay there, unable to sleep, his snores grew louder. Presently there was a knock on the bedroom door and when she quickly lit the candle and padded over the bare floor to open it, Bessie stood there in a long flannelette nightgown, saying in a loud whisper, 'Carn you keep 'im quiet, love?' Craning her neck to see into the room, she advised, 'Try an' turn 'im on 'is side. You'll 'ave to sew a button on 'is nightshirt or somethin'.'

'He wears pyjamas,' Bron told her.

'Then sew one on 'is jacket.'

As Bessie went back to bed Bron tried to wake Cyril.

When at last she did he was annoyed, denying that he ever snored, but finally she did get him to turn on to his side, breathing beer fumes into her face now so that she had to turn and grip the edge of the bed for there wasn't much room. At last she fell into an uneasy sleep.

Next morning as soon as she sat up the now familiar feeling of nausea assailed her. Grabbing her old blue chenille dressing gown she rushed downstairs, thankful that Bessie was not yet about. Upstairs again, with Cyril still asleep and snoring again, she drew the curtains over the window and poured water into the bowl, kneeling on the floor to wash. She went to wake Cyril as soon as she was dressed, bringing fresh water, warm from the kettle this time, for him to use.

'I feel awful, Bron,' he told her, running his tongue around his dry mouth. 'Any chance of a cup of tea?'

So there was another journey up and down stairs, and when he finally came down it was to grumble because there was no cooked breakfast prepared. He'd said he'd felt awful so she hadn't thought he'd want bacon and eggs, and so had only made him toast and put the butter dish beside his plate.

Bron had got up much earlier than at home, but it was now getting late and Cyril hadn't yet finished his breakfast. She couldn't wash the dishes or put anything away. While she was making the sandwiches for their lunch break Cyril wanted hot water to shave with, and she had to go out to the wash-house and wait for the kettle to warm up.

When he'd disappeared upstairs with his shaving tackle she set about clearing the table. Bringing in a bowl of hot water, she shook some Hudson's powder into it, and, stirring up the suds, washed the dishes with an anxious eye on the clock.

He came down at last in a fresh white shirt, his hair brushed until it gleamed, and Bron felt resentful for she had had no time at all to get herself ready. She thought longingly now of the house in Thelma Street, the home she'd never really appreciated, where Martha had always had her breakfast waiting, making sure everything was ready for her – freshly ironed clothes in the wardrobe, and a clean hanky for her pocket.

As soon as they'd closed the gate Cyril began to hurry, saying, 'Come on, Bron, or we'll be late.' He looked pale and heavy-eyed, and when he said, 'God! I feel awful,' she'd have liked to have reminded him that it was his own fault, but she didn't want to risk a row on this very first morning.

The rest of the staff were quick to note that Cyril was looking off colour, chiding her gently and asking her what she'd been doing to him. Some of the rougher customers, who prided themselves on enjoying a good laugh, ribbed her shamelessly, making her go scarlet with embarrassment, wishing fervently that they would just shut up.

The problem of the evening meal had to be solved. It was awkward when you weren't home to prepare it for Cyril would want a meal as soon as he got home, and anyway, apart from the little wooden safe with the mesh front that hung on the wall in the yard, and which kept the milk, butter, bacon, eggs and cheese cool, she had nowhere to store things.

He's always been used to good meals, she thought worriedly, weighing up the advantages of sausage and mash, which he'd have to wait for her to cook, and fish and chips from Pritchard's which was always delicious and piping hot.

It was late autumn. They'd be needing a fire in the grate in the evenings and she hadn't yet asked Bessie where she could keep the coal. Did the coalman deliver? She'd have to find out. Whenever they'd been short of coal in Thelma Street Will had borrowed an old pram Bertha Morgan kept for the purpose, and had gone to the sidings to get it. She couldn't picture Cyril doing that.

'I asked you for tea, love, not sugar,' the customer she was serving told her, bringing her thoughts back to the present. 'Awful absentminded you are today, Bron. It must be love.' And she chuckled to herself.

But for that evening anyway the problems solved themselves. Cyril offered to stand in the queue at the chip shop while she dashed home to make the tea and lay the table, and when she got there Bessie's coalman had been and she'd taken a hundredweight for Bron.

'There's two sheds out the back, love,' she told her lodger. 'I 'ad youers put in the first one. Got it on tick for you I did. Told 'im you were both working.'

'Thanks, Bessie,' she said gratefully, 'I was wondering what to do about coal.'

By the time Cyril came in with the meal she'd laid the table and put a match to the fire she'd hurriedly made. They sat side by side eating the delicious vinegary food, for Cyril had put plenty on in case they didn't have any, which, of course, they didn't yet.

The sticks were well alight now, and leaping orange flames were licking the coals, making even the bare room look quite cheerful. Cyril was really enjoying his meal, she could tell. After his second cup of tea, he pushed his plate aside and got up, saying, 'Pity we haven't got a couple of armchairs to draw up to the fire, Bron.'

'Well, we could go into Newport next Wednesday to buy some, or even to Canton. I think the shops open there on Wednesday afternoons as well.'

'What'll you use for money?'

'I told you my dad gave us a five pound note? If there's anything left we could save it towards a wireless.'

'Come and sit on my knee, Bron.'

When he began kissing her she didn't respond at first remembering the awful day at Llanedyrn that had got them into all this, but his lips were warm on hers and his arms tight about her, and she still loved him even though by now she was beginning to know his faults. The dining chair was hard and unyielding as they swayed in each other's arms, and presently Cyril drew away, yawning loudly, saying, 'There's no comfort here, Bron. Might just as well go up.'

'But it'll be wasting the fire.'

'It'll soon die down.'

'I haven't washed the dishes.'

'Leave them 'til the morning.'

But thinking of all there was to do before they went to work, Bron took the kettle, which she had put over the fire, and filled the bowl.

'You won't be long doing that? Go up I will then.'

I'd be quicker if you helped me, she thought resentfully as she heard him going upstairs. After all, she'd worked as hard as he had today. She put the dishes away and banked down the fire, promising herself she'd buy a guard as soon as she could.

Bron tiptoed into the bedroom, thinking Cyril might be asleep, but he was waiting for her and before she could slip her nightdress over her head he held out his arms and she went into them, nervous at first because the springs of the bed were squeaking. But his lips were hard on hers and his body so close they seemed to melt into each other.

When at last his passion was spent, he slid to her side, sighing with contentment. Almost at once he was asleep, his breath warm on her cheek.

She lay awake puzzling over this man who had come into her life. She'd been infatuated with him at first, but was no longer blind to his faults. Last night when he had left her alone and sought companionship at the pub he'd hurt her deeply, even though she knew that it was only the uncomfortable rooms that had driven him out. But the rooms had been the same for her, hadn't they? If only tonight had been their wedding night then she would have been happy. Would she ever feel really sure of Cyril? Or would their happiness always depend upon his changing moods?

Cyril had said that he wanted to go to Glas Fynydd on Sunday but she would have the washing to do. It was the only time she could do it for it would take hours to light the boiler, boil the clothes and bedding, blue and starch the shirts – and he wore a fresh one nearly every day. She had come to an arrangement with Bessie that she could wash on Sunday, ready to hang out before she went to work on Monday morning – that was, until she finished at Jessop's in a few months' time, then she wouldn't need to wash on Sunday any more.

'You put them out, love,' Bessie had said. 'Keep my eye on the line I will for you, in case it rains.'

She was getting quite fond of her landlady for she was a generous kindly soul. Poor Bessie looked much older than her years with her lank grey hair and shabby clothes, Peggy had told her she was still only in her fifties. If only she was a bit more particular, Bron thought, more like her nan.

The gas cooker in the wash-house was thick with stale grease. She'd have a go at it as soon as she had the time, and Bessie's kitchen-cum-living room always smelt of cabbage water, for she cooked all her vegetables on top of the fire.

Bron dozed fitfully, waking at intervals, hugging to herself the knowledge that she had survived, had even enjoyed, their lovemaking. Cyril would be happy in the morning. She'd get up in time to cook him a good breakfast, and next Wednesday they would go shopping to buy the two easy chairs.

The next morning they had just got off the tram and were walking towards Jessop's when Cyril said, 'Don't forget we're going home on Sunday, Bron.'

Bron sighed. It was obvious he didn't consider the rooms in Rosalind Street his home.

'I told you, love, I've got to do the washing on Sunday. It's a long job.'

'Oh, come off it, Bron. You can do that any time.'

'I can't, Cyril, Sunday is the only time I have.'

'Well, what about me? I can't hang about that place all day. Tell you what, I'll go on my own just for a few hours. I could get there in time for dinner. Mam always cooks plenty.'

Bron's spirits fell. She had planned to get a nice piece of pork, roast potatoes, make apple sauce. When she told him this, he said, 'Well, you can cook for yourself. Keep me a dinner. I'll be hungry when I get home.'

The prospect of a day's washing, cooking dinner, cleaning the gas stove first – for she couldn't fancy it as it was – was daunting. She'd be really glad when she finished work but meanwhile she wished Cyril would be a little more thoughtful. She hadn't felt really well for ages. It wouldn't have hurt him to have offered to stay home and turn the heavy handle of the mangle for her, and empty the bath she'd wash the clothes in.

When Sunday came she hadn't bothered to buy the pork, it hadn't seemed worth it for herself with so much to do anyway, and as she sat down to cheese sandwiches she was feeling really sorry for herself. Her face was shining and her hair damp and limp from the steam in the wash-house, and her back ached from standing so long at the scrubbing board. She'd been worried about turning the heavy handle of the mangle, but Bessie had taken pity on her and helped, though as yet she could have no idea that there was a baby on the way.

As she ate the sandwiches and drank her tea she pictured Cyril having lunch at his mother's house in Glas Fynydd. The snowy tablecloth, the delicious meal . . . her mouth watered as she remembered last week's lamb and roast potatoes and her favourite mint sauce. Then she remembered the view of the mountain from the front bedroom window, and how she'd seen him talking to that girl. She was convinced it had been Ceinwen.

They'd seemed to be arguing, but they could soon make things up. If Cyril meets her often enough, who knows? she told herself. Would he go every Sunday while she struggled with the washing?

Ceinwen didn't know that he was married. It was an uneasy thought.

About the time that Bron was emptying the bath with the dipper, tipping each ladleful carefully down the sink, Cyril was starting off on his afternoon walk. His mam and dad hadn't been pleased to see him without Bron.

'All right, is she?' Jenny had asked anxiously.

When he'd assured her that she was, and had only stayed at home to do the washing, she'd been openly critical.

'Couldn't you have helped her in some way, Cyril? Too much it is for the poor little thing, working all the week an' all. 'I don't approve of doing washing and such on a Sunday, but I don't see what else she could do.'

'Have you put those shelves up yet?' Idris had asked in a tone that said plainly that he knew Cyril hadn't.

But with or without Bron he'd had to come to Glas Fynydd, had to walk over the mountain in the hope of seeing Ceinwen again. God, how he wished he'd never left, especially after the conversation that had ended in her screaming at him last week, 'There's never been anyone but you, Cyril Phillips, and you know it. Just trying to get out of marrying me you are.'

Whyever had he listened to that Carrie Davies? He'd known how jealous she was of Ceinwen. They'd all been at the same school, the two girls, himself, Michael McDaid and Dilwyn James. It was natural that Ceinwen should still be friendly with the two boys. Didn't mean that they'd been carrying on together. But after what Carrie had said . . . Ceinwen's blue eyes had flashed scornfully at him for letting her down, but they'd held a look of hope as well for she'd not heard about Bronwen.

He should never have listened to Carrie's tittle-tattle and gone off to Cardiff like he had. He hadn't wanted to settle down with anyone just yet, but now he'd been fool enough to do just that, hadn't he?

Fond of Bron I am, he told himself defensively. But he and Ceinwen had been soul-mates. She'd always attracted him with her lovely fair colouring and expressive blue eyes. She had spirit that girl. Life would never have been dull with her.

He turned for home, disappointed that he hadn't seen Ceinwen today. But what good would seeing her do now when he had nothing to offer? The answer was that she still fascinated him. Even when she'd been angry last week he'd watched her with admiration, had wanted to put his arms about her and hold her close.

'Oh God!' he sighed, remembering that soon he would

have to go back to those awful rooms in Cardiff, to Bron's thinly disguised reproach for leaving her there alone. At least if he'd married Ceinwen he could have stayed amongst his own people, and gone for long walks over the mountain when things got too much.

Chapter Seventeen

The week after Bron finished at the shop, Jenny Phillips paid an unexpected visit.

'Worried I've been about you, *cariad*. We haven't seen you since the wedding. As soon as I heard you were going to be at home from now on I had to come and see that you were all right.'

'Lovely it is to see you, Mam. Did Cyril tell you that I had to do the washing on a Sunday? There's no other time. Different it will be from now on. I'm hoping to come to Glas Fynydd this weekend.'

With a sinking heart she watched her mother-in-law looking about her, taking in the grubby wallpaper which Bronwen had only made worse by rubbing with a damp cloth, and the oddments of shabby furniture, shown up even more now by the two new Rexine armchairs which were placed either side of the fire. Oh, if only they'd managed to decorate before his mother had come to Cardiff, she thought wistfully.

'I bought the paper ages ago to do the room out,' she told Jenny defensively, 'but with both of us working there was never any time. Cyril says he doesn't know anything about decorating,' she added with a laugh.

'Well, no, he wouldn't,' Jenny agreed. 'Always paid

someone to do ours, we did. Idris was never much good at it either.'

Bron brought the small wicker table, now covered with an embroidered cloth, and stood it beside her mother-in-law's chair, placing a cup of tea and a plate of biscuits on top. Glancing towards the glowing coals she was glad that she'd worked so hard over the months blackleading and polishing the grate, until now it winked and shone in the firelight in all its former glory.

'Bron,' Jenny began hesitantly, nervously stirring the teaspoon around in her cup. 'Now look, I don't want you to get offended, girl, but I want to talk to you about furniture.' She moistened her lips nervously. 'Most of this is borrowed, isn't it?'

When Bron nodded she went on, 'Like to help you we would to get some stuff of youer own. A new dining suite perhaps? Getting married the way you did didn't give you much of a chance.'

Glancing around the room once more Jenny thought, It's no wonder Cyril doesn't want to come home. But it was his own fault, wasn't it? What a fool he'd been to get involved with this girl, nice as she was.

'It's very good of you to offer, Mam,' Bron was saying, 'but there's no need to help us really. Saved a bit I did when we were both working. Not enough to buy a suite, of course, but we could put down a good deposit, only Cyril doesn't seem very keen.'

And that was an understatement! Bron thought. Why didn't she tell his mam how Cyril always lost his temper when she mentioned wallpapering the room or buying new furniture? He hadn't been like that at first, had seemed to enjoy going shopping for the two easy chairs, but lately, especially when he returned from Glas Fynydd, he was always irritable and on edge and seemed set on picking a quarrel.

Jenny Phillips wasn't very happy about her son either. Why did he prefer visiting them every Sunday to staying with his wife? Was it in the hope of seeing Ceinwen? But surely the girl wouldn't be wandering the village and mountain at this time of the year, not in her condition anyway? Why, she must be well over six months gone by now. If Jenny had ever been in that position when she was young she'd have been ashamed to show her face.

Sighing deeply, she looked into the fire. People were beginning to talk. She'd seen them huddled in little groups, and they'd stop talking suddenly when she passed by. Talk a bit more they would when he brought Bronwen with him on Sunday! Showing quite a bit she was although she wasn't yet five months. Giving a little gasp she put her hand to her mouth as she remembered that no one in Glas Fynydd knew that Cyril was married.

'Are you all right, Mam?' Bron was asking anxiously.

'Someone walking over my grave,' Jenny answered with a sad little smile.

She'd always stuck up for Cyril until lately, believing that Idris was too strict with him. Made endless excuses for him she had, always trying to put things right. Like the new furniture she'd talked to Bron about. She'd hoped to convince Idris that Cyril might want to spend more time at home if there was more comfort.

'Typical of you that is, Jenny. When will you realise that papering over the cracks instead of tackling the real trouble won't do any good? We both know why he comes here don't we? And personally I'd send him off home with a flea in his ear. Why did he go out on Sunday? Bitterly cold it was, even for January. He didn't bother about home comforts then, did he?'

'You don't think it's a good idea then, Idris?'

'Buy it for the girl I will. She looks such a child, not old enough to be married. We owe her something, Jenny, the way he leaves her on her own. And if it helps keep him in Cardiff, all the better.'

'Can I get you anything else, Mam?' Bronwen's voice broke into her thoughts. 'I could make you a sandwich – '

'No, thank you, Bron. As I told you I had my lunch in town before coming out here, and I must be getting back to start Idris's tea.'

When Bron mentioned to Cyril that his mam had called at the house he was sitting at the table. 'They offered to buy us a dining-room suite,' she told him. 'I told her it was very kind but we could manage to put down a good deposit and buy one on weekly payments.'

'What's the use of new furniture in a blutty dump like this?' Cyril roared, the set of his face telling her he was in one of his moods.

'It needn't be a dump, Cyril, not if we could get that paper I bought put on the walls – '

He jumped out of his seat and started banging his fist hard on the table, making the cutlery rattle on the plates and knocking over the sauce bottle.

'Not that again,' he yelled. 'All that palaver about blutty decorating a hole like this. If you want it done you'll have to do it yourself, you nagging little bitch. I just wish I'd never come to Cardiff, never met you. I hate this place, I do.'

Bron stared at him, her wide eyes slowly filling with tears, then, as they began to stream down her cheeks, she dashed from the room and up the stairs. She flung herself on to the bed, buried her face in the cool pillow, and sobbed her heart out.

The first few times that Cyril had lost his temper he had come to her afterwards and taken her in his arms, telling her he was sorry. But he hadn't done this for some time, and she knew he wouldn't come now.

The damp pillow had grown icy cold when she heard the middle room door being slammed and afterwards the front door, the impact reverberating through the house.

He would be going to The Bertram or one of the other pubs in Broadway. He did that more and more. Drowning his sorrows, he'd told her. Sometimes she wished she hadn't married him, but had taken the consequences like Maisie Jonas. But then she would remember gratefully that her child would have a name. The innocent who had been the cause of all this trouble wouldn't suffer the stigma that Maisie's little boy did.

Bron smiled wanly to herself. She always thought of the coming child as 'he', for Cyril had set his heart on having a boy. She hoped she would please him in this anyway.

Oh God! Please don't let him get drunk tonight, she prayed, thinking that she must watch what she said more carefully, try not to say things that would annoy him.

She got up and bathed her face and went downstairs, for the dishes would still be on the table. She knew now the anxiety that Polly must have felt all those years ago when Will would meet his brother at the pub. But Will was a gentle, loving person and wouldn't hurt a soul, with or without the drink. Cyril got really nasty when he was drunk. She'd soon found that out. Bron decided to wash up quickly and go to bed before he came back.

Lying in the darkness, sleep was far away as the thoughts spun round and round in her head. She'd hoped that they'd have got the place tidy by now and have been able to return most of the furniture they'd borrowed, but Cyril's lack of interest, and the way he spent far more than they could afford on going to the pub a couple of nights a week, and travelling to Glas Fynydd every Sunday, would make it impossible to save anything at all now that she'd finished work.

Presently the clock Polly and Will had given them began to strike the hour. She could hear it faintly in the stillness. One, two, three, four . . . she counted the strokes up to eleven when they stopped. Cyril would be coming home soon, probably staggering by this time. Not like Will had been either, singing funny songs. No, Cyril would be abusive, especially to Bessie if she happened to let him in. Bron began to tremble at the thought of having to go down and open the door, for if he was as drunk as he'd sometimes been he wouldn't be able to find the keyhole. Oh, if only she could stay here, but she daren't risk Bessie answering his knock.

Bron got out of the bed and put her old blue dressing gown on over her clothes, hoping to stop her teeth chattering. She was half-way down the stairs when she heard the footsteps, several pairs by the sound of them, outside the gate.

When the knocker banged she was there to open it, surprised to see Will and another man supporting Cyril's sagging weight.

As they almost dragged him along the dimly lit passage Cyril was trying to shrug off their arms, shouting abuse at them, glaring balefully at Bron and prodding her backwards into the room.

'Take no notice, love,' Will was saying kindly. 'Sorry 'e'll be in the morning.'

They had got him into an armchair and the other man, with an apologetic look at Bron, was making for the front door.

'Stay a while I will, Bron,' Will told her. 'Help to get

him up to bed. See that youer all right. Coming back from
a Labour meeting at the Cory Hall I was with my mate,
an' 'e was sitting on the pavement outside the pub. Shall
I try and get 'im up, love?'

'Blutty leave me alone, four eyes. I can see to myself.'
Cyril staggered up, shrugging off Will's hand, and almost
fell to the floor.

'Can I 'elp at all?' They hadn't noticed Bessie come to
the open door. 'I know what I'd like to do to this sod,
Mister, and that's chuck 'im out. But 'is pooer wife would
suffer then so I'll 'ave to put up with 'im.'

''E'll be too much for you, Mrs Evans,' Will began.

'Don't you believe it! My old man used to be roaring
every Saturday night. 'Ad plenty of practice, I 'ave,
more's the pity. 'Ate drunks I do.'

As two pairs of hands pulled at Cyril's coat to get it off
he threshed about, shouting, 'Gerr off, will you? Interfering sods!' Then glaring at Bron, 'All youer fault it is,
mealy-mouthed little bitch! You and youer blutty decorating.'

'Best stay out of the way, love,' Bessie said kindly, as
Bron went to help them. 'He might give you an unlucky
blow.'

There was uproar as they edged him slowly up the stairs
and into the bedroom, where he lay on the bed in his
shirt and underpants, muttering dire threats. When he'd
calmed down a little Will pulled the bedclothes over him,
and leaving the room Bron followed them both downstairs
where Bessie insisted on settling her in one of the fireside
chairs and went out to make a pot of tea.

'I can't leave you like this, Bron,' Will said. 'Look,
love, I'll just go and tell youer Aunt Poll, then I'll come
back an' sleep in the arm chair.'

'I'll be all right, Uncle Will, he'll sleep it off now. It

was my fault. I said something to make Cyril angry.'

'Look, love, I've seen 'im before in the pub, drunk as a lord.' He chuckled. 'I'm a fine one to talk, I know, but I learnt my lesson a long time ago and started giving my brother a wide berth – just go in for a drink now and then when I know 'e won't be there.'

'What's Nana going to say, Uncle Will?'

'We won't tell her, Bron. Not unless it gets too bad.'

Bessie was back with a tin tray on which was set a pot of tea and a tin of condensed milk with some of the contents already solidified like wax on the outside. Fetching three of Bron's cups and saucers from the shelf, she poured them a cup of tea, lacing it generously with the sticky milk.

'Youer finding those shelves I put up useful then?' Will asked, glancing towards the alcove.

'Yes, it's wonderful having somewhere to put the china. And the cupboard you put the other side is marvellous for the food and things.'

She didn't tell him that Cyril's reaction had been to threaten to go around to Thelma Street and tell him to mind his own business – only he hadn't put it as politely as that. Thankfully she'd managed to calm him down and Will was blissfully unaware that his handiwork went unappreciated in that quarter.

'Well, if youer sure you'll be all right, love, I'd better get along or youer Aunt Poll will be sending the troops out.'

When she'd thanked him again and given him a grateful hug and the door had closed behind him, Bron was undecided whether to go upstairs and lie beside Cyril, breathing in the beer fumes, or stay down here and doze in the armchair until morning, and risk even more of Cyril's wrath. But Bessie, coming through the passage just then on her way upstairs, put an arm about her, saying, 'Best go to bed, love. It will be cold down 'ere when the fire dies down.'

Following her upstairs Bron tried to apologise for all the trouble they were causing. 'Bessie, I'm really sorry – ' she began but was stopped immediately with, 'Not another word. I know what it's like, believe me. It's sorry for you I am, Bron, and that's a fact.'

Cyril's snores grew louder as they climbed the stairs. Together they turned him on to his side, and when Bessie had closed the door behind her Bron got in beside him and turned her face away. Would it be better or worse when the child came? she wondered anxiously. If she gave him the son he wanted, would he pull himself together for the child's sake?

When Will arrived at his home in Thelma Street Polly was all ready to do battle, but before she could get going he stopped her by saying, 'Listen a minute, Poll, now just listen to me. I'd 'ave been 'ome more than an hour ago if it 'adn't been for that Cyril.' And he told her of how they'd found him and taken him home. 'Nasty that boy is when 'e's 'ad a drop. Sorry for Bron I was for she doesn't deserve it. Anyway, we got 'im to bed – Bessie Evans helped me. A good sort she is. Bron is lucky there.'

'Shall we tell Mam?'

'I promised I wouldn't. Bron doesn't want to worry 'er, and it wouldn't do any good anyway.'

Chapter Eighteen

Bron didn't go to Glas Fynydd at the weekend after all. Cyril had realised with a shock that if he took her with him, pregnant as she was, then he'd have to admit to his marriage. Ceinwen will tear me apart, he thought. She'll never speak to me again. Oh, but that was being over optimistic, for being Ceinwen she'd yell after him at every opportunity! And then there was that thug of a brother of hers . . .

To protect his own interests he kept the aggravation going until Sunday when Bron felt that she couldn't face his parents while they were barely talking to each other.

Her voice heavy with disappointment, she told him on the Saturday night just before he went out, 'You'd better make an excuse for me tomorrow. We can't go together with you behaving like this.' He'd been ignoring her all week, refusing to answer civilly even the simplest question, but now he said, knowing full well it would cause further disagreement, 'Well, it's youer own fault. You started it.'

'You'd better tell your mam I'm very tired or something. Tell her I'll come with you next week.' They should at least be being polite to each other by then. If Cyril had any misgivings about Bron's promise for the following week, he didn't voice them.

When about eleven o'clock the next morning he left the house, not even trying to hide his eagerness to get away, Bron made up her mind quite suddenly to strip the walls in the room, telling herself that it couldn't look any worse than it did already. But it did. Patches of wallpaper clung obstinately to the wall, and before she was half-way around the room she was utterly exhausted and couldn't go on.

About twelve o'clock Bessie came to see her, throwing up her hands in horror when she saw what Bron was doing. She knew by now that the girl was pregnant, but she liked Bron. 'Only natural it is for a married couple,' she told herself. 'I had our Mabel when I was married only ten months.'

Bron would make a good mother, Bessie was sure of it. She wouldn't let her kids run wild like that daughter of hers.

'Get down off that chair, girl,' she cried. 'Do youerself an injury you will. 'Tisn't worth it for a bit of wallpaper.'

Bron was thankful to sit down and rest her aching back. Anyway, she couldn't do much more feeling like this. Now Cyril would have something to really create about when he came home.

''Elp you to get this lot off I will,' Bessie told her, rolling up her sleeves. 'You should 'ave done it when you moved in, before you got caught.'

They had just started stripping again when there was a knock on the front door. When Bron opened it Polly stood there, looking amazed as she took in Bron's dishevelled appearance. Scraper in hand, she gestured her aunt to come in.

'Our Glory saw Cyril going off on his own,' Polly told Bron. 'Thought I'd better come round and make sure youer all right.'

Before Bron could reply they'd reached the room. Her aunt's mouth dropped open as she gazed at the mess, before saying anxiously, 'Good God, Bron, you shouldn't be doing this! Not in youer condition.'

'It looked awful, Aunt Poll.'

'Well, it looks a darn sight worse now. Look, love, come down and have dinner with us and I'll come back with youer uncle. Done all our papering he has, with my help. We'll bring the trestles. You did say you had the paper?'

'Yes, it's here. Oh, that's wonderful, Aunt Poll! But won't he mind? Sunday an' all.'

'No. He was saying only this week that he'd offer to help only Cyril's so touchy. Anyway, it'll have to be done now so we'd better get on with it.'

They all cooked together again now that Nan was on her own once more. The pork and apple sauce, roast potatoes and savoy were delicious, but they couldn't linger. Leaving Martha to wash up and Gloria to dry the dishes, Will gathered the trestle table and the pasting brush, and Polly found a bundle of rags for wiping down and they started off for Rosalind Street.

With Polly pasting the paper and keeping the table clean with the damp rags, and Will cutting and trimming the pieces of wallpaper and putting them up, speeded somewhat by Bessie finding a pair of wooden steps in the cupboard under the stairs, they got on well. Bron kept the floor clean, picked up the discarded pieces, and made occasional cups of tea.

'Good stuff this,' Will remarked. 'Goes on a treat it does.'

'It looks really lovely,' Bron told him with satisfaction. Cyril should be pleased when it was finished, and the floor scrubbed and furniture put back in place.

Tea-time came and went and when they stopped for sandwiches they were on the third wall.

By eight o'clock it was finished. While they were admiring the paper with its dainty sprigs of flowers, Bessie came in with a bucket of soapy water and began to scrub the floor.

''Ad a good rest I did this afternoon,' she told them. 'You must all be tired out.'

Watching her carefully scrubbing every arm's reach patch, Bron wondered why Bessie didn't put some of the same energy into her own place. But she was grateful, very grateful, resolving to try and make up to them all for everything they'd done.

Polly and Will went out to wash their hands, coming back to the now tidy room to have another cup of tea and some Welsh cakes. They were sitting at the table, their eyes frequently glancing admiringly at the walls, when there was a knock at the door. Bron, thinking Cyril must have come home early for once, went suddenly cold. But when, reluctantly, she went to open the door, it was to find Martha and Gloria standing there, come to see how the decorating was going. More cups were brought from the shelves – she'd have to borrow from Bessie if anyone else came in – and Nana and Glory exclaimed with pleasure as they admired the room.

It does look nice, Bron thought, hugging Polly and Will gratefully in turn. Just then there was the sound of a key turning in the lock. Rushing to meet him, she found Cyril glowering at her – and he hadn't even seen that the room had been decorated yet. There was a sudden silence when he followed Bron in and closed the door. Then, glancing around him in disbelief, he opened his mouth and shut it again several times, his eyes fixed on the walls. But still he said nothing.

'Looks nice, don't it, Cyril?' Will broke the silence that had descended on the room. 'You'll 'ave to 'elp when I do the bedroom, then you'll soon be able to do it yourself.'

Cyril looked sullenly from one to the other, saying grudgingly at last, 'Yes, it looks nice.' He pushed aside the cup of tea that Bron had poured him and said, 'I've got a bad head. I'm going up.'

Bron, sensing that he was saving the row until they were alone, was gripping her hands together tightly under the table.

Cyril seemed to put a damper on everyone's good spirits and soon after he'd gone upstairs they all left to go back to Thelma Street. After more hugs and thanks Bronwen closed the door, bracing herself for the row she felt sure must come.

After washing the dishes and putting them away, she took a final satisfied look around the newly decorated walls and forced herself to go upstairs, feeling cold inside at what she was sure would happen.

She lit a candle to get undressed by, creeping about, opening and closing the wardrobe door carefully so as not to disturb him. There was no sound from the bed, yet she had a feeling that Cyril was awake and biding his time. Wondering when the storm would break she blew out the candle and crept between the sheets, warm now from Cyril's body, but now there was no pleasure in the intimacy.

Her head swimming with tiredness, she silently mouthed her prayers, praying that they would get on better before the baby was born, but before she had finished, her thoughts had drifted into an exhausted sleep.

Cyril lay awake staring into the blackness, his heart heavy with foreboding. The day had been a disaster. He'd never be able to show his face in Glas Fynydd again.

It had started as usual. He remembered how relieved he'd been that Bron wasn't coming to give the show away. His mam had seemed to accept his excuse for her absence, saying how tired Bron had looked when she'd gone to Cardiff to see her.

It had been a cold blustery day with pale sunshine flitting in and out of the racing clouds when he'd set out on his walk. Ceinwen had been waiting in the little hollow sheltered by trees where they usually met. It was ideal on a day like this, being sheltered from the wind.

They'd had a sort of uneasy truce for some time and he knew that she still hoped he'd marry her before her time came. They were talking quietly when suddenly she grabbed his hand and, holding it to her stomach, said, 'Feel him kicking, Cyril? Like a little footballer he is.'

Feeling the quick movement beneath his fingers, something gripped Cyril's heart. Putting his arms about Ceinwen, he kissed her tenderly. All his doubts had disappeared – the doubts that had sent him hurrying away to Cardiff and into worse trouble than before.

'You know we're meant for each other,' she was murmuring against his cheek. 'You know it's youers. There's never been anyone else, you must know that.'

When he didn't answer, she said wistfully, 'If you'd marry me now, Cyril, youer son would have a name. I'll come to Cardiff to live if that's what you want. It's awful at home now. My dad hardly speaks except to take it out on my mam.

'Oh, Cyril!' Her lips sought his again and held them in a long kiss. When they drew apart her eyes were soft and questioning as she said, 'You love me, I know, so why can't we get married?'

He gave a shuddering sigh. His voice a whisper, he said simply, 'I can't.'

'What did you say?'

And again he repeated, 'I can't. I wish I could.'

'I thought youer mam was for me. Youer over age now, you can please youerself.'

'Ceinwen, listen, you'll have to know sometime – I'm married, more's the pity.'

She'd stumbled clumsily to her feet, her face white as lint, eyes staring in disbelief as she cried: 'Youer what?'

'Yes, married I am already. Marry you like a shot I would if I was free.'

'You mean you made all those promises, got me like this – ' She was screaming now, backing away from him.

'No, it was after I went to Cardiff, after I'd been told about the other two.'

'Why couldn't you have believed me?' The dark blue eyes blazed in her white face. 'Anyway, why did you get married? You didn't have to do that.'

'I had to,' he told her, his gaze on the ground. 'Her people made me.'

'And that's what I should have done,' she screamed. 'Got my dad on to you. You begged me to wait – not to tell anyone. Youer a rotten sod, Cyril Phillips.'

Her eyes flashed with anger before, turning to leave, the wind whipped her hair across her face and tore at her full swagger coat.

'My brother will sort you out,' she called back to him. 'It won't be safe for you to walk this mountain any more.'

'Don't worry, I won't be coming to Glas Fynydd again.'

'No, but he can come to Cardiff – ' The rest of her words were borne away by the wind, then as she reached the path she turned and glared at him once more, and then she was gone.

Cyril stirred uneasily in the bed, remembering her brother's broad shoulders and girth with misgiving. Bad enough coming up against him in a rugby tackle, but that would be a benevolent affair compared to meeting him now.

The thought of never going back to Glas Fynydd made his heart heavy. Lately he'd lived for the weekends, the freedom of the mountain, the meetings with Ceinwen. If only he'd believed her, none of this would have happened. Cyril gave a little groan and turned on his side. If only he could fall asleep and forget.

Chapter Nineteen

The letter from Jenny Phillips came by the midday post.

Dear Bronwen,
We haven't been able to make any arrangement with you about buying the dining suite that we promised you and Cyril, not having seen either of you for well over a month. I understand Cyril's reasons for not coming on Sundays now, but if you feel well enough we would love to see you.

Anyway, *cariad*, would it be convenient to meet me next Wednesday in the Dutch Cafe in Queen Street at about two o'clock? If it isn't, could you let me know by return?

Your affectionate mother-in-law,
Jenny

Excitement welled up within her and Bron's eyes were suddenly bright. At last they could return her grandmother's gate-legged table and two chairs. She'd been very grateful for them but the front room in Thelma Street had looked pretty bare without them. She was thankful now that the room had been papered. Perhaps when all the things were bought for the baby, she could manage a new rug to put in front of the fire?

Bron looked around her, picturing a lovely dining-room suite in dark oak, just like the one she'd seen in Cavendish's window, set right in the middle of the room. Everything would be new now and it would all match, for the rexine easy chairs had dark oak arm rests.

Although the letter had said only to write back if she couldn't come she decided to write back anyway to show her appreciation. An hour later, putting her coat on in the bedroom, ready to go to the post office in Broadway for a stamp, she glanced at herself in the spotted glass doors of the wardrobe and was upset at what she saw. She looked awful! The coat that she hadn't been able to button for over a month wouldn't even come together now. She could have managed to buy a loose coat while she was working but it hadn't seemed important then.

Bron was remembering how her mother had always managed to look smart even if she was only going to the corner shop. In the house too she'd been neat and pretty, wearing frilly aprons to protect her tidy clothes instead of the workaday wrap-arounds most of the women wore.

Neighbours had always looked up to her mam and dad, but Bron knew that they were just sorry for her. Most of them knew about Cyril weaving his way home unsteadily from the pub night after night and those who hadn't actually seen him would surely have been told. And she felt sure that their frequent rows must be overheard, for Cyril's voice, loud with anger, would likely penetrate the walls. But the eyes that met hers in the streets were kind as well as pitying, most of the neighbours remembering the polite, well-dressed little girl who had once played with their own daughters.

Bron dreaded meeting Ivy and Peggy these days, for Peggy always looked so smart. Ivy often called in to see how she was getting on, but hadn't been able to keep the pity from her eyes. Bron felt her situation deeply, for when she and Peggy had been children, before her mother died, it was Bron who had always been the better dressed.

The reply posted, she braced herself to tell Cyril, showing him his mother's letter as soon as he came in from work.

'If they think buying us new furniture will make me want to stay in Cardiff, they've got another think coming,' he said spitefully. 'God! I wish I'd never seen this blutty place.'

'We could take the furniture with us if we ever moved to Glas Fynydd.'

'You know we can't go back there.'

Cyril had told her about Ceinwen and what had happened last time he'd visited home, and about the threat from Ceinwen's brother and what would likely happen if they should meet up.

'I'll have to try and send her some money,' he told Bron, 'a few shillings a week perhaps. She'll have things to get for the baby.'

So have I, Bron thought bitterly, I wish he'd remember that instead of spending his money in the Royal Oak or The Bertram. But a part of her understood his need to try and help this girl. Supposing Cyril had married Ceinwen and it was her left to bring up a child alone?

Martha and Polly had been wonderful, making and buying things for the layette. Bron herself had knitted matinee jackets and bootees, and Alma had crocheted a lovely shawl in a lacy design. But there was still a cot to get, and a second-hand pram . . .

'Are you going to meet my mam?' Cyril's voice broke into her thoughts.

'Yes, I've written and told her I will. Why don't you

come, Cyril? It's your half-day. We could choose it together.' But like a slap in the face the answer came back, 'To be honest, Bron, I couldn't care less.' And pushing his empty plate aside, he reached for his coat.

With a heavy heart she stacked the dishes at one end of the table and went to warm a kettle of water on the gas stove for the fire wasn't lit until tea-time.

There was no getting on with Cyril these days. He'd had the chance to marry the girl, hadn't he? If only he'd done that and had never come to Cardiff. Sulking he was because he couldn't have what he wanted, and a bit frightened too. Was he hoping that sending a few shillings to Ceinwen would keep her brother away? But no, Bron didn't believe it was that. It was more likely because he had, too late, become concerned about the girl's welfare.

If Bron had imagined all marriages were partnerships like her mam's and dad's had been, or Aunt Poll's and Uncle Will's – though theirs could be stormy at times – she was obviously mistaken. But her aunt and uncle cared enough about each other to make up and be really lovey-dovey for a while afterwards. Cyril wasn't even trying to make it work.

On the Wednesday Bron got ready as soon as she'd prepared lunch, and when Cyril came home she suggested again that he come in and meet his mam.

'Bring her back with you,' he said grudgingly. 'I don't want to go traipsing around the shops.'

Bron had prepared for this, knowing her mother-in-law must be anxious to see her son, and now she said, 'I've bought corned beef to make sandwiches. It's in the safe outside. And I've made some cakes. I expect she'd like to come back for an hour.'

It was a blustery March day of scudding clouds and fitful

sunshine. Bron walked along Broadway, self-consciously trying to keep her unfastened coat about her, wishing she had something less revealing to wear.

When she reached the Dutch Cafe her mother-in-law was waiting, and Bron was shocked to see the change in her appearance. Jenny's pleasant face was drawn and pale, and her round brown eyes had a sad expression as she greeted Bronwen.

'Is something wrong, Mam?' The anxious words were out before Bron thought.

'It's Ceinwen, Bron. Cyril must have told her, as he had to sometime, that he was married. She's making trouble. Only natural, I suppose. And that brother of hers is haunting the house in case Cyril comes home. Her father's been round to see Idris. Terrible row there was – you should have heard his language. Disgusting it was! And to think the child is to be brought up with him. It's awful, Bron.'

'How is Cyril's dad taking it?'

'Sorry I am for Idris. He's done nothing wrong. He's no longer a deacon at Ebenezer, he's given it up. Said he was too ashamed. That if he couldn't keep his own house in order he had no right – '

'Poor Dad,' Bron said sympathetically, remembering the sad-faced man she'd met that first day.

'That's enough about us. How are you keeping, *cariad*?'

The waitress had arrived with the tea and scones as Bron said, trying to be cheerful, 'Mustn't grumble but I'll be glad when the baby comes.' Then she remembered what she wanted to tell Cyril's mother.

'My aunt and uncle have decorated the room for us. It looks lovely Mam. But you'll be coming back to see Cyril?'

'Yes of course I want to see him, but I feel very angry

with him too. Poor Idris doesn't deserve what he's going through.'

When they'd finished the scones and Bron took her coat from the back of the chair, trying to get it to meet in front, her mother-in-law was watching her thoughtfully, saying as though something had just come to her, 'Oh! I wish I'd brought it with me now. It would be the very thing for you.' Then, seeing Bron's puzzled expression, she explained: 'Our Glenys – you haven't met her yet – well she had one of those swagger coats made but she can't stand it, says it makes her look pregnant it's so full. Gave it to me she did but I like fitted things too. Cherry red it is and just the thing you need, full from the shoulders and coming down to youer hips.'

'Oh, Mam, I'd be so grateful. Oh, thank you!' And she bent and kissed Jenny's plump cheek warmly.

'I could have brought it with me if I'd thought, but to be honest, Bron, you always looked so smart until now. But it's hardly worth buying with only a couple of months to go. You can still wear the coat afterwards. Fashionable they are.'

As they left the cafe and walked towards Cavendish's, Jenny said, 'You can choose any suite within reason, *cariad*, but we'll look around first.'

Bron was pleased to see that the suite she'd seen in the window was still there. The cash price on the ticket was £8/19/6. As they looked around the shop they saw a cheaper suite at less than £8 but she'd really set her heart on this with its solid-looking sideboard with a moulded design on the cupboard doors and drawer fronts.

'The one in the front of the window seems the best value to me,' her mother-in-law said, and Bronwen could have hugged her with joy. 'It's youer choice, Bron, what do you think?'

So it was paid for and Bron's eyes shone with excitement as the assistant confirmed that Thursday, the very next day, was the delivery day for Roath.

'Do you think Cyril will like it, Mam? He really should have been here to help choose.'

'If he's anything like his dad,' Jenny told her with a short laugh, 'he'll hardly notice it's there.'

When they arrived home Cyril was sitting by the fire, staring into the glowing coals. He raised his head as they opened the front room door, but Bron couldn't help noticing that, as he looked up, his gaze didn't quite meet his mother's eyes.

'I'm going out to put the kettle on,' Bron said, feeling they would like to be alone.

When she came back with a full tea-pot and the jug of milk, Cyril's face was sullen and puce coloured, and she guessed his mother must have told him how things were in Glas Fynydd.

As she was closing the door again to go back to the safe in the yard, she heard Jenny saying, 'Now look, son, it's no use crying over spilt milk. Things have happened and there's no going back. Make the best of things and don't worry about Ceinwen – I'll see they never starve.'

When Jenny left it was with the promise that she would come again the following Wednesday and bring the coat for Bron, adding, 'Glenys will be pleased it's useful to you, *cariad*. She'd like to meet you, I know.'

'That's a pretty name, Mam, Glenys – I really like it,' Bron said, but Cyril was glowering at her, saying, 'You should be thinking of boys' names, though I'll tell you now, David is my favourite.'

Bron always felt uneasy when he spoke like this. Supposing it was a girl? She didn't mind either way so long as the baby was healthy, but she'd like to please Cyril of

177

course. She saw the troubled look in Jenny's eyes. Cyril might well be building up more disappointment for himself. Why did it mean so much to him? Little girls were lovely too.

With all the wonderful things that had happened today – the dining suite, the swagger coat that her mother-in-law had promised to bring when she visited them next week – it was hard to be miserable, even when, after his mother had gone and Bron had cooked his tea, Cyril went out as soon as it was opening time.

When just after twelve o'clock the next morning the dining suite was delivered and carefully put in place, the sideboard against the wall where you would see it as soon as you walked into the room, and the table and chairs in the middle, Bron spent an hour polishing it, standing back frequently to admire the effect. She must get a tidy sideboard cloth, and one to go across the table to put a vase on. That was something else to save up for.

The room looked lovely now. The dark oak shone in the firelight and toned beautifully with the wooden arms of the easy chairs. The only thing that was old in the room was the rickety bamboo table that Bessie had lent them. Bron couldn't have managed without that before Will had made the cupboard and shelves.

Bessie was loud in praise of the suite, and pleased to have her table back. She'd missed it for it had always stood by her bed with the big green alarm clock on top, and the glass containing her false teeth ready for the morning.

Even Cyril, when he came home, agreed that the room looked very nice, and Bron resolved once more to try and get a wireless, even if it was only second hand. Perhaps he'd stay at home more often then?

The following Wednesday when Jenny paid her promised visit Bron could tell right away that something had upset her. However, first she admired the room with its new suite and then handed the parcel containing the swagger coat to Bron. When she'd tried it on and saw what it did for her appearance she hugged her mother-in-law gratefully.

'Lovely you look in that, Bron, the colour really suits you. Fits beautifully on the shoulders it does.'

Bron went upstairs to twist this way and that in front of the wardrobe mirror. It couldn't be better, falling gracefully from the shoulders over her swollen body, and swinging loosely as she walked.

Cyril still hadn't arrived home for his half-day and when Bron went down Jenny was staring thoughtfully into the fire.

'Is something wrong, Mam?'

'Not wrong, no. I saw my new grandson this morning, Bron. Ceinwen's had a little boy – not so little either, over eight and a half pounds.'

'Is everything all right?' Bron asked, but she was thinking. A boy. Cyril wanted a boy. Would it put her own child in the shade if she should have a little girl?

Jenny was saying, 'They're fine, both of them. Ceinwen's mam was a good friend until all this blew up. I wouldn't have been able to see the baby if her dad or her brother had been at home. He's the image of our Cyril – big dark eyes, and the look of his face! He should have believed her, Bron, instead of listening to that spiteful, jealous girl. A crying shame it is.'

When Bron didn't answer, she said quickly, 'Sorry I am, love, for rambling on. I shouldn't be talking to you about it, I know, but I had to tell someone.'

So, Cyril had his precious son. Bron swallowed the lump that rose to her throat. Really, you'd think Ceinwen was Cyril's wife with all the fuss they made of her. She managed to make her voice light as she told her mother-in-law: 'Cyril will be home soon.' But Jenny continued as though she hadn't spoken. 'It's funny to hold youer own flesh and blood in your arms and know that you can lay no claim. I offered to bring him up, adopt him, give him his rightful name, but Ceinwen was like a tiger with its cub. She nearly leapt out of bed, weak as she was. The baby was only a few hours old. I'll manage to help them somehow. She's going to call the baby David.'

'But that's Cyril's favourite name for a boy.' Bron's voice was filled with dismay.

'Yes, I know. And Ceinwen knows that too.'

'Are you going to tell him, Mam?'

'Well, he'll have to know. Best leave it until she's up and about, or he'll be going to Glas Fynydd and there'll be more trouble. Life's not going to be any picnic for her, Bron. We don't want to add to her troubles or yours.'

Chapter Twenty

When Cyril came home from work about nine-thirty on the Saturday evening of the following week there was an air of suppressed excitement about him. Taking a letter from his pocket and waving it in front of Bron, he said, 'Ceinwen posted this to the shop. She's had a baby boy.'

Pretending she didn't already know, Bron asked, 'Are they both all right?'

'Yes, fine. Eight and a half pounds my son was. I'm going to go home at the weekend, Bron, she wants me to see him.'

'And what about her brother?' Bron asked coldly.

'Oh, she says he goes to Merthyr Tydfil on Sundays to visit his girl. Ceinwen's old man will be at the allotment all afternoon if it's fine.'

Cyril has never considered my feelings, Bron was think-ing bitterly, but really this is the limit. Lately he'd taken the attitude that he'd done her a big favour by marrying her and saving her from disgrace. How could she ever have believed she was in love with such an utterly selfish man? It had been a madness, she realised that now, and based purely on physical attraction for she hadn't known the real Cyril at all.

The sheer nerve of expecting his pregnant wife to be sympathetic and understanding about problems relating to his former girlfriend and their baby son! Or was she former? He'd spent enough Sundays in Glas Fynydd to make her wonder about that. Tomorrow, although she herself had less than six weeks to go before the birth, he'd happily leave her all day – but she was glad to see the back of him, wasn't that the truth? Tied to him though she was now by marriage vows and the child soon to be born, she neither loved nor respected him any more.

Not sensing her mood, Cyril kept on about the letter he'd received. 'Takes after me he does according to Ceinwen – '

'God help him!' Bron muttered under her breath, but Cyril was continuing. 'She's going to call him David. She knows I like that name.'

'I thought you wanted our baby to be called David if it was a boy?' Her voice was icy cold.

'We'll have to think of something else, Bron.'

Would he be like this when their child was born? He was like a dog with two tails, her nan would have said. He just couldn't hide his excitement and pride.

Needing to do a little hurting herself, she said quietly. 'What will his surname be, Cyril? David – ?'

'Pugh, I suppose, like Ceinwen,' he said, his voice regretful. 'But he's a Phillips, that's for sure.'

Pity you weren't so sure eight months ago, Bron was thinking, but she managed not to voice her thoughts. There'd been enough rows this week already and in her present state they exhausted her.

Next morning he was up early for a Sunday, bathing in the tin tub in front of the fire while she prepared the vegetables in the wash-house.

'I'll have my dinner before I go,' he'd told her. 'I won't call on Mam and Dad this time. I'll probably be home for tea.'

Couldn't he face his father? Bron felt sad when she thought of Idris Phillips and the sacrifices he'd had to make because of Cyril's thoughtlessness.

She had put the meat in the oven by the side of the fire before he'd brought the bath in. It would be quicker now to boil the vegetables on the gas-stove rather than wait to put them over the fire.

Bron promised herself a quick visit to Alma's while Cyril was out. She hadn't seen Jackie for ages. She'd been so close to her little brother when they were at home, but with the years they'd grown apart. He was nearly twelve now, a handsome boy with his dark blue eyes and short black curly hair. He and Tom were still inseparable, and there was every likelihood that the two boys, who were keen scouts, would be out together when she arrived, for there was no way of letting them know in advance she was coming.

Cyril left as soon as he'd finished his meal, and Bron hurried to wash up and put everything away before changing into a loose dress Polly had given her and slipping on the cherry red swagger coat, very thankful that she had it for it gave her a confidence she hadn't felt for ages.

When she reached Alma's, just as she'd half expected, the two boys were out.

'Hello, Bron! Lovely to see you,' her aunt cried, ushering her into the little kitchen and putting the kettle over the fire. 'How are you, love? You're looking well.' Alma paused for breath before continuing, 'The boys have gone to some pool with a couple of jam jars. Studying pond life or something they are. There's a job I had to get them to change out of their tidy clothes.'

When she'd made the tea, set the cups and saucers on the table and brought a freshly baked sponge cake from the cupboard, her aunt took a tissue-wrapped parcel from the sideboard drawer and handed it to Bron, saying, 'Made another little coat I have for the baby. It's a bit larger than the other. It's a lacy design. Be lovely for the summer it will.'

Bron carefully unwrapped the parcel and opened out the little jacket on the tissue paper. It was made up of small crocheted squares, each one with a rosebud in the middle.

'It's gorgeous! It's beautiful!' Bron cried. 'I wish I could crochet like that.'

'I made it white so's it will do for a boy or girl, but you can sew pink or blue ribbons on it. What are you hoping for, Bron?'

'Oh, I don't mind really. I think Cyril wants a boy.' She wasn't going to tell Alma that Cyril already had a son!

She was getting ready to leave, for Cyril had said that he'd be home to tea and she wanted to avoid another row, when the boys came in holding jam jars of murky green water in which things floated about. Jackie was just going to fling his arms about his sister when Alma grabbed him quickly, saying in a reproving voice, 'Wash yourself first,' but her eyes were twinkling.

Cyril came back just after she'd got home and laid the table.

'He's lovely,' he told her excitedly, 'weighed eight and a half pound.'

'Yes, you told me. Did you meet her father or brother?'

'No, they were both out. I wouldn't have been able to see him otherwise.'

'Did you call on your mam and dad?'

'I told you I wasn't going there.'

'Your dad's no longer a deacon at the Chapel, you

could have gone to apologise to him.

'Stupid that was. It's nothing to do with him what I do. It will all blow over soon anyway.'

Was he really silly enough to believe that? But, no, she knew that Cyril was blustering, trying to convince himself.

After the meal, when she'd washed up and Cyril was reading the *Echo* she went to the kitchen to show Bessie the little coat Alma had made. It was funny. When they'd first taken the rooms she'd never have thought that she and Bessie could become such good friends. The old lady was everything her mother hadn't been – slovenly in appearance, careless over her housework, except when she did anything for Bron, then she would be scrupulous about the job. But she had a kind heart and nothing she did for her young lodger was too much trouble. Bessie could be caustic about Cyril though, especially if he got drunk, but she put up with him for the girl's sake and Bron was grateful.

When Bessie had admired the little coat, they sat down on either side of the fire.

'Isn't 'is lordship goin' out tonight?'

'Doesn't look like it, Bessie, but it's early yet.'

'Wants 'is backside kicked, 'e does. Don't know when 'e's lucky, 'aving a wife like you.'

Bron should have been annoyed, but looking at Bessie's face she had to laugh.

'He probably thinks I'm the lucky one, having a husband like him,' she said. 'Anyway, I'd better go. I've got some ironing to do.'

Bron was worried about doing her ironing on the new table, for although she would put down two thick blankets, she was terrified of marking it with the heat. To her relief Bessie said, 'Why don't you iron out 'ere on my scrubbed table? Glad of the company I'd be.'

* * *

About the time that Bron was talking to Bessie, Jenny Phillips was returning home after evening Chapel.

'Has our Cyril been here, Idris?' she asked as soon as she entered the room.

'No.'

'Well, Mrs Llewellyn says their Betty saw him getting off the train when she went to meet her friend this afternoon.'

'Well, he hasn't been here. Won't show his face either if he's wise.'

'It's no use talking like that, Idris – '

'I'm referring to that threat Ceinwen's brother made. Don't worry, Jenny, I wouldn't soil my hands. Mind you, if he's got any sense he'll stay away from Glas Fynydd.'

'But the girl saw him.'

'Well, if he's fool enough to come he deserves all he gets.'

'Look, Idris, I'd like to talk to you. We ought to help Ceinwen with that little boy. It's Cyril's all right, it's the image of him.'

'You've seen the baby then? First it's furniture for his wife, now it's money to help his fancy woman – '

'Idris, don't talk like that!'

'How should I talk then? It's a disgrace, that's what it is. I can't believe it's happened in my family. That poor little baby will be the one who suffers, believe me.'

Chapter Twenty-One

'You 'aven't forgotten what you promised, Bron?' Looking at Martha questioningly, Bron wondered what was coming.

'You know,' her grandmother continued, 'about making people think it's a seven-month baby.'

No, she hadn't forgotten. She'd thought of it often, especially now her time was near. It meant so much to her nan, Bron felt she owed her this, and of course she was hoping that people might believe it had come early for her own sake. But how did you convince the neighbours? Especially if it weighed eight and a half pounds as Ceinwen's child had. But Martha was saying pleadingly, 'You'll only have to stay indoors a bit longer with it. Just give out it's come before its time. Bessie doesn't think it's due for another two months, does she?'

That was true, but she mightn't be so sure when she saw the child.

'I'll do what I can Nan,' Bron promised without much conviction. People weren't daft, were they?

'Well it's for youer sake as well,' Martha told her.

Bron was thinking of these words about a week later. It was a Tuesday afternoon towards the end of May and she'd had a dull pain in her back since before lunch, but now for more than an hour there'd been a different kind of pain and when it came it couldn't be ignored. She knew what it was and soon she'd have to ask Bessie to go for her grandmother, and send for the midwife. But she couldn't just say to Bessie, 'I think the baby's coming.' Not if she wanted her to believe that it wasn't due for another two months.

Another contraction made her grip the arms of the chair, her face contorted with pain. She'd have to do something soon. When she could relax she glanced at the clock on the mantelpiece, surprised to find that it was nearly seven o'clock. Cyril should be home by now, she must get his tea. But when she rose slowly, she felt giddy and faint, and sank back on to the cushions, exhausted.

When there was a loud knocking at the front door she tried once more to rise but the giddiness overcame her again.

She heard Bessie go along the passage and open the door, and the tone and pitch of her voice as she cried, 'Oh, my God!' made Bronwen's blood run cold.

Then there was a shuffling sound in the passage, the door opened, and two men entered carrying Cyril between them, sitting on their entwined hands, his arms loosely about their necks.

'Oh, what's happened? Has he been knocked down?' Bron cried, rising to her feet as quickly as she could, her own pain forgotten for the moment as she stared in horror at Cyril's face.

'Beaten up he was, Missus. Some bloke that followed him off the tram. We chased the fella but 'e got away.'

'Thank you very much for bringing – ' Bron's voice faded away as blackness enveloped her and she would have fallen if Bessie hadn't dashed forward and caught her, easing her gently to the chair.

The intensity of the next contraction brought her round

quicker than the smelling salts Bessie was waving about under her nose. As she gripped the arms tightly, her teeth biting into her lower lip, Bessie cried, 'My God! The shock of seeing 'im like this is bringing the baby before its time. Better go for Martha Thomas I 'ad.'

'Where do she live, Missus?' one of the men asked. 'We'll be on ouer way now but we can fetch 'er if she lives round 'ere.'

With Bessie's thanks ringing in their ears the men left, clutching a piece of paper with Martha's address.

Ten minutes later, when Bron's grandmother rushed into the room, poor Bessie was torn between comforting Bron when a fresh spasm of pain took her, and bathing Cyril's swollen face while he winced away from her as the hot flannel made his wounds sting afresh. His left eye was closed by a puce-coloured swelling and his swollen lip was still oozing blood.

'Whatever's happened?' Martha cried, her worried eyes darting from one easy chair to the other, hurrying to her grand-daughter's side as a fresh contraction forced her to grip the arms of the chair until her knuckles grew white. Bessie's next words were music to her ears.

'Brought it on before its time 'e 'as, comin' 'ome in that state. My God, Martha! That one's nothin' but trouble.'

'Real nasty that looks, Cyril. 'Ow did it 'appen?'

Before he could painfully open his mouth Bessie volunteered, 'Got beaten up 'e did.'

Between them the two women got Bron up the stairs and into bed. Exhausted, she sank back thankfully against the pillows, then suddenly sat up again, gripping Bessie's hand. 'Please, Bessie! Cyril must be feeling awful. Would you see to him?'

'Don't go down just yet,' Martha begged. 'Stay with Bron while I get Peggy to go for the midwife.'

'Well, that boyo can wait until you come back. It's no more than 'e deserves, bringing the baby on like that.'

Bron would have liked to tell her that Cyril had been threatened, but she had no intention of putting either Bessie or her grandmother wise about Ceinwen's baby.

Martha came back just as another contraction began, and taking an old sheet she'd brought with her she tied it to the brass rail at the foot of the bed and gave the other end to Bron to pull on, saying, 'Grip it tight when it's bad, love. The way they're comin' it shouldn't be too long.'

Bessie was safely out of earshot when the midwife arrived. Examining Bron carefully she told her, 'Be back in about an hour I will. I don't think anything will happen until then. Have you got everything ready, love? Where's the cot?'

'We haven't got one, not yet,' Bron confessed, 'but I bought a new wicker clothes basket and padded it – '

'She wasn't expecting the baby yet,' Martha told the midwife, shaking her head. She'd known Ruby Bowen since she was a baby herself. She'd find a chance to speak to her when she went downstairs. No need to ask the girl to tell lies, just say something to make it seem as though the baby was premature.

But Ruby was moving towards the door, looking around her, taking in the lie of the land as she always did when she had a case. Even in her pain Bron was bitterly ashamed of the midwife seeing the room like this. She'd wanted to decorate it so much in time for when the baby was born, but there'd been no chance, not with Cyril spending money at the pub as he did and visiting Ceinwen and giving her something each week. The midwife's eyes were roaming around the room taking in the wallpaper, peeling with the damp, and the hideous wardrobe, its mirrored doors reflecting the rest of the cheerless room.

'But she must see much worse than this,' Bron told herself without conviction. 'At least it's clean.'

When her grandmother went downstairs with the midwife, Bronwen's thoughts went to Cyril. She hoped Bessie was looking after him properly. With her feelings towards him, she could be rough . . . but another contraction put an end to Bron's concern as she pulled hard on the sheet. As the pain eased, Martha came back into the room looking very pleased with herself.

'She's not a bad sort that Ruby,' Martha told her. 'If anyone asks, she's going to say "They're as well as can be expected. It must 'ave been the shock of seeing 'er 'usband like that, that started it off." And Bessie's convinced it's a seven-month baby, isn't she?' Martha concluded gleefully.

'Should we get the doctor to Cyril, Nan?'

'See 'ow 'e is in the morning. I wonder who's got it in for 'im? That boy attracts trouble.'

Bron didn't answer. She knew just who had it in for him, and he'd asked for it going up to see Ceinwen and the baby every Sunday.

'Thought you said you'd 'ave enough money for a cot?'

'I could probably manage a second-hand one. I haven't seen one for sale.'

'I'll ask around, Bron. That wicker basket will be fine for now.'

Bron was laying back exhausted after the latest bout of pain when the midwife pushed the door open with a cheery, 'Well! How are we now?'

Bron closed her eyes wearily as the agony faded and wondered how long it would be. What was happening downstairs? Suddenly she was gripping the midwife's hand, her face contorted, sweat pouring from every pore.

A scream tore from her throat and brought Martha rushing to the bed.

'It's coming,' the midwife told her calmly. 'Just another push. Come on now.'

The baby, a little girl, was born at five past one on Wednesday morning. A little while later, her agony forgotten, Bron lay back on the pillows hugging her little daughter, her cheek resting gently against the downy, silvery head. The blue eyes opened drowsily and seemed to stare at her solemnly. There was nothing of Cyril to recognise. The child was small – just six and a half pounds – and Bron was sure that she took after her own mother. And she would call her after her mother too, she decided. 'Megan,' she whispered to herself. Meg for short. It was a pretty name.

'Better tell 'is lordship,' Bessie was saying as she glanced down at the child. ''E wanted a boy, didn't 'e? Well, 'e won't get that now, but 'e'd maybe 'ave 'ad a big bouncing girl if she'd gone 'er full term.'

Bessie's eyes can't be very good, Bron thought ruefully, or she'd have seen the perfect little nails on each perfect little hand.

Presently, with Martha's assistance, Cyril came up and went over to look down into the wicker basket on a chair by Bron's side.

'You all right?' he asked through swollen lips, holding his mouth as he spoke.

'Tired,' she told him, longing for the moment when they'd all go away and she could fall asleep. 'You've got a girl, Cyril.'

He nodded, his gaze still on the makeshift cot, and with a pang of pain she knew he was comparing this baby to his bouncing son.

'We'll have to let Mam know.' The lips barely moved

and she could see how painful it was for him to speak.

'You'd better see the doctor,' she told him.

'I'll go in the morning,' he said, holding his mouth. 'I can't very well go to work like this.'

Bron didn't want Cyril about all day, but she had to agree he couldn't work in that state.

Without another look at the baby he left the room. Where was all the excitement and enthusiasm he'd shown two months ago when Ceinwen had given him a son? He hadn't even asked what weight she was: or suggested a name for her. But then, it's painful for him to speak, thought Bron. Perhaps tomorrow?

A tear squeezed past her lids and rolled down her cheeks as she thought defiantly, I'm glad it's a little girl. She'll be company, and she'll be mine, and I *shall* call her Megan after my mam. Megan Glenys. Perhaps the names didn't really go together but his sister had been so generous, giving her the cherry red coat.

When Will took her grandmother home, Polly sat in the easy chair that had been brought up to the bedroom, but now at last Bron fell into an exhausted sleep.

She woke just as dawn was putting pale pink fingers across the sky. The fire was already freshly lit, the flames dancing up the chimney and Polly, carrying the enamel baby bath half full of water, was just coming back into the room. Kneeling down on the rug in front of the guard, Polly dipped her elbow into the water, then giving a satisfied little nod, raised the baby from the basket.

Seeing Bron's eyes upon her, she said, 'You're awake, love. How do you feel? If I'd known I'd have brought you a cup of tea.'

'I'm fine, Aunt Poll. You see to the baby or the water will get cold.'

Draped over one end of the guard was a big fluffy white

towel, at the other end a tiny vest, flannelette baby gown, an embroidered cotton one, a binder, napkin, and little matinee coat.

She watched as Polly bathed the baby with sure hands, patting her gently with the towel, supporting her carefully as each tiny garment was put on. She had just lowered her into Bron's arms when Will tapped on the door to say Martha would be with them in time for Polly to see Glory off to school and then take a well-earned rest.

Will stood by the bed, beaming down at the baby.

'She's got youer mama's colouring, Bron. Nothin' like the big fella downstairs, is she?'

'Just as well.' Polly was bustling around, picking things up. 'I'm going down to get your breakfast, love. You be all right 'til I come back?'

Will was moving towards the door. 'See you tonight, love. Better make sure Cyril gets to the doctor's, go with him I will. But who would do such a thing, Bron?'

She couldn't bear the humiliation of people, especially her family, knowing that Cyril loved somebody else and already had a son by her, so she had to pretend to be mystified. Besides, it would cause more trouble if they knew, and there'd been enough of that already.

'Thanks, Uncle Will, you've all been wonderful.'

'Well, we can't leave him in that state, love. He's a surly devil sometimes, but he doesn't deserve what he got.'

Someone thought he did, Bron told herself. It looked as though Ceinwen's brother had had his threatened revenge. But would it stop at that?

When Cyril didn't come back from the doctor's within the hour Bron was worried in case anything was seriously wrong.

It was almost one o'clock when he returned, half a dozen stitches in his lip and a shade over the badly bruised eye.

'A near thing they said it was,' Will told her. 'Could have lost his eye if it had been half an inch nearer. Begged him I did, Bron, to have the doctor last night. Said at the Infirmary that he should inform the police, but Cyril won't hear of it. Filling in his form for benefit he is now and I'll post it on my way to work this afternoon.'

'What will happen about this morning, Uncle Will? I mean about you not going into work?

Will shrugged, saying, 'I phoned them from the hospital and explained.'

But Bron was worried. He'll probably have to lose half a day's pay, she thought.

When a letter came from Jenny Phillips saying she would be coming to see the new arrival on the following Monday afternoon, Cyril was determined that he wouldn't be there.

'Mam mustn't see me like this,' he mumbled, for it was still very painful for him to talk or eat. 'She'll know right away who did it, Bron, and there'll be trouble. Ceinwen's had enough of that as it is.'

Ceinwen! Always Ceinwen! It made her mad the way he kept on about her.

'I'll have to pretend that I'm at work,' he went on, 'I'll get home about seven. She should be gone by then.'

'But where will you go?'

'Oh, the pictures or somewhere.'

He can find money for that, Bron thought bitterly. There were still a lot of things to buy for the baby, special soap and talcum powder and soothing cream, and she hadn't any spare money until pay day. Cyril was behaving as though the extra expense was nothing to do with him. She must buy everything from the house-keeping, which although he had had a rise, had got gradually less and less over the months. What did he do with the money? She didn't really need to ask. The public house and Ceinwen, that's where it went.

On Monday afternoon, with the baby in her prettiest embroidered gown – thank goodness a few of these had been handed down from her great-grandmother's time – and Alma's daintiest matinee coat, Bron waited eagerly for the visit for she got on well with Cyril's mam.

It was almost four o'clock when Jenny came into the bedroom, unable to hide her dismay as she looked around her before dropping an armful of presents on to the bed.

Whatever do they do with their money? she asked herself. Cyril had a steady job, he wasn't on the dole. She'd always thought Bron was a good manager and anxious to have things looking nice. But they hadn't made any improvements to the bedroom. It was as scruffy as ever.

Gazing down at the sleeping infant she made all the right noises, but it was so tiny, such a frail-looking little thing.

'You feeding it yourself, *cariad*?'

Bron nodded. 'The baby isn't taking the milk as it should,' she told her mother-in-law. 'The midwife says she's sure it'll come all right.'

Bron wasn't happy, Jenny had sensed that as soon as she'd entered the room. She could tell the girl was ashamed of her seeing this bedroom by the flush that had come to her cheeks. Well, it had taken her by surprise, hadn't it? But there was something deeper than that. It was Cyril, of course. She'd been told he'd been seen in Glas Fynydd, and he hadn't called on them.

No good would come of that.

Bron was opening the presents eagerly, excited over the pretty cot cover and pillow case. Only where was the cot? Perhaps it hadn't been put up yet, the baby being so small? The little dresses Glenys had sent for when the baby was tucked made Bron's eyes shine with pleasure, each dainty little garment hand-embroidered and smocked. Bron exclaimed with delight over the beautiful cashmere shawl Jenny and Idris had bought, but already her mother-in-law was regretting spending the money on this when so many more necessary things were obviously needed.

The last parcel to be opened had been tied up in pale pink crêpe paper with loving care and was from young Ceridwen. Inside was a box containing talcum powder, baby soap, and an ivory-coloured rattle tied with a pink satin bow. And when Bron cried, 'Oh, that's just what I needed to buy,' Jenny wondered again. Surely they could afford a little thing like that?

Cyril's mother stayed on and on, and it soon became evident that she meant to be there when her son came home. Bron was on edge as she fed the baby, and the child seemed to sense this. Instead of going to sleep after the feed she just cried and cried, with Jenny pacing the bedroom floor massaging the baby's back.

In all the commotion no one heard Cyril come home until the bedroom door burst open and he mumbled, 'What's for my tea? There's nothing I can eat in the blutty cupboard, and there's no one downstairs.'

Then suddenly his good eye was staring at his mother, who with the shock of seeing his poor face forgot even to reprimand him for his language, crying, 'My God, Cyril, what's happened?' But she didn't need telling. Hadn't she heard the threats with her own ears? But Cyril was mumbling, 'Someone beat me up, Tuesday it was, the day the baby was born.'

'And we both know who did it,' Jenny said bitterly. 'You've only yourself to blame, Cyril. I've been told all about youer Sunday visits – ' She broke off when she saw her son stare venomously towards the bed.

'No! It isn't youer loyal little wife that told me, though it seems there's plenty to tell. Let me look at that eye.'

'Oh my God!' she cried again when he'd lifted the shade. 'They'll pay for this, believe me.'

'Ceinwen had nothing to do with it. It was him and the old man.'

'She encouraged you there,' his mother cried. 'You've never been to work in that state?'

'No. I didn't want you to see it. I didn't want to get you upset.'

'Well I am, and they haven't heard the last of this! And when youer better, Cyril, how about you getting this room decorated? I'm sure Bron's uncle would help. Pull youer socks up, boyo. Forget about that girl in Glas Fynydd. I'm hoping to persuade youer father to make her an allowance, the child is youers there's no denying, but you should start giving some consideration to youer wife and child.'

As Cyril, his face red with anger, turned on his heel and went downstairs, Jenny looked at Bron apologetically.

'Sorry I am, *cariad*, to upset you like this but it had to be said. Clear the air it will, you'll see.'

The baby, rocked into an exhausted sleep, was gently lowered into the basket and tucked in before she said, 'Go down I will and get something that Cyril can manage to eat, and what would you like with youer cup of tea?'

'Bessie would have got him something at about five

o'clock. I forgot to tell her he wouldn't be back.'

'Clear the air' her mother-in-law had said, but when she left her words would more likely bring on a thunder storm. Cyril wasn't likely to take it out on his mother, oh, no! He'd simply wait until she'd gone.

Chapter Twenty-Two

When Jenny came up to the bedroom to say goodbye she told Bron that Cyril was walking her as far as the tram.

'Youer nan's downstairs, *cariad*, come to see the baby and settle you for the night. It's a pretty name you've chosen for her. Youer mam would be pleased, wouldn't she? And our Glenys will an' all.' Kissing Bron's cheek warmly she told her, 'Don't you worry about Cyril, strong as an ox he is. It will soon heal.'

Just after Bron heard the front door close Martha came into the bedroom.

'Nice woman, Cyril's mam. Don't know 'ow she ever came to 'ave 'im.'

'Oh, Nan!'

'Gave that boy a good talking to, she did, I 'eard her. Anyway, let's 'ave Madam and put 'er ready for the night. Just top and tail 'er I will. I'll go down and get a bowl of water.'

An hour later, the baby asleep and Martha gone home on Bessie's promise to keep an eye on things, Bron was wondering where Cyril had got to, or perhaps worrying would have been a better word for she was pretty certain she knew where he had gone.

Oh, please, she sent up a silent prayer, not tonight, not until I'm up and about and can cope with things again.

Bessie was looking worn out. All they needed was for Cyril to come home drunk.

It was almost eleven-thirty when there was a loud knocking on the front door, and hearing Bessie instantly go through the passage from the kitchen Bron knew she had been waiting up for Cyril. She heard his voice and Bessie's angry shouts and fear gripped her. Oh, not again! How much more would Bessie put up with?

Just after the kitchen door closed with a bang, Cyril was lumbering up the stairs banging into the banisters, swearing loudly. Bron glanced down at the baby, now peacefully asleep, one tiny hand resting on the pillow with fingers curled.

The door burst open and Cyril lurched towards the bed. His face close to hers, beer strong on his breath, he muttered, 'What you been saying to my mam then, eh? The room's not good enough for you . . . I don't give you enough to manage on . . . What else you been whining about? And don't you deny it either. She wouldn't have lectured me like that – '

'I didn't say a thing,' Bron's eyes were blazing now, 'but it's all true isn't it, Cyril? That's why it hurts – '

Before she could dodge it his hand came out and gave her a resounding smack across her cheek. Bron touched the throbbing spot with her fingers. Her eyes wide with surprise and pain she stared at him, turning her face away as hot tears spurted from her eyes.

'Do you have to get drunk to find the courage to hit me, Cyril?' Then, as a sob took her voice, she heard him bumping into the door before opening it and stumbling down the stairs.

Praying that Bessie wouldn't come into the room until she was calm again, Bron lay down, dabbing at her eyes, and taking deep breaths, but the tears kept falling. Little

Meg who had slept through all the commotion was now stirring restlessly. If she cried she knew Bessie would come hurrying to her.

Bron lifted the child, holding her close, the tears falling like rain. The warm little body held against hers brought her comfort. At that moment she almost wished that they were alone together, like Maisie Jonas and her little boy. But glancing down at Meg she was glad at least that Cyril had given her his name.

At that moment she was sure that she hated him. If only there was some way that she could manage on her own, some way that he could go to Ceinwen and his precious son, she thought bitterly, knowing that his heart was with them and had been for a very long time. Would he have been happy with the girl if he'd believed her enough to marry her and never come to Cardiff to work?

That was what the trouble was all about, wasn't it? Cyril regretting what he'd done. And the more unattainable Ceinwen had become with his marriage, the more he wanted to be with her.

Cyril didn't come up to bed. When Bron woke the fire was already lit and Polly had brought her a cup of tea and was going down for the baby's bath.

'Your husband slept downstairs last night. I think he'd had a skinful and didn't want to disturb you.'

Bron gave her a sad little smile, and suddenly Polly was leaning over the bed, her eyes wide with horror.

'Your face, Bron. Those red marks! Looks like – he didn't?' she gasped. Surely even Cyril wouldn't have done that to a woman still in her child-bed?

But the tears slowly rolling down Bron's cheeks confirmed her fears.

'Going down I am right now to give that sod a piece of my mind,' she cried, but Bron put a staying hand on her arm, saying imploringly, 'Please, Aunt Poll! Please don't say anything. He was very drunk. It was something his mother said. He thought I'd been telling tales about him.'

'But in your condition, Bron. God, I'd like a few minutes with him. I'd black his blutty other eye.'

'Please!'

'All right. But if he ever does it again, love – '

About an hour later, when Polly had gone home, Cyril came up to the bedroom.

'I'm sorry, Bron,' he said without looking at her. 'I wouldn't have hit you if I'd been sober, but I still think you must have been grumbling to my mam.'

It was a funny sort of apology but she knew it was all she was going to get.

'I didn't say anything – 'she began, but he was already closing the door and he hadn't even glanced at little Meg. She mustn't get upset, she told herself, it was bad for the baby. Bron tried to stem her bitter thoughts towards Cyril, but it was no use. She wished that he had stayed downstairs.

Bron was surprised when Polly took her grandmother's turn that afternoon, until she explained.

'Better not let her see you like this, love. Mad she'd be and you know your nan, she'd go for him bull at a gate.'

Seeing Bron struggling with the bedclothes she helped her out and over to the wardrobe where she stared into the mirrored doors, shocked at what she saw. Touching the scarlet finger stains, she gave a gasp of dismay.

'It'll soon fade,' Polly comforted her. 'You won't be going out for a bit, love. Doesn't it hurt?'

Bron nodded as Polly tucked the bedclothes around her once more. 'It stings a lot. But I didn't think it looked like that.'

'Well, thank goodness Cyril's going back to work on

Monday and you'll be up soon. I'll take the washing home with me next week. Then the following week you should be able to manage.'

'But you won't be able to keep Nan away.'

'I know, and I can't say he was patting your cheek either, can I, Bron?'

But fate stepped in and her grandmother remained in ignorance of Cyril's spiteful attack. When Polly went home it was to find Martha lying on the sofa groaning in pain and Bertha ministering to her needs.

'My God! What's wrong?' Polly cried anxiously.

'It's my back, Poll. I've done something to it, I can't 'ardly move. Come on suddenly it did.'

'I'll go and get the doctor.'

'No need for that, girl, Bertha's been rubbing it with some of my stuff.'

'You been lifting anything heavy?'

'Only a bowl of water to wash the baby, and tea-trays and such. Felt a twinge yesterday I did when I was carrying that water from the wash house. I think we should 'ave brought Bron's bed downstairs.'

'Sciatica,' the doctor told her the following morning when there'd been no sign of improvement at all. 'You'll have to be patient, Martha, keep warm, plenty of rest. I'll give you something to ease the pain.'

'Rest, 'e says,' Martha quipped back. 'The only rest I'm likely to get is when I'm put in my box.'

'She'll live.' He looked at Polly and laughed. He liked Martha Thomas, the woman had plenty of spunk.

Polly let Bron think that it was to stop Martha from knowing what Cyril had done that she managed to keep her mother away. No sense in worrying the girl, her aunt thought, she had enough problems of her own.

It wasn't until nearly a fortnight later that Bron saw her

205

nan again, and by this time Martha was better and the marks on Bron's face had faded away.

If Bron had hopes of things improving when she was downstairs once more, they were soon dashed. Instead things seemed to get worse.

She tried hard to get the washing away before Cyril came home, but on days when the weather was bad it wasn't easy. Napkins and little garments airing over the guard were sure to cause an outburst. Another thing that annoyed him was the baby crying. In vain Bron told him that it was his loud voice that frightened her; his loud complaining voice, she could have said.

One Saturday evening he told her he was going to Glas Fynydd the following day.

'Don't look at me like that,' he yelled. 'I haven't been to the Valleys for weeks.'

'You're asking for trouble after what he did.'

'I'll take that risk. I've got to get away from here.' He flung his arm out to embrace the whole room.

It had been a wet squally day despite its being June but Bron had managed to dry everything around the fire before he came home. Now the napkins and gowns were neatly folded over the two ends of the guard, not screening the fire at all.

'Blutty fed up I am with all this. It's like a Chinese laundry. – Oh! Shut her up, will you?' he shouted as the baby began to cry.

Bron, in the middle of serving his tea, said, 'It would help if you'd nurse her for a minute –' But before she could finish the sentence Cyril had thrown down the *Echo* he'd been about to open, and snatching up his coat had made for the door.

'Why don't you have your tea first?' Bron tried to keep her voice reasonable, but Cyril slammed the door shut.

Picking up the crying baby she rocked her to and fro, remembering with a lump in her throat how her father would pick Jackie up and cwtch him the moment he came into the house. Suddenly she felt afraid for the future. Would it always be like this?

What was Cyril like on Sundays when he met Ceinwen? They must have a secret place to meet or he would be more afraid. It was obvious that he didn't treat his son with the same indifference that he showed towards Meg or Ceinwen wouldn't want to see him. She remembered how his eyes shone whenever he mentioned David. Why couldn't he find a little love in his heart for his daughter?

Bron smiled bitterly at her thoughts. Perhaps after all she only had herself to blame. Cyril had been forced into their marriage by her nan. She'd never really had a chance against Ceinwen, and as far as she could see she never would.

Chapter Twenty-Three

Walking home from Rosalind Street through the flag-bedecked streets Polly was wondering anxiously just what excuse she could give her mother this time. Oh, she'd like five minutes with that Cyril Phillips, she really would, and she'd give him more than just a piece of her mind too.

Have to think of some excuse she would, before she reached home. Bron couldn't always be falling downstairs or bumping into doors and things. Such a pity it was, too, with King George and Queen Mary's Jubilee being celebrated tomorrow, and she knew just how much the girl had been looking forward to the party in the street.

On her way to visit Bron she'd thought how festive Rosalind Street looked. The lamp-posts had been swathed in patriotic streamers, pots of red, white and blue flowers hanging from the arms. Red, white and blue flags fluttering in the breeze, strung across the street from one bedroom window to the other. Lovely it is, she'd thought, but she'd forgotten all about it as soon as she'd caught sight of Bron's face.

She'd known of course that Cyril could be really nasty when he'd had a drop too much. Since the baby was born last May Bron had had a series of black eyes, swollen lips, and bruises. Until recently, by mutual consent, they'd managed to keep Martha ignorant of the fact, but the price had been the often voiced complaint, 'She 'asn't been round for nearly a week, Poll. Think you would, that she didn't know where I lived any more.'

Then Polly would make the excuse, 'I expect the baby keeps her busy, Mam,' to which her mother would reply, 'Well she knows who'd love to mind little Meg, but she doesn't bring 'er to see me. 'Urts it does, Poll, an' after all I've done for that girl.'

Not wishing to upset Martha like this, the excuses had started that Bron couldn't come round to Thelma Street because she'd fallen downstairs or bumped into a wall. Miserable devil though Cyril had turned out to be, Polly thought, she couldn't help feeling that there was more to his behaviour than met the eye. Jenny Phillips had told them that he wasn't really a drinker until he came to Cardiff to live.

'Always went with the boys after the Rugby match on a Saturday he did. Got a bit merry sometimes, especially if they won.' But his mother obviously had no idea of how much he drank now, and how he treated Bron.

Well, he certainly never got merry, Polly thought bitterly, so what had happened to make him like he was? She didn't understand it at all. Bron was a good little wife, would have had those rooms looking a treat given half a chance. Tight he was with the money, and no wonder the way he spent it at the pub and going off to Glas Fynydd on a Sunday.

Turning the corner into Thelma Street, Polly saw her mother standing at the gate. What shall it be this time? she thought anxiously. Another fall downstairs or a bump into something?

'Bron coming round tonight?' Martha called as soon as they were within hailing distance, then as Polly reached the house, 'And don't make little Meg the excuse, girl, 'cos Bessie loves to sit with her.'

'She's had another fall, Mam, hurt her eye again.'

'You don't really believe in all these accidents, do you, Poll? Whatever's happening to that girl? Do you remember when she was courting that Chris, how smart and pretty she was? What's gone wrong do you think? Do you think 'e – sometimes I wish I'd never interfered – I don't think 'e'd 'ave married 'er if I 'adn't – but for little Meg's sake it was for the best, wasn't it, Poll?' Martha's voice was pleading.

'You did what we all thought was right at the time, Mam. It could have turned out fine. He doesn't like Cardiff I've heard Bron say heaps of times, so why don't they do something about finding a job and a place to live in Glas Fynydd? His mother could be looking out for them, couldn't she?'

There seemed to be no answer to this, and mulling over the possible reasons they went into the kitchen. Will wouldn't be home for at least another half an hour and the stew was simmering nicely on the range. Martha went out to take the washing off the line and, with a sigh, Polly sat down in a chair by the middle room fire and picked up her book. After a few minutes she put it down again, unable to concentrate, longing for Will to come home so that she could unload the burden of her thoughts.

There was a time when she would have discounted her husband's opinion, but all that had changed. Her mother's sharp tongue had told her the truth about her attitude to Will and she'd been offended and sulked about it for a while, but since then things had been different between them. It was all those years ago when she'd kicked up a fuss because he had put his arms about Bron to comfort her, the week the girl had started work at Jessop's.

'Too many of them rubbishy love stories you been reading, my girl,' Mam had said. 'Well, let me tell you this, Polly, there aren't many 'andsome 'eroes in real life, only decent 'ard-working men like youer Will who's willing to put up with youer nonsense.'

When Polly hadn't replied Martha had gone on, 'The reason youer like you are with Will is 'cos 'e loves you an' 'e shows it. Despise 'im for that, don't you, Poll? 'Cos no other man ever felt that way about you, did they? And you'd 'ave been an old maid and left on the shelf if it hadn't been for Will.'

She'd given her mother a withering look and flounced out of the room but she'd known that every word was true. Will was devoted to her and Glory. Good with the money he was too. Remembering her mother's words she'd begun to look at Will with new eyes, and the funny thing was that with her changed attitude he seemed to find a new confidence in himself; he was a different person these days, just as loving and kind as ever but their new relationship had done wonders for his self-esteem.

When he came home Will thought like her that confronting Cyril would only make matters worse for Bron. His kindly face had a worried look as he said, 'It's hard to stand by and watch, Poll, but I don't think Bron would thank us for interfering. He'd only take it out on her when we'd gone.'

It was the morning of May the sixth, Jubilee Day, and Bron was staring into the mirrored doors of the wardrobe in dismay. The shabby bedroom was reflected behind her. They had managed to get a bed of their own at last and she'd been glad they could give Ivy back the one she'd lent, but the room looked as miserable as ever. This was the least of her worries as, with her fingers, Bron traced the puffy discoloured skin around her eye. Well, that settled it, she thought, disappointed. It looked even worse than on Friday evening when Cyril had blackened it with his fist. Bloodshot it was now and puffier than ever, the dark purple bruising fading into an angry red.

She knew she'd asked for it this time but she'd been worried about finding the money for the coal-man. Cyril had just got home from work, and looking at his moody face she knew she should have left it until some other time, but the coal-man might be delivering first thing, and she'd had a hundredweight on credit the week before. And there was another worry: the baby's shoes were getting too small, and now she was beginning to toddle Bron would have to do something about it or her toes would be pinched.

'Could you let me have just enough to get some coal, Cyril?' she asked, wetting her lips nervously.

'I'm nearly skint myself,' he answered without looking up, taking a forkful of food and lifting his cup.

'He'll be coming in the morning. ˡ owe him for last week.'

'Too bad. Shouldn't have what you can't pay for, should you? Anyway the weather's getting warmer now. You don't need fires.'

'I've got to bathe the baby, and air all her things.'

'The baby! The baby! Sick of youer whining I am. God! Wish I still lived in Glas Fynydd I do.'

Suddenly, before she could stop herself, Bron was crying angrily, 'Why didn't you marry her, Cyril? You had your chance.'

Cyril had risen from the table, his flushed face dark red. Slamming his cup down so tea slopped over the cloth he came and stood over her menacingly.

'By God, I wish I had!' he yelled at her. 'I'd have been a happy man.'

'You didn't trust her, did you? That's how much you loved her then. Thought it might be someone else's child, you did.' The words she'd held back so long came tumbling out.

The blow to her eye knocked her backwards on to the arm of the easy chair and she fell awkwardly, bruising her leg. Her eye throbbing with pain she sat there head in hands, knowing that for once she'd asked for it. She'd baited him, heedless of the consequences.

She heard Cyril bang the door and stamp upstairs. Her heart full of misery, she rocked herself to and fro. It was the first time he'd ever hit her when he was sober and she'd accomplished nothing. No coal, no shoes for little Meg.

Oh, she'd been looking forward so much to the Jubilee party in the street! She'd never be able to face the neighbours now.

Remembering the remnant of material she'd been able to buy because there was a slight flaw in it, and out of which she'd managed to cut a dress for herself and one for Meg, making them up with Martha's help on the machine in Thelma Street, disappointment at not being able to go brought the tears to her eyes, and even more pain. She wouldn't be able to go, would she? It looked awful. And she hoped Bessie hadn't been spreading the news that she had fallen again. The neighbours would be thinking that she was the one who'd been drinking if they believed all the tales that had been put about.

'Those jellies you made, Bron, are they set yet?' Bessie was asking from the doorway. 'Be starting soon it will.'

Bron hurried to the safe in the yard, giving a sigh of relief when she saw that they were. She hadn't thought to look. It had been the last thing on her mind.

'Yes, they've set,' she called back. 'Best leave them here until they're needed.'

Should she go to the party and see the same look of pity in their eyes as Bessie's had held? She knew in her heart that they didn't believe her excuses. Nobody could have fallen over as many times as she was supposed to have done, unless of course there was something wrong with their balance.

'I'll 'ave Meg while you get ready Bron,' Bessie said, lifting the child and cwtching her.

Bron bit her lip, saying, 'I don't think I'd better go – '

'Don't talk daft, girl, you been paying in f'r ages, an' you made them lovely new frocks.'

'It looks awful, Bessie, worse than it did yesterday.'

'Tell you what, *cariad*,' Bessie put the baby down and started for the door, 'I got an eyeshade somewhere. Go and find it I will.'

When she came back into the room and handed Bron the pink shade, Meg crawled to her once more, pulling herself up by grabbing Bessie's long skirts, staring up at her with wide blue eyes.

'Who's a lovely girl then? Who's going to put on a lovely new dress?' Bessie cried, lifting her on to her lap. The child grew prettier by the day, she thought. Strange that Cyril didn't make a fuss of her.

With the eye-shade in place Bron felt she could face the neighbours. After all, if Bessie hadn't said anything they might just think she had a sty or something like that, and at least with the shade they wouldn't have to look at her bloodshot eye and the bruising around it.

Soon she was helping to lay the tables while Bessie took charge of Meg, sitting on a wooden kitchen chair just outside the gate, with the baby straining to get to the floor, for she had just begun to find her feet and liked nothing better than to totter between her mother's and Bessie's outstretched arms, smiling triumphantly as she reached her goal.

A slight breeze was stirring the paper tablecloths, red, white, and blue all the way down the long trestle tables in the street, so that they had to be anchored as soon as possible with heavy glass bowls of trifle, shivering jellies, rabbit blancmanges, plates of sandwiches, and a selection of various kinds of cake, from tram-line given by the corner shop, fruit cakes and sponges, to Welsh cakes still hot from the griddle. The delicious smell soon had the children crowding around, their mouths watering in anticipation of the feast to come.

When at last everything was ready a neighbour with an accordion began to play 'God Save The King', and glasses of pop and herb beer and cups of tea were raised as with one voice the neighbours and children of Rosalind Street cried, 'God save the King and Queen.'

Then everyone fell to with enthusiasm. The plates were emptied and filled again, the mounds of cakes and sandwiches disappeared and were replaced, and the big enamel teapots borrowed from the Chapel were filled up time and time again.

When at last the celebration tea was over the fun and games began, but first the trestle tables must be cleared and stacked away, after each neighbour had collected her own china, empty jelly bowl and cake and sandwich plates, glasses and cutlery. Then the tables were taken down and the street cleared for action.

No one mentioned the eye-shade and Bron was really enjoying herself. Little Meg, who had sat on her lap throughout the meal, had behaved beautifully, loving all the attention that she was getting.

Every now and then Bron glanced up the street anxiously, wondering when Cyril would be coming home from work. Mr Jessop had opened his shop supposedly just for the morning in case any street party organisers in the area wanted last minute things, but the shop must have closed hours ago.

The children were beginning to line up for the races, and on a table on the pavement were the bags of sweets the grocer on the corner had given for prizes. Next would be the Beautiful Baby Contest for which, at Bessie's insistence and without any resistance from Bron, Meg had been entered. Looking down at her now Bron felt so proud. The baby's cheeks were pink with excitement. Her blue eyes shone with happiness. Oh, if it could only always be like this, Bron thought. Later she was going round to listen to Polly's wireless when the King spoke to the nation this evening.

The races were coming to an end at last, and Bessie was whispering that the baby contest was about to start, ''Cos look, Bron, they're putting the prizes on that table now all the bags of sweets 'ave gone.'

Looking over Bron saw the lovely teddy bear that was to be first prize, surrounded by several smaller items: a rag book, a tiny doll, and a box of bricks. It seemed a lot of prizes, until looking around she saw just how many babies there were.

Taking off Meg's protective bib she patted her dress into place and gently combed her halo of golden curls. Someone called through a megaphone for the mothers to come forward for the Beautiful Baby Contest. 'When I blow the whistle,' he told them, 'will all the mothers sit down on the bench and take their babies on their knee?'

It was at that moment that Bron saw Cyril walking unsteadily towards her, and wondered anxiously how he'd managed to get like that at this hour of the day. When he reached her she saw thankfully that he wasn't very drunk. There was silence as he stood in front of her, covering one of his own eyes with his fingers, and crying, 'Now what have we here? I didn't know they were having fancy dress. Are you Nelson, Bron, or Long John Silver?'

The neighbours around her had grown silent, listening. At his words a titter went around like the sighing of dead leaves. Encouraged, enjoying the audience, he went on, 'My tea, woman. I haven't got all day. I want to go out this evening.'

'Only a few minutes, Cyril,' Bron pleaded. 'The baby competition is just starting. I've entered Meg –'

'Beautiful Baby Contest?' Cyril was reading the notice over the prize table sarcastically. 'We should have entered my son, shouldn't we? He'd have won it all right.'

One of the neighbours, thinking this was another attempt at a joke, laughed loudly. The others just looked at each other with puzzled expressions.

Bron's hand had flown to her mouth in dismay. Next moment, knowing that it was a sure way of getting his wife into the house, Cyril swung Meg roughly on to his shoulders and strode indoors, leaving Bron to scuttle after him, anxiously pleading, 'Please, Cyril, just let me have her for the competition. I'll be back as soon as it's over.'

The baby, sensing the tension, began to scream. Lifting her down and pushing her into Bron's arms, Cyril cried, 'God, doesn't this kid ever do anything but grizzle and yell?'

Cwtching Meg to her, smoothing back her curls and murmuring comforting words, Bron took her back to the street.

'Hurry up!' Bessie was calling. 'They're waiting to start.'

Bron sat down on the bench with the other mothers and

wished she'd brought the comb to run through Meg's curls. As she kissed the top of the baby's head Meg looked up at her with a dazzling smile, and kept on smiling as the judges, a couple of ladies whose own children had long since grown up, stood in front of her, writing in their books.

A quarter of an hour later, with Meg wearing the Beautiful Baby sash that someone had made for the contest, the teddy held tightly in her arms, Bron carried her back to the living room where Cyril was waiting.

For a moment she thought he was going to cuddle the child, but just then the bear which had been tipped backwards and forwards again gave an unexpectedly loud growl, making Meg's lip tremble with fright before breaking into a loud wail of dismay.

Seeing Cyril's look of impatience, Bron said quickly, 'Come and show Aunty Bessie your new teddy, Meg, while I put the kettle on for Dada's tea.'

While she fried sausage and bacon and some cold potato that she'd brought from the safe, she could hear Bessie on the kitchen side of the wash-house door, saying 'Meg, make teddy growl again for Bessie.'

Meg must have obliged for teddy's growl could be heard in the wash-house. She could hear Bessie clapping and cheering, and anxious to see what was going on she opened the door. There was little Meg sitting on the rag mat in front of the guard, clapping her hands every time that it was Bessie's turn to make the bear growl, and Bron found herself clapping too until a smell of burning made her remember the meal she was frying and she dashed to the wash-house just in time to save the bacon and turn the sausages.

When Cyril had gone out and Meg was bathed and dried with a cuddle in front of the fire, Bessie came in to say, 'Best get a move on, Bron, if you want to 'ear 'is speech.'

'I'll just put Meg up – '

'I'll put her to bed if you like, Bron. I'll tell 'er a story first.'

Meg's arms were already outstretched, so slipping the nightgown over her head Bron gave her an extra cuddle and a kiss and handed her over.

Just over ten minutes later, the eye-patch still in place, she was sitting by the fire in the middle room at Thelma Street, a plate of sandwiches on her lap and a cup of tea resting on the twinkling brass fender at her feet. Will was twiddling the nobs of the smart new wireless in its dark oak fretwork case. After listening to the crystal set that Martha still had it was a wonder indeed. No cat's whiskers, no head phones, and although there was a little bit of crackling at first, the King's voice came to them clear and firm, and when he came to: '. . . and – may I say so? – the love with which this day and always you have surrounded us, I dedicate myself anew to your service for all the years that may still be given me', there were tears in Bron's eyes, and Nana's, and even Polly's.

'It's been a lovely day, Bron,' Martha was saying, still dabbing at her eyes. 'I knew our little Meg would win that competition. You must bring her round to show us her teddy tomorrow, love, and her sash. Who made it? Was it that Mrs Joshua that does the embroidery?'

When Bron nodded, Glory said, 'We didn't have anything like that at our party, only races for the kids.'

At fifteen Glory had blossomed into an attractive young lady. The thick shining hair had taken on a bright auburn tint and was worn brushed back from her forehead and anchored at the nape of the neck with a large diamanté slide. She wore a lovely dress of emerald green crêpe-dechine, the crossover bodice flattering her budding breasts.

''Ave another cup 'fore you go, Bron,' Martha saying. 'Come out to the kitchen and I'll put the kettle on.'

When they were alone, Martha said kindly, 'What's happened to you this time, Bron?'

Bron blushed scarlet, 'It's a sty, Nan. I must be run down.'

'And I'd be a silly old woman if I believed all these excuses. It's that Cyril, isn't it? The rotten swine. I don't suppose you'll want me interfering, but don't stay away from your nan. I worry more when I don't know what's going on.'

When she got home Bessie was knitting another pair of white lacy socks. Bron smiled to herself. They must be for Meg. The socks she made for her grandchildren were of much sterner stuff.

'Where's 'e gone tonight?'

'Cyril? Out with his friends, I expect.'

''E never seems 'appy to me unless 'e's off to the Valleys.'

'He loves Glas Fynydd, Bessie, and I must admit it has something, especially in the spring and summer. Lots of open spaces, green fields and the mountain.'

And Ceinwen and little David, she told herself. Much as Cyril loved the mountain, they were the real attraction.

Chapter Twenty-Four

It was almost a month later that Bron took little Meg to Glas Fynydd to show her Nana Phillips the teddy she had won. Cyril had actually told his mam and dad about the baby winning the competition, perhaps feeling it reflected some glory on himself.

Jenny had written several times asking Bron to come and see them, but she couldn't go until the bruises around her eye had completely disappeared, knowing that if Cyril's parents saw what he'd done there'd be even more trouble. The black eye had gone slowly through the colour stages and it wasn't until even the dirty yellow that the bruise had faded to had completely gone, that she'd felt able to face them.

Bron chose a Thursday to go for Cyril would be working late. Any normal family would have gone together on a Sunday, she reflected sadly as she took her seat on the train and put an arm about Meg as she stood on the corner seat looking out of the window.

Just like the other time, as soon as they reached the Valleys the people who got into the carriage were very friendly and talkative.

'Luvly day, innit?' a smiling rosy-cheeked woman cried, taking the corner seat opposite Bron. The older woman who followed her in could have been her mother by the resemblance.

'Beautiful day,' the second woman agreed, 'but it do fag me out, Blod.'

As with a hissing of steam the train chugged out of the station, they turned their attention to Meg.

'Pretty little thing, isn't she?' the younger one said. 'Come over by 'ere, love. I got some lossins in my 'ambarg.'

'All right is it, *cariad*?' She turned to look at Bron. 'Only dolly mixtures they are. Taking them to my grandchildren I am, but there's plenty here.'

So Meg sat between them, on her best behaviour, enjoying all the fuss, popping dolly mixtures into her mouth at such a rate that Bron was forced to say, 'That's enough now, Meg. You won't be wanting any dinner when we get to Nana's.'

'Going to see her nan then, is she?'

Meg beamed at them, lifting her teddy bear and making it growl, laughing and clapping her hands like Bessie had taught her.

'Aw, she's luvly, inshee?' the younger woman said, lifting Meg to her lap and giving her a cuddle. 'Cwtch her all day I could.'

The women got off at the station before Glas Fynydd after hugging the baby and kissing her on the cheek, leaving Meg with a penny in each hand, 'To buy some lossins at the shop.'

Getting up as the train steamed into the little station at Glas Fynydd, Bron lifted down the wooden-framed, carpet-seated push-chair that one of Bessie's daughters had passed on to her now that her children had outgrown it, and once outside the station strapped the baby into it and began to push it up the steep street towards the mountain.

She was thinking of the letter she'd received from her father by the morning post. In it he'd told her that he and Evelyn could be married at last now that they'd managed to find some unfurnished rooms in the area where they wanted to live. They were to be married by special licence and he hoped Bron would be able to come to the wedding, but would understand if she couldn't as she must have her hands full with the baby.

Martha, Polly and Alma would have received letters too. Would they be going? Bron wondered. She doubted it for Coventry was a long way and there wouldn't be anywhere for them to stay. Her father had sent Meg a card with a pound note enclosed on her first birthday, and Bron had been very grateful, buying the child much needed shoes and a rag doll, and opening a post-office savings account for her with what was left, though she knew there'd be little chance of adding to it.

Suddenly she became aware of someone behind her on the pavement, and moved closer to the houses so that they could pass. It was a young girl carrying a baby. When she'd passed and was walking in front, Bron drew in her breath as she noticed the little boy resting his chin on the young woman's shoulder and staring towards her with big brown eyes. The child was the image of the baby Cyril whose photograph Bron had seen in the family album, even to the short tawny curls.

The girl obviously didn't know that Bron was Cyril's wife so she dawdled, thinking that there might be trouble if she was seen entering the Phillipses.

Ceinwen, for it must be she, looked back over her shoulder as she crossed the road and disappeared down a side turning, and as she reached the top of the street Bron saw Jenny waiting at the door of her house. She hurried forward as they drew near, lifting Meg from the push-chair, admiring the teddy, kissing the baby over and over again.

'So this is the most beautiful baby in Rosalind Street,' she cried. 'Come on, Nana's girl, come and see youer granda. He's been looking out for you for ages.'

Bron had been amazed at the difference Meg had made to Cyril's dad the few times she'd brought her to Glas Fynydd. Idris would carry her around on his shoulders, or get down on all fours and crawl about with the child on his back. And as they'd got to know each other, Bron had got on well with him, too, and had realised that he was a very proud person, a gentle, kindly man who had been deeply hurt by his son's behaviour.

Now he took Meg into his arms, saying, 'Come with youer granda, *cariad*. We'll go and see the bunnies.' These were two white angora rabbits belonging to Ceridwen that were kept in a hutch in the yard.

Oh, if only it could always be like this, Bron thought wistfully. If only she and Meg could come with Cyril on a Sunday just like any normal family would do.

When Bron had laid the table and the meal was ready Meg was strapped into the dark wood high-chair that had been kept for the grandchildren, and watching the love in their eyes as they smiled at the baby, and the way her grandfather patiently spooned the food into her mouth, beaming at the child each time a spoonful was successfully negotiated, Bron thought again what a lovely couple they were, and what a happy family they could become if only Cyril loved her, though she knew very well that he didn't.

Determined that nothing should spoil the day she put this thought behind her, and chatted and smiled as though she didn't have a care in the world. When, the dishes washed and put away, Jenny suggested they should take Meg to the shops, Bron was overjoyed. At least some good had come of Ceinwen discovering that Cyril was married. Now Bron could come into the open, take her rightful place as Jenny and Idris's daughter-in-law.

They set off in the afternoon sunshine with Cyril's mother proudly in charge of the push-chair and Bron looking about her with interest, especially at the houses in the side streets. For who knows? she thought. Perhaps one day we can come here to live. Cyril might be happy here. Then she sighed deeply. What was she thinking of? They couldn't possibly even consider it with Ceinwen only a few streets away.

They had reached the Post Office-cum-general store, and seeing the sweet counter just inside the door Bron remembered the two pennies the ladies on the train had given Meg. Taking them from her purse she bought a screw of dolly mixtures. Meg loved chocolate but always managed to get more on her clothes and hands than in her mouth, so dolly mixtures it must be.

Jenny, letter in hand, was queueing at the Post Office counter, and every time the bell on the door clanged announcing another customer the shop grew more and more crowded.

Bron looked around her with interest, amazed at the variety of things that were for sale. The Post Office counter took up the narrow wall opposite the door and window. A grocery counter took up one long wall and a display of fruit and veg and the sweet counter the other.

Damp sawdust covered the floor, and hanging from ceiling hooks behind the grocery counter was a side of smoked bacon and some salt fish, while just inside the door, in the space between that and the window, was a display of galvanised buckets and enamel bowls, sweeping brushes and mops.

When her mother-in-law left the queue, impatient with

the wait, and came over to her she was accompanied by two women, both of them bending down immediately, smiling and talking baby talk to Meg.

'Lovely she is,' Cyril's mother was saying, 'she won the Beautiful Baby Contest in Cardiff at the Jubilee celebrations.'

'Only for Rosalind Street, Mam,' Bron said modestly.

'Well, it's a very long street! And she won a teddy, bless her, and a – ' Her voice trailed away and Bron saw the rosy cheeks blanch. Glancing in the same direction as Jenny she saw the girl she had let pass her that morning, a flannel shawl about her shoulders, the baby in its folds cwtched to her breast Welsh fashion.

The girl was striding towards them, looking angry. She stared down at the push-chair where little Meg sat contentedly popping the tiny sweets into her mouth.

'Is that the reason he had to marry you?' she cried, her eyes flashing scorn. 'You must 'ave pitched him a tale. It's nothing like Cyril.'

The two women Jenny had brought across to admire her grand-daughter were staring open-mouthed, and Bron was too stunned to reply. Jenny Phillips put a gentle arm about Ceinwen, saying, 'Come along, girl, let's go outside.' But the girl shook her off angrily, crying, 'Only got to look at him you have,' she lifted her own sleeping baby for them to see, 'the image of Cyril he is. Wouldn't take my word for it, would he? Oh no! But that one there could be anyone's.'

'That's enough,' Jenny snapped at her. 'Youer not going to make accusations like that, Ceinwen. This is our grand-daughter and you'd better be more careful what you say.'

'Treated rotten I've been,' the girl cried, and by this time she had the attention of everyone in the shop. 'Told me to go again this morning, my old man did. Always at me he is. She's got everything, hasn't she? A home, a baby with its father's name. But there's one thing she'll never have and that's Cyril's love.'

The little boy, woken by all the shouting, was screaming loudly. Ceinwen strode to the door, banging it hard behind her. Jenny, her face scarlet now, was holding her hand to her mouth and Meg was whimpering to be picked up, while still putting the dolly mixtures into her mouth. The tears were streaming down Bron's cheeks as, with her mother-in-law's arm about her shoulder and the two women voicing their disgust at Ceinwen's behaviour, they left the shop.

'Trouble maker, that girl,' one of the women began, but Jenny silenced her with, 'She's got a lot to put up with, mind you. Her father treats her like dirt since she got into trouble. But she had no right at all to say that to Bron. Come on, love, we'll be getting home.'

When they reached the house Cyril's mother still had the letter she'd wanted to post in her hand. She was anxious to get indoors before any more neighbours witnessed Bron's tears. Hearing her key in the lock Idris opened the door. He beamed at Meg and was just about to unstrap her and pick her up when he noticed Bron's distress and his wife's expression. 'What's happened?' he cried. 'What's wrong?' They'd been so happy going out, he reflected.

When Jenny told him, his face flushed with anger.

'Cyril's got something to answer for,' he said, 'the amount of unhappiness he's caused.'

Tea was prepared but nobody felt much like eating; the happy atmosphere of earlier in the day had gone. While the women washed up Idris played with the baby, singing nursery rhymes and jigging her on his knee, but his eyes were sad, the old withdrawn look creeping into them.

When Bron left, Jenny insisted on accompanying them to the station.

'I'd intended to come anyway,' she said, 'but I want to make sure she doesn't get at you again. She isn't a bad girl at heart, Bron, and she really loves that little boy, but her father never allows her to forget what she's done. I'm really angry at what she said to you. We give her an allowance, you know. Cyril can't afford to give her anything and it's the least we can do.' She sighed then went on, 'Poor little David, what will the future hold for him?'

Bron was thinking about the money, just a few shillings a week, that Cyril had been giving the girl, but she said nothing. Perhaps he no longer gave it to her now that his parents were doing what they could?

When the train had moved out of the station and she could no longer see her mother-in-law, she would have liked to be alone in the carriage with her gloomy thoughts, but there was little hope of this happening on a Valleys' train and she was soon drawn unwillingly into the conversation.

'Hot today innit, luv? You been visiting?'

'Yes, my parents-in-law.'

'Isn't she luvely?' someone else said, nodding in Meg's direction. 'From Cardiff, are you?'

Bron nodded. The joy had gone from the day and even these friendly souls couldn't bring it back. She felt ashamed, humiliated, in front of her mother-in-law's friends, and she knew how upset Jenny had been. And when he'd heard Ceinwen's version of what had happened Cyril would be angry too, but it wouldn't be with the girl who had caused the rumpus. Oh, no! His anger would be directed at her. Life was so unfair.

Chapter Twenty-Five

During the cold dark days of January 1936 Bron was almost run off her feet, as first Bessie, then little Meg went down with influenza. Meg recovered quickly but was still fretful, constantly demanding to be cwtched, missing all the attention the old lady had always showered on her. But Bessie remained in bed, her racking cough echoing through the house, and as the third week of her stay upstairs began Bron grew really worried at the greyness of her friend's face, and the alarming way the fat was falling from her.

Bessie's daughters were back and forth but when they weren't there Bron looked after her willingly, upset to see her so low.

On the twentieth of January came the gloomy news of the death of King George V and Bessie, a royalist through and through, demanded that the bedroom blind be kept drawn as a mark of respect. And so with the light burning from morning to night, and sometimes beyond, Bron was kept busy endlessly searching for coppers for the meter.

Blustering March winds were blowing, twisting the endless washing around the line, by the time Bessie came downstairs. All the fight seemed to have left her as she sat huddled by the fire, a blanket about her shoulders, but Bron was still surprised when she gave in at last to her

231

eldest daughter's pleas for her to go and live with her, something Bessie had been resisting for years.

'It's on the edge of the country in Rumney, Bron,' she told her, 'and Mary says I can 'ave my own rooms. Arthur works for a builder, and 'e's added one of them glass things – you know.'

'A conservatory?'

'That's it, girl. One of them's to be my kitchen.'

'What will happen about the house, Bessie?' Bron asked anxiously.

'Well, if I was you, love, I'd get Cyril to apply.'

'Oh, we couldn't afford it, Bessie.'

'Well, they'll have a job to let the place with someone in the rooms. If I was you I'd try and get the house an' let the rooms youerself.'

'But supposing we don't get the tenancy, Bessie? Could they turn us out?'

'Don't worry, love. I won't give my notice until I'm sure about that,' Bessie said comfortingly. 'Are you going to ask Cyril about it now?'

'I think I'll leave it for tonight, Bessie. Cyril's a bit upset.'

'And what's the miserable sod upset about?' Bessie asked tartly.

Well, she couldn't tell Bessie for she'd never understand but Cyril was worried about Ceinwen, and it seemed that he had good reason to be. Ceinwen had also had the 'flu, but was still in bed after four weeks for the doctor had discovered that she had a weak heart. She'd been told not to get out of bed, not to move or exert herself in any way. When Cyril had come home this evening and told her he'd had a phone message at work, she'd asked, 'What about the baby? How will they manage?'

His eyes were filled with sorrow as he lifted Meg to his

knee, as he did sometimes now, saying, 'I've got to see her, Bron. I must go tomorrow.'

'But her father? Her brother?'

'Hopefully they'll be at work. My mother said she was asking for me.'

It was strange really the way Cyril had of talking to her about Ceinwen, of letting her know how much he loved the girl, but she was used to this by now. He'd never loved her, she'd known that almost from the beginning. She was sorry that Ceinwen was ill, of course she was, and for little David too, but she hadn't forgotten that day last year, just after the Jubilee celebrations, when she'd met the girl for the first time. And never would she forget Cyril's anger when he'd come home from Glas Fynydd on the following Sunday evening.

'What did you want to go out flaunting yourself in front of the neighbours for?' he'd yelled at her angrily.

'I didn't flaunt myself, Cyril. Your mam asked me to go to the shops,' she had shouted back, upset at the accusation.

'Ceinwen was in an awful state, I can tell you,' he'd continued. 'She nearly collapsed when she got home. It took ages to calm her down.'

Then, his tone changing, he'd asked, 'You saw little David then?'

'Yes, I saw him.' Bron had been determined not to say what she knew he wanted to hear.

Now Meg was becoming restless because Cyril, consumed with worry over Ceinwen, had stopped jigging her. Bron saw her daughter's tearful look from one of them to the other and her trembling bottom lip, and gathered her into her arms. Leaving Cyril to eat his tea, she took Meg to the kitchen where Bessie told her her news.

When she went back to the front room, Cyril was still

at the table, staring towards the fire, deep in his own thoughts. She decided, nevertheless, that she must tackle him as soon as possible, or they might find themselves without a house.

'Cyril,' she began, but he seemed to have difficulty taking his gaze from the fire. 'Cyril, there's something I need to talk to you about.'

He looked up wearily. 'Can't it wait?'

'No, it can't. Bessie is thinking of going to live in Rumney with her daughter.'

When he didn't say anything, she went on, 'We could apply for the tenancy.'

'What for? We're all right as we are.'

'But we won't be able to stay as we are, will we? The landlord will want to let the house again.'

'Leave it tonight, Bron. We'll talk about it tomorrow when I get home.'

'We needn't pay any more if we let the rooms like Bessie has.'

He didn't seem to hear her as he sat there staring before him. Sighing, Bron gave it up and began to get Meg ready for bed.

Later, the banging on the front door woke Bron from a deep sleep. Dragging on her dressing gown she glanced towards the window where a heavy grey sky was heralding the dawn.

There was the knocking again, and now Cyril had woken and was resting on his elbow.

'What the hell is that noise?'

'I don't know. I'll go and see,' she whispered, glancing anxiously at the cot where Meg was fast asleep.

When she'd unbolted the door a telegram boy was holding out a buff envelope.

'Any reply, Missus?'

Bron turned the envelope over in her hand fearfully. It was addressed to Cyril.

'Hang on a moment, I'll find out.'

But when she turned Cyril was behind her, and taking the telegram he tore it open with trembling fingers. As he read the message his face blanched of all colour and he gave a little moan of despair as the form slipped from his fingers.

He was sitting on the bottom stair, head in hands, as Bron picked up the telegram with shaking fingers and read:

Don't come to Glas Fynydd, son. Ceinwen
passed away. Will be down to see you today.

Love, Mam

The boy was looking anxiously from one to the other of them.

'Any answer?'

'No. No, thank you,' Bron said, shutting the door.

By this time Cyril had gone into the room and was sitting in an arm chair staring into the grey ashes in the grate.

'I'm very sorry, Cyril,' Bron said, putting an arm gently about his shoulder. And she found that in her heart she really was. It was a dreadful thing to have happened, and she knew that he would take it very hard. Hot sweet tea, that was supposed to be good for shock. She took the kettle and hurried to the wash-house to boil some water on the gas-stove.

When she went back to the room with the tea he was sitting, head in hands, sobbing over and over: 'Oh my God! Oh my God!' Then turning to her he said pitifully, 'I wasn't there. She needed me and I wasn't there.'

Bron pushed him gently back into the chair and put the cup between his hands, then crept upstairs for a blanket to put about his shoulders, hoping she wouldn't disturb either Meg or Bessie. How was she going to explain his grief to Bessie? Or to Nana and Aunt Poll for that matter? They still knew nothing of Ceinwen or the boy.

He didn't seem to notice when she put the blanket gently about him. The full cup still cradled in his hands, he was staring into the grey ashes.

Bron knelt down. Taking some of the sticks she'd put to dry out for the morning, she rekindled the fire, but still he sat there, tears rolling down his face.

'Try and drink the tea while it's still hot,' she coaxed gently, but he seemed not to hear.

What should she do? Bessie shouldn't be worried anyway for she wasn't yet fully recovered. And if she ran to Thelma Street – well, the situation was going to take some explaining, and they wouldn't understand her concern.

When at last she'd coaxed him to drink the tea, he looked at her pitifully. The sight of his grief moved her deeply. Why couldn't she harden her heart? she thought. This was her husband, for God's sake, crying at the loss of the woman he loved, the woman he should have married. She knew that Ceinwen had been his first and only love. Their marriage had been a mistake; even the reason for it had come about through a misunderstanding, for Cyril had always maintained that he'd thought she'd wanted it to happen. But Meg had been worth all the unhappiness, so like Bron's mam with her sunny disposition and happy smile, except when her parents argued.

Presently Cyril took his eyes from the fire and looked at Bron again, asking, 'What's to become of David?'

'I expect her mam and dad will look after him,' Bron said comfortingly.

'Oh, no! Not them,' Cyril cried. 'Her mam's kind but she's too old, and her father's a cruel devil with the belt when he's had too much.'

As Cyril dropped his head in his hands again Bron cautioned herself to stop and think carefully, and not say something she could be sorry for. She mustn't let her heart rule her head, she told herself, but she was seeing again the little boy with the big brown eyes staring at her solemnly from over his mother's shoulder on the day Ceinwen had passed her on the way from the station.

'He could come here.'

At first it was as though Cyril hadn't heard her, then he raised his head and looked at her as though he couldn't have heard right.

'You'd do that for me, Bron?' he said at last.

'For the child, Cyril,' she told him. 'I couldn't bear to think of Meg being unhappy if anything happened to me.'

'You'd really have David here? You'd look after him as your own?'

She nodded at him. 'Yes, I would.'

She knew now that her heart must be ruling her head. She'd seen the hope in Cyril's eyes. Now they clouded again as he said, 'He's Ceinwen's. Have you forgotten that?'

No, she hadn't forgotten!

'He's a child, Cyril – your child – and he's going to miss his mam. He'll need a lot of care and understanding. He'll need someone he already knows and loves and who loves him too. He needs you, Cyril.'

'Supposing they won't let us have him?'

'I thought you said the baby was too much for her mother to cope with?'

'He is, but Ceinwen's father hates the sight of me.'

'Well, see what your mam says when she comes.'

It was too late for them to go back to bed. Putting the telegram into the drawer of the sideboard, she washed and dressed then got the breakfast while Cyril prepared for work. The main thing was to get him out of the house and on his way to work before Bessie started asking a lot of questions, for Cyril's grief couldn't be accounted for by the demise of a distant friend. Perhaps he shouldn't go to work, he was in no fit state, but he needed to ask Mr Jessop for the afternoon off so that he'd see his mother when she came.

After the awful night she could hardly stay awake. She'd wanted to tackle Cyril again about asking for the tenancy of the house, yet against his awful grief it seemed of no importance. But it had dawned on her that if they had David they would need another bedroom, perhaps not right away but pretty soon. But how would they pay the extra rent, especially with another child to feed and clothe?

Cyril came home at about half-past one. It was a Saturday yet Mr Jessop had given him the rest of the day off and told him to take Monday morning as well to get his friend's affairs in order.

'What did you tell him?' Bron asked, holding her breath. She still valued Marcia's friendship.

'Only that a friend of mine had died, and there were a lot of things to sort out.'

When Jenny arrived she too looked tired and upset.

'How's he taking it?' she mouthed to Bron before going into the room.

Bron pressed her lips together and shook her head. His mother would soon see for herself. Then, as mother and son went into each other's arms, Bron went to the wash-house to make the tea.

When Bron thought she'd given them long enough together she took the laden tray into the room. When she opened the door they were talking quietly.

'Cyril tells me you have offered to have David.'

'Well, he should be with his father, he's got no one else.'

'You're a good girl, Bron. One in a million. But are you sure you can take this on? I was telling Cyril I don't think there'll be any trouble, they had their last two very late. They're both into their sixties. I don't think they'd let David go into a home or anything like that, mind, but a child needs young parents, doesn't it?'

When Bron agreed, she went on, 'Cyril was telling me about Bessie. I'm sorry she has been so ill. It would be nice if you could get the house though, wouldn't it? Give you more room.'

When Cyril's mother left, with a promise to enquire about them having David, Bron said, 'I didn't want to say in front of your mam, but we couldn't afford to keep the house to ourselves, much as we need the two bedrooms.'

'But I'll be able to give you more, Bron, enough to cover the extra rent anyway, and something towards David's keep.'

Was he going to give up spending his evenings in the pub? It seemed too much to hope for.

Will was getting ready to go around to Bron's. After what Polly had told him when Glory had been out of the room, he felt very concerned.

'Something funny there, Will,' Polly had said, 'him being that upset over a friend. Well, you wouldn't expect him to be sitting with his head in his hand now, would

you? I mean, it wasn't as though it was his mam or dad
or a brother or sister. Just a friend, she said, and they
were thinking of taking the baby 'cos there's no one to
look after him. After the way he's treated our Bron an'
all.'

That was the part that was worrying Will – them taking
someone else's baby. Bron had enough to cope with as it
was, especially the way that Cyril carried on. Well, he'd
go round and see if there was anything he could do. Perhaps Poll had the wrong end of the stick.

Bessie let him into the house, and as he chatted to her
he thought how ill the woman looked, but she seemed
quite pleased now to be going to her daughter's.

'Rum do that is,' she told him, holding him back and
shaking her head as he started towards the front room
door. 'Never seen a man make such a fuss about a friend.
His mam do tell me they're goin' to 'ave the baby and
look after it. Bron's got enough on 'er plate if you ask
me, managing on what 'e do give 'er.'

When he entered the room Cyril lifted his head from
his hands and looked at him, and Will could have sworn
that the fellow had been crying. Bessie was right. It was a
rum do.

'Come round to see if I can help? Anything that needs
doing?'

'Thanks, Uncle Will. Cyril and I have decided to look
after a baby whose mother has just died. A little boy it
is.'

Cyril jumped to his feet, his eyes blazing as he cried,
'I've had enough of this nonsense, Bron. Why don't you
tell him he's mine? It's natural that I should provide for
my own child, isn't it?'

Will knew that his mouth had opened in surprise and it
stayed open as he glanced from one to the other, from

Cyril's grief-filled face to Bron's, scarlet with embarrassment. He swallowed hard before saying, 'Well, if he's yours, Cyril, it's only natural that you should want to look after him. Before you met Bron, was it? How old is the little chap?'

'He's nearly two.' Bron was looking at him anxiously, biting her lip.

Will was trying to hide his surprise. Meg would also be two in May, wouldn't she? To cover his confusion he said quickly, 'How are you going to manage? Won't you need another cot?'

'They're sending his cot down,' Cyril told him.

Will looked at Bron. 'Pity the room isn't done out, isn't it? It will be more awkward than ever to do it once the boy arrives. Don't forget, I'll help willingly any time you want it papered.'

Cyril was staring into the fire again but Bron said wistfully, 'I wish we could do it before he comes. Supposing his nan wants to look around before she lets us have him?'

Cyril looked up anxiously at Bron's words, and when Will who'd been watching him carefully said: 'Would you help me to paper the bedroom before the little fellow arrives, Cyril?' he answered right away, showing some interest for the very first time.

'Well, it's Sunday tomorrow. We could start it then. But we haven't any paper or paint. How much do you think it would cost, Will?'

'Oh, not very much. I've got enough white paint at the house. You'll just want the wallpaper and some flour to make the paste. Tell you what, if we could get the bed and cot downstairs for tonight I could do the painting now. Leave the window open and the smell should be gone by tomorrow.'

When Cyril went upstairs, taking a spanner to undo the

bed springs, Bron gave a sigh of relief. Very glad she was that the room was to be decorated at last, but it was good too that Cyril would have something to occupy his mind. Keeping him busy doing something for David was bound to help.

They brought the bed and the cot down and put them up in the living room, then Will went home to change into old clothes and collect the paint and brushes. It is a rum do all right, he thought, the boy being only two months older than little Meg, but Bron seemed to have taken it in her stride. He hoped she wasn't taking on too much.

Glad he was that Polly and her mam had gone to Clifton Street where the shops were open until nine o'clock tonight, otherwise there would have been lots of questions and he was anxious to get back to get on with the job. Best see if Bron wanted them to know it was Cyril's son she was going to look after.

While he was getting the paint from the shed with the aid of a torch he remembered that Bron too had gone to Clifton Street after Cyril had given her some money to get the wallpaper. He wondered what she'd tell them if they met.

Chapter Twenty-Six

David's arrival at Rosalind Street was preceded by a shabby brown wooden cot, and an ancient well-sprung pram delivered to the door by the G.W.R. When on the Friday Jenny Phillips brought the child she was accompanied by Ceinwen's mother, a harassed-looking woman who, after being introduced to Bron, took her hand warmly in her own, saying, 'Had some hard thoughts about you I did, Bronwen, I must admit. But to take over little David and look after him as youer own . . .' She shook her head from side to side, tears rolling down her cheeks. Then as Bron helped her gently to a chair by the fire she looked up at her with streaming eyes, and dabbing her cheeks with an outsize hanky continued, 'Youer just as much a victim of circumstances as my pooer Ceinwen was.' Then, overcome once more by her grief, she buried her face in her hands.

Polly had been just about to let herself out after being introduced. Now she closed the front-room door quietly, thinking bitterly, Just as much a victim of Cyril's lust, she means! She'd got a good look at the child and he was a handsome little boy and looked much older than the two years Will had said he was. Oh, she hoped and prayed that Bron wasn't making a rod for her own back!

The spitting image of Cyril he is, she told herself. She'd

have known the child was his even if Will hadn't told her that night he'd been to Rosalind Street to do the painting. Mam didn't know yet though but once she saw the boy she'd guess the truth, that was for sure.

Bron had poured the tea and was trying to coax David to lift his face from Mabel's lap and drink the cup of milk she'd poured him, but the more she coaxed the deeper he buried his curly head in the folds of his nan's dress.

'Come on, boyo. I've got the cup, look!' his Nana Phillips pleaded, but he wouldn't budge.

'Don't worry,' Bron told them with an optimism she didn't really feel. 'He'll be fine when Cyril comes home.' Then turning to Mabel and offering the plate of cakes and biscuits, she said, 'You must come down to see him whenever you like. We'll be coming to Glas Fynydd some Sundays, of course, and then you can come over to Cyril's mam's.' She had no intention of risking the wrath of David's strap-wielding grandfather, or of meeting Ceinwen's brother, the one who'd beaten Cyril up.

Presently, the tea and biscuits finished, they went upstairs for Mabel to inspect the bedroom. Bron proudly pushed the door open to reveal the newly decorated room with its pretty flowered curtains fluttering gently in the breeze, the new beige oil-cloth covered beside each cot with a soft rug, the creamy wallpaper patterned with rose-buds, and the gleaming white paint. The one jarring note was the heavily varnished wardrobe which they'd been unable to replace, but at least they'd managed to drag it to a dark corner of the room.

'We've put the cots at opposite ends so that they won't always be waking each other,' Bron explained.

'A lucky little boy he is, Bron,' Mabel told her. 'Much as I love him I couldn't look after him properly, not with my back. Couldn't even push the pram up the hill. Too heavy it was.'

When they'd had tea and Cyril came home from the shop, Bron lingered in the doorway before going out to get his meal from the oven.

The little boy's eyes brightened when he saw his dad. Rushing towards him, he chuckled joyously as Cyril swung him to his shoulders. Bron saw Meg's bottom lip trembling as she put out her arms toward her father. Next moment Cyril had scooped her up in his free arm and was waltzing around the room with the two children chuckling happily.

Then, the little ones protesting loudly, he put them down to kiss Mabel's wrinkled cheek, and it was obvious they were the best of friends. But Bron had known that all along for hadn't Cyril been seeing Ceinwen and the boy most Sundays when her father and brother were away from the house?

Cyril had intended to accompany the two women to the tram-stop, but as he left the room with them David's screams filled the house when he saw he was being left behind. As he struggled in Bron's arms his father came back into the room. Taking the boy from her and sitting down, he lifted David gently to his knee and cwtched him in a way he'd never hugged Meg. She was glad his little daughter was already in her cot and couldn't see him.

Bron walked to the tram-stop with David's grandmothers, with poor Mabel in floods of tears once more. Her heart went out to Ceinwen's mother. After losing her daughter the emotional parting from her grandson was taking its toll.

When Bron got back the little boy was almost asleep in his father's arms. Bringing the enamel bowl from the wash-house and putting his flannel and soap into a dish, she undressed him gently. A lick and a promise would have to do for tonight.

The next day after Cyril had left for work, and despite all her attempts to comfort him, David yelled lustily, his arms and legs lashing out in all directions, starting Meg off too, so that they cried in chorus. Bron tried to find something to catch his interest. Even Meg's battered wooden horse on wheels received little attention as he sat on the floor banging his little fists with frustration, sobbing the same words over and over, 'Want Mama. Davey want Mama.'

Bessie came in to see what all the rumpus was about but she was no match for David and so the ructions went on. In the end she gave up and took a frightened Meg on to her lap, rocking her to and fro, singing a lullaby in the husky voice the child had learnt to love.

Bronwen, with David now back precariously on her own lap, was holding him tightly, wondering what to do next, when she felt the resistance slacken as his eyes closed wearily then fluttered open again, before he finally gave up and went to sleep.

The next few days were chaotic. Housework was left undone, washing and ironing piled up as she tried to pacify the grieving child. The moment Cyril entered the house the boy would fling himself at his father and the tears would turn to smiles while Meg would grip her father's knee, saying, 'Meg want Dada too.'

Bron knew that Cyril was enjoying all this attention as he jigged them about singing nursery rhymes, the children chuckling until they were exhausted. But next day when he left for work she knew the look of misery would return to David's eyes, as though having already lost his mam and his nan and his familiar little world, he was afraid of losing the only other person he recognised.

The children's sleep patterns were different and Bron got little chance to catch up with all the jobs she'd left undone. Early in the afternoon Meg would go happily to her cot with her beloved teddy but David would fight his obvious tiredness as she tried to hold him close, singing a lullaby as she rested her cheek against his tawny curls, murmuring words like 'precious' and '*cariad*' to him until gradually the fight would be given up and he would sleep in her arms. But he always woke up when she tried to put him in his cot.

She would never forget the day Martha came to see him a few days after his arrival. David had been asleep in the pram in the passage, it being too big to manoeuvre any further, when Bessie, who was moving that weekend, leaving them to take over the tenancy, ushered Martha into the room.

Martha had taken one long look at the sleeping child, and in her usual direct fashion said: 'Friend of the family, did you say, Bron? Anyone with half an eye can see he's Cyril's child.'

Bron had never lost the embarrassing habit of blushing and her cheeks were scarlet now. What was the use of them pretending? One look at David and everyone knew.

'Silly thing to tell people that was, girl. Now if you'd said he was a relative of Cyril's, the strong resemblance mightn't 'ave mattered.'

They were standing over the pram and the little boy's lashes had fluttered open. Looking up at the stern-looking face so close to his own, his mouth trembled for a moment then opened wide as he began to scream with fright. Bron picked him up and he struggled against her, taking nervous peeks at the unfamiliar woman who'd frightened him. Martha, retreating to an armchair, said with conviction, 'He's Cyril's, all right!'

About a week later Jenny came down and Bron was relieved that Mabel wasn't with her this time, for the sight of her familiar face, and then her leaving him again after tea, might bring back the look of misery that was slowly beginning to fade from David's eyes.

Mabel had sent some toys for the children including a much battered teddy with one ear and one eye which had belonged to David's mother. Putting out eager arms he hugged it like the long lost friend it was.

'Mabel says she doesn't know how she forgot to bring it, Bron. She didn't realise until she went into the bed-room they'd shared.'

The teddy went everywhere cwtched under one arm, and Meg, now beginning to copy everything David did, began carrying hers in the same fashion. Soon they were playing happily together, giving Bron some time at last to catch up with the chores.

The summer passed with trips in the pram to Waterloo Gardens, and sometimes on a Sunday as far as Roath Lake, but then they would go on the tram with the children wearing leather harnesses, one pink, one blue, people turning with a smile to look at them and listen to their chatter.

Bron was almost happy. Cyril hadn't once got drunk since the boy had been with them; the child had accomplished what she never could. But seeing the new contented Cyril, even though in her heart she knew that he still grieved for Ceinwen, and knowing that it was his little son that had brought this miracle about, she was prepared to reap the benefit and be happy herself.

As autumn came, mild and damp, rumours grew that King Edward VIII, yet to be crowned, was in love with an American lady, a divorcee, and that neither the Royal family nor Parliament approved. People began to take sides, but most of the women in the street, even those who had known precious little romance in their own lives, took the view that he should be able to marry the woman he loved. The King was quite popular in Wales. After all, he had been their very own Prince.

When, on November the nineteenth, Bron called into her grandmother's house, Polly was reading the headline from the *South Wales Echo* to Martha who, always feeling the cold now, was huddled over the fire.

' "Something will be done for South Wales," ' Polly read the headlines to them, 'and it says underneath that he said, "You may be sure that all I can do for you I will". King Edward VIII said that,' she repeated for Bron's benefit, 'and so he should. After all, he was the Prince of Wales.'

'What's the picture?' Martha asked.

'It's the King standing above Blaenavon Colliery – just look at the crowds. Speaking to the miners he was. It says he'd come to see for himself the appalling effect of the depression on South Wales.'

'Well, 'e's King now. Perhaps 'e'll 'ave more say,' Martha said, taking the paper to look for herself.

But, on December the tenth, just three weeks later, the King abdicated because he was unable to share the throne with the woman he loved. So much for his apparently well-intentioned words, Bron thought. Surely he must have known even then, as he stood above the colliery making promises to the suffering miners and giving them hope, that he would never be able to carry them out?

Chapter Twenty-Seven

Bron looked around the newly decorated kitchen with satisfaction. It had taken two years and a lot of scrimping and saving to get it as she wanted it but it had been *well* worth the effort. They'd only managed cream distemper for the narrow passage walls, and now she dreaded the coal-man's weekly visit when, sack on shoulders, almost bent double, he'd carry the coal through the house to the yard.

Bessie's giving her some of the kitchen furniture had been a big help, shabby as it was. As the old lady would have only a tiny conservatory and one room downstairs in her new home, she'd decided to take only the polished table and dining chairs and the plush sofa from the parlour, together with a small table and a couple of wooden chairs for the kitchen.

'Might as well 'ave some comfort from my bit of best,' she'd said, 'an' you can put that purse away an' all, Bron. If the stuff's any 'elp it's welcome you are. I know youer a dab 'and at fancying things up an' making' somethin' out of nothing.'

So Bron had set about doing just that, but with the children to see to, the endless cleaning, washing and ironing, combined with the shortage of money, it had taken a very long time. First she'd sewn cretonne covers for the cushions on Martha's Singer machine. Next she'd replaced the torn coconut matting that lay on the red and black diamond tiles, which she'd scrubbed almost back to their former glory, with two matching rugs bought in Goldberg's summer sale. But then she'd had to buy the distemper for the passage, and it wasn't until last week that she'd managed to afford the plum-coloured plush cloth and matching mantel border.

Looking back, Bron thought of the summer of 1936, the year Davy came to them, as the happiest she'd ever known. Cyril had spent time with them whenever he could. There'd been trips to the parks and occasionally to the seaside which they'd enjoyed like any happy family, giving her an insight into what life could have been for them from the beginning if theirs had been a love match.

But it didn't last. By the winter, shut up in the house with the children, Cyril had begun to get restless, picking quarrels about nothing, reminding her over and over that if it hadn't been for meeting her he'd have married Ceinwen and been able to look after her. Bron had known for a long time that his conscience at the way he'd treated the girl troubled him, but his words hurt her deeply. Glancing down at her wedding ring she'd reflect that she had paid dearly for the respectability it conferred. When he flung out of the house one winter night in 1937, for the first time since Davy had arrived she'd been dreading him coming home, but he'd returned almost sober, eating his supper in silence, still full of his grievance.

But she'd never regretted having David to live with them. He was a lovable, boisterous, little boy, and once he'd got used to her would fling his arms about her neck and hug her just like Meg had always done. Cyril, basking still in the children's love for him, rarely raised his voice in front of them and Bron was thankful for this at least.

Sometimes, in anger and frustration at her husband, she'd fling herself on to the bed, telling herself she should leave him, but where could she go?

Being almost of an age the children were hard work, especially when, too big for the pram which had now been consigned to one of the sheds in the yard, she had to walk them everywhere, the push-chair being fine for one but neither would walk while the other rode.

It was September 1938 and the news in the papers and on the wireless was becoming increasingly serious. War seemed inevitable despite the Prime Minister's two visits to Germany in search of peace. The fear of war had been building up ever since March when Hitler had incorporated Austria into the German Reich. Now it was the turn of Czechoslovakia and war was a distinct possibility.

On the twenty-eighth Neville Chamberlain was addressing a worried House of Commons, giving them a disappointing report on his two peace missions to Germany, when a message from Hitler was handed to him inviting him to fresh talks, in Munich this time, and once more there was hope. But the preparations for war went on. The British fleet had been mobilised, and the Auxiliary Air Force was at the ready. Trenches were being dug in the parks as some measure against possible air raids. The papers told of another day of tension, and Britain held its breath.

Suddenly the threat was over. Chamberlain came back with a piece of paper. Waving it aloft towards the cheering crowds he declared to a very grateful people that it meant 'Peace in our time'. So said the headlines on the first of October and the fear that nearly everyone had felt gave way to enormous relief.

Christmas was less than three months away which

seemed a long time until Bron worked out all the things she'd have to buy. She'd have to save, she told herself. But something was always needed, like shoes for the children. They didn't so much wear them out as grow out of them, especially Davy, who at four and a half was towering over dainty little Meg.

It was a Saturday, a crisp sunny day, and she was getting the children ready to go to Clifton Street to do the weekend shopping which was always a tiring affair, a battle of wills as, a little hand in each of hers, she would attempt to manoeuvrè them past the fascinating windows of Goldberg's toy shop. The window was already dressed for Christmas, an Aladdin's cave of wonder for Davy and little Meg who had hopefully already chosen a beribboned baby doll in a rocking cradle for Father Christmas to bring her, while Davy wanted a clockwork train set that went around an oval track, under painted tin tunnels and through a station platform, with little tin porters complete with luggage trucks.

Bron was worried about his infatuation with the train set which an indulgent assistant had set working for him on their last visit. Now he pulled away from her, unwilling to leave until he'd seen it racing round once more, trying to drag her into the shop. The sales girl, seeing his determination, wound it up for him and put it on the rails.

Bron was almost too late to get the piece of spare-rib pork she'd wanted for the butcher was already auctioning the leftover meat, and she had to hurry to the greengrocer's to get a savoy for they too would be closing in ten minutes.

She'd missed Bessie over the last couple of years, especially when, like tonight, she had to go to the shops, for Cyril wouldn't be home until everything had closed. Bessie would have sat with the children in the bedroom, telling them a story if they didn't go straight to sleep. But she liked it at her daughter's house. 'Pampers me she does,' she'd told Bron. 'I should 'ave come 'ere before.'

As Davy kept on talking about it Bron began to worry over his fixation with the train. He had such faith in Father Christmas bringing it for him. She'd have to have a word with Cyril about the train in Goldberg's window.

'Even if we could manage one,' she told him worriedly, 'it would only be a small one. All those tunnels and things are extra, we couldn't afford those.'

Cyril told her not to worry, he could make a little tunnel and paint it, perhaps even a station. 'I can do it in the back room at work,' he told her. 'There's plenty of wood from the boxes.'

Bron smiled at him encouragingly, trying to show a confidence she didn't feel, because if Cyril ever hammered a nail into anything it always fell out.

A fortnight later she still hadn't been able to save anything towards the Christmas presents for the children. Last week Davy had needed yet another pair of shoes, and with the winter coming she'd had to buy extra coal. Cyril had started going for a drink with his buttys again several nights a week, and seemed to think that having given her more money when Davy had come to live with them and they'd got the tenancy of the house, she shouldn't ask for more. But that was over two years ago, and what with the way that Davy at any rate grew out of his clothes and the burden of the extra rent, the money didn't allow for the extras needed at times like Christmas.

Bron had set her heart on getting the children the presents they wanted. It must be the lovely memories she had of her own childhood, she thought with a tinge of sadness. Her mam had been such a generous soul. She still sometimes wondered what had been bought with that ten pound Provident cheque. It had remained a mystery to them all, as had the purpose of the key that had been found in her purse when her handbag had been dragged from the river. Bron had carried it in her own purse now for many years as a kind of talisman.

Polly had said she was daft when she'd told her what she hoped to get the children for Christmas.

'Just like your mam used to be, you are, Bron,' she'd told her. 'Sell her soul she would for you two kids.'

'Where's the money comin' from?' Martha asked practically.

'I'm trying to save, Nan. I wish there was some job that I could do at home, just until Christmas.'

'Saw an advert I did this morning, in Pritchard's window it was. A lady in Rumney wants someone to do housework a couple of mornings a week. We could look after the children, couldn't we, Mam? 'Tisn't as if they were babies.' Polly looked toward her mother questioningly.

'Well, go on, Bron,' Martha cried. 'Get a move on, girl, or the job will be gone.'

Bron hugged her warmly, and then it was Polly's turn. Oh, if only she could get the job. It would solve all her problems.

Leaving the children with her nan she hurried to look in Pritchard's window to find out the address, then went to the Royal Oak to wait for a tram, wondering if she did get the job would she earn enough to buy presents for her nan and the others in the house in Thelma Street, as well?

It was a day of low cloud and damp mists and as the tram went over the bridge that spanned the river a sadness came over her as she stared out at the murky water flowing sluggishly between the banks of tangled couch grass. She shuddered as she always did when passing this spot. Then as the tram climbed the hill other memories stirred as she stared towards the houses trying to find the house number that had been on the card, memories of a sunny day when, holding her little brother's hand, she'd followed Mama up a long path to a house with a deep porch and a frosted glass panel in the front door. There'd been a monkey puzzle tree in the front garden, Mama had pointed it out to them before the door was opened by a sour-puss of a maid, a new maid Mrs Wilson had told them was taking the place of Gladys who had left, and who herself had replaced Bron's mam.

Suddenly she stopped to stare through a pair of wrought iron gates at a monkey puzzle tree in the centre of a front lawn, then at the number on the door, the same number as had been on the card in the shop window. A feeling of excitement gripped her. This was the house where her mother had worked and where she'd visited when a child. Mrs Wilson had given her and Jackie fizzy lemonade and cherry cake with icing on top. Fancy her remembering that!

The lady who opened the door stirred no memories at all, but hadn't Bron been told that the Wilsons had gone abroad to visit their daughter, never to come back?

When she'd explained why she'd come, the lady, who'd introduced herself as Mrs Potter, looked at her appraisingly and showed her into the lounge.

'There's just the two of us now the family's grown up,' she told Bron. 'We don't need a full-time maid. I've plenty of time on my hands. I thought if someone came in twice a week for a few hours in the morning, say from half-past nine until one o'clock, they could do the upstairs one day and the downstairs the other. Have you done any housework for anyone before, Mrs Phillips?'

'Only at home,' Bron confessed.

'Could you start next week then? See how you get on.

I'd like the downstairs done on a Friday, we have visitors most weekends. Shall we say Tuesday and Friday mornings?'

Bron felt guilty about the fact that she would only be able to stay until Christmas. Her nan hadn't said anything about having the children beyond that. Oh, but it would be wonderful to be able to get them the things they had asked Father Christmas for.

Mrs Potter was rising to show her out. She was a tall lady, her greying hair neatly waved, and her plump face wore a gentle expression. Suddenly Bron wanted to tell her. 'My mam used to work here a long time ago. A Mr and Mrs Wilson lived in the house then. We used to visit them when I was a child,' she blurted out.

'Mrs Wilson was my aunt,' the woman told her, her expression becoming sad as she went on, 'they both died in Canada while visiting their daughter. He died of a heart attack and they say she died of grief. Their daughter didn't want to come back to England, her parents were buried over there, so I took on the house.'

Murmuring her sympathy Bron was being shown out by the side door, the door she realised uncomfortably that she should have gone to when she arrived. It led into a large garden where Mrs Potter steered her toward a brick-built outhouse, saying, 'The vacuum cleaner and all the cleaning things are kept in there. I'll go and fetch the key – I've only got the one. The other key was given to someone who was going to keep the place clean while the Wilsons were away, but it was never returned. Some tragedy, I believe.'

Bron was staring at her with wide eyes. Was this the explanation? She felt let down, disappointed, as she fumbled in her purse for the key. What had she expected?

Mrs Potter watched in amazement as she took it out

and turned it in the lock and the door swung open. Then she said sympathetically, 'It was your mother then that the accident happened to? Was the name Thomas by any chance?'

Bron nodded, tears stinging the back of her eyes.

'I didn't know,' she told her new employer. 'She must have come here while we were at school.'

'Yes, that's right. My neighbour told me that she paid her wages by arrangement with my aunt. There was still a pay packet unclaimed when she heard about the tragedy, but Mrs Morley didn't know where the woman lived. Ten shillings it is.'

Bron's eyes were brimming with tears. Ten shillings a week, the exact amount she would have had to pay weekly for the Provident cheque.

Mrs Potter didn't see her tears. She was lifting some grey blankets from something in the corner resting against the work bench, to reveal a girl's bicycle and a fairy cycle with address tags tied to the handle bars. Her heart was hammering with excitement as Mrs Potter read aloud from the label, 'Mrs Thomas care of Mrs Wilson'.

But there was more, for she was now removing the wrappings from a small wooden tool-chest and inside was a set of gleaming tools. The mystery was solved!

Then Bron's elation left her and a lump came to her throat as she realised that her mother had probably been on her way to see if the presents had arrived when tragedy struck, and these gifts meant to bring such joy to them all on that faraway Christmas morning had instead cost her mother her life as she'd wandered off the path on that foggy November evening.

Chapter Twenty-Eight

Bron had been almost glad when, the week before Christmas, Cyril found out about the job she was doing. Sitting at the table, hugging to herself the knowledge that she'd managed to buy all the presents, letting the verbal abuse wash over her, she was determined not to answer back for that would only prolong the misery.

'Why did you do it behind my back?' he yelled at her.

'Because you'd have stopped me if I'd told you,' was the answer she should have given, but instead she put a question to him.

'Didn't you want the children to have those things for Christmas, Cyril? It was the only way I could get them.'

'We'd have managed them somehow,' he replied. But she knew that they wouldn't have, not unless Cyril had given up going to the pub with his friends.

Bron was dreading having to give in her notice, but at least she'd be working next week when Mrs Potter wanted the house to look especially nice, ready for her Christmas visitors.

Finding the bicycles and the tool-box had been a nine days' wonder to everyone, and Bron's heart had been full at yet another proof of her mother's generous soul. A neighbour had bought the girl's bicycle from her, it being far too small for Bron. And Jackie had told her to keep the fairy cycle until the children were old enough to ride it, so it had been wrapped once more in the blankets and put away in the shed in the yard. The tools were given to Will to use where they'd benefit all the family.

'You're not listening to me,' Cyril was saying irritably, bringing her thoughts back to the present. 'You don't have to give notice for a potty little job like that.'

'But it's only twice more, and Mrs Potter has been very good to me,' Bron said determinedly. 'I'm not going to let her down, Cyril, Christmas week an' all.'

The shilling an hour she'd been paid was good money for a cleaning job, and she'd always be grateful to Martha and Polly for making it possible by minding the children.

A few days later, pink with excitement, Meg and Davy helped her to decorate the tiny tree she'd bought in Clifton Street, and laboriously stuck together paper chains, clapping their hands with excitement as she hung them around the room. Their letters to Santa which she'd written for them had been carefully posted in the red box installed for the purpose in Goldberg's toy shop, and she'd felt a smug satisfaction as she'd watched them drop them in, knowing that the things they'd asked for were safe at home on top of the wardrobe, waiting to be put into the pillow cases that she'd hang over the brass knobs of the bed late on Christmas Eve.

Cyril was still at work, for the shop was to open late on Christmas Eve, when the children stood by her side at the scrubbed table in the warm kitchen, helping her to make gingerbread men and mince pies. She'd given them a small piece of ginger pastry each to shape into little figures, providing them with some currants for eyes. And then, their faces rosy from the warmth of the kitchen, they waited impatiently for her to open the door of the gas oven in the wash-house from where a delicious smell of gingerbread was wafting into the room.

It was a lovely Christmas. Even Cyril forgot his grievances as he watched Davy wind the train with eager hands and set it carefully on the track, tongue peeping from between his teeth with concentration. He was pleased at his son's obvious pleasure in the station and tunnel he had made with Ray's help in the back room at work.

Now that they had the house to themselves the children had plenty of room to play, and when at last Meg grew tired of endlessly rocking the cradle, she put her new doll in the shoe box that she'd pulled her beloved teddy around in ever since she could walk, dragging it about on a length of string, stopping every few minutes to settle the doll more comfortably, talking to it almost non-stop, telling her new baby that she'd have to be a good girl while Mummy had her tea.

Cyril had been really pleased with the shirt and tie Bron had bought him. He'd given her a big box of chocolates and a bottle of Evening in Paris, her favourite scent. It had been a happy Christmas, one she would look back on nostalgically for many years to come.

The new year was toasted in with optimism, but as winter gave way to spring the fragile peace Neville Chamberlain had won seemed to be clinging by a thread. It was soon obvious that Britain was preparing for possible war, having learnt her lesson in the crisis of last September. The country was rearming. Thousands of men were joining the Territorial Army, planes were being built. Gas masks had been issued. Air raid shelters were being put up. It was an uneasy peace and as autumn once more approached everyone became aware of the seriousness of the situation.

On the twenty-third of August it was announced that a

non-aggression pact had been signed between Germany and the Soviet Union. On the following day Parliament was recalled from its summer vacation and military reservists were called up. On the twenty-fifth Britain signed a treaty of alliance with Poland. Hopes of peace were fading fast.

With an uncharacteristic show of patriotism Cyril declared he would sign up right away if war was declared, with Bron begging him to leave it until he was called up. But she knew that if he made up his mind he'd do it anyway.

They were visiting Glas Fynydd the day war was declared, sitting around the fretwork wireless set while Idris twiddled the knobs. It was September the third, a golden autumn day, but the mood was grim as the Prime Minister made his solemn announcement, explaining to the nation his ultimatum to Germany that '. . . unless we heard from them by eleven o'clock that they were prepared at once to withdraw their troops from Poland, a state of war would exist between us. I have to tell you now,' he concluded, 'that no such reply has been received, and that consequently this country is at war with Germany.'

Although not totally unexpected it was an earth-shattering announcement. Bron, her stomach churning as she realised the full meaning of the Prime Minister's words, went to the wide window and gazed up at the mountain bathed in mellow sunshine, deserted now for everyone was staying close to their wireless sets. Everything looked so peaceful, so ordinary, the smell of roast dinner already in the air, a solitary child, head bent low, rolling marbles in the gutter outside. A flutter of fear tinged with excitement gripped her heart. What was in store for them all? There'd been articles in the papers, frightening articles about the possibility of terrible air raids flattening the towns. When could they expect them to start?

The children's voices came to her, high and excited, from the garden where they were pushing each other on the swing. She wanted to rush out to them and fling her arms about them protectively. Then Jenny's voice was calling her from the top of the stairs, calm and matter-of-fact.

'Come and help me hang these black-out curtains, Bron.'

After lunch Cyril went for a walk over the mountain, saying he would be calling on some of his old buttys on the way back home.

When Bron told his mother that Cyril was talking about joining up, she said, 'That's Cyril all over. Act first, think later. How about Mr Jessop? He can't just leave him in the lurch.' Jenny was standing at the window. Moving suddenly towards the door she said, 'Here's Mabel come to see David.'

'Where is he? Where's Davy?' Ceinwen's mam asked anxiously. 'He hasn't gone out with Cyril, has he?'

'No, he's in the garden, *cariad*. We can't keep them away from that swing.'

As they went through the kitchen Mabel said with a shake of her head, 'Terrible news, isn't it? That boy of mine is talking of signing up. His dad's told him he's a blutty fool. Time enough when they send for you, he says.'

Then her arms were about Davy and Bron saw the tears in her eyes. 'All right if I take him over to see his grandda, Bronwen? He won't come over since that row he had with Idris. Wish they'd make it up I do.'

'Idris feels the same, Mabel. He's thinking of coming over to see him.'

'Well, he'll find him a different man now, Jenny, all the stuffin's gone out of him since Ceinwen went.'

Bronwen watched from the doorway as Mabel, her arm about David's shoulders, crossed the street dabbing at her eyes with the edge of her apron. The boy was talking excitedly, his face eager as he looked up at her.

When Cyril returned they decided to go back to Cardiff while it was still daylight. There was a war on now and no one knew what to expect.

'Take care,' Jenny called to them, after each of them had been hugged warmly by both parents. 'Mind you talk to Mr Jessop first before you do anything, Cyril.'

266

Chapter Twenty-Nine

That autumn when the children started school Bron was very glad that it was mixed infants for it made parting with them that much easier as Meg, her hand trustingly in Davy's, walked into the classroom with hardly a backward glance.

Now Bron found herself frequently glancing at the clock, for the four journeys a day she made to and from the school meant she didn't really have time to settle to do anything. No sooner did she get home and begin to tackle the washing or cleaning, than it was time to put on her coat and fetch the children home for lunch or pick them up at the end of afternoon school.

After the very real fears of what would happen now the country was at war, the most dangerous thing encountered on the home front was the black out, when eerie figures breathing steam into the cold night air like the legendary Welsh dragon himself, would loom out of the pitch blackness of a starless night and pass by within a hair's breadth, or more likely bump with profuse apologies into someone they couldn't see.

Apart from the occasional try out of the siren, and the gloom of darkened windows even in the shopping streets, life went on almost as normal as cinemas and theatres opened their doors again and people were tempted to leave their gas masks at home. Even the black out lost some of its hazards when torches dimmed by several layers of tissue paper were allowed, the faint glow to be directed permanently at the ground.

Just before Christmas Mr Jessop's first hand, a Mr Evans who worked the provisions counter, was called up and Cyril, who'd forgotten his patriotic fervour of the day war was declared, was happy to take his place.

But the news on the wireless wasn't good. In October the battleship *Royal Oak* was sunk by a U-boat in the Scapa Flow, but in December the German pocket battleship Graf-Spee was scuttled off Montevideo. Listening to the news on the wireless became the most important thing in everyone's day.

When early in January Cyril left his lunch-time sandwiches on the table in his hurry to get to work, Bron took them with her and caught a tram to Cathays as soon as she'd seen the children into school.

It was a day of high winds and squally showers and so cold her fingers felt frozen despite the woollen gloves. She was thankful for the steaming cup of tea that Marcia put into her hands as, pointing to a sheaf of papers on her desk, she said, 'This job isn't going to be easy when they start rationing the sugar, butter, ham and bacon next week, Bron. Mr Jessop's going to be desperate for staff too when the other men are called up. I expect Cyril will go about the same time as my Chris. He's first hand at the Maypole now. Has Cyril told you that the boss has been asking if you could manage to work on Saturdays?'

'No, he hasn't mentioned it,' she told Marcia. But she wasn't really surprised, considering all the fuss he'd made when she'd been doing the cleaning for Mrs Potter.

She looked around the familiar shop wishing she could work here on Saturdays, but it was impossible anyway with the children being so small. Still, it was nice of Mr Jessop to want her, and she smiled at him warmly when she went to the warehouse to say hello. But he didn't mention the job to her although he told her that he was going to be terribly short of staff very soon, so she assumed Cyril must have said something to put him off.

As the months went by with little happening at home people were only too willing to believe Neville Chamberlain when at the beginning of April he boasted that Hitler had missed the bus.

'Perhaps youer Cyril won't be called up after all,' Martha said hopefully. 'Bitten off more than 'e can chew that 'Itler fellow 'as by the look of it.'

But within a week the Germans had taken Denmark and invaded Norway, and an attempt by the British and French to land and maintain an expeditionary force in Norway ended in disaster.

The day that Winston Churchill succeeded Chamberlain as Prime Minister, Germany attacked Holland and Belgium and it soon became clear that their missing the bus was just wishful thinking as the German forces pressed on through France and, by the end of May, had forced the British army to the beaches of Dunkirk.

Now a massive operation to rescue the stranded men from the beaches was launched, the success of which turned what for Britain was a disaster into something akin to victory, as little ships of every kind, from Channel steamers to tiny fishing boats, joined the Royal Navy in braving the mine fields to speed to the rescue. The operation, begun on the night of the twenty-seventh of May ended on the second of June, and the papers were calling it a miracle that so many got safely home.

On the eighteenth of June, three days before France signed an uneasy armistice with Germany, Winston

Churchill broadcast a solemn message to the nation. When he said, '. . . the battle of France is over. I expect that the Battle of Britain is about to begin . . .' Bronwen shivered, listening intently as he continued, 'Let us therefore brace ourselves to our duties, and so bear ourselves that, if the British Empire and its Commonwealth last for a thousand years, men will say, "This was their finest hour".'

'We're for it now, Bron,' Martha said, her voice solemn. 'I 'eard they're putting barbed wire along the beaches, an' blacking out all the place names.'

When, a few weeks later, Cyril was called up they took the children to Glas Fynydd for him to say goodbye to his mam and dad. They'd only been there about half an hour and he'd been talking to his mother in the scullery when he came back into the front room to tell Bron that he was going out.

'Shall I come with you?'

'No, Bron. This is something I've got to do myself.'

She looked at him questioningly, but he'd already turned away. Watching through the window as he left the house she saw his mother hand something to him, and as he went down the path she saw that it was a bunch of flowers. When he turned left away from the mountain and took the side turning, she knew he was going to Ebenezer and the little cemetery where Ceinwen was buried. The girl was always in his thoughts. Bron sighed, thinking there was little hope that he would ever forget her.

Jenny, watching her as she turned away from the window, came across and put an arm about Bron's shoulder.

'You mustn't mind, Bron,' she said kindly. 'She was his girl for a very long time, even when they were at school.

Unable to forgive himself he is for the way he treated her. Be patient, *cariad*, things are a lot better than they were, aren't they?'

Yes, they were better, Bron had to admit, but there'd been plenty of room for improvement, hadn't there? Still, he'd never ceased to be grateful to her for having Davy. He'd only got drunk once since, and then he hadn't been abusive, just maudlin, crying to her over the way he'd treated Ceinwen. Sometimes it seemed that in death the girl was a greater threat to their marriage than when she was alive. Bron sighed. It was something she'd have to live with, the price she must pay for Cyril marrying her and giving Meg his name.

'Come on, girl, cheer up. He'll be home on leave before you know it,' Jenny told her sympathetically, misunderstanding her mood.

Going home on the train Cyril was very quiet, his thoughts far away, so that when she spoke to him he had to bring them back from somewhere or something she couldn't share. Perhaps though he was thinking of his parents, wondering when he'd see them again? But no, she was sure that it was something else, something she had no part in. More likely he was thinking of the afternoon he'd spent in the cemetery at Ebenezer Chapel, communing with Ceinwen. It seemed to Bron that the longer she'd been dead, the more Cyril agonised over her.

They each had a sleeping child on their lap, and with the rhythmic movement of the train Bron could have fallen asleep herself but she tried to keep her mind on the last-minute preparations that had to be made for Cyril's departure tomorrow. She would be coming to the station to see him off to the army camp. Their marriage had been a stormy one, but despite everything she would be sorry to see him go. She knew that she was going to miss him.

You couldn't live with someone for over five years without missing them, and she was more than willing to forget the bad times and remember only the good, like the summer days they'd spent at the seaside last year and the year before, when they'd played on the beach with Davy and Meg.

The train was drawing noisily into the station and she had to disturb Meg, who, although crotchety at being disturbed, thankfully did as she was told, taking the steep steps from the platform carefully, then hurrying with them to the tram stop in St Mary Street.

David woke up as soon as they'd boarded the tram. Bron hoped fervently that they'd still go to bed and to sleep when they got home.

The next morning Cyril's eyes were moist as he kissed the children goodbye, telling them to be good children and help their mam and he'd soon be home to see them again. Polly had come to take them to school and as they walked up the street with her they kept turning and looking back, waving madly to Cyril and Bron. She saw Polly take their hands in hers when their final wave before turning the corner took too long, threatening to make them late for school.

The platform seemed to be crowded with people saying goodbye. Bron was conscious when the train had steamed in and was waiting at the platform, and Cyril put his arms about her to kiss her, that there was none of the desperate feeling between them that others were displaying as they clung to each other, even after the guard had raised his flag. By this time Cyril was on the train and had found himself a seat, coming to the window to wave to her as it steamed out of the station.

Bron waved until the train turned the bend and was lost to sight, feeling miserable about the way they'd parted, conscious that all around her the atmosphere was heavy with the grief and the loneliness of parting.

On the way home she called in at her grandmother's house to see how the children had behaved.

'Good as gold they were, Bron, no trouble at all,' Polly assured her. 'We were just saying the money will be short with Cyril in the army and if you'd like to take a little job again, the children would be all right with us for a while.'

When Bron told them about Mr Jessop wanting her to work on a Saturday, adding, 'But perhaps it would be awkward for you with the week-end shopping an' all?' her aunt told her, 'We can do that on the Friday, all except the meat.' And her nan added, 'They'll be fine with us, don't you worry, Bron.'

Chapter Thirty

When on the following Saturday Bron started work at the grocery store she was thankful that she'd kept her white overalls, for it would have been hard to find the money for new ones.

Mr Jessop welcomed her warmly and Marcia seemed pleased to have her back. The rest of the staff she'd once worked with had all been called up. An elderly man whom she'd heard Mr Jessop call Sid, and who must surely have been past retirement age, was managing the provisions counter with his employer's help, for there was a lot more to do with most of the items rationed on this side of the store.

Putting on her overall and going behind the grocery counter Bron was trying to imagine the fashionable Ray in ill-fitting khaki uniform instead of the smart suits and suede shoes he'd always favoured. Just then Marcia came over to introduce her to the buxom, middle-aged woman who had taken his place, and between them they carried the heavy boxes from the warehouse and filled up the fixtures, in between serving the customers.

Winnie was a friendly soul and they worked well together. She told Bron that her son had just come back from Dunkirk, but there was little time for talking as the customers queued up to be served and Mr Jessop came over to help them out.

When she overhead him saying to Marcia, 'I just wish Bron could work for us full-time. A good little worker she is,' she blushed with pleasure.

'Did Cyril change his mind about you working?' Marcia asked her as she passed the cash desk.

'He doesn't know,' Bron admitted, but she wouldn't be able to keep it from him when he came home on leave, would she? Anyway, she had no intention of letting Mr Jessop down.

During the afternoon, despite the gaps in the fixtures from goods being in short supply, and the rationing of a number of things, Bron felt almost as though she'd never left, especially when Alby, the cheerful errand boy who'd worked at the shop when she'd started there at fourteen, came in wearing Air Force uniform. There was no mistaking his cheeky grin, but he'd grown tall and looked very smart. Bron was remembering when he'd left the shop at sixteen, too old for an errand boy. He'd gone to work at the Candle King and she hadn't seen him since until now.

He came over to chat with her, surprised to learn that she was married with a five-year-old daughter.

'How about you, Al? Are you married?'

'Yes. Married last January I was, just before I went into the Air Force.' And he handed Bron a worn sepia photo of a pretty girl with long fair hair and lovely eyes.

'Embarkation leave this is,' he told her with a sigh. 'Just found out Janet has that she's going to have a baby. Wish that I could stay in this country until it's born.'

When everyone had congratulated him on the news he left, promising to call in again if he had the chance. Bron saw Mr Jessop follow him outside and push something into his hand. It looked like a pound note, but she

couldn't be sure. She watched Alby shake his head and
try to give it back but Mr Jessop pressed it on him again,
and then Alby was gone.

In the middle of the morning she realised how much she
was enjoying herself. She was loving the familiar smells all
about her, and everything had come back to her so easily:
the weighing and packing, the friendly way of reminding
the customers of what they might need. And when a fresh
batch of bread and cakes came in from the bakehouse next
door, the rich aroma took over from that of the bacon and
cheese, the vinegar still dripping into the sawdust, and
even the salt fish which hung stiff and strong-smelling just
above the bacon slicer.

Just before they'd closed for lunch a number of young
shop girls came in for something for their break, just as
they had when she'd worked here before, but without Ray
to egg them on they were a sober lot, intent on getting
served as quickly as possible, instead of hanging back until
he was free.

When at the end of the day she tucked the small pay
packet Mr Jessop had given her into her handbag, Bron
had already made up her mind to save every penny until
there was enough for winter coats and shoes for the
children. And if the coming winter was anything like as
severe as the last one they'd need scarves and gloves and
woolly hats and all, she thought, determined to pay for
the tram fare to work out of her housekeeping if she
could. But she wouldn't have Cyril's wages on a Friday
now, only the dependants' allowance that was paid to her
at the Post Office.

Cyril had written to her once, a brief note to say he'd
settled in. Anyway, she was thankful he hadn't been
called up earlier or he might have been at Dunkirk.
Winnie had told her of her son's ordeal as the men lay on

277

the crowded beaches while Stukas came in on low level sorties, spraying bullets. But now, as Bron waited impatiently for the tram to take her home, she was anxious to be with the children for it was getting late. Reaching the house in Thelma Street she was surprised to find it in darkness, until she'd read the note pinned to the door. Martha and Polly had decided to take the children back to Bron's house and put them to bed.

She hurried to Rosalind Street, hoping they had behaved themselves, telling herself that she shouldn't have left them this long. But at the house nan and Polly smiled at her, assuring her that everything was all right, that the children were already in bed and asleep, and her supper was waiting. As she hugged them gratefully she made up her mind to dip into her wages just for this week and buy them a box of chocolates.

Now with the soldiers evacuated from Dunkirk, and only a strip of water between Britain and the German forces, people were on edge as they waited for the expected invasion and for the air raids that seemed inevitable.

The Anderson shelter deep in the garden was as comfortable as Bron could make it, with blankets and cushions on the wooden benches and even a piece of oilcloth on the floor.

Just before midnight on the nineteenth of June the doleful sound of the warning siren echoed around the city. Bron, startled from a deep sleep, her heart hammering, pulled on an old coat and slippers and hurried to the children's room. Davy was already awake, his eyes round as saucers at the frightening sound, but Meg was still curled up in the bed like a puppy, her chin almost on her knees. Bron managed to get a blanket around her but by the time she'd heaved the child up into her arms and got

David to follow her down the stairs the wailing had stopped, and she thought she heard the drone of planes overhead. But when she reached the backyard, breathless from carrying Meg, there was no sound at all. Closing the shelter door behind them she sat with Meg on her lap, her arm about David, and they sang nursery rhymes until with the sound of the all-clear she rose stiffly and took the bewildered children into the house for a warm drink before going up to bed.

Now the wail of the siren became a familiar part of the evening and the night as planes droned over the city and searchlights raked the sky. The children, fretful from lack of sleep, looked wan in the dim light of the shelter lantern.

Jenny wrote, begging her to bring the children to Glas Fynydd for safety.

There are quite a number of evacuees in the village.
I shall have to take some if you refuse my offer, but
I would dearly love to have our grandchildren here
with us. Please, Bron, why don't you come too?

Bron was tempted, but there were several reasons why she shouldn't go. Cyril coming home on leave was one. That she might lose the tenancy of the house if she left it empty was her main worry, then of course there was her job at Jessop's.

A few days later on the afternoon of the ninth of July something happened to make her change her mind, at least partially. On that sunny afternoon seven dockers were killed in the hold of a ship when a lone bomber swooped over the docks. That evening she took the children to the Valleys, fearful that with daytime raids they might be still at school when the siren went.

Jenny and Idris were delighted that she'd changed her

mind, hugging and kissing them and making a fuss of them. Bron had been dreading the actual parting, fearful that she wouldn't be able to go through with it, but the children were in bed and asleep when she left, and she knew how fond they were of their grandparents and that they'd soon settle down.

It was lonely in the house on her own, and as the days passed she was often tempted to follow the children to Glas Fynydd, especially when the siren began to wail.

When Mr Jessop heard about the children going to the Valleys he asked her again if she'd work full-time, and now she agreed as long as she could have time off when Cyril came home on leave. That too became a sore point as the months went by, for Chris had had a leave and two week-end passes while Cyril hadn't been home at all. He never mentioned leave in his letters, not until she wrote and asked him about it, then he said that he was hoping to get home very soon, even if it was only for a few days.

She'd written and told him about working at the grocer's and to her surprise he didn't make any fuss at all, even remarking that the money must be very useful to her. But his letters generally were a disappointment to her. It wasn't just that they were short. They never seemed to say anything, never discussed plans for after the war, never really told her that he missed her. She had hoped that the parting might kindle the love he'd seemed to have for her before he was forced unwillingly into marriage.

When he did come home it was to be only for a few days, but she'd managed to make a fruit cake and mince pies despite the shortage, just in case he didn't get home at Christmas. Bron rushed to finish a Fair Isle jumper she was knitting for herself, sewing it up in the dim light of the shelter on the night before he was to arrive. It was lupin blue, with a pattern in deeper blue and shades of pink, and when the all-clear sounded she couldn't resist, tired as she was, rushing upstairs to try it on in front of the mirrored doors of the wardrobe. She had been knitting since the summer and had made jumpers for the children who, now that they had their new coats, were well prepared for the winter. She'd also made Cyril a Balaclava helmet and several pairs of warm socks.

Mr Jessop had kept his promise and given her a few days off. Despite being tired from a night disturbed by the siren she was up early getting things ready for Cyril's homecoming, polishing the furniture again although she had done it the day before and she knew Cyril wouldn't notice anyway. Two weeks' meat ration sat on a plate in the mesh-fronted safe in the yard and she'd queued yesterday evening at the greengrocer's around the corner from Thelma Street when Polly had rushed around to tell her that the potatoes had come in.

Bron felt as nervous as a young girl meeting her first boy as she glanced at the photo of a smiling Cyril in uniform that stood in its frame on the mantelpiece. Everyone had said how good-looking he was with his big brown eyes, his tawny curly hair cut short now and neatly brushed. Would absence have made his heart grow fonder? she wondered. Oh, she hoped so, for she still had a feeling for him, despite all the ups and downs of their marriage; despite his obsession with Ceinwen even after her death.

She had wanted to go to the station to meet him but he'd been vague about what time he'd arrive so she kept rushing to the parlour window, lifting the curtain aside to look anxiously up the street. But she was in the kitchen making up the fire when the knock came at the door. Flinging aside the copper tongs she rushed down the passage and, opening the door, flung her arms about him and pulled him inside.

'Nearly knocked me over you did,' he told her with a grin. But although his arms went about her in return there was no passion to his hug and she was disappointed. Cyril could have been greeting a maiden aunt for all the warmth that went into the embrace.

Trying to hide her disappointment, Bron busied herself making tea. She'd been going to cook the meat she'd bought for the evening meal but Cyril had planned for them to go to Glas Fynydd right away so it would have to wait until tomorrow. While he sat by the fire warming himself, the tea in his hand and a piece of the fruit cake on a plate on the table beside him, she wrapped the mince pies to take with her and put together a few other things for she would feel uncomfortable otherwise with basic food rationed. She made some sandwiches with the corned beef she'd planned for their supper, and they had these with another cup of tea before they left, for Cyril seemed anxious to get away.

His parents had been expecting him either that day or the next for they knew that he was coming on leave. The welcome was warm, and the table, despite the shortages, was soon laden with food while a couple of large pies cooked in anticipation were put into the oven to heat through.

'I find a pie the best way to make the meat ration go round,' Jenny confided.

The children, who'd been all over him when he'd arrived, wouldn't leave Cyril's side. It was pleasantly warm in the kitchen as Bron nursed her cup of tea, and soon the pies were giving out a delicious aroma. With the children's happy chatter and the pleasant conversation all about her, she contrasted this homely scene with her

lonely life at home, though of course there she could
always go to her nan's for an hour. But after the day's
work, and with jobs to do in the house when the now
expected air raids allowed her to stay indoors long enough
to do them, she was often too tired to go.

They had finished their meal with Bron's mince pies as
dessert, and the dishes had been washed and put away,
when Jenny went out to the garden, calling Bron to join
her.

'Look over there, Bron. Cardiff is getting it early
tonight,' she said, pointing to where the distant sky
glowed red. 'I wish you'd stay, just for tonight. I shall
worry if you go home in the middle of this. Let's ask Cyril,
shall we?'

'Ask Cyril what?' he queried, joining them and looking
towards where his mother was pointing.

'Your mam wants us to stay the night,' Bron told him,
'but it's awkward because we haven't brought any night
clothes or rations either.'

'Well, that's settled then,' Jenny said with a smile.
'You'll stay. We can loan you some things.'

'It would be daft to go home in the thick of that,' Cyril
decided as they all went indoors.

The children were delighted and wanted to stay up late.
They played Snap at the table, with Meg and Davy shriek-
ing with joy every time they matched a card, until presently Jenny insisted the children get ready and go up after
a hot cup of cocoa in front of the fire.

Bron undressed them, slipping on the warm night-
clothes hanging over the guard, loving every minutes for
she had missed them so much. Upstairs the two little beds
had matching eiderdowns, and as she pulled back the
covers each had a hot water bottle in a knitted case. With
the memory of the sky over Cardiff fresh in her mind she

felt a wave of gratitude towards Jenny and Idris for giving the children such a wonderful home.

The next morning she had meant them to go home early, wanting to cook the meat that had cost her so much of her ration, for it wouldn't keep much longer even in the safe, but Cyril had no intention of leaving yet and took the children for a walk over the mountain as it was a mild November day. When they returned with glowing cheeks her mother-in-law insisted Bron and Cyril stay to lunch, and when the tray of tea was brought in and the cups set out Cyril excused himself, saying he wouldn't be long. The children ran to him, begging him to take them with him again, but this time he said no and took them back to their seats at the table. Then, saying, 'I'll soon be back,' he took his coat and hurried from the house. Bron watched the window from her seat and when she saw him take the same direction as he had once before, towards the cemetery at Ebenezer, she knew where he was going.

When he returned it was almost three o' clock and she was ready to leave for the station. It would get dark early and she'd hoped to be home before that.

Jenny brought the children to the station and Bron clung to them as the train came in to the platform. Cyril was hugging his mam, then it was the children's turn, and he hugged them for so long she feared they might miss the train, but at last they were on their way to Cardiff, waving from the window until the little group on the platform was out of sight.

When they got home Cyril was very quiet. Going over to the mantelpiece he gazed for a long time at the children's photographs.

'In the best place they are, Bron,' he told her, 'and Mam and Dad love having them.'

'I know,' she nodded at him, 'and I'm very grateful.

They wanted me to stay as well.'

'Why didn't you?'

'Well, there's the house for one thing. We might lose the tenancy.'

'Don't worry. We'd find somewhere else.'

'I don't think so, Cyril. It won't be easy after the war. Lots of houses are being bombed and they're not building any more. Then there are all the people who are getting married while they're in the forces – they'll be looking for somewhere to live after the war. I'm not risking losing this house.'

Bron brought the meat from the safe, looking at it anxiously, thankful the weather was cool. It looked all right. She struck a match and lit the gas oven, then peeled the potatoes. She would bring them to the boil then roast them around the small piece of beef, just the way Cyril liked them. She was glad to be busy. She was missing the children and it was always worse when she'd just parted from them. Tomorrow Cyril would be gone too.

The table was laid and she was warming the plates and just about to slice the meat when the siren started to wail. Cyril was at the wash-house door, pulling at her arm, and she just had time to put the meat back in and turn the oven off before hurrying down the garden path.

Searchlights suffused the sky which was lit up like some tropical sunset as they hurried to the shelter and slammed the door. Bron felt carefully along the shelf Will had put up until her fingers contacted the lantern, which she lit. By its wan light they sat close together on the cushions in the damp-smelling haven and she waited with baited breath for his arms to come about her. When he merely rested an arm about her shoulders the tears sprang to her eyes. Why did she still care? she asked herself.

Last night when he'd taken her there'd been no passion,

no love play. Afterwards she'd lain awake for hours, staring at the low ceiling in his mother's back bedroom, knowing she should have been getting a good night's sleep while she had the chance, but her thoughts for the future had been anxious and she hadn't been thinking of the war.

Cyril was sleeping against her shoulder as though he didn't have a care in the world, but when the all-clear sounded she woke him and hurried indoors to see if she could salvage the dinner.

'When will it be ready?' he asked, yawning widely.

'About three-quarters of an hour, I think. I'll have to heat the oven and then get the food hot again.'

'I've gone past it, Bron. We had a good meal at Mam's.'

Bron thought of having to do without a cooked dinner all next week. Well, she could eat the meat cold for a couple of days. But when she'd sacrificed the coupons she'd had visions of Cyril really enjoying his meal. She put the food away with a heavy heart and tidied up the wash-house, then followed Cyril to bed, where he lay with his eyes closed, already fast asleep.

Chapter Thirty-One

Bron was going to Glas Fynydd straight from the shop to be with the children on Christmas Eve. She'd packed a small case and taken it to work with her, thankful that the presents had already been delivered to Jenny's safe-keeping.

Because of the black out and the air raids the shop now closed much earlier than before the war. Even on Christmas Eve customers made sure that they got everything they could get long before dusk.

The darkened train had little of Christmas cheer. The dim blue bulb did nothing to illuminate the corners, but the carriage was soon full of last-minute shoppers determined to celebrate the festive season, laughing and joking as they heaved mysterious-looking parcels on to the luggage rack.

'Glad I got that doll for our Mair I am,' a young woman was saying. 'Won't last long I know with that sawdust-filled body but she'll love it when she sees it, she will.'

'The body's only fixed to the head by a drawstring round the neck, Blod. Have it undone in no time she will,' her friend replied.

Bron listened with a sinking heart. From the description it sounded exactly like the doll she'd bought for Meg. It had looked fine dressed in the baby clothes she had made, but Meg would break her heart if the body came away from the head. Still, it could soon be repaired.

She'd hoped Cyril would get leave for Christmas for he hadn't had a full week since he'd been called up, but last week he'd written and said there was no hope. She'd packed him a parcel as soon as she'd heard, putting in a cake and some sweets and a couple of pairs of socks she'd knitted, her heart heavy with disappointment.

Bron had bought Jenny a pretty headsquare at David Morgan's in St Mary Street and added a dainty pinafore and a pair of stockings, costing six and ninepence altogether. Jenny would say one thing would have been enough, but if she'd had the money to spare Bron would have liked to buy her something really expensive. She missed the children desperately but every time the siren went she was grateful to Jenny and Idris.

Conversation was flowing all around her but for once Bron was glad to sink into the dim corner by the papered-over window and think her own thoughts.

'Oh, you shouldn't have, Bron,' Martha had said when she'd given her the warm cardigan that she'd been knitting as she sat in the shelter most nights. It was a wine colour and she'd been lucky to get enough wool which she'd had to queue for in the Arcade. Her nan's complexion was pale and she'd thought the warm shade would give her some colour. Bron was worried about Martha having to spend so much time in the damp shelter at her age, often getting out of a warm bed, bundling herself into her coat and rushing into the garden to the shelter, whatever the weather.

She'd bought Polly a headsquare just like the one she had for Jenny and wrapped it with a small box of chocolates. For Gloria there'd been a little bottle of scent, and for Will some cigarettes.

The house was in darkness as she approached because of the blackout, but as she drew near she saw that Jenny was standing waiting for her outside, hugging a coat around her.

'Won't go to bed until you come, Bron,' she said with a laugh after they'd embraced. 'Wound up with excitement they are tonight.'

They hurried into the house as Idris opened the door, putting the light back on as soon as he'd closed it again. Bron looked around her appreciatively at the lovely festive decorations which were carefully put by after every Christmas ready for the next.

The children were pulling her into the kitchen, their eyes bright with excitement, both talking to her at the same time, but she heard Meg saying, 'Daddy Christmas is bringing me a new baby doll, Mama.'

'She's been getting the cot ready all day,' Jenny laughed.

'You'll have to be in bed and asleep before he comes,' Bron told her. Suddenly they couldn't get ready quick enough.

'Pity Cyril couldn't have got home,' Jenny said wistfully, and Idris cleared his throat before saying, 'He doesn't seem to get his share of leave, does he? Especially as he's still in this country.'

Bron had often thought this herself, wondering if it was the job he'd been trained to do for Cyril was with an anti-aircraft battery in Surrey, their job being to prevent enemy planes getting through.

She had undressed Meg, folding the little garments and hugging the children in turn, realising just how much she was missing them.

What would Cyril be doing now? she wondered as she followed Jenny downstairs. Would he be on duty tonight as some of them must be, or would he be trying to celebrate Christmas with his mates? Why did the thought persist that he wasn't all that upset about not getting home? She had felt this on his last leave. It hadn't showed while they were with his parents and the children at Glas Fynydd. Oh, she hoped she was wrong and that he was just tired and fed up with all the travelling, and having to spend most of the evening in the Anderson shelter, but his letters since he'd gone back had done nothing to dispel her fears.

As Jenny went to the scullery to finish her preparations for the following day, Bron tidied the children's toys and clothes away. Idris was hidden behind the evening paper so she sat by the fire, thankful after the busy day to take the weight off her feet. But her mind wouldn't rest as she worried about her father living in Coventry which had suffered particularly heavy bombing around the middle of November. Her father had come out of the shelter after a raid that had lasted for eleven hours to find the house in which he and Evelyn had lived ever since they had married was in ruins. A week later they had managed to find rooms in a suburb of the city. It was a long way from the factory where he worked but it had been a miracle to find anywhere to live considering the terrible devastation. The ancient Cathedral had been gutted in the raid and there'd been damage all over the city.

Idris slowly lowered his paper and, looking at her over the top of his glasses, he asked as though he could read her thoughts, 'How is youer dada, Bronwen? Coventry's had a real bad time.'

'He seems all right,' Bron began but Jenny was calling her, and as she got up to go to the scullery Idris lifted his paper once more.

The next day Bron caught some of the children's

excitement. Seeing Meg rocking her new doll in its cradle reminded Bron of the wonderful Christmas when she'd gone to work for Mrs Potter in Rumney so that she could buy the children the things they'd wanted. The china doll had since been broken but the cradle had survived.

Before she left with armfuls of presents Bron made arrangements to meet Jenny in town on her half-day. The Odeon was showing the film 'Old Mother Riley' and Jenny was very anxious to see the lovable characters created by Arthur Lucan and Kitty McShane. They would have to go in the middle of the film early in the afternoon, but it was better than risking the evening when there could be an air raid. They could watch it round again to where they'd seen it anyway.

The new year came in bitterly cold and Bron was at Thelma Street to celebrate, though there seemed little to be optimistic or cheerful about. Bertha was there, looking older and more wrinkled than nan, the colour in her apple cheeks faded with all the disturbed nights in the shelter. They'd all drunk to 'Peace in the new year' but they'd known it was a forlorn hope.

On the second of January it was a cold frosty night with a full moon. The siren began to wail just as Bron had put her meal on the table. Swallowing some of the tea thirstily and grabbing a piece of toast, she pulled on her coat and hurried down the path. Incendiaries burning with an eerie greenish glow made her dash for the shelter. As she climbed down searchlights swept the sky overhead.

Bron sat in the damp, musty-smelling shelter eating her toast, her teeth chattering with the cold the moment she'd finished it. She wished she'd filled a thermos with tea the way Polly always did.

The heavy drone of planes was almost drowned out by the noise of the barrage put up by the anti-aircraft guns.

Once when she ventured to open the door a few inches to stare up at the sky, it seemed the whole world was afire as an angry red glow lit up the scene and acrid fumes filled her nostrils. The noise of planes and guns was deafening and she closed the door hurriedly and sat down shakily on the blanket-covered bench.

If only someone was here, Bron thought. Ivy had begged her long ago to share their shelter. She'd tried it once but it had been very crowded with Ivy and her husband and Peggy and hers who had a reserved job at the ordnance factory, besides an elderly neighbour who'd had to be almost carried down and who needed to rest her leg on the opposite bunk. But what had really decided Bron was the way Peggy had to wait indoors for her to arrive when she should have been in the shelter.

The heavy drone of planes was still overhead and now, above the racket of the ack-ack guns, could be heard the whine of falling bombs. Thinking longingly of the peacefulness of Glas Fynydd, Bron put her head in her hands and rocked to and fro, stiff with fright and the biting cold.

Next morning as she went to work the smell of acrid smoke still hung on the air. The tram was very late and someone at the tram-stop told her that Grangetown and Riverside had both been badly bombed and that a parachute mine had landed in the grounds of Llandaff Cathedral, doing a lot of damage.

As the tram went up City Road she saw fire engines in a side street and the smell of burning grew stronger. When she got to Jessop's everyone was strangely quiet and looking from one to the other she saw the tears in Marcia's eyes as she told Bron, 'It's Alby's wife. She was living with relatives in Riverside until he came home . . .'

Looking from one to the other Bron licked dry lips, dreading what she was about to be told.

'She was killed outright. Oh God, it's awful. He's in North Africa. They wanted the baby so much and she was pretty near her time.'

Remembering Albert's expression when he'd talked about the expected baby, Bron's eyes too swam with tears. He'd been so proud as he'd shown her the picture of his wife. She thought of him in faraway North Africa being told the awful news, and tears of pity began to run down her face.

At lunchtime Marcia asked Bron if she'd go with her to see Alby's mam.

'Lives around the corner from me she does. That's how I know about his wife. You must remember her coming in for her order when he was errand boy?'

Yes, Bron remembered the pleasant little woman she used to serve. When her son had gone to work for the Candle King she'd naturally taken her order there.

As they walked down the quiet street with its bay-windowed houses, the gardens surrounded by iron railings, Bron was wondering what she could say to comfort her. What could she say that would help in the face of such a tragedy? But the moment his mother opened the door to them she began to feel at ease, despite the woman's puffy eyes and tear-stained cheeks.

They were shown into the little parlour where a large photograph of Albert in uniform smiled at them from one side of the mantelpiece. The young woman's photo on the other side Bron recognised as an enlargement of the picture he had shown her at the shop.

'Cold it is in here,' Mrs Davies said, ushering them into the kitchen. 'Haven't lit the parlour fire since Albert was home.' She dabbed hastily at her eyes before going into the little scullery off the kitchen to put the kettle on.

Bron looked around her appreciatively, at the shining

black-leaded grate, at the brass ornaments on the mantel-piece, the polished sideboard with matching china vases either side of a half-moon shaped clock which chimed the quarter just as Albert's mother came bustling in with the tea tray and they both rose from the comfort of the chairs either side of the fire to take it from her.

'Lovely girl she was,' Mrs Davies said, shaking her head, 'wonderful little wife. Dreading what it's going to do to him I am. So thrilled he was about the baby.' And she buried her face in her handkerchief.

When they got back to the shop Bron was glad to be busy for she couldn't get the thought out of her mind of Albert being told of the tragedy. When she got home that night and had been sitting staring into the fire for some time, the air raid siren started its mournful wail and she began to shiver, dreading the hours until the all clear.

Chapter Thirty-Two

Walking along Broadway one Wednesday afternoon in the spring, Bron met Bessie Evans, her old landlady.

"Ow's 'e treating you now, love?' her friend asked bluntly.

'We're very happy,' Bron assured her quickly, not wanting to uncover old sores. She'd tried so hard to forget those early years when Cyril had sometimes been drunk and violent.

'Glad to 'ear it I am,' Bessie was saying. 'Knew 'e wasn't all bad I did. Was it 'aving that boy that changed 'im?'

Bron nodded. 'And how are you getting on?' she asked quickly, wanting to change the subject.

'Lovely it is out there, 'specially in the summer. Birds singin', and that conservatory lets in all the sunshine. Why don't you come out an' see me, Bron? The children could play in the garden.'

'They're not with me, Bessie, they're staying with Cyril's parents in Glas Fynydd.'

'Best thing too with all them raids. It's glad I am to see you, love, an' pleased youer marriage is all right now.'

Looking at her old friend Bron thought how well she looked. Smartly dressed too, for Bessie, her hair freshly washed and set in stiff ridges with a hair-net over it. Bessie was looking down self-consciously at the costume she was wearing.

'One of our Maudie's,' she told Bron proudly. 'Lucky I am 'cos 'er clothes fit me. Wardrobe full she's got.'

As she watched Bessie move away Bron frowned, thinking about what she had said about her marriage being all right. But it wasn't all right, was it? Since Cyril had stopped drinking heavily he'd been a different man, and it was years since he'd hurt her physically. But there were other ways of hurting, ways where the scars didn't heal as physical scars did. Indifference was the worst kind of hurt.

She'd tried so hard to forget the misery of those first couple of years while they'd been in rooms with Bessie, tried to forget the shame of black eyes and other embarrassments, but now her old friend had raked them up she couldn't ignore the memories she'd evoked. As usual her heart began to make excuses for Cyril's behaviour. It had been the circumstances of their marriage, the way he'd been forced into it, that had been the trouble. Cyril had felt trapped not being able to marry Ceinwen. But he loved the children. Oh, she knew he hadn't been very helpful when Meg was small, but some men weren't good with tiny babies, were they?

If only she could find a way of breaking down the barriers between them now that Ceinwen was gone, but he didn't get much leave and there hadn't been a chance with the air raid and everything last time he came home.

At the end of April, when Cyril wrote and told her he would be coming home during the following week, Bron made up her mind to do her best to bring them closer together. The time off was arranged with Mr Jessop. She knew she wouldn't have had this consideration in any other job, but sometimes wondered if with the children away she could be doing more for the war effort. But Mr Jessop had convinced her that her job was important and that when married women were conscripted, which seemed likely, he would try and keep her back.

'Take ages it would to train someone with all the ration coupons and all,' he'd said. 'Doing Cyril's job you are, Bron, keeping his place for when the war ends.'

Cyril came home on the fifth of May and this time she was able to meet him at the station. They got off the tram at Clifton Street and she slipped her arm in his, disappointed when he didn't seem to respond to her warm squeeze.

They had finished their meal and she was just making a cup of tea when there was a knock at the door and Cyril went to open it. A few minutes later he stuck his head around the living-room door to tell her, 'Won't be long, Bron. Just going to The Bertram for an hour with Eddie.' And he was gone.

Well, he was entitled to go out with his old friends, she told herself, but his leaves were so short. Swallowing her disappointment she washed the dishes and sat by the fire trying to convince herself that it was natural for him to want to go out with his buttys even though he'd only been home about an hour.

It was ten-thirty when he came in, and she tried hard not to show him how disappointed she was. After supper he sat in the easy chair gazing into the fire and Bron went across and sat on the arm, hoping he'd put his arm about her, but he just kept staring into the glowing coals.

'What are you thinking of, Cyril?' she asked at last.

'About that raid on the Rhondda you told me about when we were coming home. I was wondering if the children are safe with my mam.'

'But it was nowhere near Glas Fynydd. They say that

the Germans were ridding themselves of their load.'

'All the same – ' he began.

'Well, they're safer than they would be in Cardiff, Cyril.'

'What you really mean is you want to keep on youer job, isn't it, Bron?'

She looked at him, aghast. 'You know that's not true!' she cried. 'You were all for them going to stay with your mother.'

Cyril yawned. 'Think I'll go up. We'll have to get up early tomorrow to go to Glas Fynydd.'

Smarting from his unwarranted accusation Bron thought bitterly, He's always like this when he's had a couple of drinks. Cyril couldn't really believe she'd put the job before the children surely? But she was working hard and had managed to save all the army allowance in the Post Office for when they were together again.

After washing the supper dishes and banking down the fire she climbed the stairs slowly, her resolution to try to initiate a more loving relationship with Cyril swamped by anger at his remark and his apparent indifference to her feelings. Long before she reached the landing she could hear him snoring as he usually did after a few drinks. When she'd undressed she lay in the darkness, unable to sleep even when he turned on his side and all was quiet, as a feeling of anger, resentment, and bitter disappointment swept over her.

The leave followed the same pattern as before, the trip to Glas Fynydd where everyone was still talking about the night the bombers came to the Valleys at the end of April. Cyril played with the children for a while then walked them over the mountain to visit a friend. In the afternoon he went as usual to the cemetery, and later, having made sure to bring a few rations and a nightdress just in case,

Bron didn't take much persuading to stay the night.

Although she strove to behave normally in front of his parents the remark he'd made about having the children home hung between them, but if she expected an apology she didn't get one. It was as though he'd forgotten he'd said it.

Soon the short leave was over. Wasn't he ever going to get a whole week? Her resentment had stopped her once again from showing her love for him. Now they were on the platform and she watched the precious minutes tick away by the platform clock. Hearing a whistle she thought the train must be approaching and flung her arms about Cyril in desperation. She pressed her lips to his. For a moment he seemed to respond, but then he pushed her gently away. Surprised and hurt she looked up to see an unhappy expression in his eyes as he said, 'For God's sake, don't make it any harder for me, Bron.'

The train belching steam was now drawing into the station, and picking up his haversack and kissing her on the cheek he made for the nearest carriage.

Following him in a daze, the probable reason for his behaviour slowly dawned on her. Of course, this might be embarkation leave and he hadn't wanted to worry them. Oh God, if only she'd known. She'd spent the whole of the leave feeling resentful towards him. Poor Cyril, keeping up a brave front. He never had been much good at showing his emotions towards her. Pushing her way through the crowd to get near his carriage she got there just as the doors were slamming and the guard was about to blow his whistle. She searched anxiously for a glimpse of Cyril as the men crowded the window, smiling and waving as it began to move away.

As the train gathered speed, Cyril sat down and rested

his head in his hands. Why did he always seem to make a mess of things? He'd been daft enough to promise Karen that he'd ask Bron about getting a divorce. He wouldn't have promised her only she'd found out about him being married and had threatened never to see him again. He'd met Karen just after he'd been posted to Surrey. His heart had nearly stopped when she'd turned to serve him in the NAAFI and he'd seen the uncanny likeness to Ceinwen. He soon found she was like Ceinwen in other ways too, a spirited girl and warmly loving, until someone had told her about Bron, then she'd wanted nothing more to do with him.

By this time he'd been taken home to London to see her mother and he'd got on well with the family.

'She'd better not find out I've been going around with a married man,' Karen had shouted at him. 'I'll get a divorce,' he'd promised without really meaning it. He'd managed to spend the end of each leave with Karen, sometimes passing a night at her home if she herself was on leave. It had been a game at first, but here he was now head over heels in love with the girl. He hadn't the heart to ask Bron after all she'd done, especially after the way she'd taken young David to please him, and she'd been all over him when she'd met him at the station. Thinking of Karen he'd been forced to pick a quarrel with Bron, implying that she didn't want the children home when he knew very well she worshipped them. It had done the trick though, she'd been quite cool with him after that, but he still hadn't said anything to her.

Cyril took out his wallet and gazed down at the photo of Bron and the children. He must leave it out, pack it in his kit-bag or something so Karen's mother wouldn't see it. She thought it was marvellous the way he went home to see his mam every leave. She had no idea that he was married.

Arriving at Paddington he saw Karen waiting for him before she saw him, her lovely blue eyes intent on the occupants of the carriages as they tumbled from the train. Then they were fighting their way through the crowds towards each other, flinging their arms about each other when they met, oblivious of the people milling about them. And holding her close, Cyril knew that, whoever it hurt, he had to spend the rest of his life with this lovely girl.

They were leaving the platform making for the underground when she asked anxiously, 'What did she say, Cyril? You did see her?'

'Yes.' Then seeing the hope come into Karen's eyes, and knowing much as she loved him she'd probably refuse to see him again if he admitted that he hadn't even asked, he added, 'She's going to think it over, love.'

Karen couldn't hide her disappointment, but he put his arm about her shoulders and told her that he was disappointed too, and was rewarded with a sad little smile.

'Where are we going?' Cyril asked as they came up from the underground where a queue of people were waiting to go down to shelter for the night. Karen was taking a turning that he knew by now wasn't her usual way home.

'To the pictures or a cafe. Anywhere where we can be alone, Cyril. I don't know why you spend so much of your leave in Wales, feeling the way you do about your wife. Anyway my parents will be queueing for the shelter by now. God, Cyril, I don't know how they stand it. It's awful, night after night.'

They chose a table in the far corner of the cafe and as they drank their tea and ate their toast, she went on, 'It's a wonder there's any East End left, though other parts of London are getting it badly too. I've been going to the tube with Mum and Dad every night since I've been home. It's a good place to shelter but it's awfully cramped. Some people spend every night there.'

Cyril was glancing anxiously at his watch, saying, 'I think I should be getting you to a shelter, Karen.'

Before she could answer the warning siren began its rising wail. As it swelled around them he grabbed her arm, dragging her to the little crowd who were pushing their way through the doorway.

In the darkness, apart from the searchlights sweeping the sky, they rushed along with the others. There was the heavy throb of planes and the noise from the barrage was deafening. Flares began to fall in the street around them, bathing it in a sinister green light.

'Where is it?' Cyril gasped breathlessly, looking around him wildly for they seemed to be alone now. 'Where's the shelter?'

'Next turning.'

Incendiaries were falling on the roads and pavements, lighting up the street, hissing and burning with bluish white flames. And now there was a new sound to add to the cacophany, a sound more terrifying than the heavy throb of planes or the bombing of the barrage, a sound that made Cyril grab Karen and drag her deep into a doorway as bombs began to whistle through the air.

Chapter Thirty-Three

After Cyril's train had gone Bron left the station in a daze. Why hadn't he told her he was going abroad? She would have known then why he was so edgy and unsettled. Poor Jenny and Idris. They'd be upset at not being told. Best not to say anything until she was sure. She'd known though that he had something on his mind, and what was it he'd said just as they were parting? 'For God's sake, don't make it any harder for me, Bron.' And she'd never forget the look on his face as he'd said it.

Turning the key in the lock she went into the empty house. In the living room the fire had gone out, and the dishes they'd left in their rush to get to the station were still on the table, waiting to be washed. She sat down in a chair and gazed into the empty grate, tears of disappointment blurring her vision. She'd had such hopes of improving their relationship this leave. Now, if he went abroad, she wouldn't have another chance.

Why had she let him niggle her like that? She'd known he was always quarrelsome after a few drinks. She'd known too how much he'd resented her going to work. Why had she shown her feelings at his remark, spoiling their chances of a new understanding?

She was remembering the way he'd hugged the children when they were leaving, as though he would never let

303

them go. Now, with hindsight, she thought she understood.

Bron went to answer a knock on the door and opened it to Polly.

'Thought you'd be feeling a bit low with Cyril gone back,' she said, following Bron into the living room. 'Wash these dishes up I will while you get the fire going again, then we'll have a cup of tea. Look, *cariad*, there's no need for you to stay here on your own. Youer nan worries about you alone in that shelter.'

'It's too far to run round to Thelma Street when the siren goes.'

'I know, but you ought to go in with your friend, Ivy's girl. You said they'd invited you.'

'Yes, they did, but it's overcrowded anyway – the elderly couple next door go with them, and I don't like Peggy having to wait in the house to let me in.'

'Well, anyway, come back with me now and have some dinner. I put a vegetable pie in the oven, youer nan's watching it for me. I got the recipe from the wireless. Hope it'll be all right.'

'Are you sure there'll be enough?'

'Of course there will. I put in plenty of vegetables and flavoured it well. There's not much fat in the pastry but it'll be all right if it's eaten while it's hot.'

Polly had proved herself versatile at making something out of almost nothing, following all the wartime tips she'd heard or read about, like beating cornflour into the meagre butter ration to stretch it further, and making the coal go a long way by mixing coal dust, clay and water to make briquettes. She took papers like *Woman and Home* every month just for the advice and recipes, cutting them all out carefully and sticking them in a scrap book. Her meatless soups were delicious, and the sponges she made with a little dried egg rose to perfection. Bron didn't need a second invitation to share the vegetable pie.

'Enjoy 'is leave, did you?' Martha asked, looking pleased to see her.

'Yes,' Bron admitted, 'but it wasn't nearly long enough.'

'How were the children when you went to Glas Fynydd?'

'Fine,' Bron told her, feeling guilty for not coming to see her nan while Cyril was home, but she knew she'd never have got him to accompany her and she couldn't have left him in the short time they were together.

'You'd hardly recognise Meg,' she told them. 'She's getting quite a tomboy. She's looking forward to her seventh birthday.'

'And David?'

'He's fine too. They get on really well, but that's mainly because Meg worships him. Still, he's a nice little boy, and they're company for each other.'

The pie was delicious and she begged the recipe from Polly, leaving as soon as she'd wiped up the dishes, for it was a Saturday and Mr Jessop would be glad of her help.

As she went home along Thelma Street neighbours she'd known since she'd gone to live there as a child greeted her in a friendly way. She wished she was on such friendly terms with her neighbours in Rosalind Street where she'd been born and brought up until she was eleven. She wasn't bad friends with anyone, had never had words over anything, but she'd wanted to be respected as her mam had always been.

In the beginning when she'd taken the rooms with Bessie she'd been so pleased to be going to renew old acquaintances and meet new ones, but with Cyril often drunk in those days and sometimes giving her black eyes and bruises her pride had made her keep her head averted, and as she'd become convinced that the whole street was talking about her and Cyril she'd been reluctant to do more than nod her head to people she didn't know well.

It had been against Bron's nature for she'd desperately wanted to be friends, but the few times she'd been forced to go to the shops sporting bruises to her face she'd seen the pity in their eyes and had held her head defiantly high. She knew they thought of her as stuck up and wished that somehow she could reverse the situation. It had been a long time ago but somehow because of it she had never got on really friendly terms with any of them except Ivy who had been her mother's best friend, and whom she still saw from time to time.

When she got to work she felt guilty when she saw the stack of orders waiting to be put up and heard the customers grumbling about having to wait to be served. The time flew as everyone was rushed off their feet. Bron was glad, for while she was working there was no time to miss Cyril.

On Monday morning Bron was getting ready to go to work when she heard the letter-box and found a long white envelope on the mat. She opened it curiously, stiffening with shock when she read with growing horror the letter from his Commanding Officer telling her that Cyril had been killed in London on the way back to his unit when, during a heavy raid, the building he'd been sheltering in was demolished by a bomb. His papers and photos, etc had been sent back to them at base. He very much regretted . . .

Shaking all over, Bron read it through again. There must be some silly mistake. What had he been doing in

London? Had he been changing from one station to another? But surely he could have done that by taking the tube?

There was a greyness in front of her eyes, then blessed oblivion as she slumped forward in her seat at the table, her head falling on her outstretched arms.

Carrie Williams – the same Mrs Williams who'd stood in the street wiping her eyes on her apron on the day Bron's mother had been found in the river – saw the telegram boy banging on Bron's door. When he'd been knocking for some minutes she put down her scrubbing brush and went across the road. Bron must be in, she told herself. Doing her front she'd been for ages, having had a chinwag with her neighbour before getting down on her knees to scrub the patch. Bron couldn't have left for work or she'd have seen her. Telegrams were important. She'd go and see if Ivy had a key.

'Hang on,' she told the boy as she passed, 'I won't be a tick.'

Ivy bent down and peered through the letter box, calling: 'Bron! Bron!' But with nothing to be seen or heard she got up stiffly, saying, 'You sure she isn't gone to work?'

Carrie nodded decisively. 'See 'er I would if she'd gone, Ivy.'

'Well, I don't suppose she'll mind, but I've never done it before, not even in her mam's time,' Ivy said doubtfully, pulling the key through the letter-box and opening the door.

When Carrie heard her cry 'Oh, my God!' she grabbed the telegram from the boy who was now standing by the open door looking curiously down the passage, and dashed into the house, stopping at the living room where she could see Ivy bending over an inert Bron who had fallen forward over the table in what appeared to be a dead faint. Together they lifted her to the armchair and put her feet up on a stool. As Ivy was loosening her clothing Bron's eyes flew open and she looked around her in surprise. When her gaze fell on the letter the colour that was coming back to her cheeks drained away once more, leaving her face chalky white.

Seeing the telegram in Carrie's hand she took it with shaking fingers, fainting once more as the fateful words sprang at her from the page, confirming the letter she'd read. Carrie dashed back to her house for smelling salts and Peggy sent the telegram boy away – then dashing upstairs for a blanket, she wrapped it around Bron, for although it was a warm morning the girl felt icy cold.

Despite her bulk her neighbour was back almost at once, and while she waved the salts about under Bron's nose Peggy put the kettle on the gas ring and made some tea, sweet and strong. But Bron took ages to come round. It was almost as though she knew she was better off unconscious than coming to terms with the awful news.

By the time she was finally sipping the tea, her nan and Polly had arrived and someone had been sent for the doctor though there was little he could do to ease her grief, except to treat the shock and to stop the shivering that persisted despite the blankets and hot drinks.

The day passed with long periods of sleep from which she woke to a fresh realisation of what had happened.

'Would they have let his parents know?' she asked.

'Well, you are down as next of kin,' Polly told her. Someone was sent with a telegram and Bron tortured herself with pictures of Jenny or Idris opening it. Oh, she should have told them herself, but when she got out of bed, she fell back again exhausted. The pills the doctor had prescribed were doing their job. Later in the afternoon she tried again and as she went slowly downstairs, hanging on to the banister, Polly came to guide her down, saying, 'You should have stayed in bed, love.'

'I've got to go to Glas Fynydd, Aunt Poll. Poor Jenny, poor Idris. I've got to be with them and the children.'

'Youer in no fit state to go, Bron. Wait until tomorrow.' She knew her aunt was right, but she didn't want to go back to the bedroom to be alone with her terrible grief and disturbing thoughts. She blamed herself now for letting him upset her with his silly remark, for spoiling the leave that she'd meant to be so wonderful. If they'd only been happy while he was home. If only she had that to look back on.

The day seemed endless now as she sat in the armchair rocking herself to and fro, being plied with endless cups of tea and sympathy. She was grateful, indeed she was, only it was Jenny's shoulder she wanted to cry on. They could comfort each other, but nothing could bring Cyril back, and they'd quarrelled, hadn't they, over his remark? But he must have cared the same way she did, else why should he have said, 'For God's sake, don't make it any harder for me, Bron?' What else could he have meant but their parting?

Her grandmother insisted she go home with them, they didn't want to leave her in the house alone, though she wouldn't have minded. She just wanted to sit and think of Cyril. She made up her mind to go and see Jenny and Idris tomorrow. She knew what they must be going through.

The next day Polly insisted on going with her to the Valleys and, still doped with the tablets the doctor had given her, she was glad. Nan had sewn a black arm-band on her light blue summer coat but she must get something black, more suitable to mourn him in.

As soon as they reached the house the door opened and she fell into Jenny's arms, while Meg hid her face in their skirts and David stood watching them, his mouth trembling.

When they went into the big kitchen-cum-living room Idris rose to greet her and Bron was shocked to see how much he had aged since she had seen him last week. His eyes were dark hollows in his head, his face lined with grief. As they talked, like Bron he couldn't understand why Cyril should have to go across London. Why he couldn't have reached the station he wanted on the underground.

'But in wartime, who knows?' he said, as though trying to console himself. 'I can't see my boy spending a night in London if he didn't have to, not with all the raids they're having.'

Jenny's eyes were puffy from crying but she showed her concern for Bron, saying, 'You look all in, love. It's a pity you can't come and stay with us.'

'We shall be having a service at Ebenezer,' Idris told her, 'perhaps at the week-end. I got in touch, Bron, but we won't be able to have a proper funeral – '

Suddenly he was stopped as Jenny cried, the tears spurting from her eyes, 'A direct hit it was. Oh, my God!'

Bron was thankful the children were with Polly in the scullery where they were helping her to get the tea tray ready. Looking up she saw Ceridwen in the doorway, a look of horror on her face at her mother's words. Cyril's youngest sister was now nineteen, an attractive dark-eyed girl who was nursing at a military hospital and got home whenever she could get leave. Bron was remembering the first time she saw her, when Ceridwen had rushed from the house to fling her arms about her big brother whom she'd obviously adored. They'd always been close. Poor Ceridwen, it would hit her hard.

Polly was coming in with the tea tray, the children following behind, one proudly carrying a plate of sandwiches, the other a plate of cakes. They talked in low voices, murmuring platitudes, as though afraid of their own haunting thoughts, but Bron's were still with her for she couldn't get out of her mind the way Cyril had died, it haunted her by day and woke her from her dreams. Not even a grave in the cemetery. War was so senseless and cruel.

When at last it was time to go home she and Jenny clung to one another, their tears mingling on each other's cheeks.

Chapter Thirty-Four

The memorial service was to be held at Ebenezer on the following Sunday and as Bron had not yet felt able to return to work she arrived at Glas Fynydd on the Saturday afternoon to stay the night, longing to be with Meg again, for, as she told herself, the children were all she had of Cyril now.

When she walked into the house it was like a shrine, with pictures of Cyril, in wooden and brass frames, flanked by vases of flowers, set about everywhere.

'Determined I am that the children won't forget him, poor little mites,' Jenny told her. 'People have been bringing flowers all week. Lost they are with there not being a proper funeral for them to send wreaths to.' And she burst into tears.

Next morning as they set off to walk to the Chapel in the warm sunshine Jenny was dressed in black from head to toe, the sombre veil floating from a pill box hat drawn down over her tear-ravaged face. Idris supported her on one side with Bron, wearing her new mourning outfit, her long fair hair topped by a black turban, on the other. Ceridwen walked between the children who looked solemn and a little important when neighbours greeted them as they passed.

In the Chapel the scent of flowers was overpowering,

and the words of the hymns, meant to be comforting, tore at Bron's heart. Jenny hardly lifted her head as, the veil pushed back, she buried her face in a black-edged handkerchief. As they were leaving after the service friends surrounded them, putting their arms about Jenny and pressing Bron's hand sympathetically.

As they came out and walked down the path she glanced towards the cemetery, thinking of all the times that Cyril had come here to visit Ceinwen's grave. Looking at the little boy who was so like him, and who had lost both his parents, her heart went out to him.

Back at the house they glanced through the old photo albums, the same ones Bron had been shown on her first visit, and Jenny kept calling the children's attention. 'Look at Dada when he was a baby,' or, 'Here's youer dada building a castle at Barry Island,' or, 'Look at him holding the cup with the rugby team at school.' She confided to Bron as the children moved away that she was determined they would never forget him, but looking at the solemn little faces Bron felt disquiet. They were too young for such sorrow. She wished that it was safe enough to take them home.

Despite Jenny and Idris pleading with her to stay, Bron left after an early tea, for although everyone told her it was much too soon she'd made up her mind to go back to work the following day. Mr Jessop had been wonderful, coming to see her and telling her to take as long as she needed, but she knew how short-staffed he was and she was the breadwinner now. It wasn't any longer Cyril's job that she was keeping open but her own, for the army pension she would receive wouldn't be enough. Bron made up her mind to work full-time until the children came home again and save as much as she could. Perhaps

after the war Mr Jessop would give her a Saturday job
again.

The following morning she was just packing her sandwiches to take to work when she heard the letter-box
click. Perhaps it's another letter from Dada, she thought,
going into the passage to pick it up. He'd written her a
lovely letter as soon as he'd read the news in Polly's, and
wrote to tell her he was very upset at being so far away.
As soon as he heard if he could have time off he'd write
and let her know when he'd be down.

But the letter wasn't from her father, she could tell that
by the writing and the London postmark. As she tore the
envelope open a photograph fell to the floor, and bending
down to pick it up she was mystified to see the picture of
an attractive young girl. Had the letter been delivered to
her by mistake? It was a photograph of a stranger, yet
there was a resemblance to someone she either knew or
had seen. Hurriedly she turned to the address but there
was no mistake. It was addressed to Mrs Phillips. Then
she remembered that it was Ceinwen the photo had
reminded her of, and turned to the letter for an explanation.

Dear Mrs Phillips,
I just had to write to you because our children meant
so very much to each other and it should be a bond
between us. I know Cyril was a good son to you by
the way he spent most of his leave with you in Wales.
My daughter Karen was in the NAAFI stationed near
his unit. I thought you'd like to see her photo seeing
that they were talking of getting engaged, though no
date had been settled. She would one day have been
your daughter-in-law yet you'd never met her, but I

know you would have loved her on sight.

I would love to meet you sometime as we share a deep, mutual sorrow. Our children died as they wanted always to be in life, together.

I got your address from my daughter's pocket book which was how they were able to identify her, and which has been returned to me.

Anger mounted as Bron read, and she was barely able to contain herself. The woman was sincere, she had no doubt of that. But what game had Cyril been playing, pretending she was his mother? How could he do this to her? She'd known he had something on his mind. Was this what he'd been wanting to tell her when he'd asked her not to make it any harder for him?

Suddenly she lifted her arms and and grabbed at his picture on the mantelpiece, staring at the handsome, smiling face with something akin to hatred. In sudden revulsion she was about to dash it to the floor when a thought stayed her hand. Jenny and Idris must never know about this, it would break their hearts. No one must ever know, then the secret would be safe. In death his mam and dad had found their ideal son. She must never disillusion them, must keep this knowledge to herself.

Bron put the picture back on the mantelpiece, knowing it would be missed and cause speculation. For her own sake too it would be better no one knew. She wanted no more pity, no whispering as she passed. This last week the neighbours had opened their hearts to her, shown her sympathy and friendship. That she had been glad to take, but not their pity, she'd had enough of that in the past.

Trembling with anger and feeling slightly sick at the way he'd deceived her, she thought of the poor woman whose daughter had died with him. She would be expecting a reply but she wouldn't be getting one. She would put the photograph and the letter in a fresh envelope and send it back to her, scribbling across it, 'Opened by mistake. Mrs Phillips gone away'. Better to disappoint her than to break her heart. She herself had had enough heartbreak to last a lifetime. As the anger fumed inside her she told herself that she'd lost Cyril now, even his memory, for that had turned out to be a sham.

A glance at the clock made her shrug on the black coat that hung over the chair. She must wear it for a while if she wished to keep up the charade. It wasn't going to be easy. The customers would be constantly voicing their sympathy, telling her what a nice young man he'd been when he'd worked at the shop. She'd have to respond to Mr Jessop's sympathetic glances too, and Marcia's spoiling, and there wouldn't be any break at home either for Aunt Poll, Uncle Will and her nan, expecting her to grieve, would surround her with love and understanding.

It was the thought of going to Glas Fynydd that troubled her most of all. She pictured the sickly sweet room with its masses of flowers and photographs of Cyril, and the sickly sweet talk there would be of their wonderful son, the sadness and worship in Jenny's eyes as she glanced from one photo of Cyril to another. But wasn't Bron still sorrowing too, for the husband she'd never really had, and the dreams that had all gone sour?

Suddenly she could stand it no longer. Picking up a vase Cyril had given her one birthday, she flung it down with force, smashing it to smithereens.

Chapter Thirty-Five

As the months went by Bron sometimes woke from
dreams, her heart swamped with grief. Then she'd
remember the letter she'd received just after Cyril was
killed in the air raid and it would be like waking from one
nightmare only to be plunged into another, only she knew
this one was real.

For a long time now she'd been worrying about Meg.
The little girl, once so happy and boisterous, was becoming a solemn, silent child as Jenny, determined the
children would never forget their father, kept Cyril's
memory alive for them with endless stories of his exploits
and the increasing number of photos that had found their
way out of the albums and into frames.

Now it was Christmas and Bron was staying at Glas
Fynydd over the holidays but there was little of the festive
spirit. This first Christmas after Cyril's death it was under-
standable, but with two children in the house Bron
thought they could have had a few decorations. Poor
Jenny, Bron knew how she was suffering. She had
changed from a friendly, outgoing woman to one obsessed
by memories. Cyril had died last May, but time had only
sharpened her loss, such was the intensity of her grief.

It was Christmas Eve, and they were getting the
children to bed. Bron was feeling worn out after a day at

the shop before Mr Jessop had let her finish at half-past four. The journey, and now the effort of keeping up the pretence of her feelings for Cyril, was telling on her.

Several times she'd wanted to scream, 'You didn't know him at all. He was your son but you've no idea what he was really like.' Especially when she heard Jenny tell the children to go straight to sleep for their dada would be watching over them. After their hot milk Bron had gone upstairs with them and tried to lighten their mood by telling them a funny story she'd made up about the antics of a puppy. It made them both laugh, but when she'd hugged them and had her hand on the light-switch, Meg whispered, 'Stay with me, Mama, please!' And David said, 'Nana lets her have a night-light now 'cos she's frightened of the dark.'

But Meg had never been afraid of the dark. She was growing into a nervous child. What was happening?

'There's nothing to be afraid of, love,' Bron told her little daughter. 'You're safe here in this house, and David's only over there.'

Meg's lips were puckering and her eyes filling with tears. Bron's arms went about the child, and as she hugged her David told her, 'It's Dada watching over her all the time that she's afraid of. Afraid of being naughty she is 'cos he'll know, won't he?'

Overwhelmed by the anger that rose in her Bron felt like dashing downstairs and confronting Jenny, trying to make her realise just what she was doing to the children. Did she really think that they'd be comforted by the thought of someone, even their father, watching over them all the time? It had got to stop or, air raids or no air raids, she would take the children home. Well, Meg anyway. She had no legal right to take David.

Bron decided to ask Jenny to be careful what she said

in front of the children, but her mother-in-law's reply was typical. 'What I said was meant to be a comfort to them, Bron. You don't want them to forget Cyril, I know. Noticed I have that Meg seems a bit nervous these days, but she's bound to be upset at losing her dada, isn't she, *cariad*?'

Bron never could stay angry with Jenny for long. She'd been so generous, taking the children into her home and always worrying about Bron's own welfare, begging her over and over to leave Cardiff and stay with them until the war ended, but it was more important than ever now to keep the tenancy of the house, for it wouldn't be easy to find a landlord willing to take on a woman on her own, especially with two children.

But sitting in the train on the way home Bron couldn't get Meg's sad little face out of her mind. There were still air raids over Cardiff and long shivering nights in the shelter to endure. Most of the children had stayed in the city with their parents, but they probably had no option. Jenny had given her the chance to send them away from the raids. Wouldn't it be wrong to bring the child back into danger?

Bron thought of Mr Jessop and how he had come to rely on her, for with the extension of rationing there was a lot of extra work to do. In November a points' system had been brought in for the fairer distribution of canned meat, fish and vegetables, with customers able to choose how they spent the twenty points they received each month. Mr Jessop had told her there was more to come, that in January the points would be extended to dried fruit, rice and tapioca. But despite her loyalty to her boss, Bron knew that for Meg's sake she would have left the shop and brought her home if it hadn't been for the continuing air raids.

When she reached home the house was icy cold so she put the kettle on the gas stove while she lit the fire. With a cup of tea before her she began a letter to Albert. She had written to him after his wife was killed in the raid, telling him how sorry she was, but when he'd replied thanking her she hadn't answered, for she knew Cyril wouldn't have understood her sympathy. When Albert came home on compassionate leave he didn't come to the shop, and his mother had told them that he spent most of his time with his wife's people. The correspondence would have stopped with those two letters but when Cyril died Albert had sent her a letter of sympathy. The letter had a Plymouth postmark. His mother had told them he'd not been sent back to Africa after his compassionate leave but had been sent to the South coast. The letters had been spasmodic at first with Albert writing two to her one, but Bron had tried to write to him more often, knowing that what he really wanted was a shoulder to cry on. His letters were still full of Janet and the baby they'd been looking forward to so much, and she knew that Albert felt comfortable about writing like this to her because he assumed that she was suffering in the same way over the loss of Cyril.

When at the beginning of the following week Mr Jessop called her to the phone in the shop, Bron approached it with a mixture of fear and curiosity. She'd never had anyone call her before, though she'd used the telephone outside the Post Office to call the doctor to the children once or twice. As she took it in her hands and lifted the ear-piece fear was uppermost in her mind for no one would call her at the shop unless it was urgent.

Ceridwen's voice seemed normal enough, as she explained in her pleasant lilting tones that she was at home for a few days' leave and could Bron meet her tomorrow on her half-day at that cafe near the Friary?

As she agreed Bron was looking anxiously towards Mr Jessop, wondering if he thought it was a nerve for someone to ring her at the shop?

'Is anything wrong, Ceridwen?' she asked worriedly.

''Course not, *cariad*,' Ceridwen assured her. 'Tell you what it's about when I see you.'

So there was something, she thought, wishing she could get on the next train. But surely her sister-in-law would have said if either of the children was ill?

She went home, anxious for tomorrow afternoon to come. Placing the blanket on the kitchen table to do the ironing, she put the heavy iron over the hottest part of the range, trying to guess what the visit was about. When she'd finished the ironing she washed her hair quickly, praying the siren wouldn't begin to wail as soon as she'd got it wet, remembering the misery of sitting in the cheerless shelter on more than one occasion, with soapy water running down her face while trying to dry her hair with an already damp towel.

Bron was sitting in the cafe, her eyes on the entrance, twiddling a teaspoon round and round in the cup of tea she'd ordered while waiting for Ceridwen. Then she saw the attractive leggy girl, her dark eyes lighting up as they rested on Bron. She wasn't in uniform today, no doubt glad to get out of it for a while, but the black coat she wore couldn't dim the bright colour in her cheeks or the smile she gave Bron as she sat down and they ordered their meal.

'What is it, Ceridwen?' Bron asked anxiously as soon as they'd been served.

'Well, Mam won't ask you herself, Bron, because you were so good about taking him . . . oh, look, I'd better come straight out with it – she wants to adopt David.'

Swallowing hard, Bron said, 'The children get on so well together, it's a pity to part them now. I've grown to love him too.'

'She keeps saying that David is so much like Cyril was at his age, Bron. The doctor says that Mam has never got over the shock, but I know this would help. It would be like having Cyril over again if she could keep him.'

'She'll spoil David the same – ' Bron began unhappily, but the girl broke in quickly, 'No, Bron, she's promised Dada she won't, and he's such a nice little boy.'

'Meg will miss him terribly when she comes home.'

'Well, you can visit whenever you like – stay weekends.'

'What can I say, Ceridwen? I've no claim on the child; we didn't get around to adopting him, though we talked about it often. Anyway, what do Ceinwen's mam and dad think about it?'

'They're all for it. Dreading the time he'll have to come back to Cardiff they are. They see plenty of him now.'

'Poor Meg,' Bron said with a sigh. 'She's going to be very upset.'

'He can live with Mam then, Bron?'

'Well, I don't see how I could prevent it if I wanted to, and he's settled with them now so there won't be any upheaval.'

Ceridwen gave a big sigh of relief. 'Well that's a load off my mind, Bron. It means so much to Mam. It will help her get over the loss.'

Looking unhappy, Bron said, 'It's Meg I'm worrying about. She's so nervous these days. I wish your mam wouldn't keep on to them about Cyril watching over them. She doesn't realise . . .'

'I have told her about that,' Ceridwen broke in quickly. 'I don't think she's said it since. She didn't think, Bron, and with the weather we've been having they're shut indoors too much. Tomorrow if it's fine I'll take them for a walk over the mountain. They'll enjoy that.'

When she'd said goodbye to Ceridwen at the station Bron made her way slowly to the tram-stop, walking behind two couples, their arms linked, eyes only for each other. She felt the old familiar loneliness that she had experienced often enough even when Cyril had been by her side, except perhaps for that all too brief summer, the first one after David had come to live with them, when he couldn't do enough to please the boy and everyone had benefitted from the trips to the parks and the country-side, not to mention two wonderful days by the sea.

She hadn't even the satisfaction that they'd ever been happy together, she'd lost him to Ceinwen before they'd even met, and when the girl died she'd had to play second fiddle to a ghost. Yet the ghost, it seemed, had soon disappeared when he went into the army. She looked with longing once again at the young couples so wrapped up in each other. They didn't even look up as she had to push her way past.

Sitting on the tram, staring out of the window, her thoughts went back to David. But it's only common sense, Bron told herself. Jenny and Idris can give him so many advantages that I can't, and he's used to Glas Fynydd and likes the school in the village where he's lots of friends. But the children were so close. How would they react to being parted? Who would tell Meg? She dreaded the time when they'd have to be told, yet she longed too for the time when the raids were a thing of the past and her daughter was home with her again.

The house felt damp and chilly as she went through the passage to the kitchen, thankful that she'd found the time to lay the fire before leaving for work that morning. She shivered as she took off her coat and knelt to put a match to the paper, putting her hand out to the blaze as she watched the flames licking around the sticks. Getting up from her knees, still hugging herself for warmth, she went to the wash-house and put the kettle on the gas-ring.

Back in the kitchen, with a cup of tea resting on the fender, she looked around her at the furniture, most of which Bessie had left behind. The room looked cheerful now that the coals were glowing, with its lumpy cushions sewn into bright cretonne covers and matching curtains at the window covering the black-out ones, the big range black-leaded and polished until you could see your reflection.

Bron drew the curtains, and putting an old cardigan about her shoulders for extra warmth flopped down again on the sagging cushions of the armchair. Staring into the glowing, shifting coals she was lost in thought. Cyril had been dead now for seven months and she'd given no one cause to talk, but lately the longing for company – yes, male company, she admitted to herself – was strong. Remembering how envious she'd felt of the young couples leaving the station this afternoon, she longed for someone with whom to share her life and her thoughts as she'd never been able to with Cyril.

Nobody knew that she felt like this. To everyone she was a grieving widow. Martha and Polly would be shocked if they could read her thoughts, but then they didn't know the truth about the way Cyril had died. Sometimes she thought that she had played her part too well. The letters, for instance, that she'd been exchanging with Albert for the last six months. He'd naturally assumed that she was as heartbroken as he was himself, and their correspondence had been initiated to comfort each other. In his last letter Albert had told her he was due for a leave very soon, and Bron found that she was really looking forward to seeing him again, remembering the kindly thoughtful boy who'd shared her lunch breaks and made no secret of his fondness for her. She was remembering, too, the last time she'd seen him when he'd visited them at the shop: a tall young man in air-force uniform, full of hopes for the future, hopes that had been dashed for ever by a German bomb.

Glory had been going out with a Canadian soldier for a few months now. There'd been a fuss at first, but he'd soon won Polly and Will round with his charm and good manners and little presents of chocolates and cigarettes.

When Bron had been introduced to him she'd thought him a very nice boy. He'd only looked about twenty. Last week Glory had wanted her to make a foursome with Mel's friend who was about Bron's own age.

'It's just a bit of fun,' she had pleaded. 'There's no harm in it, Bron.'

Shocked her nan and Aunt Poll would have been if she'd accepted. Bron smiled to herself, remembering what had happened at the pictures last week. She'd been sitting alone watching the Pathé news when a hunk of a fellow wearing a smart khaki uniform had pulled down the seat beside her. They'd been halfway through the feature film when she felt his hand touch hers gently. She'd shaken it free and looked around for an empty seat but she couldn't see one. When presently the lights went up for the interval he'd noticed her wedding ring and said apologetically, 'Sorry, Ma'am, I didn't know.' And when she'd smiled at him to put him at his ease, he'd pressed a bar of chocolate on her.

His short fair hair had been clipped ridiculously short, and his blue eyes had been so friendly she wished she could have strolled out of the cinema on his arm. She smiled, remembering the warning her nan used to repeat often before she was married: 'Never allow yourself to be picked up, Bron. It's dangerous to go out with anyone you haven't been introduced to.' Well she'd been introduced properly to Cyril and just look how that had turned out!

Bron blushed as she remembered how she'd felt that day at the cinema. Her emotions had been stirred by the touching love scenes in the big picture, a wartime love story of partings, suffering and misunderstandings, which ended with the lovers falling rapturously into each other's arms at the same spot on the station platform where it had all begun. The film had emphasised her own loneliness and isolation from the company of people her own age.

The coals stirring and falling low in the grate brought her to her feet to switch on the light and make up the fire, then she went to the wash-house to rinse her hands and get something for tea.

Ten minutes later, back in the armchair by the fire with a plate of bread and butter and a slice of cake on a plate on her lap, the worry that she had been crowding out with her thoughts refused to go away. David was to stay with Jenny and Idris, that had been decided today, and she supposed that was as it should be. But when would they tell Meg? Poor Meg, she'd be heartbroken. Wouldn't she want to stay at Glas Fynydd as well? The children had been brought up together since they were two years old, they thought of each other as brother and sister – they *were* brother and sister. She should have insisted on being there when Meg was told. Oh, if only it was safe to bring her home now. If only the raids would stop altogether. If only this horrible war was over. If only . . .

Bron got up and shook the cushions impatiently into

shape before going to the wash-house to make a flask of tea in case the siren began to wail.

Chapter Thirty-Six

The hours dragged until Saturday evening when Bron could take the train to Glas Fynydd. She prayed they hadn't told Meg about David's staying on with his grandmother when she came home to Cardiff, dreading the effect the news might have on the already troubled child.

As the train steamed into the station Jenny and the children were waiting on the platform. Bron slammed the carriage door and Meg and David came rushing towards her, arms outstretched, crying: 'Mam! Mam!' in high excited voices. She knew by Meg's happy smile that she hadn't yet been told.

David had called her Mam, or Mama, ever since he'd come to live with them when he was two years old. What would he call her, she wondered sadly, when Jenny and Idris had officially adopted him?

The difference in Jenny was remarkable. She linked her arm in Bron's as the children ran ahead.

'Grateful I am, *cariad*, for youer understanding,' she told Bron. 'We haven't told David yet because of Meg. They're still grieving over their dada, poor little things. Upset she's going to be, I know, but she'll get over it once it's safe for her to go home.'

'I'm glad you haven't told her, Jenny,' Bron said, wishing she could add, You haven't given her much chance to

331

get over losing her dad. She'd little doubt that the flowers and photographs would still be on display in every room in the house.

They'd hardly got into the house and the kettle been put on for a cup of tea when the photo albums were brought out, but this time only the ones that held pictures of Cyril as a baby and a young child.

'Isn't David the spitting image of him, Bron?' Jenny cried, taking a photo of her grandson from the mantelpiece and holding it against one of Cyril at about the same age. The dark eyes looking back at Bron from the photos were the same, large and solemn. The pictures were in sepia but she knew that the short springy curls in both were in reality a rich tawny gold.

'Please don't spoil him, Mam,' she found herself saying, blushing scarlet at her nerve. 'Remember, he's David not Cyril. There's a lot of Ceinwen in him too.' Bron was surprised to find she felt no bitterness at mentioning the girl's name.

'I've learned my lesson, Bron,' Jenny assured her. 'Cyril always had his own way right from the beginning. It was being an only boy in a family of girls, I suppose. Ruined he was, *cariad*.'

On the Sunday afternoon when she had to say goodbye, Bron clung to Meg, wishing she could take her home. The air raids had been less frequent lately although there were still a lot of alerts, keeping everyone in the freezing shelters until the all-clear sounded. It would be silly to take chances.

Anyway, she thought, Meg is bound to benefit from Jenny's new cheerfulness and the atmosphere will be less morbid now, though apparently the flowers and pictures were to remain. The summer posies, and later autumn chrysanthemums, had been replaced when no longer available by artificial silk flowers and these, carefully arranged, flanked photographs of Cyril wherever there was space.

Spring came at last and at the beginning of April, while making one of her regular week-end visits to Glas Fynydd, Bron was seated at the table with the rest of the family when Ceinwen's mother came in. David jumped up and, flinging his arms about her, cried: 'Nan! Nan!' and Bron was surprised to see Meg doing exactly the same.

'She thinks if Mabel is David's nan, then she must be hers as well,' Jenny laughed.

When the children had gone back to the table Mabel stood behind David's chair, her hand affectionately on his shoulder, saying, 'Saw ouer Blod I did yesterday, Jenny. Surprised she was that young David's going to be living with you and Idris from now on. Pleased she is that he'll be brought up in Glas Fynydd where he belongs.'

There was a deathly silence as the children stared at Jenny who had gone very white, then David cried, 'But why can't I go back to live with Mam and Meg?'

'Youer happy here, aren't you, boyo?' Jenny asked anxiously. 'Lots of friends you've got now youer at the boys' junior school. Don't you want to stay, David?'

The boy put his arm about his tearful little sister.

'Meg and me want to stay together.'

'Meg will have lots of friends herself at her new school, won't you, Meg?'

She burst into fresh tears and flung herself at Bron, sobbing, 'I want to come home – with you, Mama. I want to go back – with you now. Why can't David – stay with us?'

'Nana's lonely,' Bron whispered against her hair. 'We'll have each other, Meg. But you can't come home, love, it isn't safe yet.'

'Youer mama's right, love,' Jenny began, but Meg
pulled away from her and ran upstairs, sobbing loudly.

'Whatever possessed you, Mabel?' Jenny asked crossly
as Bron rushed past her after Meg.

'Sorry, love, I forgot,' she heard Mabel saying, as she
took the stairs two at a time.

Meg had pulled the bedclothes over her head but when
Bron pulled them gently down she raised a pathetic little
face and said, 'Nana loves David more'n me.'

'Of course she doesn't,' Bron told her, cwtching her
close and rocking her to and fro.

Jenny was coming into the room. She seated herself on
the side of the bed and said, 'There's sorry I am, Bron.
Mabel shouldn't have burst out with it like that. Look,
Meg, youer nana loves you very much, but youer mama's
just longing for when it's safe for you to go back to her.
And David will still be youer brother.'

Bron was looking at her watch in dismay. She must be
at the station in twenty minutes, but Meg clung to her
pathetically, crying, 'Take me home, Mama, take me with
you.' What could she do? She'd have to go soon, but she
couldn't leave the child like this. Would it be wrong to
take her home just for a few days? She could talk to her
then, make her understand about David. Things had been
pretty quiet this last week, only a few alerts and nothing
much happening. How about Mr Jessop? She'd be letting
him down, but Meg's happiness must come first.

'She'll be all right,' Jenny was assuring her. 'You get
along, Bron, or you'll miss the train.' But Meg was gripping her tightly and sobbing even louder.

'Suppose I just take her until Wednesday?' she said to
Jenny, with her eyes on the clock. She'd have to leave
soon.

'I don't think you should give in to her, Bron,' Jenny

told her. Meg clung to her all the more.

'I can't leave her like this,' Bron replied, pleading for understanding.

'Well, I can't stop you. I'll put some things in a case, but you'll have to hurry.'

They got to the station just in time to see the train steaming away from the platform, and with a sinking heart Bron realised there wouldn't be another for two hours. It would be very late when they got to Cardiff. Supposing a raid began before they reached home?

It had been a bright sunny spring day, but now the evening had turned bitterly cold and an icy wind was blowing along the platform which was little more than a halt, not even having a waiting room.

'We'd better go back, Meg,' she began. The remark brought a torrent of tears, and she sat down on a bench and took the child on her knee.

'What is it, love? You've always been happy with your nan.'

'It's Dada,' the child sobbed. 'He watches me all the time. All the pictures watch me. Take me home with you, Mama.'

Poor little Meg, Bron had hoped she'd got over her fear.

'We'll freeze if we stay here, love,' she said lightly. 'We'll have to go back until it's time for the next train.' She got up and took Meg's hand, but the child wouldn't budge.

'Come on, don't be silly.' Bron moved towards the steps, pretty certain that Meg would follow her.

When she opened the door and saw them, Jenny cried, 'There's glad I am you've changed youer mind.'

'We missed the train,' Bron told her. 'But I'm still taking her for a few days. I've promised her, Jenny.'

Bron wished she could tackle her mother-in-law about the photos of Cyril on show in the bedroom where Meg slept. Two on the mantelpiece, one on the chest of drawers, and another on the bedside table. But it was awkward with Meg sitting beside her. She decided to talk to Jenny when they came back on Wednesday.

This time they left with plenty of time to spare. There were few people travelling and they had the darkened carriage to themselves. The dim blue light hardly pierced the gloom, and with the windows blacked out Bron counted the stations to Cardiff General.

Meg cwtched up to her, talkative now that they were on their way at last, excited at going home.

Telling her mother again about the junior school she'd moved to at the beginning of term, she said, 'I've got a best friend now, her name is Olwen. She likes our David.'

'That's nice, her liking David.'

Meg giggled. 'It's soppy.'

Relieved that the child seemed to be back to normal, Bron laughed too.

They arrived at the tram-stop to find the tram already gone. When Meg began to shiver Bron decided that a brisk walk to the stop in Queen Street would be best.

They were half-way along St Mary Street when the siren began its mournful wail, and as the sound swelled and seemed to engulf them and searchlights swept the sky, Meg was looking all around her in wonder, asking her mother what the lights were for.

'We'd better hurry, love, you'll have to run. We'll go to the Castle dungeons, that's the nearest shelter.'

'What's a dungeon, Mama?' But Bron didn't answer for now the rat-a-tat-tat of ack-ack fire replaced the noise of the siren. When, panting, they reached the shelter there were few people taking refuge as yet but more were arriving all the time, and as they sat down Bron was blaming herself bitterly for being foolish enough to bring the child home.

Two women came and sat on the bench beside Meg and began talking to her. One of them rummaged in her handbag and produced a bag of sweets.

As people pouring out of the cinemas took refuge the shelter filled up rapidly, and Meg was soon the centre of attention as she chatted and laughed excitedly. Remembering the weeping child who'd left Glas Fynydd Bron thought, Jenny was right, she would have got over the upset, given time.

A man stood up unsteadily, swaying to and fro, a rosy-cheeked man, jolly in his drink, waving his arms about, urging everyone to sing.

'Come on, now – altogether. "It's a long Way to Tipperary . . ."' And a few of the older people joined in, others taking it up before they reached the end. Then someone started 'We'll Meet Again' and everyone began to sing, and when that was finished the jolly drunk, determined to have the songs of the First World War, waved his arms about as though conducting a choir and began singing 'Keep The Home Fires Burning' and everyone sang with gusto.

In the dim light of the shelter Meg's eyes shone, her tiredness forgotten as she sang her own garbled version of the songs. When at last they came out to the pitch black town there were no more trams and they began the long trek home.

The house was cold with no fires in the grate for a couple of days. First Bron put on a kettle for a hot drink and a water bottle for the bed. Meg would have to sleep with her tonight, it was too late to warm the bedclothes, and make up a bed for her.

While she undressed the child talked excitedly, and Bron reflected ruefully that she seemed more afraid of her father's ever watchful eye from the photographs than she'd been of the air raid tonight.

Next morning as Bron was going downstairs there was a knock at the door and when she opened it Polly stood there.

'Worried I was, love. You weren't here when I knocked last night.'

When Bron had explained, her aunt said, 'Was this wise to bring her home? Oh, well, she's here now, but what are you going to do about going to work?'

'I thought I'd go and see Mr Jessop this morning.'

'Look, Bron, if it's only for a few days we'll have Meg. She's always got on well with us. Go into work today and perhaps he'll give you some time off to be with her.'

Meg was coming down the stairs, rubbing sleepy eyes. Despite the time she'd been away she hadn't forgotten Polly and ran straight into her arms.

Delighted to see the child again, Polly cwtched her warmly, saying, 'Remember when you used to play with our Glory's dolls, love? Well, they're still up in her bedroom.'

After that Bron had difficulty in persuading Meg to stay and have breakfast.

Ten minutes later, watching them go down the street hand in hand, her daughter beaming up at Polly, Bron thought what a lovely warm-hearted family she had. They hadn't always seen eye to eye, and Polly had mellowed with the years, but they'd always been there when needed and she'd been grateful.

She got to work early and when she explained to Mr Jessop about having Meg home for a few days, he said, 'Well, if we could get some rations weighed up in advance

I think we could manage without you for, say, tomorrow afternoon and Wednesday morning. You'd be back Thursday ready for the week-end rush.'

Bron felt like flinging her arms about him. Instead she thanked him warmly, adding, 'I'll get on with weighing up the rations right away.'

Tuesday afternoon she took Meg to Clifton Street, and to her favourite shop when she'd been at home, the Penny Bazaar, where she took ages choosing a present for herself and one to take back to David, from the more expensive end of the counter, and they went to town where Bron used some of her precious coupons to buy Meg a pretty dress, and a shirt and trousers for little David, despite the fact that now in the spring the coupons were being cut from sixty-six a year to just sixty coupons to last over fifteen months. She just felt happy at making this little sacrifice, for Jenny had her work cut out keeping them well-clothed on their own ration coupons, and Bron knew that her mother-in-law often used her own, and sometimes her own money too.

Bron feared there might be a fuss when the time came to take Meg back to Glas Fynydd, but her fears proved groundless for on the Wednesday morning when she came down to breakfast Meg suddenly put her hand to her mouth and asked anxiously, 'What day is it, Mam?'

'Wednesday, love. Why?'

'It's Olwen's birthday on Thursday. Can I go back today?'

Bron nodded, saying, 'Why didn't you say, love? We could have bought her a present in Clifton Street.'

'Oh, I bought one for her with Nana last week. I gave some of my pocket money towards it. Will I get back in time to see Olwen tonight?'

'We'll go early this afternoon, Meg.'

She sighed with relief. 'I wonder what Olwen's doing without me?'

'Making eyes at David, I expect,' Bron told her with a smile, and Meg giggled.

'Can I wear my new dress to the party, Mam?'

'Yes, of course you can,' Bron told her, thankful there wasn't going to be a fuss about her going back. She was determined to tell Jenny this time about the effect of the many photos of Cyril in Meg's bedroom, but she knew that it was really the words Jenny had used when she'd said her father was watching over her that had done the damage. Meg was such a sensitive little thing. She'd have to be careful how she broached the subject though; she didn't want to upset Jenny who she knew had made the unfortunate remark to comfort the children.

When they arrived early in the afternoon Bron was thankful to discover that there was no need to say anything at all, for after they'd all hugged Meg and she'd taken the child's case up to her bedroom, she found the photographs had disappeared from the room where Meg slept.

Jenny, who'd been following behind and had seen her surprise, said, 'I should have done it before, Bron. I've been very thoughtless. David told me what was upsetting Meg. I didn't think, girl. You know me.'

'You did what you thought was for the best, Mam,' Bron said, giving her a hug. 'Meg will always remember her dada. She doesn't like to think he's watching her all the time, that's all.'

'I'll explain to her that I didn't mean that at all,' Jenny said. 'I suppose I did get a bit carried away.'

This time when Bron had to leave Meg was playing happily with her friend Olwen, a dark-eyed little girl with plump cheeks and short bobbed hair. She hugged her mother, and the three children waved until Bron was out of sight, and she gave a sigh of relief that there was to be no fuss.

The silence in the house in Cardiff seemed strange after Meg's lively chatter and she switched on the wireless and let the music fill the emptiness of the room.

The next day there was a letter from Albert to tell her he would be home the following Saturday; his train should arrive in Cardiff at about half past seven in the evening. Bron read the letter through once more. He must want me to meet him, she told herself excitedly, then her spirits fell. She wouldn't finish work in time. She didn't get away from the shop until well after seven o'clock, except when she was going to Glas Fynydd for the weekend. Mr Jessop was always very good about that.

I could ask him, she thought, but instantly dismissed the idea. Why should she want time off to meet Albert? Mr Jessop wouldn't understand.

What would they talk about when they met, she wondered. They'd have to find something besides their mutual grief. She wasn't grieving any more, hadn't done so since the letter she'd received from London. But it was different for Albert, wasn't it?

Chapter Thirty-Seven

Albert's mother came into the shop and straight up to Bron.

'You've heard he's coming home on Saturday? I think Albert would like you to meet him at the station, Bron. Done him the world of good it has, you and him writing to each other.'

'I won't be able to finish work in time, Mrs Davies,' Bron told her reluctantly, her mind already working on how she could put it to Mr Jessop.

Mrs Davies went across to the other counter and soon Mr Jessop was smiling and nodding his head.

'A good sort youer boss is,' Mrs Davies told her, when she returned to Bron once more. 'Real generous he was to Albert when he came in to see you all one day.'

Marcia was looking at her questioningly. As soon as she was able, Bron went over to her.

'It's Albert,' she told her friend. 'Remember I told you he was coming on leave? His mam wants me to meet him at the station.'

'Will you go? You've been writing to each other for ages, haven't you?'

'Well, he wrote with his sympathy when Cyril died, and we've been corresponding ever since.'

When Saturday arrived, knowing she wouldn't have

time to go home and change before going to the station, Bron wore her favourite pale blue dress under her black coat. This was the first time she'd worn a colour since Cyril's death, but she'd stayed in mourning only so as not to upset other people, especially his mam. As the time drew near to leave the shop, she was feeling nervous. Was she taking too much for granted in going to meet him? But Mr Jessop was calling to her, 'You can go now Bron,' and she hurried to the back room and washed her face at the sink, patting it dry with a clean handkerchief – she didn't fancy the grubby roller towel hanging behind the door.

Moistening her lips with a pale lipstick and pressing them together, then dabbing her nose lightly with a powder puff, she gazed into the spotted mirror and pulled the ribbon from her hair, letting it fall loosely about her shoulders.

'Tell him we'd like to see him while he's home,' Mr Jessop said, when she came into the shop ready to leave, and Marcia smiled and nodded agreement.

The train was over half an hour late. She watched as another train came in and the platform was enveloped in steam, doors slamming, people rushing forward to greet their loved ones. People in uniforms were everywhere, and Bron's nervousness grew. Then she was thinking of the last time she'd been on this station, seeing Cyril off, remembering his words: 'Don't make it any harder for me, Bron.' Misunderstanding, she'd wondered if he was going abroad and hadn't yet told her, when all the time he was going to London to meet that girl.

Another train was hissing into the station, and she pushed the bitter thoughts to the back of her mind while she moved forward and peered into the carriages as it slowed to a halt. She recognised Albert as soon as he stepped from the train, the blue eyes smiling in the freckled face, as he came towards her, fair hair shining with brilliantine beneath the smart air-force cap.

'Bron! I hoped you'd come.' He kissed her awkwardly on her cheek, blushing as their eyes met.

'You must be glad to come home. Your mam was really happy when she came into the shop to tell me.'

They'd reached the bottom of the steps leading from the station when he turned to her, saying, 'You don't know what it meant to me, your writing like that.'

'Me, too,' she told him.

'I was always seeing you as you were when we worked together, Bron. I had the love-bug badly, remember? You were my first love. I've always had a soft spot for you.' He grinned at her.

When they'd left the station and were at the tram stop, Bron wondered if she should go home with him. His mother hadn't seen him for months. When a number two tram was pulling into the stop she said, 'There's my tram, Albert. I expect your mam would like to have you to herself tonight.'

Albert put a staying hand on her arm, and there was no mistaking the disappointment in his eyes as he said, 'Please, Bron! I was hoping to see a lot of you on this leave . . . perhaps it's too soon after . . .'

The tram going to Whitchurch Road arrived at that moment, and they shuffled forward with the queue. When they'd got on and Albert had put his kit bag on the rack and they'd found a seat together, she said quietly, 'No it isn't too soon for me Albert. We weren't that close, Cyril and me, not like you and Janet.'

'You'll never know what your letters meant to me, Bron. You were the only one who really understood. Then I began looking forward to your letters in a different way; not just for the sympathy and understanding they brought. I was going to ask you for a photo to take back.' He put his hand over hers and squeezed it gently.

Mrs Davies was at the gate as they turned the corner of the street, and when she came to meet them Bron hung back. Albert folded his arms about his mother, and when at last he released her she put an arm about Bron's shoulders and they all walked towards the house.

The kitchen table was draped with a white damask cloth, and Bron saw that three places had been laid. A well-risen sponge cake had pride of place in the middle of the table, and she saw by the lacy pattern on top that a little of Sarah Davies's precious sugar ration had been sifted through a paper doily.

When the warm plates were brought in, each with a lean pork chop, than a dish with roast potatoes, one with cabbage and another with apple sauce, followed by a steaming gravy boat, Bron felt guilty knowing just how much of his mam's rations it must have taken; but the savoury smell was tantalising her taste buds, for she'd only eaten snacks all day.

Soon the plates were cleared, and, while Albert and Bron were voicing their appreciation, large slices of sponge cake were put on their plates.

'However did you get it to rise like that?' Bron asked, for with eggs in short supply she'd found it difficult to make a successful sponge herself.

'I added bicarb and cream of tartar,' Sarah told her. 'I can give you the recipe if you like, Bron.'

The evening had turned chilly, and after the dishes were washed and put away Bron was glad to sit beside Albert on the sofa that had been drawn up to the fire, with his mam in the comfy armchair, while firelight mellowed the brightness of the steel fender to warm amber. The conversation flowed, and Bron, glancing at her watch from time to time was feeling loth to go. When she could put it off no longer, Albert rose to get his coat, saying, 'I'll take you home, Bron.'

'You'd be too late to get a tram back here,' she told him, and saw his mam's grateful look as he compromised by just seeing her to the tram.

Arriving home, Bron went straight to bed and dreamt of Albert's arms about her. He had kissed her gently before she'd got on the tram, and asked if they could meet tomorrow, but she'd had to tell him she was going to Glas Fynydd to see Meg. He had insisted on meeting the train when she returned. She'd have loved him to meet Meg, but she didn't want to court trouble. Jenny would never understand.

The days of his leave passed much too quickly. On Wednesday they went to Penarth and walked along the promenade, but there was a keen wind coming from the sea, and they put their arms about each other for warmth and laughed, especially when a gust took Albert's cap and he had to run after it. Each time he put out his hand the cap flew into the air, and Albert was off again in pursuit. When, out of breath, he finally caught up with it they decided to call the walk off and sat in a café by the window watching the windswept promenade. Another man was chasing his hat now, a trilby, and as they watched his fruitless efforts from the comfort of the café they could afford to giggle.

By Friday evening the leave was almost over. When the blind of the shop was drawn there was still a customer to be served and Bron sighed in despair, thinking they would miss the last house of the cinema. Marcia rushed over from the cash desk, saying, 'I don't mind, Bron, really I don't. With Chris in the Middle East, I'm in no hurry to go home.'

'Thanks,' Bron murmured fervently, knowing she would do the same for Marcia when she needed it. She put her coat on and hurried away to meet Albert.

It had been a wonderful week; both she and Albert had soon lost their shyness, and Albert had opened his heart to her, telling her of the depth of his despair when Janet had died.

'When you lost Cyril, Bron, I felt I knew just how you'd be feeling,' he told her. Then, taking her hand and squeezing it gently, he said, 'Weren't you happy with him, love? . . . you said . . .'

'We didn't get on very well,' was all she'd admit to.

They sat in the cinema holding hands, and presently she rested her head on his shoulder. When the film ended and the lights went up, Bron sat primly upright watching the adverts on the blind that had been drawn down in front of the screen. She realised that she'd no idea what the film had been about. Her mind had been elsewhere, wondering how she would get through the long months until Albert's next leave.

'What time is the train tomorrow?' she asked, hoping she could come to the station.

'It's due out at half past one.'

Could she manage it in her dinner hour? It would be mean to Mr Jessop to be late back when he'd been so kind. But she knew that she must be there to say goodbye.

Next day, as the train drew into the station, they clung to each other, all their shy restraint gone. The guard had raised his flag before Albert rushed for the carriage.

'Write to me, Bron,' he yelled, as with a burst of steam

the train clanged into motion and began to move away from the platform.

'I'll write tonight,' Bron yelled back.

Albert gave her a final wave, then patted his breast pocket in an exaggerated way, and she knew he was telling her where he kept the photograph she'd had taken for him at Jerome's.

In return she had received a photo of Albert, and smiled tenderly as she saw the self-conscious smile he'd given the camera.

When she got home she stretched up to the mantelpiece and took down Cyril's photo. Taking it out of its frame, she replaced it with the one of Albert. The family will have to know sometime, she told herself uneasily. She was expecting Jenny to make a fuss, at any rate, for Cyril's mother knew nothing of her son having a girlfriend, or that he'd been with her when he was killed in the London Blitz. Jenny rarely visited Cardiff now; there was no need, with Bron going to Glas Fynydd every weekend. Besides, she was tied by the children's school hours.

Bron would have loved to have taken Albert to her nan's while he was home, but she was afraid Martha would consider it too soon for her to be going out with someone new, and might show her feelings. But now, placing Albert's photo on the mantelpiece, she felt defiant.

Polly was the first to notice. 'Who's that?' she cried, surprised and curious at the same time.

Bron took down the polished wooden frame and handed it to her. Gazing down at it, Polly asked, 'How long have you known him then?'

'Ever since I was fourteen,' Bron told her, her eyes twinkling. 'Albert was errand boy at Jessop's when I first went to work there. His wife was killed in an air raid,

Aunt Poll. It was before Cyril died. I wrote and sent my sympathy, and he did the same to me.'

'And you've been writing ever since?'

Bron nodded. 'At first it was mutual sympathy.'

'He looks a nice boy,' Polly said approvingly, putting the photograph back in its place.

'He's in the air force, a rear gunner,' Bron told her. 'Do you think Nan will be upset?'

'She'll be pleased for you, Bron. Mam's always worrying about you being on your own, especially when the war is over.'

'I'll have to tell Jenny soon. I know she'll think it's too early for me to be thinking of somebody else.'

'When is he coming home again?'

'It'll be at least three months, I should think.'

'I'd leave it 'til then if I were you.'

'He wanted to see Meg, Aunt Poll. I wish I could have her home.'

'Well, I know it's been quiet lately, but I don't think it's all over yet.'

'Albert's mam lives near the shop so I can call in there on my way home. She's a lovely person. You'll all have to meet her.'

Months passed and the days grew warmer, and Bron began to scan Albert's letters eagerly for a mention of his next leave. She was thrilled when he asked her if she'd get engaged the next time he came home.

Now she dawdled outside every jeweller's window and dreamt of the day he'd put the ring on her finger. Whenever she heard the droning of planes she pictured him, crouched in the tail of some plane, though she just had to use her imagination, for she had no idea what his job really entailed. She tortured herself with the picture of enemy searchlights seeking the plane out, and fiery bursts of *ack-ack* fire.

Albert came home at the beginning of May. When he stepped off the train they went into each other's arms and kissed and hugged as though they'd never let each other go.

I love him, Bron thought happily. But she'd loved Cyril once, hadn't she? Only that had been different, she told herself sternly. She'd been young, impressionable, infatuated with his good looks. She hadn't known the real Cyril at all, not as she knew Albert. Polly had said, 'Albert looks a nice boy,' and he is nice, Bron thought, through and through. That evening she took Albert to meet her family, and Martha and Polly had done them proud, making a sherry trifle, and Welsh cakes despite the rationing, and preparing a lovely salad served with a tin of red salmon Martha had been hoarding for a special occasion. 'And what's more special than my grand-daughter getting engaged, I'd like to know?' Later she whispered to her grand-daughter, 'He's a nice young fellow, Bron. You can see that right away.'

The conversation never flagged, especially when the remainder of the Christmas sherry was brought out and poured, with an especially generous measure for Albert.

He was so deep in conversation with Will that he almost missed the last tram home, and Bron heaved a sigh of relief when he jumped on just as it was pulling out of the stop.

This time, determined Albert should meet Meg, Bron had written to Jenny telling her she was bringing a young man with her on Sunday and giving Jenny no time to reply.

The next day, which was a Wednesday and her half day, they decided they'd go to Newport to choose the ring. That night Bron couldn't sleep for excitement, realising more than ever what she'd missed with Cyril.

At lunch time she dressed carefully in a dove grey suit that emphasised her slim waist, and a cream, lace-trimmed blouse. They got off the train at Newport, and when they turned in to Commercial Street they stopped at every jeweller's, bemused by the glittering displays, for the black out wouldn't be drawn until it was dusk. Halfway along, they went into the shop they liked the best for her to try some rings on, and as she spread out her hand for Albert to see the half hoop of diamonds set in platinum, the glitter of the ring under the hooded counter lights was matched by the brightness of her eyes.

When they went into a café to celebrate, Albert led her to a secluded table screened by a tall potted plant, and when the waitress had brought their order and they were alone they toasted each other with tea, and Albert slipped the ring onto her finger and kissed her. Then they ate the buns filled with mock cream, and left the café to take the train back to Cardiff; and when they were seated in the carriage, Bron rested her hands in her lap, her eyes on the ring. That was until, realising they were to have the carriage to themselves, Albert put his arms about her and his lips to hers, murmuring that he couldn't wait to add a wedding ring to the one he'd bought today. And when she looked up and saw the longing in his eyes, she didn't want to wait either.

'How about us getting married on my next leave, Bron?'

'I'd love to but – '

'There mustn't be any "buts", Bron.'

'I was thinking of my mother-in-law,' she told him. 'She'll need time to get used to the idea.' Jenny would have to accept it, but Bron didn't like to spring it on her like this. Jenny had been so good to her, she didn't want to upset her.

When, on Sunday, they climbed the steep street to Jenny and Idris's house, she was feeling nervous. The engagement ring was in her purse, for now she felt guilty about not telling her mother-in-law about Albert before. Meg and David dashed from the house to greet her, both of them hugging her tightly at the same time, almost taking her breath away, especially after the steep climb. Albert was smiling at the children and putting a hand in his pocket he brought out two twists of sweets, saying, 'Better not eat them all before you have your dinner.'

When Jenny thought no one was looking, Bron saw the look of sadness on her face, and wondered if she was remembering the day Cyril had taken Bron to meet her for the very first time. But when she'd introduced Albert, and told her how long she'd known him, Jenny had smiled at him warmly, saying to Bron, 'I'm glad, *cariad*. It's been very lonely for you.'

When Albert went out to push the children on the swing and talk to Idris, who was in the garden, Jenny said, 'I like him Bron, I really do, but be sure, *cariad*, before you think of getting married. You've Meg to consider. How would she take to having a stranger in the house?'

'But he isn't a stranger,' Bron was quick to defend him. 'I've known him ever since – '

'I know, love, told me, you did. It was Meg I was talking about, *cariad*.'

But by the end of the day, when Albert had fixed the arm of Meg's favourite doll, and repaired the clockwork spring on David's train, it was Albert the children wanted to tell them their bedtime story, and they almost missed the train home because of his determination to please them.

Bron felt bad not telling Jenny about their engagement, but she knew it had been something of a shock for her as it was. She promised herself she'd tell her next week. Let her think it had been decided after their visit, and get used to the idea in easy stages.

On the train going home, Albert confided his ambition to own a grocery store of his own with living accommodation.

'I've been saving for years, Bron,' he told her. 'When Janet went, it knocked me for six. I lost interest in everything. I didn't have the heart to plan for anything. Went to night school for years, I did, taking book-keeping and other subjects, and I've been in the grocery trade all my working life. But perhaps you've had enough of shops, Bron? Perhaps you'd just like to be a housewife when we settle down.'

'I'd love us to work together,' she told him. 'Mr Jessop says there'll be rationing for a long time even when the war's finished, and I do understand that part of it.'

'I hadn't thought about there still being rationing. That would be a big help, Bron.'

For some moments there was silence, then Albert changed the subject, asking, 'Where would you like the wedding to be?'

She thought for a few moments, wrestling with the regrets she'd felt last time at not having a white wedding and a service in church. But that would cost money, lots of it, and then there'd be the reception for all their friends, and that would cost too. She couldn't expect her nan to help on just her pension, and she had very little saved herself.

'A register office,' she said firmly. After all, if they wanted they could always renew their vows in Church at a later date.

* * *

When Albert had gone back she made up her mind to have Meg home for a few days the following weekend. Monday was always a quiet day at the shop, and Mr Jessop offered her the Monday off if she would come in on the following Sunday morning to help with stock-taking.

The air raids seemed to have quietened down, although just when you thought they were over there'd be another, but she felt it was quiet enough now to take the risk, and Meg had enjoyed it so much last time.

She wasn't prepared for Meg's tears when she told her her plans.

'I don't want to leave Olwen, Mama. She's my best friend,' she cried.

'But it's only for the weekend. When the war is over Olwen can come and stay with us if she likes.'

'Can she really, Mam? And can I come and stay at Nana's sometimes?'

'Yes, of course you can, love.'

'I'm just going to tell Olwen,' Meg cried eagerly, rushing to the front door.

It was already dark when they arrived home, and Bron was thankful that no air raid had spoilt their homecoming this time. In the kitchen, she felt her way around the table to draw the curtains at the window before putting on the light, remembering that Peggy had been fined five shillings at the Magistrates' Court only a few weeks before, for showing a light in the front room for little more than a moment.

In the houses in Rosalind Street the brass light switches for the parlour, middle room and passage were all in a row outside the middle room door. Peggy had thought that the parlour curtains were drawn. She'd dashed to pull them across as soon as she'd entered the room and realised they weren't, but a conscientious warden had already noticed, and was hammering on the front door yelling, 'Put that blutty light out!'

Now Bron knelt and put a match to the fire laid ready in the kitchen range, then hurried to the wash-house to put the kettle on the gas-ring.

Twenty minutes later, making toast on the long-handled fork in front of the now glowing fire, she was in no hurry to get Meg to bed, for she was enjoying the child's company and her evident pleasure in being up late with the prospect of the game of Snap her mother had promised to play after supper.

The firelight was turning Meg's silky fair hair to fiery gold. Later, when they'd finished their meal, as she'd watched the eager little fingers carefully laying down each card, and Meg's excitement when she could call 'Snap!' she'd wanted to hug her close. But at last bedtime could be put off no longer, and they climbed the oil-clothed stairs together.

'Olwen can sleep in David's bed when she comes, can't she, Mam?' Meg asked, putting her arms about her mother's neck.

Meg recognised the picture of Albert. 'I like him, Mam,' she said. 'He's fun. Is he going to be my new dad?'

'Would you like him to be, Meg?'

'Well, it's nice when it's just you and me, like now, but I wouldn't really mind. I heard Nana telling Grandad you must be lonely. Are you lonely, Mam?'

When she'd gone to Glas Fynydd to fetch Meg home, she'd shown them the engagement ring, and it had been much admired. She should have known that a generous soul like Jenny would understand, though Jenny had cautioned her again. 'Make sure, Bron, that it isn't too soon for Meg,' she'd said. Now, sounding Meg out, Bron felt encouraged.

'When Albert comes home and we're married, we may have a grocery shop. Would you like that, Meg?'

'Would I be allowed to weigh things up on the scales?' she asked eagerly.

'Yes, of course you would, love. You could be a big help too, sweeping up the sawdust and spreading fresh on the floor,' Bron told her, fanning her enthusiasm.

'When will Uncle Albert come home again, Mam?' Meg had decided to call him uncle all on her own, but Bron was determined he would be Dada after they were married.

'I wish I knew,' she told her daughter wistfully. 'We may get married when he comes home next time, then he'll be your dada.'

'Can I be a bridesmaid, Mam? Will you wear a long white gown?'

But Bron had to curb her excitement. 'It won't be that sort of wedding, love,' she said, 'but I promise you shall have a pretty new dress.'

Chapter Thirty-Eight

As Meg's birthday approached she made it known that she wanted a toy grocery store for her present, but Bron knew that by this stage of the war such a toy would be very difficult to find. When Will heard about it he set about making one from some wood he had in the shed, while everyone else in the family sacrificed a week's sweet ration to fill small bottles begged from neighbours and friends. The bottles were of all shapes and sizes, and weren't to the same scale as the shop, but this seemed of little importance as they added dummy boxes of tea, sugar, and other commodities, that they'd made to fill the fixtures with merchandise.

When Bertha Morgan brought in a set of toy scales and weights that one of her grown-up granddaughters had long forgotten, the shop was complete. It only consisted of a small counter with fixtures behind containing the dummy packets and small bottles of sweets, and one of Bron's old shop coats that Polly had cut down to size, but Bron knew that Meg, who had only asked for a little toy model, would be over the moon that she could really stand behind the counter and serve.

The shop was a great success. On her birthday Meg donned the white coat and happily weighed sweets into the little three-cornered paper bags that Martha had begged from the corner shop. Then she would serve the mock packets of sugar, tea and flour, putting them all back again afterwards, ready for the next customer, and the sweets disappeared slowly but surely, and had to be replaced.

There were other birthday presents, of course – books, a box of paints and some clothes – but the shop was the main attraction. Now she wanted to come home every weekend to play with it, for it was too heavy for Bron to carry to Glas Fynydd, and she hoped very soon to have Meg home for good.

It was the middle of August before Albert had leave again. All the wedding arrangements had been made well in advance, except of course for booking the actual date and time at the register office, and Bron saw to that as soon as Albert's letter arrived.

Bron had chosen a cream costume, fitted at the waist, with which she would wear a beige lace-trimmed blouse, and a pillbox hat with a veil. Cream court shoes and a matching handbag completed the ensemble. Meg was so excited about her new pink dress and white shoes, and this time at the register office Bron knew she'd have no regrets.

Once again the wedding guests consisted only of family on both sides, Marcia, Peggy and her mother. The parlour table was piled high with gifts: towels, bedding, cutlery, tablecloths, and a dainty bone china tea service – this last from Polly and Will. The bedding was from Martha, the full set of cutlery from Sarah Davies, and Gloria gave them an enamel washing-up bowl filled with household things.

Meg was to stay with Martha for the night, Polly was to take her back to Glas Fynydd in the morning. Soon it was her bedtime, and Bron and Albert tucked her in and took turns to hug her goodnight. When they were finally ready to leave, as they were going to the door Meg cried happily, 'Goodnight Mam, goodnight Dad,' and to Bron and Albert it was the best wedding present of all.

Back home in the bedroom, which she had decorated with Will's help using pretty flowered paper, having at last managed to replace the hideous wardrobe with a good second-hand walnut bedroom suite, Albert was very quiet as they prepared for bed. Suddenly he pulled her down to sit beside him on the bed, and putting his arm about her shoulder, he said, 'There's something I've got to tell you, Bron.'

She looked up anxiously. What was wrong? Was he thinking of Janet. Was that why he looked so sad?

'Look, love,' he went on after a pause, 'perhaps I should have told you before. The truth is this is embarkation leave. I'm going overseas again. Oh Bron! I didn't know until just before I came home.'

Her arms tightened about him, as she told him, 'We'll have to make the most of this week then, love, but why didn't you tell me?'

'I didn't want to upset you, love. You looked so happy.'

Their arms tightened about each other and their lips met, but presently he gave a long sigh.

Bron's heart plummeted as she thought, there's something wrong, I knew it couldn't last.

'Look, love,' he said, hugging her to him, 'I may be abroad a long time. I'll have to be careful – you know – I don't want to leave you pregnant. You'll have enough on your plate as it is.'

Her arms went about him then, but before her lips sought his she murmured, 'Oh Albert! I can't think of anything more wonderful than to have your child, something of you to cherish, and if I get my wish it will make our parting a little easier to bear.'

Seeing the love and longing in each other's eyes, they embraced.

Chapter Thirty-Nine

Albert had long departed for his unknown destination by the time Bron realised her hopes of having a baby were to be fulfilled. She was ecstatic with joy, a joy not even slightly dimmed when Martha told her, "Ave youer 'ands full now, you will, my girl. You should 'ave waited until he came back.'

Despite the slight bouts of morning sickness, which had finally confirmed her pregnancy, she felt quite well and happier than she'd been for a long time, except for worrying about Albert, and her longing, very soon to be fulfilled, to have Meg home with her.

Just after Christmas, when things had been fairly quiet for some time, she told Mr Jessop that she wanted to give up work, adding, out of gratitude for all he'd done for her, 'I'll stay until you find someone, of course.'

Bron soon wished that she hadn't said those words, as the weeks dragged by. Several customers offered their services, but as they had no experience and only a personal acquaintance with rationing Mr Jessop had refused their help. Then a few weeks later a young man who'd trained as a grocer before going into the army and being invalided out, saw his advert and was welcomed with open arms, although rationing had been in its infancy when he'd been called up.

* * *

On the day Bron said an affectionate goodbye, she went home laden with presents, a little sad at leaving workmates and customers she'd grown fond of, but feeling elated that Meg was coming home at last.

So, on a day towards the end of February 1943, wearing a new swagger coat to cover her increasing bulk Bron went to Glas Fynydd to fetch Meg home. The little girl was sad at leaving Olwen, her friend for so long, and went to her house to bid her a long goodbye, coming back to tell her mother regretfully, 'Olwen's mam won't let her come to Cardiff until the war is over.'

'I told you that myself, Meg,' Bron said. 'Never mind, perhaps it won't be long.'

It was an optimism she didn't feel. The war seemed to be dragging on and on. She didn't know what Albert was doing apart from the fact that he was back in North Africa. She listened to every news broadcast on the wireless, and watched the Pathé News anxiously whenever she went to the cinema.

Meg wanted to bring all her things home with her, but it was impossible to carry all the toys she'd accumulated since she'd been with Jenny and Idris.

When Bron hugged David she watched for any signs of regret that he wasn't going home with her, but there were none. He was a happy, contented little boy with lots of friends, and Bron was thankful.

The following week, Bron waited outside Stanley Road School to meet Meg after her first day there. When the children came tumbling out, Meg was arm in arm with a small blonde girl of about her own age.

'This is Daisy,' Meg told her proudly. 'She lives at the top of Thelma Street. Can she come back and have tea with us, Mam?'

Two pairs of blue eyes regarded Bron hopefully. Feeling dismay at the prospect of having to make a quarter of corned beef into enough sandwiches for three, but delight at Meg having found herself a friend, Bron answered, 'Yes. So long as Daisy tells her mam.'

After that it was Daisy this and Daisy that from morning to night. The girls were inseparable, playing with Bron's shop or dolls, or at Daisy's home. Bron had met Daisy's parents and found them a nice couple, and Meg loved to take her turn at pushing Daisy's baby sister Molly along the street in her pram.

Soon it was May, and Bron, now near her time, was feeling exhausted, especially as the weather grew warmer. She was also worried about Albert; only his frequent letters calmed her, aiming each week to reassure her he was still alive. Polly came in at all hours of the day and evening to make sure that she was all right.

'Why don't you come and stay with us until it's over, Bron?' she asked. 'You're coming home to have the baby anyway.'

But she didn't want to leave the house just yet, soon enough to bring the bed down to Martha's parlour when they had to. She'd have liked to have had the child at home, but had given in because it would be easier for Polly and Martha to look after her at Martha's house.

On the seventeenth of May, Meg was sleeping the night at Daisy's house. Staying at each other's houses was something they loved to do. When, later in the evening, Polly paid Bron a visit, she tried to persuade her to come and spend the night with them. 'I don't like you being alone, *cariad*,' she told her. 'It's no trouble for Will and me to bring the bed down. We're thinking of getting it ready anyway.'

'I won't come tonight, Polly. Supposing Meg comes

back before I get home?' she told her. 'I'm going up to bed soon anyway.'

'I'll come and see you in the morning. You look tired, love. I should get upstairs if I were you,' Polly said, kissing her goodnight.

Bron didn't bolt the door; Polly might be round before she was up. Bron made herself a cup of tea and then struggled up the stairs. The house seemed empty without Meg. If she needed anyone during the night she'd arranged with Mrs Coles next door that she'd bang upon the party wall. Her neighbour knew all about the key, for hanging it behind the door was the practice of the neighbours too.

She felt exhausted and was soon asleep. She was dreaming a dream in which Albert was with them at the seaside, and Meg was paddling in the sea. There was a lot of noise, not seaside sounds at all. Something was impinging on her dream, a wailing, a familiar and dreaded sound. Her mouth dried and her heart gave a sickening lurch as the air-raid siren brought her wide awake, sitting up in bed.

She put on her dressing gown, and, gathering a blanket from the bed, went downstairs as quickly as her cumbersome body would allow, through the kitchen and the wash-house, picking up the matches on the shelf above the cooker, then out to the yard. The wailing noise was rising to its peak, and searchlights were sweeping the sky, bathing the garden in eerie light as she made her way down the path to the shelter, wishing she'd kept Meg with her now. But they were sensible people with children of their own to protect. The throbbing of enemy planes was almost drowned by the *Whang! Whang!* of anti-aircraft guns, and, as she climbed clumsily down into the shelter, descending parachute flares bathed the scene in sinister light.

With a final horrified glance at the sky, Bron slammed the door shut, wrinkling her nose at the musty smell. She hadn't been down here for some time; it was icy cold too, and she draped herself in the thick blanket and sat down. Fumbling with the matches she lit the lantern with shaking fingers, wishing she'd prepared a thermos of tea as she used to when the raids were frequent. Now she held her hands to the lantern for warmth, her worried thoughts dwelling on Meg. I shouldn't have brought her home, she told herself, praying Meg wasn't too frightened, for she wouldn't be as used to the raids as Daisy was.

The guns kept up a non-stop bombardment as planes droned once more overhead. Every now and then shrapnel would pepper the roof of the shelter, as though it was raining nuts and bolts.

During a brief lull, she opened the door and saw part of the sky covered in a pall of crimson oily smoke, shutting it quickly at the sound of planes droning in the distance. Then the barrage started up again and she thought of Meg, wishing she could comfort her.

When next Bron opened the door it was to see flames reaching skywards, incendiaries and bombs having done their worst.

Her back ached, with the cold she supposed. It was a sickening ache that was quickly getting worse. What time was it? She'd noticed that it had been just past two thirty-five by the kitchen clock when she'd been on her way to the shelter. Her mouth was so dry it was a job to moisten her lips, and the sickening pain made her want to cry out.

Bron had been feeling frightened for some time now, but not of the bombs that were whistling through the air, albeit at a distance. The baby was starting, she was sure of it now. A fresh spasm of pain gripped her and she broke out in a sweat. Dear God! why hadn't she listened to Polly and gone home with her? But she hadn't been expecting it to happen for another fortnight at least. Now, as she moaned and rocked to and fro, she prayed for the raid to end. But what could she do even then? She was in no fit state to fetch the midwife or Polly.

During a particularly bad spasm of pain the all clear sounded, but it was some minutes before she could even move. Then she lay back against the cushions gasping for air, knowing that she must move for the baby's sake, but all her energy seemed drained away. Trying to open the shelter door a fresh wave of pain gripped her. Bron was resting after this particular bout, when she heard running footsteps and the door burst open to reveal a white-faced Polly with Will behind her.

'Aunt Poll,' she croaked from her parched throat, 'how did you know?'

'I was worried, Bron, after the night we've had. The sky's red with fires. Why haven't you gone back to the house?'

But Bron doubled up with a fresh spasm of pain, and gasped, 'The baby's coming.'

When the pain eased they got her to the house, where Polly decided right away that they'd never make it home.

'Best for us to get her upstairs, Will,' she told him. 'Then you'd better dash for the midwife. It's Ruby – you know where she lives.'

'I went there when you 'ad Glory.'

Lowering Bron gently to the bed, he was gone.

It was a worrying ten minutes for Polly until Ruby arrived, with Bron moaning and sweating with pain, and the kettles to put on and things to get ready. But when the midwife arrived and put down her bag and began to time the contractions Polly regained her confidence. Ruby was a good midwife, none better.

'I'll stay with her now. It won't be very long. Put some kettles on, Polly, we'll need hot water.'

'I've put two on the gas stove and a saucepan.'

Suddenly Polly remembered that the case Bron had packed ready for the confinement was at their house.

'Will!'

He came halfway up the stairs. 'Anything I can do, Poll?'

'Yes. Get that case Bron left at our house, will you? I'll have to get things ready and there's no fire in the bedroom. I could do with several pairs of hands.'

'Well you got mine, girl. I'll be back in a minute, and Martha with me, I expect.'

Twenty minutes later, the room cosy now, with flames dancing around the coals in the grate, the baby was born. Just as a pale sky tinged with pink was heralding the dawn, Bron heard his first cry.

'It's a boy, Mrs Davies. A lovely little boy,' Ruby beamed down at her.

As soon as the baby was bathed and put into Bron's arms, the horror and pain of the night receded. A warm glow of happiness filled her whole being as she looked down at the sleeping child. Albert would be so happy.

When the baby was tucked into the cot that had been Meg's, Bron fell into an exhausted sleep, and hours later was just floating half in and half out of consciousness when she became aware of light footsteps running up the stairs.

Meg was pushing the door open, crying, 'Mam! Mam! Uncle Will brought me home. Where is he? Where's my little brother?' She came round the bed to peep into the cot, whispering when she saw the baby was asleep. 'Ooh! isn't he lovely?' Putting out a gentle finger she tenderly stroked the baby's cheek.

Epilogue

The station was bathed in warm sunshine on the spring day in 1946 when Bron and the children rushed up the stairs to the platform to welcome Albert home. Pushing through the crowds, Bron, slim in a new turquoise-blue dress, warm blonde hair glinting in the sunlight, held tightly the hand of a curly-haired boy of three with wide blue eyes and a peppering of freckles on his cheeks.

'How long before the train comes in, Mam?' Meg, tall now, blue eyes bright with excitement, fingered lovingly the filigree necklace that spelt her name in silver letters, one of the many presents Albert had sent her since he'd been abroad.

'Any time now,' Bron told her, trying to sound calm, as she bent to tuck the top of Alun's little knitted suit into his pants.

With the sound of a whistle shrilling in the distance, the crowd shuffled forward, but Bron held Meg back, saying, 'Alun might get hurt in that crush.'

Hearing his name, the small boy grinned up at them, the expression on his face so much like Albert's it caught at Bron's heart.

As the train steamed in, amidst all the bustle and clamour, the slamming of compartment doors, the joyful

371

shouts of reunions, Bron's eyes anxiously searched the crowd. Then Albert was pushing towards them, dropping his kitbag and flinging his arms about her, but not before she'd seen the look of love and pride at the first glimpse of his son. Now he scooped the child up with one arm, putting his other arm lovingly about Meg's shoulder. Alun, wondering what all the fuss was about, struggled to be free. Presently, when his dad had given in to his struggles and he was once more clinging to his mother's skirts, he lifted one of his new brown sandals proudly for the man called dada to admire.

Ever since Alun could remember his dad had been a picture on the mantelpiece, a picture he kissed each night before he went to bed. As soon as he'd finished his mug of cocoa his mam would lift the photo down and say, 'Kiss night-night to your dada, love.' If he made the glass wet with his lips, she'd laugh, and tell him, 'I'll bet he enjoyed that one, boyo,' and they'd all laugh – him, his mam and Meg.

Hearing a whistle Alun wanted to see the train steam out, all he could see from here was people's legs. He pulled hard at his dad's hand and looked up anxiously, then he was swung up to his shoulders, and his dad was calling up to him, 'Is that all right, son?'

It was great, he could see everything. The train was beginning to pull out, there was a lot of noise and steam floating over the platform. Men with trolleys piled high with luggage were wheeling them away, people were moving towards the steps that led to the street.

He could see the chocolate bar machine, but he knew it would be empty. Mama had told him it was 'cos of the war, but his dad was fumbling in his pocket bringing out two bags of sweets. His mam had looked pleased when he'd remembered to offer them first, and his father had lifted him down and given him a hug. It was nice after all, having a real dad.